Also by S. W. Perry

The Jackdaw Mysteries
The Angel's Mark
The Serpent's Mark
The Saracen's Mark

The Heretic's Mark

S. W. PERRY

CORVUS

First published in Great Britain in 2021 by Corvus, an imprint
of Atlantic Books Ltd.

This paperback published in 2022.

Copyright © S. W. Perry, 2021

The moral right of S. W. Perry to be identified as the author
of this work has been asserted by him in accordance with the
Copyright, Designs and Patents Act of 1988.

10 9 8 7 6 5 4 3 2

A CIP catalogue record for this book is available from the
British Library.

Paperback ISBN: 978 1 78649 900 4
E-book ISBN: 978 1 78649 902 8

Printed and bound by CPI Group (UK) Ltd, Croydon, CR0 4YY

Corvus
An imprint of Atlantic Books Ltd
Ormond House
26–27 Boswell Street
London
WC1N 3JZ

www.corvus-books.co.uk

For my family

When these prodigies do so conjointly meet,
let no men say 'These are their reasons, they are natural':
For I believe they are portentous things...

WILLIAM SHAKESPEARE, *JULIUS CAESAR*

Prologue

The White Tower, London, 7th June 1594

They come for him shortly before dawn with a showy rattling of keys loud enough to wake the ghosts on Tower Hill. He rises stiffly from the first proper rest he has had in weeks, his joints reclaiming the pain the cold stone floor has borrowed while he was asleep. 'Anon, anon!' he protests as they take him by his chains. 'All in good time. Incarceration is no friend to old bones.'

'Old bones or young – it matters not,' says his gaoler with the wistful familiarity of the prisoner's confessor. 'You're wanted at Whitehall.'

'Whitehall?' he replies. 'Has Her Grace the queen spoken for me? Does the Privy Council accept my innocence? Are they setting me free?'

But no answer comes as they hurry him down the wet, slime-covered steps towards the waiting wherry – only the sharp-tongued screeching of the gulls from the darkness of the river.

After months in captivity, Dr Roderigo Lopez has almost forgotten what it is to look out upon a horizon slowly prising itself from the grip of night. He stares about in cautious expectation. By the time they approach Westminster there is enough light for him to see, to his left, the pale mass of Lambeth Palace rising above the reeds. To his right, the grand houses along the

Strand are taking shape. He knows them well. Within their private chambers he has administered to the greatest men in England. Powder of Spanish fly to help the Earl of Leicester in the bedchamber when his ardour failed to match his ambition; mercury to cure young Essex of the French gout; enemas to ease old Burghley's fractiousness at the dinner table. The rewards had been handsome, if only to buy his silence: a good house, a certain prestige, money, even the queen herself for a patient. But they had never truly seen him as one of their kind. In his heart, Lopez had always known it.

At the Westminster stairs the boatmen hand him over to a brace of uniformed halberdiers in crested steel helmets. He almost laughs. Do they think a single white-haired old Jew might threaten the very realm itself? Do they not know that, after months of confinement, he can barely walk unaided?

In a panelled chamber with an embossed ceiling painted blue and studded with yellow plaster stars wait two members of the Queen's Bench, Attorney General Coke and Chief Justice Popham. They are grave men in ermine-trimmed gowns. No smiles. Barely a greeting. They sit behind a table spread with expensive crimson cloth. It is bare, save for a leather-bound Bible and a roll of parchment with a tail of golden ribbon and a grand wax seal attached. Lopez notes the seal has been broken.

Let them think you're the last man on earth to bear a grudge, he tells himself. They might find a little mercy in their cold hearts.

'You're up early, gentlemen,' he says, smiling.

'This is not a business for late sleepers,' Coke says.

'Have you brought Her Grace's letter of pardon with you?' Lopez asks, glancing at the parchment.

But their hard, formal faces tell him that whatever this document is, it does not carry his salvation. The pain in his joints, temporarily forgotten in the blossoming of hope, begins to scream at him again: *Fool... fool for ever thinking they would find mercy in their hearts for a man like you.*

With indecent haste, Coke and Popham put him through a perfunctory second trial, as though the first – it seems an age ago now – had somehow failed to stick, like the colour in a badly dyed shirt. A detestable traitor, they call him. Worse than Judas. There is no crime on earth more heinous than plotting to poison a monarch anointed by God. He was guilty of it in February, he is somehow even guiltier in June. And so he will hang by the neck until half-choked, suffer the severing of his privy organs and disembowelment by the knife – all while there is enough life left in him to appreciate the executioner's skill at butchery. And if that doesn't convince him of his perfidy, they will quarter his torso with an axe, burn the sundered parts and throw the ashes into the river. He will have no grave. Only his head will endure a strange immortality: set upon a spike on the southern gatehouse of London Bridge as a warning to future would-be regicides.

Why do I not fall to my knees in terror? he wonders. Perhaps it is because terror has become such a familiar companion during his lonely imprisonment. He knows it like an old friend. It cannot bite him any harder now.

Until they tell him it is to be today. At Tyburn.

✠

There is an etiquette to an execution for high treason. Whether it be a solemn confession or a passionate protestation of innocence, an address to the mob is required. And the condemned man must stand naked as he prepares himself for the leaving of this world, just as he was when he came into it.

The executioner tears the dirty shirt from Dr Roderigo Lopez's back. He turns the pale, trembling body to the crowd. *Look*, he seems to be saying, *can you not see the stain of guilt on the puckered white flesh?*

'I love the queen as well as I love our Lord!' Lopez cries out.

'Papist traitor!' someone shouts. Others pick up the chorus: 'Vile Hebrew... Spanish assassin...' This last insult hurts him more than the others. He is Portuguese, not Spanish. The Spanish are his enemy, as much as they are to the people now hurling their abuse and spittle at him.

As the executioner places the rough hemp noose around Lopez's frail neck to begin the slow gruesome journey, the words of the man who lit the fire that sustains the queen's religion – Martin Luther – echo in the physician's lonely, tormented soul: *Every man must do two things alone... his own believing, and his own dying.*

In a different life, the man watching from the crowd had been someone of substance. But that was before his fall.

Grand in stature with a voice to match, he too is a physician – once the most renowned anatomist in England. There had been a time, Sir Fulke Vaesy recalls, when he had been a proconsul of the medical profession. A time when he could afford to attend an execution in silk-lined hose and imported Bruges shirts. He has shrunk a little since then. His reputation has gone, and with it the income. The manor house at Vauxhall has gone too, sold to some upstart warden of the Fishmongers' Guild. The expensive brocade doublet he had worn on his imperious strolls down Knightrider Street to the College of Physicians is now patched and faded, like the covering of an old chair. He no longer has the spare cash to replace it. Now he is reduced to giving purges and drawing blood, like a country barber-surgeon.

Sir Fulke Vaesy knows exactly who is to blame for this ruination. Being a man who values careful accounting – at least when he had property and possessions to account *for* – he has drawn up a proper reckoning. It does not exist on paper. It cannot be presented as a bill. Nevertheless, the columns are neatly ordered in his head: every humiliation, every slight, every averted eye and unanswered greeting, every cancelled invitation... all assigned a price and entered in the ledger.

And where, now, is the fellow to whom this bill should be presented? In the pay of Sir Robert Cecil, that is where. Physician to Lord Burghley's ill-formed younger son. Favoured by the queen herself, if what Vaesy has heard is true – though how Her Grace can bear to listen to the man's wild, heretical ideas he cannot imagine. These undeserved endowments are, in Vaesy's mind, the interest on the debt the wretch owes.

With detached professional interest, Vaesy observes the executioner take up his knife and geld the struggling old man on the scaffold. He nods at the practised ease with which the wrinkled white belly is opened up, spilling the hot pearlescent billows onto the planks. He watches the blood spill over the edge of the platform. For a moment he sees himself climbing the steps and instructing the crowd on the inner workings of the human body.

The axe begins to swing, quartering the Jew's still-breathing body with a sound like someone dropping four heavy sacks of flour in quick succession. Then one final blow finishes the grisly masque for good. The executioner holds up the head by its now-crimson beard.

And in that moment the man watching from the crowd forgets the crush of sweating bodies that press upon him with such rude familiarity. The stink of unwashed common broadcloth and half-eaten coney pies, of cheap ale and rotten gums, fades entirely from his nostrils. In its place, as if carried sweetly on a sympathetic summer breeze, Sir Fulke Vaesy thinks he can smell the faint but distinct scent of revenge.

PART 1

Falling from Heaven

1

'Tell us, Dr Shelby: when did you first conspire with the executed traitor Lopez to poison Her Grace the queen?'

The questioner wears the livery of Robert Devereux, the young Earl of Essex. He is a large man. He has to stoop slightly in this dank low-ceilinged former monk's cell. His face reminds Nicholas Shelby of an oval of badly cast glass on a grey day, cold and impenetrable. Judging by the foot-long poniard he wears at his belt, the noble earl has not hired him to wait at his table or tend his privet hedges. His companion is also armed. He stands close to his master, as though he hopes a little of the other man's menace might rub off on him.

Even in summer the hospital warden's office has the dank stink of the river about it, the walls cold and slippery to the touch, a place more suited to burial than the administration of healing. Now, in the shocked silence that follows the man's accusation, it has for Nicholas the stillness of a freshly opened crypt. Before he can reply, the warden gives a frightened little harrumph. His eyes, set unnaturally close to the bridge of his thin nose, hurriedly fall to the ledgers on his desk. He seems to think that the harder he studies the inky scrawls, the further he can remove himself from the implications of what he's just heard. 'I have no knowledge of Mr Shelby,' he mutters to the pages, 'other than of his duties at this hospital. Beyond that, I am not of his acquaintance.'

Nicholas thinks: that's exactly the kind of betrayal I might have expected from a man I have always imagined more as a pensioned-off Bankside rat-catcher than a hospital warden, a man who sneeringly refuses to understand why a physician who now serves Sir Robert Cecil, the queen's privy councillor and secretary, should still care enough about healing to visit St Thomas's Hospital for the sick poor of Bankside on a Tuesday and Thursday, without even asking for the shilling a session you grudgingly paid me when I was down on my luck.

He keeps his reply calm and measured. Bravado will be as incriminating as hesitancy. 'Who are you to speak with such impertinence to a loyal and obedient subject of Her Majesty?'

The man gives a smile that is very nearly a sneer. 'Judging by what Master Warden has just said, it would appear you must account for yourself without an advocate, Master Shelby. Please answer the question I put to you.'

'It is not a question,' says Nicholas. 'It has no merit. It is an insult. And as a member of the College of Physicians, to you I am *Mister* Shelby.'

A contemplative nod, while the man considers if this has any bearing on the matter at hand. Then he looks at Nicholas with eyes as sharp as the poniard he carries at his belt. 'Then as a physician, *Mister* Shelby, you must know what hot iron can do to a man's fingers. How will you practise your physic with burnt stumps?'

'This is risible. I will hear no more of it.'

Nicholas moves towards the door, intending to leave. A thick, leather-sleeved arm blocks his way. Not suddenly, but smoothly – as if the body it is attached to has seen all this before and knows precisely how this measure is danced.

'Did you not see the recent revels at Tyburn, Mr Shelby?' asks the younger of Essex's men, a hollow-cheeked fellow with lank pale hair that hangs down each side of his face like torn linen snagged on a thicket. He mimics the lolling head of a hanged man, while one fist makes an upwards-slicing motion over his own ample belly. He dances a few steps in feigned discomfort, as though he's stepping over his own entrails.

As ever when Nicholas is raised to a temper, which is not often, the Suffolk burr in his voice becomes more evident. 'No, I did not! Let me pass. I have borne quite enough of this nonsense.'

'That is a pity, Dr Shelby,' says the owner of the arm. 'It might have proved an instructive lesson – for your likely future.'

Nicholas bites back the reply that has already formed in his mind: *What you call a revel was nothing but the murder of an innocent old man.* In these present times, to express sympathy for a condemned traitor is almost as dangerous as committing the alleged treachery yourself.

'You would be advised to give a proper account of yourself to Master Winter here,' says the mimic with the lank hair, nodding towards his friend. 'When did the executed traitor Lopez seek to enrol you in his vile conspiracy?'

'Do you *really* expect me to answer that?'

The warden seems to deflate into an even smaller huddle over his ledgers. He shakes his head as if trying to cast off a bad memory, or perhaps to show Essex's men that he never wanted Nicholas Shelby anywhere near St Tom's in the first place, however far he may have risen since.

The one named Winter says, 'Oh, be assured, sir, you *will* answer the denouncement – before me, or before the Queen's Bench: the choice is yours.'

Denouncement. So that's it, Nicholas thinks. Someone has made a false accusation against me. He tries to think who it might be.

He has few enemies, and none made willingly. Perhaps some minor member of the aristocracy has taken offence that the new physician to Sir Robert Cecil refuses to purge him for an overindulgence of goose and sirloin.

'Who has laid this false charge against me?' he demands to know.

Winter's reply is non-committal. 'I am a servant of His Grace the earl, not a market-stall gossip.'

'And I am in the service of Sir Robert Cecil,' Nicholas reminds him. 'I am physician to his son. Now let me go about my lawful business.'

Winter puts one thick hand on the hilt of his poniard and lifts just enough blade from the sheath to show he means business.

'I am sure Sir Robert can find another doctor to attend his son, should the present one lose his life resisting arrest for treason. You are to come with us to Essex House.'

Nicholas has a sense of falling – the warning the stomach gives the brain of coming terror. He remembers that old Dr Lopez made a similar journey not so many months ago, and from there to the Tower. As he follows Winter and his boy out of the dank little cell and into the June sunshine the warden's head does not lift from his ledger, as though Nicholas Shelby has been already condemned and forgotten.

✠

In her apothecary's shop on Bankside's Dice Lane, Bianca Merton is preparing an emulsion for Widow Hoby's inflamed ear. She takes up a bottle of oil of Benjamin and pours a generous measure into a stone mortar, which she sets on a tripod over the stub of a fat tallow candle. Then she breaks up some mint, marjoram and oregano, pares a few leaves of wormwood from a stem and drops the mixture into the gently warming liquid. As she begins to grind the pestle, the scents spill out in profusion. She inhales. She smiles. There might be an open sewer outside, but in her modest premises the air is always exotically fragrant.

Some who live in the teeming warren of lanes that cluster around the Rose playhouse on the south bank of the Thames would think it a shame to pour such a fine oil into the ear of an old woman with barely the clothes on her back to her name, but Bianca knows Widow Hoby has a good soul. Her husband was one of the more than ten thousand Londoners who were carried off by the pestilence that ravaged the city last year. She deserves a little luxury.

On Bankside, indeed throughout Southwark, there is a certain air of mystery – not to say notoriety – about Bianca Merton. For a start, she looks different. Her skin has a healthy caramel sheen to it, a hint (or so her mother always told her) of a family line that ran from the Italian Veneto across the Adriatic to Ragusa, and from there into Egypt, or Ethiopia, or even far Cathay. (Her mother had never been *entirely* specific on the subject.) But it is more than just her complexion – which admittedly has paled a little under the unpredictable English sun – or her startling amber eyes and the thick, dark convolutions that spill from a high, determined brow that mark her out as exotic. Whether her customers come for oil of bitter almonds to ease a ringing in the ears, a decoction of plantain, sorrel and lettuce for a nosebleed or simply for a chat, they cannot help but wonder if the rumours are really true: that the daughter of an English spice merchant and an Italian mother can mix a poison as deftly as she can a cure.

Being what the rest of London refers to disparagingly as denizens of 'the Turkish Shore' and thus used to the unusual, these same Banksiders have long since taken to Bianca Merton. Southwark admires a certain dash, a measure of what it likes to call 'assurance'. Man or woman, poor or poorer (there are few enough in the city's southernmost ward who are rich), they don't much care if it's not shown by their clothes. A jaunty cap worn at a rakish angle, a flash of bright ribbon, a string of polished oyster shells sewn to the collar in place of pearls will do, if it's all one can afford. What is important is that you walk down Bermondsey Street or along the riverbank with your chin up, as though the Bishop of London, the queen's Privy Council, the Lord Mayor and his Corporation – along with all their petty laws – can go straight to the Devil in a night-soil waggon, for all you care. And in this, Bianca Merton suits them down to the ground.

For those who have learned of it, and Bianca has done her utmost to ensure there are few, the only thing that might raise a doubting eyebrow is her faith. In a realm whose present queen is still under a pope's sentence of excommunication, and whose former sovereign, the bloody Mary, burned three hundred Protestant martyrs before her own departure into a richly deserved hell, Bianca Merton's Catholicism could well be viewed with suspicion. Not so much now, of course. Not since she purchased the Jackdaw tavern with the money her father had left her. There are few heresies a Banksider won't forgive, if the price of his ale is competitive. And besides, you'd be hard pressed to find one who *doesn't* have something in their larder they'd rather not share with the world across London Bridge.

The one thing they are all agreed upon is that they cannot quite bring themselves to address this comely young woman with the interesting past by her new, married name. She came to them as Mistress Merton, and Mistress Merton is how they see her still, regardless of their happiness at the match. Goodwife Shelby just doesn't seem to fit.

When the oil infusion is complete, Bianca adds it to the rest of the medicines she has prepared for tomorrow's early customers. She locks her shop and goes out into the warm summer air. She walks the short distance to the pleasant lodging she and Nicholas rent close to the river by the Paris Garden. On the way she passes the place where her Jackdaw tavern had stood for centuries – until that summer night last year, when the trail of mayhem caused by her new husband's association with Sir Robert Cecil brought about its incineration and her own close brush with death. Recovering in the splendour of Nonsuch Palace, the home of Nicholas's friend, John Lumley, she had often wondered how she would feel when she looked again on the ruins of the place she'd bought with her father's inheritance when she arrived in London from her former life in Padua. She had suspected it would break her heart, despite the fact that Nicholas, after his return from the Barbary shore, had the means to rebuild it. To her surprise, she had dismissed the blackened skeleton with a shrug. New starts, she had realized, were nothing new to her now. They were to be embraced, not feared.

She stops to inspect the work. She observes the freshly hewn oak posts set into the scorched foundations, the frame upon which the new Jackdaw will rise, and checks that the masons have run the first few courses of bricks straight. Not *too* straight, mind; the Jackdaw was never about symmetry – that had been part of its charm. Announcing her satisfaction to the foreman in charge of the reconstruction, she walks on towards the Paris Garden.

Arriving at the lodging, she finds two notes left for her. The first is from Nicholas himself – their love is still fresh enough to leave each other *billets-doux*. She reads it, learns that he expects to return from St Tom's by five and tucks it into the neckline of her gown, where she imagines the feel of it against her skin is instead of the warmth of his touch.

The second note is from Rose Monkton.

Mistress Moonbeam, as Bianca is wont to call her friend and former maid, has returned to Bankside to help her while the

Jackdaw is being rebuilt. The note informs her that Rose has gone across the bridge, on an errand to visit an importer of spices on Petty Wales whom Bianca knows to be that rarity amongst Thameside merchants: an honest man. Too many of them these days are not above bulking out their wares with powdered acorns and other counterfeit dusts. This one does regular business with his counterparts in Venice, the middlemen in the trade from the Levant and Asia. It is a useful conduit for Bianca's letters to her cousin in Padua, Bruno Barrani. All it costs is her continued custom, and free medicine for the merchant's hermicrania. She checks to see if Rose has taken her latest letter with her, because Rose is liable to forget her own name if the wind changes direction suddenly. She has.

There has been a lot to tell Bruno since last she wrote – most of it impossible to put in a letter. So Bianca had confined herself to a report of daily life on Bankside, and for his greater interest – because Bruno likes to hear of strange phenomena – she had mentioned the mercifully brief fresh outbreak of plague in the spring; the great storm at the end of March that had torn up so many trees and ripped off so many roofs; and the fearful rains and gales of early April. Her final words, before closing with the usual expression of familial devotion and commending Bruno to God's merciful protection, had touched on the matter closest of all to her heart: *as yet, no sign of our hoped-for bounty...*

That had been harder to write than she had expected. But the fact remains that, despite lying with Nicholas that night of the fire, and on many joyous occasions since, her belly is still as flat as it has ever been.

As Bianca sits in the window seat of the parlour, looking out across the unusually quiet lane to the close-packed timbered houses and the spire of St Saviour's beyond, she hears the church bell ring four times. The slow, deliberate chimes remind her how time seems to be passing ever more swiftly. She has already seen the back of thirty. Only God knows how many years she has been allotted. As each one ends, so the possibility of bearing a child – *their* child – diminishes. To give Nicholas a healthy child would be the final laying of his first wife's ghost.

To fill the time while she waits for him to return from St Tom's, Bianca picks up a printed sheet purchased a few days ago from a bookshop near St Paul's. It is the new poem by Master Shakespeare. She had been lucky to find a copy. They are flying out of the stationers' faster than the presses can run them off. She lets her eyes skim over the words to get a feel for the piece, before reading it more attentively.

She does not get beyond the second verse before a dark and uncomfortable sense of foreboding comes over her, no doubt brought about by remembering what she has left out of her letter to her cousin:

O comfort-killing Night... Black stage for tragedies and murders fell...

Whispering conspirator with close-tongu'd treason...

Make war against proportion'd course of time.

✠

Returning from delivering Mistress Bianca's letter into the hands of the merchant on Petty Wales, Rose Monkton hurries south across London Bridge. She prefers not to linger in the narrow parts where it runs beneath the buildings that perch upon it as if they are teetering on the edge of a precipice. The crowd squeezes in so tight that you have to fight your way through the shoppers, the hawkers and the cut-purses. She prefers the few open spaces where there is a chance to look at the river sweeping beneath the great stone piers on which the whole implausible edifice is built.

Then she can breathe properly. Then she can gaze east towards the Tower, or west towards the grand houses lining the northern bank around Westminster.

Rose has grown accustomed to grand houses recently. She's developed a taste for them. Born in the narrow maze of lanes between the Paris Garden and Long Southwark in the shadow of the playhouse whose name she shares, she has always found the crush of the timber-framed tenements oddly reassuring, as comforting as the wooden walls of a cradle to a swaddled infant. But then, in the aftermath of the fire, and with plague still rampant in London, Master Nicholas had accepted Lord Lumley's offer of sanctuary at Nonsuch Palace. True, she and her husband Ned dwelt in the servants' quarters, but even they were grander than their former rooms at the Jackdaw.

The thought of Nonsuch makes her hanker for the comforting vastness of Ned's huge frame. She will have to wait a little longer, she thinks with a resigned smile; Mistress Bianca still has need of her. A body can't run an apothecary shop that tends to the needs of half of Bankside and watch over the rebuilding of a tavern by herself – not with the way that London day-labourers are wont to behave. And Bianca Merton is, after all, more an older sister to her than a mistress.

As she emerges from beneath the bridge gatehouse into Long Southwark, Rose takes care not to glance up at the traitors' heads crowning the parapet like a macabre grinning diadem. She presumes the one unburnt relic of poor Dr Lopez is up there now, blackening in the summer sunshine.

She has heard Master Nicholas tell how he doesn't believe the old man was guilty of trying to poison the queen. And to her mind it seemed a monstrous way to treat a physician. The barber-surgeon who pulled that diseased tooth of hers when she was eleven, perhaps. But not a doctor.

As she leaves the gatehouse and turns right towards the Pepper Lane water-stairs, eyes fixed straight ahead in an effort to resist the uncomfortable urge to look back and up over her shoulder, Rose sees a familiar figure coming towards her from the direction of Long Southwark.

He's the last man you'd take for a physician, she thinks. She imagines men of medicine – like magistrates, priests and schoolmasters – to possess a stern gloominess brought on by all that book-learning, probably tall and lugubrious, and definitely old. Master Nicholas is none of these. How could he be? He'd never have won the heart of Mistress Bianca if he was.

He looks exactly what he told her he was before he became a doctor: the younger son of a yeoman farmer. Thus, being of a romantic mind, Rose imagines him made out of the same solid earth that sprouted the men who fought with the fifth Harry at Agincourt, or who now captain the ships of Drake, Hawkins and Raleigh. He looks as though he'd be more at home wielding a scythe than a scalpel, though she suspects he'd do it with the same careful diligence, allowing himself just the occasional flourish to show that he's not all earnest sobriety, that he can laugh at himself, when required.

He's wearing that old white canvas doublet of his, the one he came to them in, a twenty-eight-year-old foundling abandoned by the river he'd thrown himself into to escape his grief. It had taken her ages to clean the mud off it, while Mistress Bianca tended his battered body upstairs in the attic of the Jackdaw. He looks a lot different now, of course. He has the grateful eyes of a man who knows the value of a second chance. Now, even his coarse black hair and his tightly cropped beard know better than to sprout piratically, as Rose herself would prefer. But Mistress Bianca won't have him looking like a felon, and has told him so more than once.

But who are these two fellows with him? She hasn't seen *them* before. Not as big as her Ned, but large enough. And by the way they crowd him, they do not appear to be friends.

Rose becomes certain something is amiss when Master Nicholas does not smile at her. In fact he stares straight through her, save for a very brief shake of his head, as though he's trying to tell her not to acknowledge him. Keeping her eyes off his, she waits until she feels it is safe to look back. She watches in horror as they bundle him down into a waiting wherry as if he's the most wanted criminal in all London. In indecent haste the wherry pushes off into the current.

But not before Rose has had the opportunity to spot the embroidered design on the leather tunics of the two men. It is a mark she has seen before, when the young man whose livery it is made one of his many vainglorious processions through the city, graciously accepting with a wave of his gloved hand the hosannas of the admiring crowd.

2

The Strand, London. Later the same day

Essex House stands on the north bank of the Thames, between the Middle Temple and the eastern end of Whitehall. Like many of the great houses that line the river to the west of Temple Bar, it once belonged to a bishop. But that was before the queen's father, the eighth Henry, decided he preferred his men of God – if not their monarchs – frugal. It has a grand banqueting hall, more bedrooms than the city has wards, and fine gardens that sweep down to the water's edge, where two private water-stairs jut out like serpents' tongues tasting the air for treason.

All London knows Essex House wears two faces. The first is cultured and fashionable. Poets and musicians come here, lavish masques are held amid the topiary. The dancing is exquisite. As are the boys who serve the wine.

The other face is darker. Like its equivalent, Cecil House, home of that other great faction of England, it is a centre of intrigue and politics, of foreign entanglements and alliances that shift forever like quicksand. Hidden away in places where a guest is unlikely to stray are the expert cryptographers, forgers, intelligencers. A few of these men are also practised in the application of a skill that would turn the stomachs of the more rarefied visitors who come in via the front gate. Their domain lies below ground – so the screams won't disturb the neighbours.

Nicholas arrives by the water-stairs that serves this other face. As the wherry rocks against the piles, Winter gives him a helping shove that will leave bruises on his back for days. He almost falls at the feet of two other men waiting for him on the planks. They are middle-aged, of middle height and from the Middle Temple, judging by their dark legal gowns. Ominous, thinks Nicholas with mounting alarm. If they are Essex House lawyers, they may have been sent simply to intimidate. But if the noble earl has brought them in from the Temple, then the accusation may already be public knowledge. It could have gathered a momentum that will be hard to stop. It could be that the letters of his arraignment have already been prepared.

They lead him up the gently sloping gardens towards the great house. He sees gardeners in linen smocks trimming the topiary; clerks and messengers moving purposefully along gravelled pathways; a gaggle of expensively dressed young gentlemen practising archery, their arrows speeding deep into a straw target set against a shady elm tree, honing their skills in the hope the earl will take them on his next expedition to the Low Countries. Or Lisbon. Or wherever else glory and riches may be had, by those with an appetite for risk.

Looking back, he sees Winter and Lank-hair trailing him like a pair of wolves trying to anticipate which way their prey will break. In the distance, out on the river, two tilt-boats glide past incongruously, their passengers enjoying a pleasant picnic beneath the awnings.

The lawyers seem to be the only two of their profession in all London disinclined to speak. In silence they lead him towards an area of stables and storerooms. It is shady here. Nicholas feels a chill in his blood, though whether real or imagined he's not sure.

They stop before a low lintel that caps a door studded with iron. One of the lawyers produces a heavy key from the folds of his gown. He inserts it into the lock-plate and tries to turn it. The lock does not yield. He tries again. And when that too is unsuccessful, a third time.

'Are you sure this is the place?' he asks his companion.

'The old carpenter's store – that is what His Grace's secretary told me, Master Rathlin,' the other replies.

Rathlin tries the key a fourth time. Withdrawing it, he stares at the intricate metal maze of the bit, until Winter steps forward, takes it from him, puts it in the lock and calmly turns it in the opposite direction. Nicholas stifles a grin. They can't believe me to be that much of a threat, he decides. They clearly didn't think it worth sending their best legal minds.

Inside, the chamber smells of wood-shavings and old animal pelts. It is bare, save for a furrowed carpenter's trestle. Here and there little curls of paper-thin shavings poke through the dust like wavelets on a frozen pond. It looks as though it was last used when the Earl of Leicester owned the place, and he's been dead almost six years.

'They said there would be chairs,' says Rathlin, as Lank-hair wipes the dust off the trestle with his forearm. 'Why are there no chairs?'

Lank-hair is dispatched and returns a few moments later carrying a bench just big enough to seat two. He places it before the trestle with elaborate care, as though this were the Star Chamber and not an outhouse. The lawyer without the key gives a petulant little tut, motioning to the other side of the trestle. 'We're questioning the accused, not the wall,' he mutters under his breath, a small triumph of petty revenge.

'I beg pardon, Master Athy,' mutters Winter, as though Lank-hair is not to be trusted to make his own apology.

This inept confusion gives Nicholas no comfort. It is not Rathlin and Athy who will pass sentence upon him. That will be left to Chief Justice Popham and Attorney General Coke. Not that it matters much. No matter how sound the accused's protestations of innocence, treason trials tend to have only one outcome.

With Winter and his friend stationed behind him, blocking the exit, Nicholas stands before this mockery of the Queen's Bench, trying to look as though he's being kept from more important business. Rathlin, apparently the more senior man, looks around the mean little chamber, gives a sigh of resignation and begins.

'You are Dr Nicholas Shelby, of Barnthorpe in the country of Sussex, accredited to practise physic by the Bishop of London, and a member of the College of Physicians. Is that correct?'

'No,' Nicholas says, sucking in his cheeks. 'I'm Richard Tarlton.'

This causes Rathlin to look at Winter with a severe furrowing of the brow. 'What's this, Master Winter? Have you brought us the wrong fellow?'

Athy put his hand over his mouth and gives a lawyer's sonorous cough.

'Richard Tarlton was a comedic *actor*, Master Rathlin – at the playhouses. He's dead.'

Rathlin looks surprised. 'Oh, a jest.' Then, disapprovingly, to Athy, 'The playhouses, you say?'

'I do, Master Rathlin.'

Rathlin studies Nicholas through narrowed eyes. 'Sinful places, playhouses. Given over to those who rejoice in lust, and impertinence towards their betters.'

Nicholas sighs inwardly. *That's all I need: a lawyer and a Puritan.*

'It is alleged, Master Shelby,' Rathlin continues, 'that you were an accomplice in the recent vile conspiracy made by the Jew Lopez, a native of Portugal given shelter in this realm, to administer to our sovereign lady, Elizabeth, a concoction fatal to Her Highness. This plan was thwarted only by the diligence of her Privy Council and the intercession of the Almighty. What say you – guilty?'

'I say the Trinity term must be a barren one for you lawyers, if you have time to waste on such a wild fabrication.'

'The allegation came from a reliable source,' says Rathlin.

'Did it really? Would you care to name it?'

'You think perhaps we have fabricated this charge on a whim?'

The evasion gives Nicholas a glimmer of comfort. An anonymous denunciation, he thinks. 'I'd put my money on it coming from someone I refused to purge for a bellyache brought on by overindulgence,' he says. 'Prove me wrong.'

Athy looks down his nose at the accused. 'This is not a trivial matter, Mr Shelby. We are speaking here of treason.'

Nicholas shrugs, a gesture that carries more indifference than he feels. 'I get more than a few of such charges, now that I am in the service of' – a pause to make sure they are paying attention, then a slowing of the voice as he plays the only card he holds – 'Sir Robert Cecil, Her Grace's secretary.'

But Temple lawyers are not so easily distracted. Rathlin says, 'But you have oftentimes been in close proximity to Her Highness's person, have you not?'

'*Oftentimes?* No; I'm not her personal physician. Not yet.'

Nicholas remembers Robert Cecil's warning last year when he returned from Morocco. The queen had expressed an interest in having him speak to her of the Barbary shore and how the Moors practised their physic. 'Don't get your hopes up,' Cecil had warned him. 'She makes invitations like that to every young man whose appearance pleases her.' But Cecil had been wrong. Elizabeth *had* summoned him: once to Windsor, once to Whitehall and twice more to Nonsuch. The memory of their first conversation springs into his mind now. 'Are you *sure* you are a physician, sirrah? You do not have an academic look to you.'

He'd taken it as a compliment.

'Master Baronsdale tells me he considers you a heretic,' he hears the queen saying, her white cerused face – almost as unmoving as a mask in a morality tale – creasing slightly with amusement at the expression on the faces of the assembled courtiers who are wondering what manner of fellow she'd commanded to appear before her. 'In matters of physic, I mean.'

'It is the privilege of the president of the College of Physicians to judge us humbler doctors as he chooses, Majesty,' he had replied, head down out of deference. But to his horror that had enabled him to see that he was wearing an old patched pair of woollen hose. In the pre-dawn darkness when he'd dressed, Bianca had been half-asleep. Kissing him goodbye had taken preference over ensuring he'd been properly attired to meet his monarch.

Rathlin's voice pulls him back to the present.

'Nevertheless, you *have* been granted privy access to Her Grace's chamber. We presume she did not call upon you to have you read poetry to her. What did you do there?'

'We spoke of how the Moors of Barbary organize their hospitals. She was interested.'

'The Moors have *hospitals*?' asks Athy, as though the possibility has only just occurred to him.

'For longer than we have had them. The one I visited was better than St Tom's. Certainly cleaner.'

'How remarkable.'

'Not really. Many of our procedures come from Moorish physicians of old, or from the books of antiquity they saved from destruction by the barbarians.'

Rathlin asks, 'And during these visits to Her Majesty, did you administer any foreign substance to her body?'

'No.'

'Nothing at all?'

'I think I might have remembered. So might she.'

'Did the traitor Lopez suggest such a thing to you?' This from Athy.

'Of course he didn't.'

'But he *was* present.'

'Only at the first summons. After that, he was elsewhere – latterly in the Tower. I see you are not taking notes.'

'This is a preliminary interview, Dr Shelby,' Rathlin says. 'There will be time enough for testimony later – when you appear before the Queen's Bench.'

'Were you *ever* alone with Her Grace?' Athy asks.

'Is that an offence? I hear tell the Earl of Essex is often in her privy company.'

'Answer the question,' says Athy sourly.

'Then, never. I was always in the company of either Baronsdale or Beston.'

Rathlin raises a lawyer's eyebrow, as though he's found the fatal flaw in the defence. 'So there were *others* in this conspiracy?'

Nicholas manages not to laugh. 'Master Baronsdale is president of the College of Physicians. Beston is one of the Censors, responsible for testing our professional knowledge. Are you suggesting the entire membership of the College conspired to poison the queen, Master Rathlin? All of us?'

'You could still have secreted your poison in some innocent-looking vessel, Dr Shelby.'

Now the laugh cannot be restrained. 'Master Athy, Censor Beston might not be the sharpest of scalpels I've come across, but even *he* would manage to make a connection between a junior physician administering an unapproved draught to Her Grace and her subsequent demise.'

Rathlin leans forward across the trestle, the elbows of his lawyer's gown leaving a snail's trail of dust as they move. He steeples his fingers under his chin as he looks up at Nicholas with his cold judicial eyes. 'Perhaps, being a medical man and not of our profession, Dr Shelby, you do not know that even *speaking* of the queen's death is tantamount to sedition. It is forbidden.'

'If you're going to accuse me of seeking to poison her, and I am to defend myself, it's a little difficult not to.'

'Are you saying you deny the charge?'

For a moment Nicholas does not answer. Wearily he raises his gaze towards the low ceiling. Inches above his head a row of rusty iron hooks hang from a rafter like the sagging eyes of a dropsy patient.

'Is that what you did to poor Dr Lopez – decide he was guilty from the start?'

Rathlin seems caught by surprise. 'I cannot tell you, Dr Shelby,' he says. 'Neither I nor Master Athy was party to the examination of Lopez. That was conducted by the earl himself, and Sir Robert Cecil.'

The news gives Nicholas a glimmer of hope. Perhaps a formal charge has not yet been laid against him. Perhaps this really is a consequence of nothing but malice – a fiction uttered carelessly by someone who bears him a grudge. But even if it is, Nicholas knows this can still end in a lethal outcome. After all, the queen herself had not agreed to Lopez's execution until the worm of doubt had been woken in her. What if the Earl of Essex is at this very moment in her company, reassuring her that another conspirator has been caught before he can strike? Poor Lopez had been her personal physician for more than thirteen years before she abandoned him. What hope could there be that she would lift even a single bejewelled finger to protect a young man who had been in her presence just four times, a man whom she had already called – perhaps only half-jokingly – a heretic?

Equally concerning to him is how far Robert Cecil will go to protect him. Lord Burghley's son does little that is not in defence of his queen. For all the service Nicholas has given him over the past four years – service that has put his life in jeopardy more than once – he knows that in that crooked little body is an iron-willed ruthlessness. After all, Lopez himself was once Robert Cecil's man. And look where that got him.

'Master Winter,' he hears Rathlin say in a voice he might well use when closing a prosecution, 'I think it time to convey the accused to a place where he may be confined while he considers the wisdom of his defiance.'

And as he senses Winter and Lank-hair move to grip his arms, Nicholas Shelby understands that his ordeal has only just begun.

3

As evening approaches, Bianca Merton waits at the Falcon stairs for a wherry to take her across the Thames. The warmth of the day is fading; a chill is settling on the city. After half an hour her feet are tapping out a tattoo on the planks while the river mocks her impatience with dancing waves turned orange by the setting sun. Then three tilt-boats arrive from the northern bank almost simultaneously. A spirited but good-natured jostle with feet and oars breaks out amongst the boatmen for the best mooring post. 'What are you doing on the water, Tom Frear? You'd be safer pushing a plough,' shouts the first. 'Mercy, good sirs,' says the second to the passengers in another boat, 'you're the first lot today that Jack Tomblin ain't managed to drown.' Tomblin, not to be outdone, roars with good-natured scorn, 'Make way for a proper waterman, you lubbers! Neptune hisself would weep to see such clumsiness.'

By custom, Bianca Merton would watch this tussle with mild amusement. But this evening she is desperate for the wherries to empty. She knows from experience how hard it is to get a private audience with Sir Robert Cecil.

Five young gentlemen from Gray's Inn are the first ashore: trainee lawyers looking for diversion from their studies. To Bianca they look ridiculously young to be chancing purse and body on Bankside. Their beards are meagre and they have more pimples than a freshly plucked goose. She wishes the Jackdaw was still open. At least she'd be able to keep an eye on them, tell them which dice-dens and bawdy-houses to steer clear of, which alleyways to avoid if they should end up alone. But this evening it is all she can do to stop herself shouting at them to get out of her way. When the boat she has chosen is empty, she calls down to the waterman, 'Good morrow, Master Frear. Will you take a fare to the Savoy hospital stairs?'

The boatman looks up. 'You, Mistress Merton? The Savoy hospital? Nothing amiss, is there?'

'Nothing amiss, Master Frear,' she lies. He's noted the agitation in me, she thinks. She tries to compose her features. 'I have some business at Covent Garden, that's all.'

'Shall I wait for a full load to take upriver, or are you in a hurry?'

'A hurry, Master Frear – if that's not a burden to you.'

'Then you're in luck, Mistress. The tide's still on the flow.'

Bianca does the best she can to settle on the cross-bench. Realizing her left hand is drumming on the plank, she fumbles inside her gown for her purse.

Leaning into his oars without breaking rhythm, wherryman Frear shakes his head. 'There'll be no need of that, Mistress Merton. You and Dr Shelby cured my Mags of the tertian fever. Twelfth Night last, it was. Say the word an' I'll row you to Oxford and back, an' twice on Accession Day, all for gratis.'

Bianca gives him a grateful smile. It hides a cold swell of fear in her belly that has nothing to do with the rise and fall of the wherry as it strikes out past the Paris Garden towards Whitehall. From the moment Rose Monkton came flying through the door, her mistress has been pondering the likelihood that one of the most powerful men in the kingdom will happily lay aside whatever occupies him this evening just to grant an audience to a Bankside tavern owner without a tavern.

In the event, she doesn't recognize the gatekeeper on duty at

Cecil House. He, in turn, does not recognize her. And even if he did, Bianca knows he is but the first thorn bush in a whole thicket set around the queen's secretary that grows denser, the more one tries to penetrate it. She adopts a tone she thinks might sound authoritative.

'I am the wife of one of Sir Robert's physicians,' she begins. Even now it sounds strange to her. 'I must speak to Sir Robert. It's urgent.'

'Sir Robert's physician, you say?'

'Dr Nicholas Shelby. You must have seen him pass through these gates before now.'

The gatekeeper nods. 'The young fellow who don't look like a physician?'

'That would be him.'

'And you're his wife?'

'Yes. I am Mistress Merton.'

'But you said you were Dr Shelby's wife.'

'I am.'

'So why are you Mistress Merton and not Goodwife Shelby?'

'I am both,' she says, having little time for the English practice of subsumption by marriage.

'How can a body be two people at once?'

'I *have* to speak to Sir Robert.'

'What about?'

'A privy matter.'

'I'll have to know more before I can pass a message.'

Bianca's jaw stiffens. 'I told you, I'm the wife of his physician. It's about a pustule that needs lancing.'

Even in the dusk Bianca can see the relish in the gatekeeper's eyes. He's savouring how the revelation will play with the other servants when he tells them the son of the Lord Treasurer has a boil somewhere on his august person.

'A pustule – whereabouts?'

Bianca smiles sweetly at him.

'It's guarding his gatehouse.'

Less than ten minutes later she finds herself sitting on a window seat beside a tall column of mullioned glass stained orange by the setting sun, staring fixedly at a mantelpiece carved with the Cecil insignia, and trying to slow the frenzied beating of her heart by silently counting the monotonous ticking of a fine French clock.

✠

Nicholas has no idea how much time has passed since Winter pushed him through the door of this new chamber. But at least his accommodation has improved. They have taken him from the old carpenter's store to a minor wing of Essex House. He can sense, perhaps by the stagnant closeness of the air, that it has been used as a depository for things no longer necessary to the earl's comfort: furniture that is out of fashion, boxes of clothes that now fail to dazzle, people... The floor is tiled, a white-and-red zigzag that makes him think of blood running over the planks of a scaffold. He wonders if this is where they kept Lopez while they plastered over the gaping cracks in their case against him.

He is lying on single narrow cot, not quite wide enough to take a fully-grown man. The coarse woollen sheet scratches through the linen of his shirt. It fails miserably to soften the hardness of the boards beneath. If he rests his arms by his sides, the limbs are forced inwards across his body; if he extends them, the edges of the cot are hard against his elbows. Either way, he cannot sleep. Perhaps that's the aim. Wear him down. Exhaust him. Confessions can be wrung out of a man without recourse to hot iron or cold fists.

Sometime after Winter had left he heard a key turning to unlock the door. Thinking the interrogation was about to begin again, he lifted himself off the cot, preferring to face them on his feet than prone like a beaten dog. But it had only been a servant bringing a plate of bread and cheese and a pot of small-beer.

He wonders if Rathlin and Athy will come again. Perhaps Essex will send someone more significant. If it is Chief Justice Popham, or Attorney General Coke, or even Essex himself, then the thread of hope will unravel. His greatest fear is that they will come accompanied by the infamous Richard Topcliffe, the queen's tame torturer.

To master the fear inside him, and to suppress his longing to be with Bianca, in his mind he runs through his knowledge of Italian vocabulary. In their time at Nonsuch over the winter, she helped him improve his limited skill in the language. For him it had been just a diversion. His real motive had been to strengthen the muscles in her throat, to aid her recovery from the laryngotomy he had been forced to perform in order to save her life, after the smoke from the fire that destroyed the Jackdaw had almost killed her. He reaches *benefico* before something resembling sleep takes him.

✠

A key turning in the lock brings him suddenly awake. Two faces emerge from the blackness, each turned into a devil's mask by a sudden flare of candlelight. One of the masks speaks.

'You are to come with us, Dr Shelby.'

The voice is Rathlin's. Nicholas presumes the second demon is Athy. Rising stiffly from the cot, he asks, 'What hour is it? Where are you taking me?'

He receives no answer. Despite his aching limbs, he thinks of punching the closest devil's face and making a break for it.

But beyond the compass of the candlelight there is nothing but blackness. He has no idea where to run to. So with Rathlin leading and Athy as rearguard, he walks hesitantly into the depths of Essex House.

After a meandering journey that costs him barked shins and several harsh prods in the back, a door looms out of the night, framed by the faintest sliver of light. Nicholas almost walks into Rathlin's back as he stops. He sees the candle flame move diagonally, extinguished and then relit as it passes across the silhouette of the lawyer's body. He hears Rathlin's fist rap twice on the door. The next moment he is standing, blinking furiously, in a grandly appointed room lit by more candles than he can count. Their flickering light makes a dancing cloudscape on the gleaming white plaster ceiling, casting shadows from the ornate moulding. On the far wall, an oak gallery extends from one side to the other above a row of paintings that he takes to be leading members of the Devereux family.

In the centre of the room stands a tall man, a little younger than himself. He sports a sandy-coloured beard and a doublet seeded with more pearls than a diver could harvest in a year and still have lungs to breathe with. He eyes Nicholas with detached disappointment, as though he's bought a hunting dog on a false recommendation. Nicholas knows him at once. It is Robert Devereux, the Earl of Essex.

But it is the familiar little figure beside him, reduced even further by his neighbour's magnificence, his crooked stance a blemish on this otherwise-pristine canvas, that truly draws Nicholas's attention. It is Sir Robert Cecil.

Nicholas's heart sinks. He has always known that friendship and loyalty would mean nothing to Lord Burghley's crook-backed son if he thought the realm's safety was at stake. Look how he had turned his back on old Lopez.

And then, to his astonishment, he hears a woman's voice. It comes from his left, in a pool of shadows the candlelight has not penetrated. And it is even more familiar to him than Cecil's broken outline.

'Mercy, Husband!' Bianca Merton says. 'I let you out of my sight for one moment and you wander off like a brainless goat in an olive grove.'

✠

Robert Cecil's men have brought a spare horse for Nicholas to ride the short distance from Essex House to the Strand. He wonders grimly if that's because Cecil and Bianca had expected to find him beaten and unable to walk unaided.

A footman leads the way with a horn lantern. The queen's secretary, Nicholas and Bianca ride together, almost stirrup to stirrup, their mounts picking their way carefully through the night. Three grooms make up the rearguard a short way behind. The sky is clear, an intense black velvet broken only by a quarter-moon and a scattering of attendant stars. Along the broad earthen path, grand houses loom like abandoned temples in an ancient landscape. Owls call like lost souls from the fields of Covent Garden.

The Lord Treasurer's son rides with an ease that makes the twisted curve of his shoulders seem a natural facet of his horse's movement. For once, he appears supple. To Nicholas, he looks like a creature who belongs to the night. He seems strangely good-tempered for a busy man called out when he should be abed.

'I have not bested the handsome Earl of Essex for a while,' Cecil says as they emerge from Ivy Lane onto the Strand. 'We can expect tantrums at court, of course. Strange how such a well-made shell can hold so petulant a yolk.'

'I cannot thank you enough, Sir Robert,' Nicholas says, for what must be the fourth time since leaving Essex House. He turns towards Bianca. 'I despaired of seeing my wife again.'

'I thank God all heretics are not so determined, else I might begin to fear for our realm's safe continuance.' It is said with humour. But Nicholas knows there had been a time when Robert Cecil would have spoken those words in all seriousness. 'Your wife is not a woman to be dismissed easily, Dr Shelby,' Cecil continues. 'She insulted my gatekeeper, put one of my grooms in fear of his soul with her threats of witchcraft, refused to let my secretaries have a moment's peace until they fetched me... What is it like, being married to a shrew?'

'That is not strictly true, Sir Robert,' Bianca interjects. 'I confess that I *did* imply to your gatekeeper that he was a pustule, and I *might* have told that groom I have a distillation that makes the privy member shrink, and that I would put some in his ale if he didn't fetch me someone with a little authority. But your secretary punished me for it, by having me sit in an empty chamber for two hours until I could stand it no more and went in search of you myself.'

'Do you know who denounced me, Sir Robert?' Nicholas asks.

'Not yet. It appears Devereux's secretaries acted impetuously. I *suppose* I should commend their enthusiasm.'

'I'm surprised he let me go so willingly.'

'In the correct order of things, I should have deferred to him – Devereux being an earl. But I am the queen's privy councillor and secretary, and my father carries the queen's favour more securely than he does. I interrupted our noble young friend at a late supper with the Earl of Salisbury.' He laughs. 'A main course of poetry, followed by an unexpected dish of indigestion. To my mind, all very satisfactory.'

At Cecil House the servants are used to visitors in the small hours, expected or not. There are returning ambassadors, envoys, intelligencers, agents of influence and a host of others who need to rest after delivering their secrets to the Cecils. A guest chamber in the south-eastern corner tower is swiftly made ready. It is small, but finely furnished with a carved tester bed and Flanders hangings. Cold brawn and hippocras arrive, as if from nowhere, to quell the hunger and slake the thirst.

'You *do* know it to be a lie: that I conspired with poor Lopez to poison the queen?' Nicholas tells Robert Cecil as he bids them good rest.

'Of course. I never doubted it. Why would I turn out in the dead of night to haul you away from Robert Devereux, if I had?'

'Slanders can be hard to erase, these days.'

'We shall speak tomorrow. Perhaps by then one of my clever fellows will have learned more about the identity of your accuser.'

When Cecil has departed, Nicholas stretches out, laying his head back on the bolster. It's a blessed comfort after the confines of the narrow cot at Essex House.

Bianca crawls around him on all fours, drawing the tester's curtains – enclosed; confined. 'You have Rose to thank, not me,' she says, her face cut by a thin line of candlelight penetrating through a gap in the fabric.

'She must have recognized Essex's livery.'

'For once she was paying attention to something other than the fancies in that head of hers. I shall have to stop calling her Mistress Moonbeam.' Bianca sits beside him on her haunches, though in the darkness he can barely see her outline. 'You *didn't*, did you?'

'I didn't what?'

'Seek to poison the queen?'

'No!'

For a moment he thinks she might doubt his innocence. Then she adds, 'You do realize there can be but one poisoner in our union, Nicholas? You're the healer, I'm the poisoner, remember? My mother, God save her soul, would turn in her grave in Padua if she thought I'd broken the family chain.'

He laughs. 'You've never *really* poisoned anyone, have you?'

'Of course not.'

He can't see if she's smiling, or if she has that steely glint in her amber eyes that comes whenever she's decided to keep something to herself.

'Well, not a *fatal* poison. But there's always a first time for everything, Nicholas.'

'Sir Robert will summon us in a few hours,' he murmurs. 'We should sleep, or else—' He breaks off to yawn. In the darkness within the tester he feels Bianca's weight as she places herself astride him.

Then he hears her say, 'I think I choose the "else".'

4

The view from Robert Cecil's study windows on the fourth storey of the north-western tower affords a fine panorama of Covent Garden fields. Beyond the stands of ash, oak and elm, Nicholas can make out Longacre and the hamlet of St Giles, greyed by a mid-morning shower. On Cecil's desk is the squat golden box of a clock, just like the one Bianca had seen during her wait the previous evening. It has a dome for a bell on top. The single hand – counting off the hours – is an elongated, stylized ray of sunlight radiating from a central Helios with a human face. With a little mechanical cough, the sunbeam slips above the Roman numerals XI etched around its circumference. From within comes a whirring of coiled springs and the biting of ratchet teeth, followed by the tinny tolling from the bell. Cecil looks up from his papers and catches Bianca looking at the apparatus.

'A fine horologe, is it not, madam?'

'*La misura del tempo*,' Bianca reads from an inscription below the face. 'The measure of time.'

'Of course, you read Italian. I had almost forgotten you were a foreigner to our realm. Padua, was it not?'

'Yes. That is where I was born. But we could not afford a machine to tell us the hour, Sir Robert. We had to rely on the church bell. We managed, I seem to recall.'

'It is a brother to one I presented to the queen,' Cecil says proudly. 'The mechanism was made by the late Master Urseau,

Her Grace's clockmaker. But I imported the cases from Florence. She prefers things Italian to French. She still thinks Master Urseau came from Turin. She will hear nothing to the contrary.'

'Do we *really* have need of such devices?' Bianca asks. 'Should we not rely on nature to tell us when to get up or go to bed, when to sow our crops and when to harvest them? I'm content with the church bell and the rising and setting of the sun. It seems more in tune with how things should be.'

'My wife has better intuition than many,' Nicholas says. 'Perhaps that is because her senses are sharper.'

Cecil gets up from his desk. He points to the Molyneux globe in the corner of the study, a model earth made of wood and lacquer set on its axis in an elaborately carved frame. It is the one on which he described the journey Nicholas was to undertake to Morocco the previous year. 'Senses are all to the good,' he says. 'They are given to us by God, so that we may see His world in all its majesty. But if my cousin, young Master Francis Bacon, is right, we are entering a world in which the new learning – measurement, precision, discovery – will give us answers to phenomena that are, at present, mysteries to us. I happen to think he is right. Why, there are now clever artisans who can make a clock so small that a man may carry it in his purse. My father has one. Soon we may be able to measure accurately not just the passing of the hours, but minutes – even the theoretical second.'

Nicholas thinks: you've come a long way from the day, almost four years ago, when you thought that because one of my medical books was printed in Italy, the knowledge in it must be heretical.

'Why would we want to do that?' Bianca asks. 'Do our lives not speed by far too quickly as it is?'

Nicholas winces. The Cecils are not accustomed to being questioned by their inferiors, least of all by a female recusant. But Sir

41

Robert has developed a grudging respect for Bianca Merton and gives her nothing more reproachful than an indulgent smile.

'It is all about measurement, Mistress Merton,' he explains. 'As an example, measurement might help us learn if Master Copernicus was right when he claimed the earth is not still, and that instead of being fixed at the centre of the cosmos, it moves about the sun in a great orbit.' He shrugs. 'Though why we don't all fly off as it travels, he failed to tell us.' Glancing at Nicholas, perhaps for respite, he adds, 'Given your wild views on some matters of physic, Nicholas, I presume you favour the Polack's claims.'

'I believe they merit further consideration, Sir Robert.'

'Don't tell the bishops that, or there are bound to be more anonymous accusations made against you.'

Nicholas stiffens. 'You have news?'

Cecil gives him a look of regret. 'Not much, though I fear what I have been able to determine is not good.'

'Please be frank with me, Sir Robert.'

'There was more than one letter sent. But they are all in the same hand.'

Nicholas closes his eyes. 'Sent to whom?'

'Sir John Popham, Chief Justice of the Queen's Bench.'

Nicholas winces. 'Oh, *Jesu!*'

'And the Attorney General, Sir Edward Coke. There could be others.'

Bianca grips her husband's arm. She leans into him, telling him without words that he does not face this new danger alone.

'What can I do?' he asks.

'I can keep Essex at bay a little longer,' Cecil tells him, returning to his desk. 'But with Popham and Coke demanding further investigation, I fear I may be outfought.'

'Then I am still in danger of arraignment?'

Cecil looks pained. 'I will do my utmost for you, Nicholas. I promise it. I do not wish the only physician I trust – not to mention a particularly useful intelligencer – to fall because of malicious tittle-tattle.' A sigh, followed by an opening of the palms to show that even a privy councillor has limits to what he may achieve. 'But if they succeed in convincing Her Grace not to heed my defence...'

'What do you suggest I do, Sir Robert?' Nicholas asks, unable to keep a trace of desperation from his voice.

'Until I get to the bottom of this slander, I think it would be wise for you disappear for a while.'

Bianca turns her head away from her husband. She doesn't want him to see the shadow of fear that has clouded her eyes. Since the day he came to her – a living corpse covered in river mud, a man who had sought to destroy himself because his physic could not save his first wife and the child she had been carrying – Nicholas has left her only twice. On both occasions he brought violence and death clinging to his shadow when he returned.

'I could go back to Suffolk,' he says. 'I'm not much of a farmer, but my father will put on a brave face and tell me he's grateful for the extra pair of hands.'

'I wasn't thinking of Suffolk,' Cecil tells him.

'Then where?'

Cecil nods in the direction of the Molyneux globe. 'Somewhere that Essex, Coke and Popham will consider it too much of an expense to bother you. Somewhere across the Narrow Sea. I think it's time you left the realm awhile.'

✠

His minor victory over the Earl of Essex seems to have inspired an unusual, jovial generosity in Robert Cecil. Before it has a chance to fade, Nicholas accepts the offer of his private wherry for the journey back to Bankside. At the end of the jetty he and Bianca see two oarsmen rigging a canvas awning against the threatening showers. Beyond, the river slides reluctantly towards the east, glassy under the noon sun.

They remain silent for most of the journey. They sit slightly apart in the stern, each lost in their own thoughts. There is a purpose to their silence: great men place spies in the households of their competitors. For all Robert Cecil's diligence, who is to say that one of these boatmen has not been placed in his service by an Essex, or a Coke, or a Popham? So when they do speak, Nicholas and Bianca confine themselves to inconsequential talk: the rebuilding of the Jackdaw and how the head carpenter prefers chattering to chiselling; how the Lord Chamberlain players have amalgamated with the Lord Admiral's men to perform at Newington Butts, and whether it will affect business at the Rose theatre on Bankside; whether Master Shakespeare will write something a little less stomach-turning than *Titus Andronicus*, because frankly Bianca is getting a little weary of having to turn out to treat people whose constitution can't handle all that stage-blood, yet are happy to turn up to watch a performance of a more realistic nature at Tyburn or upon Tower Hill.

From the Falcon stairs, they go directly to their lodgings by the Paris Garden. Catching sight of their approach, Rose almost topples her pail of water as she rises too abruptly from scrubbing the flagstones.

'Mercy, I thought you'd both been taken by the fairy folk!'

'You did well, Rose,' Nicholas tells her. 'I'd still be at Essex House if you hadn't recognized that livery.'

Rose scowls. 'Robert Devereux may be the 'andsomest man in all England, an' an earl an' everything, but that don't give 'im no right to 'ave his bully-boys manhandle Master Nicholas. A right pair of rufflers they looked. Whatever was they about?'

'Someone wrote some lies about me, Rose, that's all. He sent them to Essex and others.'

'Does this saucy rogue 'ave a name?'

'Anonymous, I'm afraid.'

Rose's black ringlets swirl with a defiant will of their own. Her plump cheeks colour with anger. 'Well, you tell me where this Master Nonny-mouse lives, an' I'll call my Ned back from Nonsuch to 'ave one of his friendly words.'

Nicholas smiles, glad she's on his side. 'I'm home now, Rose. That's all that matters.'

'For a little while,' says Bianca with a cautionary tone. 'Sir Robert Cecil says that Master Nicholas should leave the city, as a precaution. And for the very first time I find myself in agreement with him.'

Rose seems suddenly short of breath. 'But he *can't*!'

'Why not?' Bianca asks.

Rose looks close to tears. 'When he went swanning off to the Barbary shore last year, you almost *died*, Mistress.' She turns to Nicholas, her chest heaving beneath her gown, her eyes wide with anxiety. 'And when *you* went off to Gloucestershire that time, you almost died, too.' She thrusts her open hands out towards them, as though offering a precious gift. 'Can't you *see* – going away ain't good for either of you!'

'Don't be silly, Rose,' Bianca says. 'No one is going to come to any harm. It's only for a while.'

'How much of a while?' Rose demands to know, withdrawing her hands and balling them against her hips.

'Just until Sir Robert has managed to find out who's making these unfounded accusations against Nicholas.'

'Ned and I shall come with you,' Rose announces. 'To keep you safe.'

Bianca is touched by her fervour, but adamant. 'I will need you and Ned here, to watch over the work on the Jackdaw.'

'You're going *with* 'im?' Rose squeaks as the realization strikes her.

'Of course I'm going with him,' Bianca says, taking hold of Nicholas's arm. 'He's my husband.'

✠

It is evening, and far away from Bankside – across the Narrow Sea in fact, in a small city to the north-east of Antwerp. A young woman dressed in a threadbare brown kirtle stands gazing up at the façade of a cathedral, steeling herself to enter. The city is called 's-Hertogenbosch, known more simply to Brabantians as Den Bosch, and the maid's name is Hella Maas.

In years she is closer to Rose Monkton than to Nicholas Shelby or Bianca Merton. But there the similarity ends. Where Rose is the very picture of pastoral pulchritude, this young woman has a severe, broken beauty. It is a beauty forged in grief. Her eyes are deep and dark, bulbous, as though too many bad dreams are pushing against them from the inside.

From the great tower that soars above her, the cathedral's bell begins to ring out its sonorous invitation. The deep, bass voice makes the warm evening air quiver, as though it has a pulse, as though it is alive. Hella knows that in the narrow channels of the Binnendieze, running through the city the way veins and arteries run through her own body, the water will be rippling in concert. It will make the shadows dance beneath the little bridges that seem to spring between cliffs of mossy brickwork.

Hella has come to the great cathedral of St John the Evangelist because she has heard what lies within. Were it not for Father Vermeiren, she would have come sooner, but the priest is large in frame and voice, and his scowl frightens her. She would not put it past him to give her up to the Spanish garrison as a troublemaker, and she knows only too well the extent of their cruel depravities.

Her self-inflicted banishment has cost her dear. She has missed being present at Mass, and she knows God will have witnessed her absence. But today she has summoned all her courage. Because today is the one day of the week when Father Vermeiren stands before the congregation and opens God's window to let everyone see a glimpse of His great plan.

Hella waits silently while the inhabitants of Den Bosch hurry past her into the darkness beyond the great door. She sees the stolid cloth merchants, their faces lined with furrows of resignation from the endless battle to compete with English imports; the tough little beef farmers who can find grazing pasture even on soil made spongy by too much rain and too high a water table; the well-dressed men of commerce who now look for their profits to Antwerp rather than Cologne; the Spanish soldiers of the garrison, even more pious than the local clerics and just as dangerous. Some meet her gaze with a flicker of recognition, though fewer now than when she first arrived in the city.

There had been a time, barely a month ago, when they would have gathered in the Markt square in their hundreds to hear her preach. Then they had pressed in upon her, straining to hear her words, marvelling that God would choose such an insubstantial vessel through which to let His voice flow. Now, if they recognize her at all, they turn their heads away. They place themselves between her and their children, as if she carries a contagion. They no longer want to hear her warnings. Yet warnings are what Hella knows she was put on this earth to deliver.

For as long as she can remember she has understood the power of portents. Even as a child, she could link something bad happening to a recent storm, or a flood, or a fire brought about by a lightning strike. Had not her very birth occurred in the year that a new star had blazed into being in the night sky?

She does not think this second sight of hers is a gift. For Hella, to be permitted glimpses of the future but be unable to alter it, to gain knowledge only to watch helplessly as the consequences bring death in their wake, to see things she would rather not see, is a curse. Sometimes she thinks she would be better off blind.

Every day, for the past thirteen years, she has castigated herself for failing to use this ability to warn the people of Breda, her home town, of the catastrophe that engulfed them on the very day she turned eight. *Eight*: a number that the Bible associates with resurrection. Her sister Hannie had taught her that, and Hannie – five years older and twice as clever – had shared her delight in the magic of numbers. But Hannie is dead, along with almost six hundred other citizens of Breda, amongst them nearly every other member of the Maas family. *Six hundred*: the number of chariots that Pharaoh sent to hunt down the Israelites.

In the years that have passed since that day, Hella has turned the guilt, the self-reproach, to good use. Whenever the ghosts of her family drifted across her vision, which was every single day, she would imagine they were encouraging her from heaven to warn the living that God does not want us to lift the curtain. He doesn't want us to go searching for what might lie behind it – like so many of those pursuing the new learning, the new sciences. *Tell them*, sister Hannie would whisper to her, *that I was wrong, that there are some things it is best not to know.*

In Den Bosch, the crowds who came to listen to her had soon begun to thin. The first to go had been the ones who shouted back that she was frightening their children. More followed. Every day there would be fewer gathering around her in the Markt square. She had wondered if Father Vermeiren from the cathedral was behind it. Had he warned his parishioners that it was not proper for a woman to preach? She knew for a fact that he had led a delegation of city burghers to the Beguinage, the community of pious women who had given her shelter and board, suggesting they expel her, because that was exactly what they had done. She had been forced to sleep under a bridge, to hold out her hand for food like a beggar. Soon she had found herself addressing hardly anyone but the town drunks and the worst sort of men, who insulted her with obscenities and derision.

And then she had learned the true reason why most of Den Bosch had abandoned her sermons: they had only been listening to her because she was a novelty. They had their own window into God's plan for mankind. And it lay inside their own cathedral. And now she has summoned up the courage to defy Father Vermeiren and see it for herself.

Waiting for a gap in the flow of people passing through the great arched entrance, Hella picks her moment and slips inside.

The nave is cast in shadow, the pale slender columns reaching into the canopy of the roof like a forest made of stone. She can smell incense burning in sconces, and the dusty scent left by centuries of pious feet rubbing against the flagstones. Taking her place as close to the altar as she can, Hella pulls her plain cloth gown over her head, so that Father Vermeiren, should he see her, will take her for just another of the Beguines, come to hear his homily on how to live a pious life.

The painting stands behind the altar, resting on a gilded screen. As tall as Hella herself and half her height again in length, it is a triptych, its two outer panels folded inwards to hide the centre section. Thus, as Hella stares at it, wondering how it can possibly draw the citizens of Den Bosch away from God's word as channelled through her, it reveals to her only the forms of two saints, each one painted entirely in shades of grey on the back of its folding wings. Their lack of colour reminds her of the images that often appear in her own head, images of her sister Hannie, of her parents: ghostly, insubstantial, always in danger of slipping away when she tries to fix them in her memory. Images of the dead, slain because she, Hella, hadn't had the wisdom to heed the portents properly, hadn't warned them of what was coming.

Hella can sense the growing excitement in the congregation as Father Vermeiren moves towards the altar, his deep booming voice calling them to penance. Two of his priestly procession move to the triptych and begin to open the side-panels, slowly, as though what lies within might blind them if revealed too suddenly.

The ripple of gasps that flows through the worshippers sounds to Hella like a cold wind blowing over tall grass in the dead of night. What they are seeing, most have seen before, but that does not stop the congregation giving a collective shudder, as if they are all part of the same frightened organism.

After that, Hella Maas hears nothing, not even Father Vermeiren's great voice as he begins the liturgy. She feels nothing, not even the elbow of the person beside her as he pushes forward to get a better view. If she were a martyr, she wouldn't feel the pain of the arrow as it strikes or the sword as it falls. Nothing exists except what she sees laid out before her on the now-open triptych. She feels a great wave sweep her up, carrying her into the images burning themselves into her eyes.

But it is no wave of holy exultation. It is a wave of terror. True, the window has been opened, and Hella Maas is staring through it. But she is staring not into heaven, hoping to see an imagined glimpse of sister Hannie and her parents – she is staring directly into hell.

5

In the privacy of their bedchamber, Bianca sits in the single chair and swings her legs so that her feet are resting on the edge of the bed. Her kirtle falls back over her knees.

'Can Lord Lumley not help us?' she asks. 'Surely he can tell the queen you're innocent.'

'John Lumley may have her favour, but he's still a recusant. The Privy Council will try to persuade her that he's protecting a traitor. I won't risk making things more hazardous for him. We've seen, with Dr Lopez, how easily the queen's trust can be undermined.'

'Then where do we go, Husband?'

'I know the Low Countries well enough, from the summer I spent as a surgeon to the army of the House of Orange in the war against the Spanish occupation.'

'Holland? But it's crawling with English agents, isn't it? You've told me before: the Privy Council has its watchers and informers everywhere.'

'That's true. And if the purse was heavy enough, they wouldn't hesitate to take us by force.'

An idea pops into Bianca's head, like a sudden flash of sunlight from behind a raincloud. 'Then we choose somewhere where my own faith is in the ascendancy. A Catholic country.'

Nicholas considers this for a moment. Then he says, 'You know very well that I have no time for religious factions, sweet. But I'd be exposed as a heretic the moment I opened my mouth.'

'I can help you pass for a good Catholic, Nicholas,' Bianca says with a bright laugh. 'If you'll chance your immortal soul.'

'According to Robert Cecil, it was damned the moment I fell in love with you.' He grins. 'But you know, it might just work. You're a marvel, Mistress Merton.'

'Do you have anywhere in mind, Nicholas? Please don't choose some dull, provincial backwater. I would lose all joy in such a place.'

He thinks hard. 'We need somewhere that Spanish rule is not too arduous; somewhere accustomed to foreign merchants and traders coming and going at will. A town where two new faces are scarcely worth remarking upon.'

'Can you think of such a place?'

'Without a moment's pause, Wife. We'll try Antwerp for a while.'

It is the obvious place, Nicholas tells her. It even has an exchange where they can convert English coin into *gulden* or *ecu* – though since the queen's father debased the English currency, they will have to swallow the punitive exchange rate.

'I've heard Antwerp is a fine city,' she says, remembering three Dutch brothers who drank at the Jackdaw before the fire, Protestant weavers who had fled from the Spanish occupation.

'Then Antwerp it shall be,' Nicholas says. 'Where better to lose ourselves than in the Duchy of Brabant?'

Bianca frowns. 'But first we have to escape from England. What if they put a watch on the ports?'

Nicholas runs a hand through the black wiry tangle of his hair, as though to plough a disciplined furrow through his thoughts. 'We must put our trust in the fact they have not issued a formal arraignment against me. That gives us a few days' head-start. But we can't delay.'

'And if Essex, Coke or Popham sends men after us?'

'We must misdirect them – lay a false trail.'

'Then are we already fugitives?'

'It would be foolish,' he answers, 'to think ourselves otherwise.'

✵

The Tabard inn lies just off Long Southwark, south of the great stone gatehouse at the foot of London Bridge. You can spot it from a hundred yards away by the garish sign of a man's tunic quartered with heraldic insignia. It boasts good lodgings, decent ale and livery stables where you may leave your horse if you are rich enough to own one, or rent one if you're not. It is a pilgrims' tavern. It marks the start of the spiritual road to Canterbury and on to St Peter's in Rome, though with the queen's new religion now firmly established, fewer use it for that purpose. Now it caters mostly for visitors bound for the city across the bridge.

Bianca Merton has always considered it a model of what a tavern in the Liberty of Southwark should be, although she baulks at the landlord's toleration of the more brazen type of Bankside doxy. However, on the morning of the day after Nicholas's release from Essex House, its greatest recommendation for Bianca and Nicholas is that the husband of Jenny Solver – Southwark's most efficient gossip – is a regular.

They enter the stable courtyard as St Saviour's bell tolls eight. Yesterday's showers have brought out the sweet ammoniacal smell of manure from the stalls, along with the musty tang of old leather and horsehair. The ostler, Tom Prithy, greets them warmly. He is a man wholly suited to his role, with a long equine face and wide, trusting eyes arched by eyebrows too delicate for his runnelled complexion. He even has a habit of stamping his left foot when making a point, like an impatient courser. Prithy is a good man, and Bianca is reluctant to take advantage of him. But needs must.

First, she engages him in a pleasant exchange about nothing in particular. Then she asks after his daughter: does she need any more of the posca of vinegar and herbs for that cold distemper of the stomach? Prithy thanks her warmly and says no, his daughter is restored to her former good health, thanks to the efforts of Dr Shelby and... he tries to say 'Goodwife Shelby' but gets no further than 'Goo—' before reverting thankfully to 'Mistress Merton'.

Then Nicholas asks, 'Do you have two sound mares we can hire? We have to make a journey – the day after tomorrow.'

'Must be important, to miss the Midsummer Day revels.'

'A physician is always on call, Master Prithy.'

'These mares – short legs or long?'

'Long enough for Dover.'

'Dover?' says Tom Prithy with a lift of his lugubrious eyebrows. 'They must be paying you well, this patient. Ain't Dover got no physicians of their own?'

Before Nicholas can answer, Bianca says with uncharacteristic vehemence, 'Dover? I thought we'd agreed *against* Dover.'

'No, Wife. I told you quite clearly it must be Dover,' Nicholas says with laborious patience.

'But Dover is a hateful little place! Even in the sunshine it's beset by French gales. The streets stink worse than they do here; and the *people* – I can't even bring myself to think of the people.'

Nicholas says sternly, 'I have decided we are going to Dover. Have you forgotten, so soon, that you are now a wife? A measure of the proper obedience is required from you.'

Bianca purses her lips. 'If you command it, Husband, then I *suppose* it will have to be Dover. But I still loathe the place.'

'You're only saying that because my brother's wife comes from Dover. You've never liked her. You've always made that clear enough.'

This is a fiction. Nicholas's sister-in-law is from Woodbridge in the county of Suffolk. Bianca has yet to meet her.

'Why would anyone like your sister-in-law anyway?' she snaps petulantly. 'She's a harridan.'

Nicholas draws a slow breath to prepare himself. He says slowly and deliberately, in case Tom Prithy might mishear: 'That's rich talk, coming from the daughter of an Italian witch!'

The slap that lands against Nicholas's face echoes around the stables, bringing forth whinnies of alarm from the stalls, and a look of utter astonishment on Tom Prithy's face.

Later, in the crowded taproom, he will tell his master the landlord – in public – that Dr Shelby and Mistress Merton had their very first argument within his hearing.

'Well, they always were an ill-matched couple,' the landlord will say. 'I'm surprised it's lasted this long.'

'It were all about Dover,' Tom Prithy will say, shaking his head slowly as he marvels at what some folk will find to fall out over.

'Dover?' says the landlord.

'Oh yes,' confirms Tom Prithy, as the customers – including Jenny Solver's husband – crowd even closer to catch the yeast of the gossip, ''twere definitely Dover.'

✠

'I didn't realize you actually meant to strike me,' Nicholas says as they walk back along the riverbank to the Paris Garden. 'Was that really necessary?'

The red mark between his left cheek and the line of his tightly trimmed black beard has yet to fade.

'I thought it would add some authenticity.'

'Authenticity? I think it might have added a loosened tooth.'

'But it did the job, didn't it?'

'There's no question about that,' Nicholas admits, rubbing his cheek.

Bianca leans across and plants a chaste kiss on the red weal. 'A husband striking his wife in the heat of an argument would scarcely draw comment on Bankside, or anywhere else in London

55

for that matter. But a wife striking her husband...' She gives Nicholas a sly grin that he finds just a little alarming. 'Master Prithy will be speaking of it for days to come. And unless Jenny Solver has lost her hearing, or her husband is struck dumb before he gets home—'

Nicholas nods. 'At least, if Essex's searchers come here asking questions, there will be plenty of people to tell them where we've gone. It will take them days to discover we never went within twenty miles of Dover.'

'But if we're not going to Dover to take a ship for Antwerp, where *are* we going to take it from? So far you haven't deigned to tell me.'

'We're going to my father's farm, at Barnthorpe.'

'Are you planning to have me sit in a muddy farm waggon all the way to Antwerp? You do know the Narrow Sea is in the way?'

He takes her teasing in good spirit. 'Woodbridge is barely five miles away. Dutch herring boats and wool traders regularly put in there. We'll pay for a passage on one of those.'

'I suppose it's only right to tell your family you're leaving the realm for a while,' Bianca says with a compassionate nod. 'It will be good to meet them at last.'

Nicholas remembers how he disappeared into a shadowy life of drunkenness and vagrancy after his first wife, Eleanor, died in childbirth. He still finds it hard to forgive himself for the pain he put his family through. He says, 'They deserve to know the reason for my dropping out of plain sight for a while. Besides, they will have to learn at some point quite what a tempest I've married.'

Bianca wonders if he has really given his plan the critical scrutiny it requires. 'Have you forgotten the searchers – the ones the Privy Council send to watch the ports for Jesuit infiltrators?'

'Woodbridge is small. They'll be concentrating on Ipswich or Lowestoft. And they'll be looking for Jesuits trying to *enter* the realm, or papist tracts and pamphlets being smuggled in. A Dutch wool merchant and his wife going home in the opposite direction from a little town on the Deben won't raise their suspicions.'

'Dutch? How do you propose we pass ourselves off as Dutch?'

'Easily. I can muster enough of the Hogen-mogen language – from my summer with the army of the House of Orange. You'll have to speak Italian. I cannot imagine they'll know the difference.'

Bianca is still not convinced. 'But once they learn we didn't enter Dover, the very next place they'll search for us is your family home. And what if they decide to put someone at Aldgate, to keep watch on the road east? They'll take us before we've even left the city.'

It is not often that Nicholas is ahead of his wife in matters devious. He grins. 'We're not taking the road from Aldgate, either.'

'Then short of sprouting wings and flying out of London, where exactly *are* we going?'

But, to her ill-suppressed fury, Nicholas refuses to be drawn.

Time, thinks Nicholas. It is all a matter of judging the falling of the hours. Linger, and Essex might change his mind and come after him. The Chief Justice and the Attorney General might discover an urgency that is usually quite alien to their grand offices. But act too hastily, and flight will look like an admission of guilt. And without preparation, he and Bianca could face the prospect of impoverishment and destitution in a foreign realm. These are the thoughts that drive Nicholas Shelby as he prepares for their departure from London.

'What shall we do for money?' Bianca asks, over a breakfast of brawn and bread.

'We still have plenty left from the prize I brought back from Morocco. Then there's my stipend for attending Sir Robert's son – he owes me for three months.'

'But a heavy purse will draw thieves like a carcass draws flies.'

'We'll take just enough for our immediate needs.'

'And when that runs out?'

'I'll ask Sir Robert to put the Cecil seal on a letter of credit. Antwerp might be Catholic, but she still trades with England, and the great banking families of Europe have agents there. We'll not starve.'

Then there are the mundane practicalities of leaving Bankside. Who will ensure that the fingers of a carpenter's mangled hand are straight and useable, rather than twisted and inflexible, if Dr Shelby is not there to splint them? How will the victim of a street robbery bear the pain of his beating if Mistress Merton is no longer around to provide a decoction of henbane and mandragora? Who will make the powder of cinnamon, myrrh, white amber and *cassia lignea* to help with a difficult childbirth? And if Dr Shelby is not on hand to diagnose a case of bladder stones, and Mistress Merton is not there to mix the fennel root, lovage, black peony and motherwort to dissolve them, how is relief to be found? There are few Banksiders with the money to bring in a physician from across the river. And anyone in Southwark claiming to have studied medicine at Oxford, or Cambridge, or Paris, Basle or Uppsala – or Thebes on the River Nile, for that matter – is without doubt a charlatan.

Throughout the next day Nicholas and Bianca attend to these and other questions. Nicholas returns to St Tom's. He takes great pleasure in announcing his freedom to the warden, telling him that he won't be around for a while as he intends to travel to Dover.

'There's no hospitals in Dover, Shelby – just whores, fishermen and sailors,' the warden points out with a noisy sniff, as though this is the end he's always imagined for Nicholas. 'I trust you'll not be after any of St Thomas's mercury.'

'No hospitals, but plenty of ships,' Nicholas counters, explaining that he's on his way to Paris to take up a position as physician to a rich Huguenot. Dover... Paris... the trail will have any Privy Council searcher tied in knots for weeks.

Leaving the warden to enjoy his sour jealousy, he seeks out a competent barber-surgeon he trusts. He offers the fellow enough out of his own purse to cover his twice-weekly consultations at St Tom's.

Meanwhile Bianca enlists the help of some of the older women of Bankside. She chooses carefully: women of sound common sense who've spent a lifetime caring for children, husbands, parents; women she can trust to prepare a serviceable poultice, plastrum, syrup or tincture. She gives up a few of her secrets in exchange for a clear conscience. Then she sends Rose across the bridge to ensure a line of credit with an apothecaries' merchant in Blackfriars who can provide ingredients.

But what to do about Rose herself? The woman can barely pass a minute without her eyes welling with tears, or loud snorting noises issuing from somewhere deep inside her misery. She has reverted to her former feather-brained self – the persona Bianca calls Mistress Moonbeam. Now Rose is forever misplacing or dropping things and getting her words jumbled up.

'Ned and me... when you leave... that you're safe... how shall we know...?'

'Dry your eyes, Rose, dear.'

'But how long...? You won't even *say*.'

She is only partially mollified when Bianca requests that Rose writes to her husband Ned at Nonsuch, summoning him back to Southwark. 'I'm entrusting the reconstruction to the Jackdaw to you both,' Bianca tells her. 'If Nicholas and I have not returned before it is completed, I want you and Ned to manage it for me. You may have our lodgings here, until the Jackdaw is fit for you to move into.'

Nicholas encloses Rose's note in a letter that he writes to his friend John Lumley, asking him to release Ned from the Nonsuch household. He also asks Lord Lumley to read Rose's words to her husband, because Ned does not have the learning to read them for himself.

Then there is the matter of what to carry on the journey. Nicholas has purchased a collection of pouches and bags from a saddler in Bermondsey. But what to put in them? For him, the choices are made within minutes: his sturdy white canvas doublet that has seen him through all manner of tribulations, three shirts, a change of under-breeches, a knife and spoon, a plate and, for defence against cut-pads and thieves – or, God forbid, any bounty-hunter the Privy Council might send after him – the wheel-lock pistol he brought back from Morocco, along with powder and ball.

Bianca, too, has little to take. Most of her belongings were lost in the arson that destroyed the Jackdaw. Since the fire she has purchased only two new kirtles, one of bottle-green linsey, the other of scarlet mockado, a damask doublet-bodice dyed a fine golden-yellow, two pairs of boots, a farthingale of canvas and whalebone (which will be utterly impractical on a journey on horseback) and some linen under-smocks, plus essential personal items such as a hair comb and eating utensils. Mercifully, on the day of the disaster she had left her favourite carnelian bodice at the Dice Lane shop. Her father had bought it for her on her eighteenth birthday. He'd chosen one of the best tailors in Padua, though he had been far from wealthy. It would have broken her heart to have lost *that*. That will have to come.

There are some items, she decides, that are frankly indispensable. She will not consider going without her own lip colouring, which she makes out of alum, cochineal and gum arabic. Nor will she forgo the little casket in which she keeps the cloves, candle-soot mixed with crushed alabaster and civet, and the application cloth that she uses to clean her teeth. A fugitive she may be, but a Paduan woman has standards to maintain, regardless of the current state of catastrophe.

But what to do about her father's books and his silver Petrine crucifix, also saved because – thank God – they, too, were at Dice Lane?

The books are far too cumbersome and heavy to take. But the cross, on which a finely worked St Peter is being crucified upside-down because he feels unworthy to die in the same manner as his Lord, is barely six inches long. Sentiment, alone, would recommend it. And it could well be useful once they are across the Narrow Sea, adding credibility to the story Nicholas has contrived to explain their arrival in the Catholic territories of the Low Countries: that they are recusants, forced to flee from the cruel oppression of Elizabeth's Protestant ministers. So the cross comes, too. Everything else – hers and Nicholas's – goes into their wooden chest for safekeeping.

Deciding that the hardest leave-taking should be tackled soonest, she takes herself down Black Bull Alley to the little patch of ground she owns tucked away behind an ancient brick wall close to the riverbank.

She stands before the old, lopsided wooden door awhile before entering. The air here is heavy. It is freighted with the essences of a vast weight of muddy grey-brown water sliding past on its way to the sea, bearing with it the detritus of London: a cat that drowned at Esher; a memento that a grieving lover cast in at Kew; a shattered wheel from an old cart abandoned up at Richmond; a rack of rib bones from the shambles at Lambeth Palace; the hopes and fears – and yes, the waste – of two hundred thousand Londoners, and all those souls who people the riverbank along its journey from Avalon, or Eden, or wherever else the English think it rises.

But once Bianca steps inside her little physic garden the air changes. It seems to thrum to the competing scents of thyme and catmint, wormwood and lavender, and all the other herbs and plants she nurtures here, for her balms, concoctions and infusions.

And so she takes a sad farewell of the place she calls her 'other heart'. The place where she can speak her most privy thoughts out loud and know they will receive a safe, warm, fragrant – and, most of all, unjudging – reception.

How will you be, when I see you again? she wonders. *Will you be old and weary, your leaves drooping on their stems like the lank strands of an old woman's hair? Will Rose, whose mind flits as heedlessly as the insects that dance upon your petals, let you die while I am somewhere far away?*

Unable to hold back a tear, Bianca turns and walks back through the little stone archway, locking the door upon the one thing in her life she cannot entirely trust to another's care.

✠

'Antwerp?' says Cecil, as though weighing the word and finding it heavier than he expected. 'I already have a man in Antwerp.'

'That was not my motive for choosing it, Sir Robert – if you recall.'

Cecil nods pensively. 'It's close. I can call you back with ease. And you should be safe enough from the likes of Coke and Popham. But according to my man's dispatches, several high-ranking officers from the Archduke of Austria's household have been seen in the city. The Dons have appointed him governor of the Spanish Netherlands, and he could be planning to make it his headquarters. It might prove too hot for an Englishman. And your new wife does rather have a habit of drawing attention.'

'Then we'll go to Paris, or into the German states. Maybe the Palatine.'

Cecil considers this for a moment. Then he takes up a quill and paper. 'I'll write the letter of credit you have requested – on one condition.'

I wouldn't have expected otherwise, Nicholas thinks. With Robert Cecil, there's always a condition.

'Keep your eyes and ears open,' Cecil says. 'Well-dressed Dons talking loudly in taverns – that sort of thing. Their galleons putting in, or making sail. Bodies of troops arriving or marching out.'

'I don't speak Spanish, Sir Robert.'

Cecil taps the corner of one eye. 'You know what I mean.'

'And on the slight chance that I do learn something, how shall I pass it to you?'

'Let me know where you settle. Use the cipher we agreed upon when you went to the Barbary shore for me last year. Apart from that, write nothing down. I'll inform my agents. They'll seek you out. It's safer that way.'

Not necessarily for me, thinks Nicholas. You don't want me travelling the roads of Europe with a list of your agents in my head.

In the late afternoon he returns to Bankside, richer by six months of stipend, plus his back-pay. The money is a mix of English nobles, florins and *ecus*, drawn from the fund Cecil uses to pay his agents abroad. Along with the purse is a letter of introduction to the banking families with whom the Cecils have dealings in Paris, Rotterdam and Montreux. Nicholas also bears a passport letter with the Cecil seal attached, permitting him to leave England, though Sir Robert has warned him that if Essex, Coke or Popham were to persuade the Privy Council to issue a charter of arraignment, then their document will take precedence and the safe-passage will be worthless.

'So if we're not really going to Dover, and we're not going out of the city to the east by Aldgate, then where *are* we going?' Bianca demands to know, staring at the gleaming coins. 'Are we taking wing to Barnthorpe, like angels?'

'We're going to Gravesend,' he says.

Bianca gives him a puzzled look. Gravesend is separated from the road into Suffolk by the cold and turbulent Thames, ever widening as it flows towards the open sea.

And then she remembers a cold, foggy April night three years past. She and Nicholas had been searching the lanes below the Hythe for a tavern in which to lay their heads. They had gone to the little town that lies to the east of King Henry's great royal shipyard at Woolwich, in the search for a witness to a monstrous crime. She remembers that night not only for the reason behind their visit, but also for the fact she had thought it was to be the night Nicholas would – at last – find the courage to bury Eleanor's ghost and lie with her. It hadn't happened, of course. It had been too early, she had realized. But as the memories of those hours fall into place in her mind, she smiles.

'I think I know why we're going to Gravesend,' she says, her amber eyes gleaming with mischievous light. 'We're going to see Porter Bell.'

6

Nicholas has chosen the perfect day to leave. A misty dawn gives way to a clear blue sky, trimmed at its southern rim by a thin white fleece of cloud. The day has other things to commend it than simply the weather. In the old faith, it is the feast day of St John the Baptist. But to Banksiders it is Midsummer Day, the twenty-fourth of June. Last night was St John's Eve. On the Pike Garden a great bonfire had been lit, and the smell of roasting meat hung on the night air until well after midnight. Knock-down and mad-dog, stitch-back and dragon's milk flowed down thirsty gullets by the barrel-full. Those whom the locals call maltworms were swiftly relieved of their purses whenever they subsided into drunken slumber in a doorway or under a hedge. In the months ahead, more than a few Southwark lads and lasses would find themselves standing nervously before the priest at the entrance to St Saviour's. Bianca had mourned her last evening in Southwark not just because she was leaving, but also for the profit the Jackdaw might have turned, had it still been standing.

She and Nicholas had been careful to keep a clear head. It had been easy for him; he still drinks only carefully, after his descent into Purgatory when Eleanor died. Vagrancy is not a state he has any intention of returning to. As for Bianca, she limited herself to a couple of glasses of Rhenish at the Turk's Head, taking care to sit with her back to the window, so that she might not see the skeleton of the new Jackdaw rising from the ashes a little further down the lane and lose her nerve.

This morning much of Bankside is still abed, snoring through its inebriated dreams. Those who are already up are preparing for the day's continuing celebrations: more feasting, drinking, dancing. A robust game of football has been planned in the Paris Garden, though today Dr Shelby will not be around to treat the broken limbs, squashed noses and flayed knuckles.

When he and Bianca arrive at the Tabard's stables in the clear light of early morning, Tom Prithy sees they have put their domestic spat behind them. They favour him with a cheery wave as they ride out of the Tabard's livery stables towards the Kent road. Dr Shelby's had a word with her, the ostler thinks. He's reminded her of the wifely station ordained by God. Let's hope the peace lasts until Dover.

They ride at a comfortable pace. Hurrying will only serve to draw attention. As they ride down Kentish Street and into the Surrey countryside beyond, the only traffic they meet are laden farm carts coming into the city. The sun is up, the buttercups speckling the fields like gold coins scattered from heaven. Nicholas unlaces his white canvas doublet a little. He has left the more expensive one he'd purchased for the wedding last August in his clothes chest at the Paris Garden lodgings; there's no point looking like a fine prize for a cut-purse.

'I never knew you could ride like a man,' he says, observing how Bianca has chosen a man's saddle, hitched up her gown and now sits astride her horse with a confidence he finds thrilling. He knows he should be scandalized, but he rather enjoys the way she disregards convention.

'In Padua I wanted to ride in the annual horse race,' she tells him, her face lighting up with the memory. 'The boys let me practise with them; but I beat a few of them, so they wouldn't let me compete. They said it was an affront to decency. I quite like being an affront to decency.'

At St Thomas-a-Watering they pass the black, rotting remnants of the traitors and thieves hanged on the gibbet there and left as a warning for wiser folk. It reminds them of what they're fleeing – the price of failure.

At Blackheath they let the horses quench their thirst from a stream, lingering until a drover and his flock have passed out of sight and the way is empty. Then, unobserved, they turn off the Kent road and strike north-east across the heath, towards Woolwich, where the new galleons of the queen's navy are rising from their wooden cribs. Before they reach the dockyard, it is Nicholas's intention that they should join the eastern road to Canterbury. He thinks they can be in Gravesend by dusk.

'I hear tell this place is notorious for felons and cut-purses,' Bianca observes anxiously as they pass along a rutted track between banks of wickedly barbed gorse.

Lifting the flap of a saddle pouch to reveal the polished wooden stock of the wheel-lock pistol, Nicholas smiles. 'It's the pistol Captain Yaxley of the *Marion* gave me when I returned from Morocco. I've already loaded it with powder and ball,' he says confidently. 'If we see cut-purses ahead, all I have to do is take the turning wrench, crank the wheel, prime the pan, set the dogtooth... and give fire.'

'Well then, Husband, that fills me with the *greatest* confidence,' Bianca says with a smile of encouragement. 'Just as long as they don't come at us at the gallop.'

✠

Nicholas's judgement proves sound. In the tranquil dusk of Midsummer Day they enter Gravesend. The little town is still a scene of revelry. On the Hythe, the gravel strand that thrusts out into the river, a crowd of citizens is singing its way through a repertoire of bawdy songs, most of which involve anatomically impossible acts of copulation between the Pope, the King of Spain and a variety of animate and inanimate objects. Inside the Mitre tavern an uneasy Midsummer Day truce is in play. The sailors from the foreign ships anchored off the Hythe keep to themselves, heads down, enjoying their ale in silence, lest their foreign tongues attract attention. The rest of the trade is in boisterous mood. The drinkers are making the most of the day; the field or the river, the furnace or the lathe, will reclaim their labour soon enough. Nicholas and Bianca push their way carefully through the taproom throng. An overturned shovelboard or an inadvertent elbow interrupting a game of hazard will not go down well here: there's enough sharpened steel being carried to armour a porcupine.

Nicholas scans the faces. Porter Bell is not a large man. He could be hard to spot. When they had first seen him here, Bianca thought she was looking at a ghost. Porter's treatment in Holland at the hands of his Spanish captors, and the loss of a son to their muskets, had turned him into a husk of a man, a husk half-drowned in drink. He had lost a second son to a murderer. What must he look like now?

But Nicholas has a feeling that revenge might just have saved Porter Bell, a revenge he himself had contrived, though he has never told Bianca of it. And so he is looking for a face with the first colour of rebirth in it. And indeed, when he turns in response to a tug at his sleeve, he sees that his hopes were well founded.

'Good morrow, Dr Shelby. An' Mistress Merton, too. I'd not thought to see you two again.'

The smile Porter Bell gives them is heartfelt, but uncertain – the smile of a man trying to remember how to do it. But the eyes are not as shrunken as once they were. The skin is no longer spectrally translucent, as though the suffering of the body had thinned the life-force within the flesh.

'You look well, Master Porter,' Bianca says.

'And you may thank the man beside you for that, Mistress.'

For an awful moment Nicholas thinks Porter Bell is going to reveal the cause of his recovery, right here in a crowded tavern. So he says, as nonchalantly as he can contrive, 'That parcel I sent you some time ago – it must have been almost three years...'

'The foreign one,' Bell says, understanding at once.

'Yes. I trust it arrived safely.'

Porter Bell gives him a contented nod. He glances towards the river. 'All that needs saying is that it was successfully delivered to an appropriate destination.'

'Was anyone around to witness its delivery?'

'It was pitch-dark,' Bell says, shaking his head. 'But I'd warrant there's more than a few of us who fought in the Low Countries who would willingly raise a jug in praise of what you did, Dr Shelby.'

Nicholas gives an awkward smile. 'And others who would wish me dead for it, so let us speak of other matters. Are you still a waterman?'

'I am. An' I prosper at it now.'

'I'm glad to hear it.'

Bell gives him a sly glance. 'I don't suppose *you* had anything to do with Lord Lumley sending me that generous sum?'

Nicholas just smiles.

'Well, it was the mending of me, Dr Shelby, that's all I can say. Now I have *two* boats: the old skiff, an' a new pinnace for carrying goods. An' trade on the river is always brisk.'

'You'll be putting the ferry to Tilbury out of business, Master Porter,' Nicholas says with a grin.

'There's room on the river for us all,' Bell says. 'Besides, there's some folk who care not to be seen on the official ferry, if you understand me – on account of it being, well, *official*.'

'Then it seems that fortune has favoured us both,' Nicholas says. 'Because that is exactly what we've come here to talk to you about.' He hails a passing potboy and orders a bottle of sack to celebrate Porter Bell's resurrection.

In the opaque dawn light the shingle promontory of the Hythe disappears in front of them, a path leading to the lip of an unseen chasm. The fog has stolen the river away, along with all the ships moored upon it. To the east, a thin spread of misty gold lies like the first stroke of a painter's brush on a new canvas.

Nicholas and Bianca walk their horses down to the water's edge. At the extent of their reins, the horses have already begun to fade from view, as though the unseen river is washing away their substance, dissolving them.

'How will we see him?' Bianca asks.

'We won't have to. He'll see us. He told me once he can tell where he is on the river even in the dead of night – even if there's not a single lantern lit in any of the ships. One hundred paces to the east, he said.'

'But how shall we know east from west in this fog?'

'We keep the Hythe to our backs. If our feet get wet, we turn a little to the right.'

They pace carefully a short distance, until shingle begins to give way to tufts of sedge and rising ground. Looking back, Bianca sees the Hythe has disappeared, with only a scattering of rooftops and masts visible above the fog bank.

A low whistle comes out of the whiteness somewhere close by, as Porter Bell hears the sound of their horses at the water's edge. A dark shape looms ahead.

The pinnace is about twenty feet long, flat and ugly in the water, a tub for transporting bales of wool and other light cargo across the river. Bell has chosen a place on the bank where the earth has slipped into the water. He has grounded the pinnace on the riverbed, so that the blunt prow is just about level with the land. Even so, it takes a deal of coaxing to get the horses to step down onto the wooden planks of the hull. At first Nicholas fears the clatter of hooves and the shrill whinnying will wake all of Gravesend, but the fog and the river seem to steal away the sound.

When the horses are aboard and tethered, and Bianca has been assigned to calm them, Bell sits on one of the two cross-benches and motions Nicholas to take the other. At each bench is a pair of sturdy oars. Nicholas wonders if two men will be strong enough to get the pinnace away from the bank.

'We'll float off when the water rises,' Bell says confidently, as though reading Nicholas's thoughts. 'It won't be long, if I've timed it right.'

'Today is not the first time you've done this, Master Porter,' Nicholas suggests.

Bell laughs. 'Throw a stick on the Tilbury marshes an' you're like to hit a horse-thief on the noddle. As I told you last night, they like to steer clear of the ferry.'

Within a few moments the pinnace begins to shift, her keel sending up the sound of iron on gravel from the riverbed like the groaning of a sea monster fighting to shake off its chains. How Bell guides them across the river, Nicholas has no idea. He can see nothing beyond the stretch of his oars, hear nothing but their watery slash as they rise and dip. The river itself is silent. It is back-breaking work; he would never have thought the sinewy figure behind him, calling out encouragement, capable of it. But there is a hardness in Porter Bell's body that is not apparent at first sight. He has endured a Spanish cell in the Netherlands. Pain of his own choosing is easy for him to bear.

Bell has just announced they are approaching the northern shore – though how he knows is a mystery – when the pinnace strikes something in the water. One of the horses begins to panic. Its head tosses wildly, threatening to yank the reins out of Bianca's hands. The huge chest begins to rise; the hind legs flex; the wide black eyes roll; the nostrils gape. The horse is on the verge of rearing. In the next instant it will hurl itself into the river. Worse, thinks Nicholas, the fear will spread to its neighbour and they'll all be dashed beneath the flailing hooves. And Bianca is the first one in the way of a ton of terrified horseflesh.

He lets go of the oars. Caught in an ungainly crouch between sitting and standing, he can only watch in horror as the horse begins to rise.

And then all is calm again. The horse is standing foursquare, its pupils no longer the size of angel coins, snorting as if it's the humans causing all the fuss. Its companion goes back to scratching its lower lip on the gunwale of the boat.

And there is his wife: as slender as one of those boys who play the female parts at the Rose, calming the beast with a caressing hand on its neck. From the sleeve of her gown she had produced – with the skill of a Bankside street trickster – a sprig of camomile and is wafting it under the horse's nose.

'Something else you learned from the young jockeys of Padua?' Nicholas asks, half in jest, half in stupefied admiration.

'Preparation, Husband,' she says with a sweet smile. 'A horse is much like a man. You have to think ahead for them.'

As the north bank of the river appears out of the fog – another magic trick, he thinks – Nicholas cannot help but wonder if what Southwark says about his wife's supernatural abilities might not, after all, be true.

✠

Porter Bell has brought them to a safe landing spot, far enough from the ramparts of Tilbury fort and the ferry jetty to slip unnoticed into the county of Essex. He wishes them good fortune and vanishes back into the foggy river, a diminutive Charon who's found a way back from his own personal Hades.

'How do we find our way from here?' Bianca asks as the sound of the oars striking the water fades. 'I can barely see my hand in front of my face.'

Nicholas explains his plan. They will take the track that runs from Tilbury to Chelmsford, then join the old drovers' road to Melton, crossing the Suffolk border below Nayland. The Tabard's palfreys are sturdy beasts, accustomed to long distances. Three days, he reckons, if the weather holds.

But striking out from the shore into the white soup of early morning would be insane, he adds. It might just be possible to keep the golden blur of the rising sun to their right as they head north, but the Tilbury marshes are dangerous. Lose the path, and there any number of stinking creeks waiting to suck the unwary down into the ooze. Better by far to wait for the fog to burn off a little. So they hobble the horses and settle down to wait.

And within a short time the fog begins to dissolve, like breath left in the air on a cold day. Nicholas wonders if it's another of his new wife's skills she hasn't yet told him about.

✠

In the long shadows of evening, Nicholas and Bianca take shelter below the treeline of Botwulf's Wood on the outskirts of the little hamlet of Barnthorpe. The setting sun burnishes the thatched-roof houses and the tithe barns with a soft golden light. It is dusk on the third day following their crossing of the Thames, as Nicholas had anticipated. But he is not yet ready to announce his arrival.

Bianca knows why he's hesitating. He's waiting for the villagers to come in from the fields; then they won't have to lie, if the Privy Council's men arrive to ask them if they've seen one Nicholas Shelby, son of this hamlet, wanted for the wholly fictitious crime of attempting to poison their queen.

When the way is clear, they walk the horses quietly down into the courtyard of Yeoman Shelby's farmhouse. Through the little leaded windows Nicholas can see his mother and his sister-in-law, Faith. They are laying out the board for supper, heads slightly bowed as they chatter while they work. He goes to the porch, stands for a moment in its familiar shelter before knocking.

It is Faith who opens the door. She stares at him in the gathering darkness, refusing to believe what her eyes are seeing. Then she cries out, 'Mercy! Jesu and all His saints save and protect us!' A pewter dish slips from her hand, rattling itself into stillness on the flagstones. Then she flings herself at him.

'Faith, whatever is it?' his mother calls out.

And when Faith draws enough breath to answer, Nicholas is forced to endure a warm and enveloping scrimmage of arms and cheeks and hands and bosoms before he can utter a word. He catches a melee of images: Faith beaming as rosily as an apple hanging ripe from a bough; his mother, eyes bright with tears; his father holding him at arm's length to get a proper look at him – once he's laid aside his long-stemmed clay pipe, something he doesn't do even when Parson Olicott comes to call; his brother Jack taking him in a well-meaning headlock as if they were boys again; and what seems to be an ever-growing litter of Jack and Faith's children, who shriek in delight at the return of Uncle Nicholas and insist on being hoisted aloft, protesting tearfully at any imagined favouritism whenever they're not staring in silent awe at the slender, comely young woman with waves of dark hair who stands silently, but smiling slightly, in the doorway.

'And this must be our new daughter,' his mother says, when he has been allowed to disentangle himself.

Now it is Bianca's turn to endure the emotional avalanche. 'You are right welcome, child,' Goodwife Shelby says, embracing Bianca as though they've been friends for ever. 'My son does not write much' – a glance of reprimand in Nicholas's direction – 'but when he does, it's mostly about you.'

As they fuss over her, Bianca feels a sweet pain grow inside her. The comfort of family has been denied her for so long. Her father and mother are both dead, her own birthplace is in a different land. She surrenders to this unconditional welcome, aware that her own familial past has never felt more distant.

Later, when the horses are fed and stabled, the dust of the ride has been brushed from doublet and gown, bellies filled with steaming lamb pottage, thirsts slaked with ale and sack, and Faith has taken Bianca away to show her the chamber where she and Nicholas will sleep, Nicholas and his father share a moment together.

'You've hardly said a word, lad, all evening.'

'That's not true!' Nicholas protests. 'I've barely had a moment to put food in my mouth.'

'I mean about why you've come back.'

'I thought it was time you met Bianca,' Nicholas says, feeling the guilt warm his cheeks.

'Nothin' to do with that fellow they put to death in London – the queen's physician?'

'Why would you think that?'

'Oh, I don't know. Perhaps because you're a physician, too, an' you work for Sir Robert Cecil, an' you've had audiences with the queen 'erself, an' 'er old physician just got himself quartered for tryin' to poison her, an' you don't make a habit of dropping by out of the blue to discuss the price of wool at Woodbridge market. Will that do you?'

'I hadn't imagined you'd heard about Dr Lopez up here.'

'This is Suffolk, Nick, not the moon. Jed Blackwell took a flock down at the end of May; got home the day before yesterday. He told me folk down there spoke of little else.' His craggy face, scoured by salt-marsh and the east wind, darkens. 'How could a man of medicine plot to poison the queen? He must have had the Devil in his heart.'

'He didn't poison anyone. They butchered an innocent man.'

Now there is real fear in his father's eyes. 'Are you involved in this somehow, Nick? Is that why you've come here, without a word to warn us?'

'Yes. And it's only for tonight.'

A cruel payment, he thinks, for such a welcome.

'Deal straight with me, boy,' Yeoman Shelby says, leaning forward across the table. 'Are you a fugitive?'

Nicholas considers his answer before speaking. 'Not yet. Sir Robert Cecil is still for me.' He shrugs. 'But for how long...'

His father takes a draw of his pipe. For Nicholas, the scent of the smoke he exhales brings back a flood of childhood memories, all the more poignant for knowing he cannot seek shelter here.

A look of sad admonishment from his father. 'What, in the name of all that's holy, have you got yourself mixed up in, Nick? And you with that sweet new bride of yours. I had hoped you'd found a new, happier life for yourself – after Eleanor.'

'I have.'

'Then why are you on the run?'

'I was denounced. An anonymous accusation. It has no merit.'

His father says, 'It's not your way to run from a fight, boy. Remember those bloody knuckles you got at Cambridge, when the "gentlemen" mocked you as country-pate?'

'This is different, Father. There's such a madness amongst the Privy Council these days – they see plots against the queen even when there are none. That is how innocent men go to the scaffold.'

His father gets up from his chair and walks to the window. He peers out into the dark night as if he expects to see men-at-arms already dismounting in the courtyard. 'We'll hide you here at Barnthorpe – in the old priest hole.'

Nicholas remembers the tiny space under the parlour stairs where, as a boy, he'd played hide-and-seek. His grandfather had fashioned it during the reign of the sixth Edward, to hide any Catholic priest who might manage to slip into the county by way of the Deben river. His father, though obedient to the new religion, has never bothered to seal it up.

'No, Father,' he says. 'I'll not put the family in danger. I'm going back to the Low Countries. It will be safer for me there.'

'How long?'

'Until Sir Robert can unmask the source of this slander against me.'

'Will you tell me where?'

'Best if I do not – for your own sake.'

'Exile then?'

'For a while. When Bianca and I are safely sheltered, I'll send word to Sir Robert, ask him to tell me when it's safe to return.'

His father turns back from the window, jabs the bowl of his pipe in Nicholas's direction. 'Have you no mind for the sorrow that will bring your mother?' It is not in Yeoman Shelby's nature to speak of the sorrow it will bring him, but Nicholas can see it in his eyes.

'It will be safer for everyone if we don't tarry. We plan to leave tomorrow. Before the sun comes up.'

Yeoman Shelby sits down at the table board again. He picks up his pewter jug and tips the last of the ale into his mouth. The old, familiar stoicism of the farmer comes over him again. 'Well,' he says, 'I suppose I'll have to be the one to tell your mother. By the sound of it, you've enough trouble of your own to worry about.'

✳

For a man almost universally feared for his size and his volcanic temper, Ned Monkton looks at this precise moment like a child deprived of a treasured toy. If Rose didn't know her husband better, she would swear those are tears brimming in his eyes.

He has come from Nonsuch like a whirlwind. But even whirlwinds can arrive late. As Yeoman Shelby prepares to break the bad news to his wife, Ned Monkton stands in the doorway of the lodgings by the Paris Garden, looking around as though he half-expects Nicholas and Bianca to jump out from the kitchen. *It was just a prank, Ned. See what a new sort of fellow you've become – quite unafraid to laugh at yourself.*

'Surely they could 'ave waited a few days?' he says in a hurt voice that seems to belong to a far smaller man.

'Master Nicholas was denounced, 'Usband,' Rose says, looking up and seeing little but the swell of his chest and his great auburn beard. 'Some villain wrote a letter to the Privy Council – said he'd intrigued with Dr Lopez in the matter of the queen's poisoning.'

'The queen's been *poisoned*?' Ned growls in astonishment. 'This is worse than I feared.'

'No, 'Usband, the queen has *not* been poisoned,' Rose explains carefully: Ned, alarmed, can be a tad unpredictable. 'But that didn't save Dr Lopez. Now Master Nicholas has 'ad to flee abroad to escape the same fate.'

'Because he was denounced for something he didn't do?'

'I think you've got the tail of it, 'Usband,' Rose says with a relieved smile. 'Now 'ang on tight, in case it wriggles free.'

'Are you making merry with me, Wife?' Ned says, enfolding Rose in his huge arms.

'Mercy, never!'

'Where 'ave they gone?'

'We're not to know that, 'Usband – in case the Earl of Essex come here asking.'

'When will they return?'

'That depends on how long it takes Sir Robert Cecil to find out who did the denouncing and make him confess he was lying through his poxy arse.'

Ned considers this with a dark scowl. 'Then I must start at first light, Wife.'

Rose's eyes widen. 'Start what?'

'I owe Master Nicholas my life,' Ned says. 'The least I can do is find out who's slandered him.'

Rose marvels that such a fearsome carapace can hold such a good heart. She sighs and shakes her head. 'Master Nicholas needs you here, to help me make sure the labourers don't rebuild the Jackdaw with the roof on upside-down. Besides, I know what you're like. You'll be no use to him if you're arrested for affray.'

'But I must do *something*.'

'We'll put our heads together after you've rested from your journey,' Rose says. 'You must be tired.'

'Tired of being an 'usband without a wife,' Ned says, scooping up Rose in his arms as easily as if she were filled with goose-down – which, on bad days, Bianca claims is nearer the truth than it should be, especially the head part. He carries her towards the stairs like a prize.

'Been hungry while we've been apart, 'ave you, 'Usband?' she asks coyly.

'Ravenous,' he replies, opening his mouth like a great fish. 'Them Nonsuch servant maids are all bone and gristle.'

'You'll need something you can get your teeth into then, I suppose.' She gives his beard a playful tug. 'Serious, though – someone needs to find the wretch what denounced Master Nicholas, else your fine mane will be grey as winter before he and Mistress Bianca can return home.'

'I shall give the matter my most careful attention,' Ned promises as he starts to climb the stairs, 'right after I've 'ad a good rummage through the larder.'

✣

The two Spanish soldiers leaving the cathedral of St John the Evangelist in Den Bosch are clearly men of some mark. It shows in the quality of the corselets and padded breeches they wear, slashed to reveal stripes of crimson silk, and in the silver hilts of the swords of fine Toledo steel at their belts. It shows, too, in the haughty disdain with which they look down upon the burghers and their womenfolk. Provincial, they would call them contemptuously. Utterly lacking the *vivacidad* of the Spanish.

'Take as an example that peasant girl there,' says their leader, a somewhat portly Castilian of middle years whose burnished breastplate has been let out more than a little since he was first fitted for it at the Escorial in Madrid, 'the one staring at the cathedral as though she's never seen a house of God before. Comelier than most Netherlanders, I'll grant, but just look at that scowl. To think that we shed fine Spanish blood trying to save the likes of her from the Lutheran heresy!'

'I know her, Don Antonio,' says his companion, the captain of the city's Spanish garrison.

'You've had her? I hope you washed her first.'

'Mercy, no! The swineherd doesn't lie with his pigs, does he?' the captain of the garrison replies. 'She preached here, in the square, until Father Vermeiren put a stop to it.'

'Preached? She knows her Bible? Surely a vagrant such as she cannot read.'

'She was railing at the likes of the Pole, Copernicus, shouting at the top of her voice that man has no business delving into our Lord's plan for the cosmos.'

'Well, at least the wretch knows heresy when she hears it,' Don Antonio says with a hearty laugh.

'She said it serves only to let Satan deceive us. The parts I heard sounded very shrill.'

The Castilian shakes his head in wonder at the manner of barbarian he has been set amongst, and then forgets the wild-eyed maid as though she had been a mere shadow and not a woman at all.

Don Antonio considers himself a man of no mean station. He is well educated, widely travelled and cultured, especially in matters of the arts. He has been sent to Den Bosch by Archduke Ernst of Austria, currently enjoying the pleasures of Antwerp in the aftermath of his triumphal entry at the head of a Spanish army into that city. And he has more important things to think about than a young woman in the threadbare gown of a Beguine staring like a mad thing at a cathedral.

'Speaking of Satan, Don Antonio,' says the captain of the garrison, jabbing a gloved finger back over his shoulder, 'the fellow who painted that thing in there... what sort of man could possibly imagine such depravity? No Spanish church would tolerate a blasphemy like that for a moment. We'd burn it – and the painter along with it: palette, brushes, oils, pigments... the lot.'

'Brabantian food and Brabantian weather,' suggests Don Antonio. 'They rot the mind. Quite why His Excellency the archduke wants it in his collection is beyond me. But that's an Austrian for you.'

'If it were hanging on my wall, it would give me nightmares,' says the captain of the garrison. 'The deepest mineshaft is where I'd put it, or in a weighted crate at the bottom of the sea.'

'Ah, but you know little about fine art, my friend,' says Don Antonio. 'And what an archduke wants...'

The two men reach the place where the grooms are waiting with their horses – Andalusian stallions, each with a hindleg bent slightly and resting on a tilted hoof, for all the world like a pair of bored courtiers awaiting a royal audience.

'I shall return in a few days, to make the appropriate arrangements with the Church authorities,' the Castilian says, presenting the offered stirrup with a foot clad in the supplest Valencian leather. 'But one thing is clear to me. Be it the food, the weather or the imaginings of a deranged mind, if Signor Hieronymus van Aken is correct in what he has depicted in that painting, we'd best start offering the Lord rather more Hail Marys than we do at present.'

7

Next morning in Yeoman Shelby's farmhouse there is a sombre mood, at odds with the joyousness of the night before. Quiet farewells are said. Leave is taken, embraces exchanged. Tears are shed, visible and secret. A cart is prepared and harnessed to the placid old Suffolk punch that does the heavy lifting at Barnthorpe, ready to carry Nicholas and Bianca to Woodbridge. Nicholas knows, from his conversation with his father last night, that there is a Dutch herring boat moored there. But there is no safety to be had by announcing their entry into the town, so they will remain in the cart, hidden beneath a sheet of tarred flax until the last practical moment.

'The horses we brought – you'd best cover up their brands,' Nicholas tells his father. 'It's unlikely a Privy Council searcher would know the Tabard's mark, but better not to take unnecessary chances.'

He gives the members of his family one last embrace and climbs aboard the cart. He settles down with Bianca on the hard wooden planks and pulls the sheet of flax over them. He hears Jack's muffled voice urging the punch forward, feels the wheels turn and the cart lurch. He cannot bring himself to lift the sheet and look back.

✣

'It's safe,' Jack Shelby calls as he brings the old Suffolk punch to a halt in a narrow lane by the Bell tavern in Woodbridge. 'There's no one about.'

Throwing back the cover, Nicholas and Bianca climb down from the cart. Jack helps them unload the bags they've taken off the Tabard's horses. 'Don't leave our parents to wonder what's become of you, Brother,' Jack warns. 'Not like you did when—' He stops, glancing at Bianca.

'It's all right, Jack. She knows all about Eleanor.'

Jack nods in understanding. 'Aye, well, not as long as that, eh?'

'I promise.'

'What do you want me to do with the horses?'

'Next time there's a flock being driven down to London, have someone take them to the Tabard in Southwark. Put out the word they were found on Blackheath.' He hands Jack a few half-angels. 'Here, that's to pay for the trouble. They might even get a reward from the landlord.'

A brief, brotherly clasp of hands – nonchalance hiding the pain – and the cart moves away down the lane towards the river. Nicholas watches it go for a moment, then he hoists the bags over his shoulder, wraps the fingers of his free hand over Bianca's and leads her down to the little quayside in search of their means of escape.

Moored below the old Tide Mill are a couple of English wool hoys and the Dutch fishing boat that Nicholas's father told him about. The air is heavy with the putrescent stink of tidal mud. The estuary echoes to the scream of gulls.

The skipper is easy to spot: tall and thin, with a nose like a heron's bill. When he walks, he looks like one, too – as though he's about to take wing. He wears a grubby leather tunic stained with fish oil. He is supervising the unloading of casks off the tubby little herring buss.

'We're trying to reach Antwerp, Meneer,' Nicholas explains in his imperfect Dutch. 'But we need discretion. There's a father who doesn't approve of a marriage. And a jealous brother.'

The man looks them up and down. Beneath the sharp features he seems a friendly fellow, perhaps a decade older than Nicholas. He nods in sympathy. 'Can you pay?'

Nicholas says, 'We can pay. Can you give us passage?'

'If you don't object to the smell of herring.'

'We'll live with it.'

'I am Jan van der Molen,' the skipper says, extending a hand for Nicholas to shake. It is slippery to the touch. 'You are English, not Dutch, yes?'

Nicholas confesses that he is.

'A Lutheran or a Catholic?'

'Does it matter?'

'Not to me. It might in Antwerp.'

Nicholas is about to tell him that he and Bianca are prepared to take the risk, when the sound of horses' hooves and the jangling of harness echoes over the river. Turning his head, he sees a troop of ten mounted men-at-arms come clattering down the quayside. A sudden reappraisal of his prospective passengers is clear in van der Molen's face. His eyes narrow as he steps back to put distance between them.

The troop dismounts a few yards away. A sergeant in breast-plate and pikeman's pot-helmet orders two of his men to guard the horses while the rest fan out along the quayside. Nicholas glances towards the Tide Mill, gauging his chances of slipping away unobserved. Even as he does so, one of the men calls out, 'Stay where you are, Master. Seek not to thwart the queen's business.'

Bianca glances at her husband, alarm written clearly on her face.

'Surely they can't have found us already,' she whispers. 'Have we been betrayed?'

Nicholas weighs the possibilities. If the attorney general or the chief justice has moved with uncharacteristic speed, then it is quite possible that he and Bianca are the quarry these men seek. But, equally, simple ill fortune may have brought this group of searchers to the harbour at the worst possible moment.

'I'll speak Dutch, you speak Italian,' he says between clenched teeth. 'We'll bluff our way out of trouble.'

While his companions board the vessels moored against the quay, calling with imperious voices for the crews to stand aside and let them search, the soldier who challenged Nicholas is approaching. 'I am commanded to search this vessel and all here for evidence of papistry,' he shouts in a thin voice.

Nicholas lets out the breath he's been holding. 'It's alright,' he whispers to Bianca. 'It's not us they're after.'

She gives him a frightened glance. 'No, it isn't. It's very far from alright.'

He stares at her, confused. 'What do you mean?'

'If they search my bags, they'll find my father's Petrine cross. They'll know I'm a Catholic.'

The perplexity in Nicholas's eyes turns to horror. 'You *packed* it?'

'You said they'd be searching for Jesuits trying to enter the realm, not leaving it.'

The soldier is now only a few paces away. There is no time left for Nicholas to think of a plan that won't unravel the moment it's attempted.

'State your business here, Master,' the soldier commands.

Up close, Nicholas can see he is a slight lad of no more than eighteen. His head is almost enveloped by the steel pot he wears. It makes Nicholas think of a cockle peeping out of its shell. But he is armed, and his companions more than make up for what he lacks in stature.

Nicholas can think of only one way of forestalling the imminent discovery of Bianca's Petrine cross. But it means he cannot pretend to be Dutch, and it will place him irrefutably at Woodbridge. All the subterfuge, from the argument at the Tabard to the perilous crossing of the Thames at Gravesend, will have been in vain. It would have been less trouble, he thinks, to send Lord Popham or Sir Edward Coke – even Essex himself – a map of their journey.

'I am on Privy Council business, Sergeant,' he says, favouring the boy with a rank he clearly does not hold. 'As such, I am entitled to pass without hindrance.'

'You have proof of this, Master?' the lad asks, showing an unwelcome but commendable refusal to be cowed.

'I do,' says Nicholas. He reaches into one of his bags and takes out a small square of parchment with a heavy wax seal attached and offers it to the searcher. It is Robert Cecil's letter of safe-passage.

Whether he can read the pass or not, the lad stares at the heavy wax seal, clearly in awe.

'It is the seal of Sir Robert Cecil,' Nicholas says helpfully. 'And when I next see the queen's secretary, I shall commend you to his favour, Sergeant...?'

'Lambarde, Master – if it please you,' the lad says, wide-eyed. 'Henry Lambarde, of Ipswich. But I'm not a sergeant.'

'Then I shall recommend to Sir Robert that you ought to be,' Nicholas tells him, trying to sound as lordly as he can, and hoping the lad won't wonder why someone on official duties is wearing an old canvas doublet. But young Henry Lambarde of Ipswich just grins with delight. 'Then pass, on the queen's business' – a glance again at the letter of safe-passage – 'Dr Shelby.'

'And you can tell your officer there's no call to search Master van der Molen's vessel. I can vouch for him,' Nicholas says, thanking whatever lucky star is at this moment hanging precariously above his head.

When the soldier has gone, the master of the herring buss says, 'So, you're planning to elope with the daughter of the English queen's minister! That takes some courage, I must say.'

The Dutch word *weglopen* is close enough to the English meaning for Nicholas to comprehend its meaning. 'No,' he says with a contrite smile. 'We're already married. And Sir Robert has but one child, a son. He's about three.'

'He's a famous man in Holland, Sir Robert Cecil,' van der Molen says in admiration. 'We count him up there with the late Earl of Leicester. They have given us goodly assistance against the Spanish. You could have told me the truth; I'd still have taken you.'

'Thank you, Master van der Molen. I would have been more open with you, but as you can see, I am on Sir Robert's business.'

'I won't enquire further,' the Dutchman says. 'You'd not be the first Englishman who wanted to be put ashore in the Spanish provinces in secret.' He gives a sad smile. 'My father was one of the Sea Beggars. He took almost as many Spanish ships as he did herring – till they caught and hanged him. Bring your fine lady and your bags and come aboard.'

The stink of fish is even more prevalent once Nicholas and Bianca are on deck. The herring buss is a plump old lady of the sea, almost as broad as she is long. Her prow and stern are as well rounded as any Amsterdam matron. She has two masts and a little wooden cabin on the afterdeck. She offers the troubling prospect of a rolling, pitching journey across the Narrow Sea, but she looks sturdy enough to take it.

'Antwerp, you said,' muses van der Molen as the last of the herring casks have been rolled onto the quay.

'If you can; we'll make it worth your while.'

'Oh, the son of a Sea Beggar will be taking no coin from another enemy of Spain. Have no fear on that score.'

'That's very generous of you, Master van der Molen.'

'But I'd steer clear of Antwerp, if I were you.'

'Why?'

'We've come from there. The Archduke of Austria rode into the city a short while back, at the head of a body of Spanish troops. He's making Antwerp and Brussels the twin centres of his authority in the Spanish Netherlands. His spies are everywhere, making sure the rebels don't slip inside the city and take a potshot at him.'

Bianca has picked up the word *Antwerp* and seen the cautionary look on van der Molen's face.

'What's wrong, Nicholas?'

'He's saying Antwerp is too dangerous for us. We'll have to think of somewhere else to go ashore.'

'Tell him to think of somewhere they have shops and dancing,' she says. 'I'll follow you anywhere, Nicholas, as long as it's not tedious. I draw the line at tedious.'

'Can you land us somewhere else, Meneer?' Nicholas says in Dutch. 'Somewhere my wife won't go mad with boredom.'

The master laughs. 'I'll take you to my home town. It's just below the River Maas, around twenty leagues from Antwerp. It's still occupied by the Spanish, but the garrison is small. Not so many spies.'

'That sounds perfect,' Nicholas says, thanking him. 'I know the Low Countries a little. What is the name of this town?'

''s-Hertogenbosch,' van der Molen says proudly. 'But we call it Den Bosch.'

8

Southwark, London, 29th June 1594

Ned Monkton watches the labourers at work on the reconstruction of the Jackdaw and thinks himself the least
gainfully employed man on Bankside. He is overjoyed
to be back with Rose, but Mistress Bianca's wish to have him
here to help oversee the work seems something of an extrava-
gance. There is not a soul who would dare short-change Bianca
Merton. Most of the men at work here are former customers.
More than a few have had need to visit Bianca's apothecary shop
or call upon Nicholas's healing skills, if not for themselves, then
for their families. They want to see the Jackdaw open again as
much as anyone. Indeed, the brickwork is already climbing like
a red creeper between the stout oak posts. The thatchers come
by almost every other day to ask when they will be needed. Ned
wishes only that he could let Nicholas and Bianca know how the
project has become a source of pride throughout the lanes south
of London Bridge.

Ned is not the wisest man on Bankside, though he is far from
being the dullest. He does, however, possess a mind made brutally efficient through hardship. And he is determined to track
down and expose the man who denounced Nicholas as an
accomplice of the unfortunate Dr Roderigo Lopez. He has asked
everyone he can think of if they have heard even the slightest
rumour, from the wherrymen who ply their trade on the river to
the cut-purses who send their customers back to the other shore

with nothing but neat little tears in their cloaks as a memento of their visit. But they can tell him nothing. He has even pestered Jenny Solver, Bankside's foremost peddler of gossip, until she has begun to avoid him in the street. But so far he's been unable to pick up even the faintest of scents.

And he thinks he knows why.

Anyone who can write a letter to the Privy Council denouncing a physician is not the sort of person who moves in his sphere. It must therefore be someone of a higher station. And that, in all likelihood, means a world closed to a former mortuary porter, even one who has spent several months in the domestic household of Lord Lumley at Nonsuch Palace. If it is a *gentleman* – the word makes his tongue sour – then the Ned Monktons of this world are unlikely to get so much as a toe across his threshold. Rose was right: he'd probably end up in the Clink or the Marshalsea, accused of assault.

Ned tries hard not to let the realization sink his mood as he turns to walk away from the building site. He tells himself to dwell on the day when the Jackdaw opens its doors again. Absorbed in his thoughts, he notices the man watching the construction work from the side of the lane only in the instant before he sends him flying. The man stares at him in terror, which folk are often wont to do when about to collide with Ned Monkton.

'Forgive me my carelessness, Master,' Ned says, extending a great fist to clutch the man's sleeve in an effort to stop him toppling. 'I did not see you. I'm sorry.'

For a moment there is confusion in the man's eyes, something else Ned is used to whenever he apologizes for being clumsy.

'Too many thoughts, not enough head,' he adds apologetically. Then he steps back and gets his first proper look at the fellow.

Ned can see now why he failed to notice him. He is a small man, and although small does not necessarily mean insignificant, in this case he is just that. His jerkin is patched and his hose made of the coarsest wool, his narrow head bald save for a few strands of grey hair that fall forward of his ears. He holds himself in tense expectation, as though chastisement is an hourly experience. A man accustomed to being shouted at, Ned thinks.

'Is this the Jackdaw tavern?' the fellow asks, mustering the fractured pieces of his courage.

'Aye, it is,' says Ned, letting go of his sleeve and stepping even further back so as not to intimidate any further. 'But as you can see, if you're after a quart of mad-dog, you're a little premature.'

The man gives him a sickly smile, to show he can take a joke. 'And the owner... er... Shelby – Dr Shelby... is he here?'

Something in the way the man speaks makes Ned think it is not his own question he's asking, but another's. He's been coached.

'Who wants to know?'

'No one of any matter,' the man says hurriedly. 'I simply wondered if he was still on Bankside.'

'He's gone abroad.'

A sudden flicker of vicarious interest in the little eyes. 'Might I ask where to?'

Ned remembers what Rose had told him on his return from Nonsuch when he'd asked the same thing: *We're not to know that, 'Usband – in case the Earl of Essex come here asking...*

But Ned has seen more than a few Privy Council searchers in his time, and they tend not to look like small, hard-done-by domestic servants. 'He didn't see fit to tell me,' he replies. 'Are you in need of physic, by any chance?'

'Physic?' the man echoes.

'If you're one of his patients, there's a barber-surgeon at St Tom's who's agreed to give service in his absence.'

'Are you quite sure Dr Shelby is abroad, and not imprisoned?' the man asks tentatively.

Ned raises one bushy red eyebrow. 'Why would you think he might be in prison?'

'No particular reason,' the man says, again a little too quickly for Ned's taste. Then, after a contemplative sucking of the teeth that seems staged, or is intended to give him thinking time, he adds, 'St Thomas's, you say – this barber-surgeon who's seeing Dr Shelby's patients?'

'Aye,' says Ned. 'If you're in need.'

'Yes, he will do, if Dr Shelby is not here.'

Then, with mumbled thanks, the man turns away and hurries off down the lane, revealing as he goes two large damp patches on the back of his hose.

When are folk going to stop thinking I intend to murder them? Ned asks himself sadly. The poor fellow's pissed himself.

He calls after the man to stop, but that simply adds impetus to his pace – something else Ned Monkton is used to. Which hurts him a little. Because all he was trying to do was tell the stranger that St Tom's hospital lies in quite the opposite direction.

✠

An hour later, in a modest little house on St Andrew's Hill, a short walk north from the Blackfriars river stairs, the once-great anatomist puts his servant – whose name is Ditworth – through an inquisition of which any Spanish cardinal would approve.

'Tell me again, sirrah,' Sir Fulke Vaesy insists, 'did this rough fellow you spoke to have no knowledge of Shelby's whereabouts? None at all?'

'No, Master. I swear it. He said he had none, other than abroad.'

'You're sure he's not been arraigned to any prison on Bankside?' Vaesy demands to know, yet again.

'No, sir. I visited them all: the Clink, the Counter, the Marshalsea, the Queen's Bench... no prisoner by the name of Shelby anywhere.'

Vaesy returns to his seat by the window. Outside on St Andrew's Hill where it gives onto Thames Street, Londoners are hurrying about their business. Not one wastes a single glance on the very ordinary home of the man who once held the chair of anatomy at the College of Physicians.

Vaesy thinks: if Nicholas Shelby – he can't bring himself to call him Doctor – hadn't poked his nose into my wife's affairs when he did, revealing a nest of serpents I hadn't for a moment suspected existed, I'd still be that man. I'd still be welcome in the grand houses of London. I'd still have the favour of the queen. Nor would I be reduced to bleeding or leeching the very worst sort, people who once would have stood aside as I passed. And to think that the man whose meddling brought about this calamity was very nearly appointed the queen's physician! At least my letters to the Privy Council put an end to that.

In his heart, he hadn't really wished Shelby to suffer the same tribulation as the late Dr Lopez. He wasn't a vindictive man. A few months in the Tower, while innocence was eventually established, would suffice. Just enough of a fall to bring ruin in its wake, the way Shelby's interference had ruined him.

Vaesy has tried hard to find out if his denunciation has had the desired effect. He's asked around. But his old colleagues at the College of Physicians, who had once bowed their heads to him, now won't give him the time of day. Nor will the courtiers with whom he was once on first-name terms. So he has been forced to send Ditworth across the river to Bankside to see what he can uncover.

Remembering that the hapless Ditworth is still standing in the chamber waiting to be dismissed, Vaesy says, 'Abroad? Just abroad?'

'Yes, Sir Fulke.'

Vaesy sighs. Well, exile is better than nothing. An eye for an eye...

'Did you ensure no one could have known it was I who sent you to Bankside?'

'Yes, Sir Fulke. I did.'

'You weren't stupid enough to mention my name, or give your own?'

'No, Sir Fulke.'

'And you did not take the same wherry out and back?'

Ditworth assumes the expression of a man who has overcome his enemies by superior guile. 'I was most careful not to, Sir Fulke. Besides, the big fellow I spoke to at the building site was naught but a common labourer. He wouldn't have had the brains to be suspicious.'

✠

As they lie abed in the Paris Garden lodgings, Ned says to Rose: 'The fellow who came to the Jackdaw asking questions about Master Nicholas – he wasn't a Banksider. I'm sure of it.'

Rose turns over and throws an arm about her husband's chest. Her fingers barely reach his breastbone. She grasps the wiry auburn hairs that coil there, as though trying to stop herself sliding down a steep woodland bank. 'You've been kicking my ear about that fellow all evening,' she says sleepily. 'What makes you think so?'

'He didn't know where St Tom's was, an' he seemed to think it was Master Nicholas who owned the Jackdaw, not Mistress Bianca. Everyone on Bankside knows the Jackdaw belongs to her. An' all that wanting to know if Master Nicholas had been taken up in irons. There's something amiss. I *know* it.'

Rose says, 'You think he might be the fellow who wrote the denouncement?'

'Wouldn't 'ave 'ad the balls. He was naught but a little arseworm.'

Rose's mouth turns down in disapproval. 'Sometimes they're the sort to start an anonymous slander.'

'Are you telling me he was checking to see if it 'ad done its mischief?'

'Why else would he bother to come across the river, just to ask where Master Nicholas is?'

'Maybe if I could find the wherryman who brought him, they could tell me whereabouts on the north bank they picked him up,' Ned says.

'But what if he saved himself the risk of a soaking and walked across the bridge instead?' Rose says. 'You'd never trace him then.'

Ned sits bolt upright.

'What is it?' Rose asks, gazing up from his lap into a tangled auburn canopy.

'He came across the river! He *definitely* came across the river.'

'How can you be sure, 'Usband?'

'Because I remember now: the back of his hose was soaked. I thought he'd wet himself. But he could either 'ave slipped getting in or out of the wherry or – more likely – the boatman 'ad some sport with him on the crossing. So they might well remember 'im.'

Rose reaches out and lays a cautionary hand against her husband's chest. 'Promise me, if you find him, you won't go back to your old ways,' she says. 'I don't want to lose you to a noose, Ned Monkton.'

Ned leans down and kisses her. ''Av' no fear, Goodwife Monkton,' he says gently. 'This Ned's a different man to the one he once was.'

9

For Nicholas and Bianca the first two days of the voyage across the Narrow Sea are like waiting for a jury to reach a verdict. Every time another sail is sighted, their hearts beat faster: is it a fast galleon dispatched to apprehend them?

By Nicholas's reckoning, the voyage should take less than three days. It ends up taking almost five. It is not the weather that delays them, as the sea is unusually benign. But a fisherman must make a living. Van der Molen meanders the tubby little vessel through waters he knows to be rich in fish. Nicholas and Bianca give as much assistance as they can without getting in the way, hauling on nets, shovelling the slippery silver bounty into casks of salt, washing the blood off the deck with buckets of brine.

Even when they make landfall it is not really land at all, more like scraps of marshy carpet floating on the sea, with only the occasional stunted tree to break the bleak skyline. Eventually these islands off the Brabant coast close in, forming a recognizable river. Even so, Van der Molen announces they have another twelve leagues to run – perhaps a day's travel, if the wind holds – before they enter the waters of the River Dieze.

Bianca is worried about the letters of safe-passage and credit that Nicholas carries. She fears the reverse of the shock they had at Woodbridge.

'If you are a recusant, and you're fleeing abroad because your Catholic faith means you can't practise in England any more, why are you carrying letters of safe-passage and credit from a queen's minister?'

Nicholas has thought this through. 'Because I was his physician. Because I have cared for his child. Despite our different faiths, he feels bound to help me, knowing the accusations laid against me are false. He's offering me a new start.'

'Conscience? That doesn't sound like the Robert Cecil I know.'

'It's close to the truth – and that is the best cover I can have.'

That evening, as they eat salted fish and hard bread beneath the darkening sky, the herring buss rolling with a motion that has Bianca feeling permanently queasy, Nicholas asks Jan van der Molen how it is that a Protestant still calls a Catholic town his home. Just as they have since leaving Woodbridge, they communicate with a rugged but efficient mishmash of Dutch and English.

'I could have left with all the other Lutherans and Calvinists – gone north into Holland,' Jan says. 'But I was born in Den Bosch. I'm damned if I'll leave simply because the King of Spain, the Bishop of Rome or the Holy Roman Emperor says I must believe in their heresies.'

'Do they not persecute you?' Nicholas asks.

'We keep our voices low and our faith to ourselves: those of us who remain. On the surface, we pretend to be good Catholics. But inside – well, you don't eat a fine plump herring for the skin, do you?'

When Nicholas translates this for Bianca, she laughs. After six years in Protestant England she knows exactly what he means.

Like all fishermen, van der Molen is at heart an optimist. It is only in the afternoon of the second day following their sighting of land that a town slowly begins to emerge from that hazy membrane between earth and sky. It appears to be moving slowly across the flat land, propelled by little wheels that turn out – as they draw closer – to be the turning sails of a multitude of windmills.

The little vessel moors in the shadow of the Pickepoort, a magnificent multi-spired gatehouse set into the Den Bosch ramparts. Beyond the sloping walls and the modern brick bastions, the slate roofs of fine houses and the slender spires of churches pierce the wide summer sky. Nicholas tries again to offer Jan van der Molen money. He refuses. 'It might be wiser if you avoid the obvious lodging places,' he says. 'The owners like to keep in with the Spanish by reporting on the movements of newcomers.'

'Where would you suggest?'

'Why, my house, of course. If you don't want the citizens of Den Bosch to think all Englishmen and their wives stink of gutted herring, you'll need the services of my Gretie and her washing tub.'

With a grateful smile, Nicholas hoists the bags over his shoulder and nods to Bianca to follow. As he crosses the wooden bridge into the town and the shadow of the Pickepoort swallows him, he has the sense that his exile has truly begun.

Across town, Hella Maas sits in the doorway of a merchant's house in the Markt square, huddled in her Beguine's gown. She holds her arms tight around her body, like a vagrant trying to stay warm in winter. The stone step is brutally hard against her flesh. She is hungry. She hasn't eaten much above a stolen bun for days, and she aches as though she's been beaten. She takes in the scene before her in stiff jerks of her head, as though she fears calamity might pounce the moment she relaxes her guard. She studies the fine façade of the cathedral of St John the Evangelist, and the surrounding merchants' houses with their zigzag eaves like dragons' teeth or a flight of stairs, seen end-on. She envies the pigeons that fly up to settle upon them, because – if she could follow – she would climb those stairs into the pale-pink wash of the Brabant evening and sit with the angels amongst the clouds.

That is where Hella has imaged her sister, Hannie, and her parents have been sitting for the past thirteen years – where they will sit for all eternity. But now she knows differently. They are suffering a never-ending torment, the like of which she has never imagined even in her worst nightmares. And it is all her fault.

From her vantage point she has a good view across the square to the front of the cathedral of St John the Evangelist. She watches the burghers and their families, their faces solemn yet expectant, disappear inside. When she closes her eyes the image of the great Gothic façade remains etched into her mind. So too does the image that she knows lies within.

Why, she wonders, has God not seared the truth of it into the eyes of the congregation, the way He has into hers? How can they go willingly into the cathedral, see what she has seen and come out again as though there is nothing amiss? Why do they not fall to their knees and weep in terror?

She tilts her face towards the sun, thinking she might stare straight into it, so that the image of hell that is so dazzlingly clear to her might be burned away. In the moment before Hella's eyes fill with blinding sunlight, a dark shadow falls across the doorway in which she crouches. She senses someone standing over her, though all she can make out is a blurred silhouette. And then the silhouette speaks.

Hella recognizes the voice at once. It is a voice from her past, deep and masculine. A voice she had thought she would never hear again. A voice from a time of sorrow.

'Well, little Hella, I should have thought to find you here, so close to God's house,' it says. 'Do we have time left in which to speak? Or is Judgement Day already at hand?'

10

For three days Nicholas and Bianca lodge with Jan van der
Molen, his wife Gretie and their strapping twins Johannes
and Willem, who clamour endlessly to be allowed to
accompany their father on his next voyage even though they have
yet to reach their tenth birthday. The family occupies the lower
two floors of a narrow-fronted, five-storeyed house beside the
Binnendieze. Its back wall is a cliff of brick descending into the
canal. The window of the guest chamber gives only three possible
views, all limited: a sliver of sky, a slash of dark water beneath
their washed clothes drying on a rope beneath the sill, or the wall
of the house opposite. But the hospitality is unstinting. Though
not rich, the van der Molens can offer their guests a plentiful
supply of eggs and cheeses, tasty meat pies and sweet *appeltaerten*.
Salted herring, it seems, can sustain a man only so far.

On the third day Bianca can no longer disregard the ache that
troubles her. It is not an ache of the bones, but of the soul. And it
has got worse since the day she first entered Den Bosch.

'I haven't prayed before a Catholic altar since I left Padua,' she
tells Nicholas. 'The last time I made confession was when Cardinal
Fiorzi came secretly to London. I need to seek absolution.'

'Shall I remain here?' Nicholas enquires.

'No. Come with me. If you're going to pass for a recusant,
you ought at least to be familiar with the interior of a Catholic
church.'

Nicholas knows exactly what Robert Cecil would say about him accompanying her: that he is endangering his immortal soul even by setting foot inside such a place. That the Roman Mass – and all the flummery that attends it – is nothing but the Antichrist's means of luring foolish folk to their eternal damnation. And that the so-called priests who perform it do so only to line their purses, stealing the hard-earned coin of those too simple to see they're being gulled.

For his own part, having lost his first wife, Eleanor, and the child she was carrying, he has asked himself too many questions about God's plan to find an easy way back to Him. He has read a little Lucretius. He knows that he is not the first man in the world to doubt the existence of the Almighty. But there again, why should he not accompany his wife if she has need of spiritual comfort? And she is right about his need of education.

When he asks Jan van der Molen, the Brabantine nods in approval. 'The burghers will expect it of you both, if you're not to raise too many eyebrows,' he says, assuming that the request is part of his guests' need to pass themselves off as papists. 'Even more necessary if you plan to make a living here.' He claps Nicholas on the shoulder. 'God will know what is truly in your heart. He does not expect us all to be martyrs.'

'Where should we go?' Nicholas asks. 'I saw a lot of spires when we arrived.'

'Oh, that's easy to answer,' the fisher of salted herring says. 'You should go to the cathedral of St John the Evangelist.'

✳

Before Bianca can make confession, she must first find a priest who can speak English or Italian. She would prefer the latter. Her mother's tongue has been the language of the confessional all her life, and a Catholic priest in Brabant is as likely to have been ordained in an Italian seminary as a Spanish or a French one.

Gretie van der Molen makes some enquiries amongst her neighbours. An appointment is made.

Four days after arriving in Den Bosch, late in the afternoon, Gretie takes Bianca and Nicholas to the great cathedral in the Markt square. There they are met by two priests wearing the black cassocks and four-cornered birettas of the Church of Rome. The older of the two is a plump, ruddy-faced man of fifty. He has a dour look about him, as though the hearing of other people's sins serves only to add to his general disappointment with humanity. Bianca thinks: no matter; he's a man of God. A confession is a confession, whatever the character of the priest who takes it.

'So you are the husband and wife who have fled the realm of the excommunicated whore Elizabeth,' he announces uncompromisingly in English, his Dutch accent almost inaudible. 'I am Father Vermeiren. I studied at the English College at Douai.'

Hearing his queen so described sends a little shiver of alarm through Nicholas. Such words, spoken aloud in England, would have every Privy Council informer for miles queuing up at Whitehall to claim the reward.

'Mevrouw van der Molen tells me you had to flee England in haste.'

'We were denounced,' Nicholas says, enlisting a truth in the service of their cover.

'It is the duty of every man, woman and child in England to obey the papal Bull *Regnans in Excelsis* issued by our Holy Father Pius the fifth, and rise against the heretic whore Elizabeth,' Vermeiren says helpfully. 'Yet we see that they do not – save for a very few who know their duty to God.'

'It's really not that easy,' Nicholas says defensively.

'Tyrants are not in the business of making their overthrow *easy*,' Vermeiren announces, implying they haven't tried hard enough. 'Nevertheless, you are welcome here.'

Gretie van der Molen looks at Bianca apologetically. Clearly she had no idea Father Vermeiren spoke English.

'I have come to you because I am ready to make my confession, Father,' Bianca says, though she suspects – given that Father Vermeiren doesn't appear to have a forgiving bone in his body – that she'll be saying Hail Marys till Judgement Day.

'I would receive it myself,' Vermeiren says with an apologetic frown, 'but my duties here prevent it. An important visitor is expected at any moment.' He glances at his companion, a much younger man. 'Father Albani here studied at Bishop Borromeo's seminary in Milan. He hails from that city. He will take your confession, Daughter.' With a curt nod, he leaves them in the care of the younger priest.

Father Albani is a youthful, handsomely made man. He has a studious face, with boyishly smooth skin, mirthful brown eyes and receding hair. Bianca feels a twinge of embarrassment. He's far too good-looking to hear the secrets in her soul.

'From Padua, child?' Albani remarks in a quietly grave manner that speaks of trust and reassurance. 'A daughter of the Veneto.'

Child. He can't be more than a half a dozen years older than herself.

'And, afterwards, does your husband wish me to hear his confession also?'

When Bianca translates, Nicholas gives a grim laugh. 'Only if he's not busy. It might take a while.'

'Perhaps later,' Bianca says in Italian. 'My husband is still getting used to the freedom here. In England, confession is forbidden – unless it's to confess you are a lamb of the one true faith; in which case, they employ not the confessional but the rack.'

Father Albani shakes his head sadly.

Gretie van der Molen bobs a farewell to the two priests and heads off to the square to browse the market stalls for vegetables. Nicholas settles into a pew while Father Albani leads Bianca to the confessional. Alone, he lets curiosity lead his gaze. It is not the first time he has been inside a papist church, but it is the first one he's entered that hasn't been visited by a victorious band of Protestant mercenaries. The pews are intact, not torn up for firewood; the saints still stand serene in their niches; the altar is intact, not desecrated; the great pillars reaching to the vaulted ceiling are a pristine milky-white – not smeared with graffiti or excrement. Even the stone-scented air is clean, untainted by the stink of soldiers' bodies, stabled horses or spilt blood.

The interior is in shadow now, the images in the grand stained-glass windows of the sacristy flat and lifeless. The insubstantial forms of worshippers move around him, taking their places quietly in the pews; sitting, heads bowed in prayer; rising unburdened to leave. Two nuns, hooded in pale-brown habits tied at the waist with knotted rope, take turns to light candles with a single glowing taper, their footsteps lost in the echoing cavern of the nave. Nicholas feels an oddly comforting pressure working upon his body, as though the prayers of centuries still linger.

It is curiosity, not impatience, that makes him rise from the pew and wander along the nave's southern wall. He responds with cautious courtesy to the murmured acknowledgement of a tall man in a dark-blue civic gown and starched ruff who passes him in company with a much younger woman who could be a wife, a daughter or a servant; her impassive face gives him no clue. He returns the watery smile of a rotund burgher of immense dignity whose every step is tapped out with a walking cane as though it were a point of order in a courthouse. He knows he should think of them as heretics, but they seem so ordinary: people going about their lives and hoping to find here the promise of salvation. Eventually he finds himself in the grip of a sensation he can't quite place. A sense of *returning*? Surely not. He has helped thwart Catholic plots against his own homeland, served a man as implacable to the heresy of papistry as it is possible to be. And yet Nicholas must admit to himself now – in his own act of confession – that he has always been a reluctant recruit to Robert Cecil's holy war. And how can a faith be heresy, when the woman he loves more than life itself embraces it?

Pondering these questions, he finds himself standing before a narrow archway set into the cathedral wall. The door is open, held back by a solid iron hook. Inside, candlelight dances to some unfelt draught. Again out of curiosity, Nicholas peers in.

He is looking into what once might have been a side-chapel, a disused shrine whose saint has fallen out of fashion and been removed. The plain stone walls show blank shapes where frescoes might once have stood. There are holes in the floor for railings to keep the devout at a safe distance. A thick stone buttress – part of the bones of the building – cuts it almost in two, leaving part of it in darkness. But it is the thing immediately opposite the door that seizes his attention. For a few moments Nicholas can make no sense of what he's seeing.

Later, he will say it was curiosity that made him enter the little chapel. But in his heart he will admit it was something darker. Because, when the images writhing before him suddenly fall into place in his understanding, Nicholas realizes that he is looking directly into hell itself.

✠

'And finally, Father, I confess the sin of lust. I lust after my husband. I enjoy the pleasure he gives me...'

There is silence beyond the little grille of the confessional. It is a silence that demands filling. Bianca feels her face begin to scorch with embarrassment.

'... frequently.'

There. She's said it. And to a handsome young priest.

To her surprise, she receives a warm chuckle through the lattice of the screen. This startles her, because if God is speaking to her through this man, then God is chuckling, too.

'"How much better is thy love than wine? And thy oils better than spices?"' The voice is mellifluous, but surprisingly knowing. 'The Book of Solomon, child,' Father Albani explains. 'It tells us that God weeps at a loveless marriage. There is no sin in what you describe.'

This is not how she had expected the confession to end. Still blushing, Bianca adds, 'And I confess the sin of impatience, Father.'

'Even God is sometimes impatient, Daughter. It is a very small sin.'

'I mean I fret because I have not yet fallen with child.'

It is true, she reminds herself. She is not getting any younger. A woman in her early thirties should, by now, have given her husband a son. Another omission in the long line of faults she thinks she ought to confess to Father Albani.

'I am sure there is plenty of time left,' Father Albani tells her.

Time. In her mind, Bianca can see the little clock sitting on the table in Robert Cecil's study, its mechanism clicking away relentlessly. She can see the printed words of the poem by Master Shakespeare that she had been reading while Nicholas was being dragged to Essex House: *Make war against proportion'd course of time...*

'And judging by what you tell me,' Father Albani is saying, the humour brightening his voice, 'you seem to be making every... *effort*... to remedy the situation.'

'We are, Father. *Every* effort.'

'Then you must not wish to hurry. He has set time upon a straight path, child. The mile markers on that path come to us at a rate only of His choosing. All in life will arrive at its appointed hour.' The priest's voice takes on a tone of solemn warning. 'So it is from the moment of our birth... until the Day of Judgement.'

✶

Judgement Day. That, Nicholas realizes, is what he is looking at – a triptych, a three-panelled painting for an altar, at least the height of a man, propped against the far wall, its panels open, as though waiting for someone to come and collect it. But it is no ordinary work of religious devotion. It is a searing representation of the torments facing the sinner on the day of God's final reckoning. And it seems impossible that a human mind is responsible for its creation. It looks to Nicholas as though the Devil himself has instructed the artist what to paint, guiding his hand as he conjures in brilliant colours – made all the more vivid by the flickering light of a stand of candles – a cast of the most monstrous characters. Approaching the painting, he wonders if he has not fallen into some terrifying dream.

The left-hand panel shows a scene from the Garden of Eden. But even here something is not right. There are storm clouds gathering in the pastel blue sky. And instead of falling rain and hail, angels are tumbling down towards the earth. Some are pure, their arms outstretched, buoyed on gossamer wings. But others are dark and demon-like. Beneath them, Adam and Eve are already fleeing paradise.

But it is the central and right-hand panels that truly shock him. Where he might expect an inspiring image of the Resurrection, here there is something entirely at odds with heavenly mercy. In a dark, fiery landscape, naked sinners are undergoing an extraordinary series of torments. Demons in the form of lizards, birds, fish and creatures too fantastical to name – though all with something frighteningly human about them – visit horrors upon the little naked sinners that sear into his mind. A green lizard standing on its hind legs drowns a drunkard in a wine cask. A beetle the size of a man rides a sinner's bare back. A demon in the shape of a hunter in a blue coat, his head that of a long-billed bird, carries a naked human trussed to a pole – the prey turned predator. In the centre of the main panel, a machine like a huge pepper grinder is crushing living bodies to make oil for the frying of fellow sinners. And on the right-hand panel: more suffering, more torment, all in an even darker landscape that is unmistakeably hell itself.

Nicholas is not a superstitious man. He is a physician, a man of the new science. He is a rational man, not some Suffolk peasant who sees the Devil's hand at work when the crops wither or the milk sours in the pail. He has little time for tales of witches and demons. But this is so finely executed, so overwhelmingly *real*, that he can feel the terror already turning his stomach to ice. He can only imagine what nightmares this work must give the good burghers of Den Bosch. Transfixed, he stares at the triptych, scarcely able to comprehend from what fevered imagination the images painted upon it have sprung.

And then he hears muted voices from just outside the chapel.

What makes him slip quietly into the darkness behind the buttress will be easy for him to explain to Bianca, when later she asks him why he hid. He will tell her that for all his pretence at being a recusant, he is still a heretic in this land, an enemy of its faith. To some, his mere presence in this cathedral is a mortal offence. And given that there has been hardly an hour since that night at Essex House when he has not expected the sound of a fist hammering on a door, or a rough hand seizing his arm, he has long been in the grip of a certain anxiety. A small part of him will say that he was so absorbed in the images before him that, upon hearing the approaching footsteps, he had half-expected the Devil himself to step through the little stone archway. Whatever the true reason, he will later agree with Bianca that his instinctive decision to dart behind the thick column and into the darkness very probably saved his life.

Leaning back against the stonework, he tries to steady his breathing.

By the voices he hears, he knows that two men have entered the chamber. They are speaking Latin, a language Nicholas is well versed in from his days at petty school and his medical studies at Cambridge. It is the common language of lawyers, physicians and the clergy. Are they priests then? Certainly one of them is Father Vermeiren, because Nicholas can make out those solemn tones. The other man has a slight sibilance in his voice that could almost be Spanish. He must be the important visitor Vermeiren had spoken of earlier, the reason why the priest couldn't spare the time to hear Bianca's confession.

'I had thought to find the piece ready,' Nicholas hears. 'Why is it not packed up and ready?'

'Bishop Gilburtus is protesting against its removal, Don Antonio. It has been part of the cathedral's fabric since it was first painted.'

'Protesting?' the other man says. 'The bishop should consider it an honour to be able to present it to His Imperial Highness, the archduke. Though I have to say, God alone knows why anyone would want to keep such a grotesque thing.'

'It was painted by Hieronymus van Aken, a son of Den Bosch,' Vermeiren is saying. 'The lord bishop believes this is where it should remain.'

'That is of no interest to my master,' the Spaniard says dismissively. 'If you wish this cathedral to remain a cathedral, and not become a byre for cattle, you will have your workmen cover it up and load it on the cart, so that I—'

As the Spaniard stops mid-sentence, Nicholas hears more footsteps on the flagstones. Father Vermeiren calls out, reverting to Dutch, 'Who are you? What do you want? Can you not see I am busy here?'

The next moment comes a sound like someone crying out from a sudden attack of stomach cramp: a deep, groaning gurgling, followed immediately by the dull impact of a human body against hard stone. Then the sudden clatter of a steel blade on flagstones, followed by a single high-pitched scream – masculine – filled with agony.

Behind the pillar, Nicholas reacts without thinking. His physician's instincts overcome his desire to remain unseen. His legs move without the will's command. As he steps out from the shadows of the stonework he is almost knocked off-balance by a man fleeing the chamber, disappearing into the dark body of the church.

Now he can see that, besides himself, three people remain in the chamber. One of them is Father Vermeiren. He is lying on his back, one arm thrown out behind him, the other across his belly, his legs twisted sideways. His eyes stare sightlessly at the vaulted ceiling. By the amount of crimson spreading over the black cloth of his cassock, he appears to be in the process of transmuting into a cardinal before Nicholas's eyes.

The other man – portly, with a sunburnt face and neatly trimmed beard – lies close by, his head almost touching the priest's. Nicholas can see by the yellow corselet and breeches, expensively slashed to show the silk lining, that he is no priest, but a Spanish officer. Like Vermeiren, his eyes are wide open. But there is still a measure of stunned life left in them, a guttering candle flame that looks moments away from extinction. His throat appears to have been slashed. The blood pumps thickly from a severed artery, anointing the flagstones. Close by lies a dagger, the blade the length of a man's forearm. It is slick with blood.

The third of this sanguinary trio is the only one very much alive.

Nicholas is looking at a dark-haired young woman with a high, domed brow and eyes that seem almost too large for the face, though he puts this down to terror. Her plain cloth gown is liberally spattered with the gore the killer has so generously spread about the chamber. For a moment he can almost believe she is one of the tormented sinners, escaped from within the picture into the world of the as-yet-unjudged. She only makes her reality indisputable when she begins to scream.

11

For Nicholas, the next few minutes pass in a maelstrom that pushes the torments portrayed in the triptych out of his mind entirely. He has real horrors to attend to. Despite his best efforts to stem the blood pumping from the Spaniard's throat, the man's eyes slowly dull. Eventually they reflect nothing: no pain, no fear... no life.

By then the chamber is full of people shouting in Dutch or Spanish. Save for Father Albani and Bianca, they achieve nothing other than stirring the chaos like witches around a cauldron. The captain of the Spanish garrison arrives, his sword drawn even in this house of God. Judging by his wild gesticulating and the whey-faced and trembling response it brings from the assembled priests and nuns, he appears to want to hang everyone from the trees around the Markt square. Nicholas, who has tended wounded Spaniards taken from the field of battle, shouts '*Médico!*' at him, which at least delays their immediate lynching.

Bianca and Father Albani are doing their utmost to soothe the terrified young woman in the blood-soaked kirtle. She has stopped screaming, but her crimson hands shake as though she's contracted a severe case of the palsy.

When it is clear that the Spaniard has passed beyond earthly help, Nicholas steps away from the two bodies. He turns to the captain and opens his bloody hands, shaking his head sadly to show he has done all he can. 'Imposible… lo siento,' he says regretfully. The man glares at him, his anger only slightly mollified.

Freed from the need to fight for his patient, Nicholas sees a picture of the slaughter emerging in his mind. Father Vermeiren has been killed instantly, by a sudden knife thrust between the ribs and into the heart. The blow must have been unexpected, Nicholas thinks, because the priest's hands are unbloodied, and there are no telltale rips on the sleeves of his gown, indicating that he tried to defend himself.

The dead Spaniard seems to have been slashed across the throat, a sweeping arc of a blow that has torn through the larynx and the carotid arteries, also before he'd had a chance to act.

The captain of the garrison begins yelling again. The rapidly changing expressions on his dark face are easy to read, even if his words – delivered in a strangely high-pitched tirade – are incomprehensible. He wants to know what Nicholas is doing here, what he has seen, what account he can give of the murders. But Nicholas has little more to give, even if he had the language.

The man's shouting subsides only when two deputies from the town assembly arrive, prosperous men with a civic solemnity about them that not even two bloodied corpses in their cathedral can shake. They escort Nicholas, Bianca and the bloodied, terrified apparition in the peasant's gown down an echoing stone passage to a windowless storeroom. It is not exactly a dungeon, but with the iron grille that serves as a door closed behind them, it might as well be. The maid has started trembling again. Bianca calms her as best she can.

One of the councillors holds aloft a tallow light, to study Nicholas's face by. 'Who are you?' he asks in Dutch. 'The captain said you are a physician, but I have never seen you before.'

It seems to Nicholas that there is no profit to be had in lying. At least, not about his identity. 'I am an Englishman. And this is my wife.' He nods towards Bianca, who is clasping the maid to her breast, stroking her tangled hair like a mother with a child who's woken from a nightmare. 'We are refugees.'

'Ah, you are the couple Meneer van der Molen brought us. We have heard of you,' the other councillor says, as though observing some rare phenomenon of nature. He speaks good English – a wool merchant used to dealing with the heretics across the Narrow Sea, Nicholas guesses.

'He told you?' Nicholas asks, wondering if his trust in the owner of the fishing boat has been misplaced.

'He did not have to. It is our job to know what occurs in our town. Why did you come?'

'We fled out of England because I was denounced as a Catholic,' Nicholas says, sticking to the story he and Bianca have contrived. 'They accused an innocent old physician I knew of seeking to poison the queen. They tortured and executed him. I could have been next.'

The burgher nods in sympathy. He says, 'God will punish them, when He is ready. But it would appear you have inadvertently brought some of the heretics' malevolence with you.'

'What do you mean?' Nicholas asks.

'The Protestant rebels in the northern states – I would hazard they are responsible for this.' He regards the two corpses sadly. 'It would not be the first time they have sent an assassin to murder a prominent Spaniard. But to commit sacrilege in God's house, and slay an innocent priest while they do it: for that they will be damned to the eternal fires.'

'Can you tell us what happened here?' the councillor asks.

'Not really. I didn't see the actual attack,' Nicholas says. It occurs to him that hiding in the shadows inside the little chapel might not look like the behaviour of an entirely innocent man. 'I was merely taking a look at your fine cathedral while my wife was at confession.'

The man nods. 'So you cannot describe the assassin?'

'Not really. A man pushed past me, but I didn't get much of a look at him. Then I heard this poor girl screaming. As for the rest of it, well, the priest was clearly dead. I did all I could to save the other gentleman—'

'He was more than just a gentleman; he was Don Antonio de Cantagallo, an officer in the household of the Archduke of Austria,' the councillor says. 'He had come from Antwerp to arrange the removal of that altarpiece.' He looks at Bianca. 'And your wife – she also saw nothing?'

'I was at confession,' Bianca says. 'Ask Father Albani.'

In the tallow light, Nicholas has the chance to study the maid a little more closely. Her trembling has ceased, but she keeps turning in the direction of the little slaughterhouse, as though she fears the killer might come after her to finish his task. Her face has a haunted look about it. The eyes fill their sockets like those of an injured animal, wide, hurt and uncomprehending; the narrow cheekbones below seem about to push through the skin. Her dark hair looks as if it's been hacked with a blunt knife. To Nicholas, it is a face that a painter had intended to be beautiful, but while his back was turned some unseen hand had mixed a terrible wash of pain and solemnity into the colours.

'Well, we know *you* well enough,' the councillor says, coming nearer and ramming his thick hands into his hips like an angry parent.

Bianca puts one defensive arm around the girl's shoulders, pulling her closer.

'You are the child who keeps frightening our citizens with what awaits them on the Day of Judgement,' the burgher says, still speaking English, presumably for Nicholas's benefit. 'You're the one who believes everything she sees in a painting. Did you come here to cause trouble for us with the Spanish, by defacing Master Hieronymus's altarpiece?'

The maid's darting gaze comes to rest on the burgher, as if she's seeing him for the first time. To the surprise of both Nicholas and Bianca, she answers in English that is even less accented than the councillor's. 'I came to ask Father Vermeiren to burn it, before the Spanish take it to Antwerp and infect the souls of even more of God's innocent lambs.'

'How very public-spirited of you. What happened, then?'

'The rebel – he burst in... pushed me aside...' She covers her eyes with her hands as though trying to block out the image. 'He lashed out with his knife at the Spaniard. When... when Father Vermeiren tried to help him, the man thrust the blade into his breast.' Inspecting her blood-smeared palms as though seeing them for the first time, she adds softly, 'I *tried* to hold him up. I swear it, on all that's holy. But he was too heavy. I had to let him go—' She turns her face from the spread fingers as though blaming them for the failure.

'Describe this man.'

'I *cannot.*'

'You cannot, or you will not?'

'I saw only his eyes. The rest of his face was covered by a cloth.'

'What was he wearing?'

'I can't recall.'

'How convenient.'

Tears turn the blood left by her palms into watery smears of crimson. 'It... it all happened so suddenly. I was frightened – terrified.'

'The girl is clearly distraught, Meneer,' Nicholas says. 'Would it not be kinder to allow her some time to recover her composure?

And somewhere more comfortable. Surely there is no cause to keep us here.'

The councillor is practised at turning down petitions and suits laid before the city assembly. He has a stock of gestures and expressions designed to garner sympathy, even while he disappoints. 'Sadly, no,' he says. 'I cannot release you until our Spanish friends agree – not after His Imperial Highness the archduke loses one of his favourite officers to an assassin in our humble cathedral.'

The councillor gives the barest hint of a bow of regret. Placing the tallow light on the floor, he gestures to his companion to follow. Closing the iron grille behind him, he leaves Nicholas, Bianca and the maid to whatever thoughts they are brave enough to conjure from the surrounding darkness.

✠

'The Spanish will hang us all,' the young woman says resignedly, when the echo of the closing door has been subsumed by the ancient stones of the cathedral. 'We'll never leave here alive. You must tell them I'm innocent. Perhaps they'll listen to a physician.'

Trying to take her mind off her fear, Nicholas asks, 'Where did you learn to speak our language, Mistress...?'

'Maas. My name is Hella Maas,' she says, drawing a blood-stained sleeve across her eyes even as she avoids his question. 'And if I spoke only Dutch, I could *warn* only the Dutch.'

'Warn them about what?' Bianca asks. 'Do you mean Spanish retribution for the assassination?'

'I mean the day when we are all judged. The day we are condemned to everlasting torment.'

It is said in such a matter-of-fact tone that she could be speaking of market day rather than Judgement Day.

'Oh, you mean the triptych,' Nicholas says, rather more sceptically than he intended. 'I admit it was troubling, compelling even. But it is just a painting.'

Hella says, 'Do you not see now how dangerous it is, to have such things revealed? If you, a physician, can be drawn to such images, imagine what damage they might do to a soul that is less educated. That is why I have to warn the people of Den Bosch. Knowledge is not always a gift—' She breaks off as they hear the sound of a key turning in a lock and the discordant, mournful cry of the iron gate opening.

'Holy Mary, Mother of God, they have come to hang us, just as I said they would,' Hella whispers.

A single figure emerges out of the shadows, a rushlight clasped in one hand. The flames cast demon's claw-marks across his face. For a moment Nicholas wonders if the maid is right and the captain of the garrison has sent a priest to give the condemned the Viaticum.

But it is only Father Albani, come to tell Bianca that he has managed to convince the captain and the burghers that she and Nicholas are nothing but innocent passers-by, caught up in a wicked attack by a deranged Dutch rebel. Numerous people – from the Sisters lighting the candles in the cathedral, to worshippers approaching from the Markt square – all testify to a solitary man fleeing into a side-street. The Spanish are searching for him at this moment. So Nicholas and Bianca are free to go. So too is Hella Maas, although on the subject of the triptych it might be safer for everyone if she keeps her warnings to herself for a while. The Bishop of Antwerp will have enough on his mind, grieving for his murdered priest, without being troubled by an itinerant maid preaching the imminent arrival of the Last Judgement.

And Father Albani has a warning, too, for Nicholas and Bianca.

'When the archduke hears of this,' he says in that Lombardy accent that tugs at her memories of home, 'he will send his people here to investigate further. I would not care to be a foreigner – an outsider – when they come, no matter how innocent. Or from what persecution you happen to be fleeing.'

✳

In the Markt square the citizens of Den Bosch are gathering, attracted by the news. They come alone, in pairs, in little groups of friends and family, coalescing, separating, swirling like leaves carried on the surface of an eddying stream. Are the rumours true? Have the rebel provinces of the north sent an assassin to our peaceful town to commit murder? Is it true that Father Vermeiren lost his life wresting with the killer? Is there no abomination to which the heretic rebels of the north will not stoop? And now the Spanish have doubled the guard on the city's gates. They will send inquisitors from Antwerp or Brussels. They will treat us like enemies instead of subjects.

As Nicholas and Bianca descend the steps of the cathedral, Hella Maas close on their heels, they can already see Spanish soldiers stopping the younger men in the growing crowd. They are aided by the Den Bosch watch. What is your name, young fellow? Are you a native of this place? Account for your movements in the past hour...

'I don't like the look of this,' Nicholas says in a low voice. 'We've found ourselves in the midst of an upturned wasps' nest.'

'They have no cause to blame us,' Bianca protests. 'You fought to save that Spaniard. We're innocent.'

'That's of little comfort. Your handsome Italian priest was right. We can't stay here – it's out of the question. Think what would have happened if that Spanish captain had ordered a search of our room at the van der Molens'. If they'd found the wheel-lock pistol and Robert Cecil's letter of safe-passage, then not even your Petrine cross would have been enough to save us from the gallows.'

'I have no fear left to spare for *that* consideration, Nicholas,' she says. 'Inside, I'm still shaking from the thought that if the assassin hadn't dropped his knife, he might have killed you, too.'

As they cross the square, Bianca notices how people stare at Hella Maas. Even though Father Albani has managed to borrow a brown cloth gown from one of the Sisters to cover her blood-stained clothes, they still nudge each other, glower at her with cold, suspicious eyes.

'I think you would be wise to stay off the streets,' Bianca says to her. 'Do you have a family you can go to?'

'None. I am alone here.'

'Where do you live?' Nicholas asks. 'We'll walk with you. It might help.'

'I live between the water and the sky,' the maid says mysteriously.

'You'll have to be a little plainer than that,' Bianca says.

'There is a bridge. I live in an old wreck of a boat, underneath it.'

Nicholas has to stifle a disbelieving laugh. 'You live under a *bridge*?'

'Do I look to you as though I live in a palace?'

'Forgive me, I didn't mean—'

But it seems the maid is used to hasty judgement. 'It is safer for me there. The people do not bother to trouble me.'

'Well, first we must clean you up,' Bianca says. 'Father Albani will want the gown returned, and we can't leave you looking like the victim in a Greek tragedy.'

They are leaving the square now, entering a cobbled street barely wide enough for a single cart to pass. It runs down towards the canal and the van der Molens' house. 'Perhaps Mistress Gretie can assist,' Nicholas suggests.

A few yards ahead of them Nicholas sees a wool merchant's warehouse, as familiar to him as any in Woodbridge. Two storeys above the cobbles, a sturdy iron bracket thrusts out from the wall, rigged with block and tackle. Directly beneath its eye, all but blocking the lane, is one hessian-wrapped bale waiting to be hoisted. There is no sign of the labourers. Nicholas guesses they've either skived off to the Markt square or they're skulking in the nearest tavern because the wool merchant is out of town.

He is about to lead Bianca and Hella Maas past the abandoned bale when he hears a shout from behind. Turning, he sees they have been followed into the alley by three men and two women. Clad in cheap broadcloth, the men are bare-headed and look malevolent. The women wear dirty linen coifs on their heads. None of them seems particularly rich when it comes to the possession of teeth.

'You – Satan's bitch! We want a word with you,' one of the women calls out in coarse Dutch.

'Burning's too good for Lucifer's whore,' shouts the second woman.

One of the men notices the pulley rope looping down from the high bracket to a shackle lying on top of the wool bale. 'But hanging will suffice,' he calls eagerly. 'Your vile blatherings have brought death into God's house. It's time to choke off your wailing once and for all.'

Bianca instinctively pulls the maid towards her, as if the two of them together might outmatch the hatred of five. Without even thinking, Nicholas moves to shield them, pushing them towards the narrow gap between the bale and the wall of the warehouse. 'Take her to the van der Molens',' he says urgently. 'Tell Jan I might need some help. It's not far – *hurry!*'

Even as he speaks he knows he's wasted his breath. Bianca Merton does not run from danger. And she has seen what he – until this instant – has not.

Hanging from the shackle at the end of the rope is a bale-hook, a curved iron rod used for manhandling the great parcels of wool. It has a wooden T-handle at one end. The other is sharpened to a wicked point. With one arm around Hella Maas's shoulders, Bianca lifts it from the bale and brandishes it at the three men.

'Nicholas, what's the Dutch for "One step nearer and I'll geld you all like spring-born lambs"?' she asks through gritted teeth, her amber eyes blazing.

But there is no need for Nicholas to translate. The look of murderous intent on his wife's face is universal, and she is wielding the bale-hook as expertly as if she's been taking lessons in swordplay at Signor Bonetti's school at Blackfriars.

The women goad their menfolk on. But there is no mistaking the personal harm Bianca intends to do them if they choose to chance their luck. They hang back, like feral dogs confronted by a burning brand. A moment later two labourers appear at the opening below the iron bracket and demand to know what's going on. The would-be lynch mob breaks and runs, back towards the Markt square, hurling insults over their shoulders that Nicholas thinks best not to translate.

As the narrowness of their escape hits her, Bianca bends her knees and takes deep and steadying gasps of air, as though recovering from a sprint. The arm thrown protectively around Hella relaxes. Instantly the maid slips her grasp. She flees down the lane towards the canal, oblivious to Nicholas's calls for her to stop.

From the upper floor of the warehouse, one of the labourers delivers a stream of robust but good-natured Dutch.

'What's he saying?' Bianca asks.

Nicholas laughs, partly in admiration and partly in relief. 'He wants to know what it's like being married to a harpy. And can he have his bale-hook back?'

Bianca lifts her gaze towards the labourer and raises the hook to her lips. She gives the iron shaft a bawd's kiss and throws it onto the top of the bale.

For a moment the two labourers can do nothing but stare down into the lane in disbelief. Then, their courage fortified by height and distance, they break into roars of joyous approval.

Playing the affronted husband, and failing miserably because it is all he can do to smother the laughter bubbling in his throat, Nicholas takes Bianca gently by the arm. 'Come, Wife,' he says. 'You're not on Bankside now.'

✠

'Goodness, child! You look as though you've been gutting a barrel of herring all by yourself,' exclaims Gretie van der Molen as she surveys the state of Hella's gown. Shooing Nicholas and Bianca away, she leads the girl into the parlour, calling on the twins to heat a cauldron of water on the fire. An hour later Hella is sitting at the van der Molens' table, looking like a freshly scrubbed novice in the plain cloth gown Father Albani loaned her and tucking into a plate of Gretie's appeltaerten.

In need of a stiff drink to settle their nerves, Nicholas and Bianca find a tavern in a little cobbled square close to the Dieze, a few minutes' walk away. There are tables outside and the evening is warm, the sky a soft vermilion.

'Did you hear about the Spaniard and Father Vermeiren?' the potboy asks when he brings their drinks.

'Yes, we did,' says Nicholas in the best Dutch accent he can manage.

The potboy gives him a suspicious stare. 'You're not from Brabant, are you, Meneer?'

'No. But neither am I the assassin. We've already made an account of ourselves to the captain of the garrison.'

'I was only asking,' the potboy says with a shrug. He disappears inside the tavern, but not before casting another glance over his shoulder to make a note of their faces.

'How long will it take for the Spanish to send their investigators from Antwerp?' Bianca asks under her breath, after they have spent a while tiptoeing around the shadows of the day's events.

'I should think they'll be here sometime tomorrow.'

'If it's too dangerous to stay here, then where do we go?'

Gazing into his cup, Nicholas considers her question in silence. 'We could go north, into the Protestant rebel provinces,' he says at length, his voice full of doubt. 'But Holland is teeming with agents of the Privy Council. All it will take is a word sent from Essex, Coke or Popham, and they will be fighting amongst themselves to be the first to claim the bounty. No, I fear the north is closed against us. We could go south, into France – Paris, perhaps. Or east, to the German states. Then there's Bohemia, and the Palatine.'

Bianca considers the choices as she sips at her glass of jenever. 'Paris might suit,' she says unconvincingly. 'I hear tell Paris is a fine city.'

'Paris it will be then.'

'But not so fine that I would consider wearing out my shoes to get there,' she muses, hearing once again Father Albani's voice in her head, a voice redolent with the mellow warmth of Italian sunlight at eventide.

'So, not Paris.'

'Probably not.'

'You have somewhere else in mind, do you not?' he says, with a perceptive smile.

'I might do.'

'You have that look in your eyes.'

'What look?'

'The one you use to disguise what is really in your thoughts.'

Draining her glass of jenever and savouring the taste of juniper in the back of her throat, Bianca says confidently, 'The Via Francigena.'

'That's the old pilgrim route down through France, across the mountains and on to St Peter's in Rome,' he says, giving her a quizzical look. 'Why would we go to Rome? I'm content to play a Catholic for a while, but I'm not sure Sir Robert Cecil would ever employ me again if he knew I'd been *that* close to the Pope.'

For a moment she just looks at him over the top of her jenever glass.

And then – as her true intention dawns on him – a knowing grin spreads across his face. 'But it's not Rome we're heading for, is it?'

'No, Husband,' she says sweetly, her eyes gleaming. 'It is not.'

Nicholas has often suspected that one day she would come to this decision. Even on Bankside, where the roots of her new life seem so vigorous, he has always known there is a part of Bianca Merton that the Veneto has not relinquished. And from the very moment he first considered what would happen when she realized it, he has always known he would go with her. A river may encounter any number of narrows and rapids on its journey, but it cannot ever stop itself seeking the open sea.

'It's Padua,' he says. 'You want to go *home*.'

She searches his face, unsure how her suggestion has been received.

'Just for a while – until this is all over and we can return safely to Bankside. Is that such a terrible thing to admit?'

'No. Deep in my heart, I think I have always known. Why didn't you suggest it at the start, rather than agree to Antwerp?'

'I thought you'd want to be close enough to England to return easily when you're exonerated. And Padua is a very long way away. It will take us weeks of walking.'

In truth, he rather likes the idea. He knows of Padua's reputation as a city open to the new learning. It has a fine medical school. Nicholas is aware – from the latest letter to arrive on Bankside from Bianca's cousin, Bruno Barrani – that a purpose-built anatomy theatre is being constructed there for the great Fabricius, the university's professor of anatomy and surgery, and that Padua has tempted away from Pisa a brilliant young mathematician named Galileo Galilei, whose fame, according to Bruno, is already spreading beyond Italy. Nicholas can think of worse places to spend a few months in exile, even if it is much further away from London than he had planned. And it will be good to renew his friendship with the diminutive Bruno. Yes, Padua it shall be.

Nicholas is about tell Bianca he wholeheartedly approves, when a sudden movement close by their table drags his eyes from hers.

How long Hella Maas has been there, neither Nicholas nor Bianca can say. Nor how much of their conversation she has overheard. But people at the surrounding tables are already nudging each other, pointing in the maid's direction. And all their faces tell the same story: Hella Maas is trouble. It would be better for everyone if she made herself scarce; stopped alarming decent folk with her dire warnings of the Devil's imminent return. Better, perhaps, if the Spanish hanged her in lieu of a rebel assassin.

'I am a pilgrim, too,' she says to Nicholas, her gaze so penetrating that he wonders if perhaps she can see things that reveal themselves to her alone. 'You saved my life once. Now I ask you to do so again. Let me come with you.'

✠

A world away from the little town of Den Bosch, the day's heat is leaching out of the hot stucco walls of a grand, elegantly arcaded building on Padua's Piazza delle Erbe. The Palazzo del Podestà is the official residence of the city's civilian governor, who holds his authority from His Serene Highness Pasquale Cicogna, Doge of Venice.

As a liveried minion escorts Bruno Barrani up the wide stone stairway to the Podestà's audience chamber on the first floor, Bianca's cousin is quietly confident. How hard can it be to convince the doge's representative in Padua that his master should count himself amongst the select owners of a marvel of the new sciences? These days a prince's reputation – a doge's reputation – is judged as much by his patronage of the arts and learning as it is by his prowess on the field of battle.

The servant stops before an imposing pair of wooden doors that reach from floor to ceiling and, for all Bruno knows, keep on going through the roof and up to heaven. He gives a discreet knock and pushes open the left-hand door. 'The merchant Signor Barrani,' he says in a soft, reluctant voice, the sort he might employ when announcing to mixed company the arrival of the pox doctor.

The chamber is simply furnished, though certainly not frugally. The huge desk is made of imported Indian teak, carved to within an inch of its life by clever guildsmen of the *Arte dei Carpentieri*. A Christ of African ivory hangs crucified on the wall behind the desk, his head turned down towards a window open to relieve the heat. The Podestà is standing at the sill, observing the crowd in the piazza, as though he's checking on their mood for the figure on the cross. He turns towards Bruno, his fleshy lip pursed into a cod's pout. Sixty if a day, Bruno reckons, a barrel of Venetian dignity wrapped up in a red gown of office, a black silk cap draped across his white curls. He looks like a prosperous cardinal with a questionable past.

'I have read your letter with interest, Signor Barrani,' he says in a whistle that makes Bruno wonder if there isn't a tame flautist hidden somewhere to accompany him. 'I have to say I am not versed in matters astronomical. The questions I have are purely practical.'

'I shall endeavour to answer them to the fullest of my abilities, Your Honour,' Bruno says, making a second sweeping bow in as many minutes.

'First, is such an engine even possible?'

Bruno takes a step backwards, as though presented with an obstacle he has only this moment seen. 'Possible?' he says, feigning surprise. 'More than possible, Your Honour. It already exists.'

'In Florence, you say?'

'And also in Madrid. The Medicis have one. So, too, does King Philip of Spain. New wonders of discovery are being made almost every day. Surely we cannot permit the Serene Republic to remain deficient.'

The Podestà nods wisely. Hooked already, thinks Bruno.

'How did you come to hear of this apparatus, Signor Barrani? You are not from Florence?'

'Heavens, no! A loyal Paduan, born and bred.'

'Nor, I understand, are you from the Palazzo Bo.'

'Trade has been my university, Your Honour.'

'A merchant, I am led to believe?'

'Indeed, Your Honour. A very humble merchant. One who keeps his ears open on his travels, particularly when the Fiorentini find it impossible not to boast about their latest acquisition in the new sciences.'

'And you wish to set up a guild with the express purpose of building one of these – these *engines* – for His Serene Highness?'

Bruno gives the Podestà an engaging smile. 'The *Arti dei Astronomi.*'

'It has a good ring to it, I'll give you that,' says the Podestà.

'If we are not to remain in thrall to the Fiorentini indefinitely – a state of affairs that I presume His Serenity would consider most injurious to the Republic's reputation – then a guild should be enrolled at once.'

'With you to lead it?'

'I thank God I have eyes clear enough to see my duty when it beckons, Your Honour,' Bruno assures him.

'Have you actually seen this device? Are there plans in existence?'

'That is why I have come to you, sir. I intend to visit Florence again at the first opportunity, in order better to study Signor Santucci's achievement.'

'Santucci? I haven't heard of him. Who is he?'

'The architect and constructor of the device, Your Honour.'

'A Florentine?'

'I fear so.' A sad shrug. 'And Florence is a long way off, and the price of lodging there extortionate. In short, I need a patron.'

The light of understanding flares in the Podestà's watery eyes. 'You want the trip financed? Is that it?'

'As I told you, Your Honour, I am but a humble merchant. Sadly, my humility is down to its last few ducats.'

The Podestà returns to the window and looks out into the piazza, as though he might see His Serene Highness there, ready to give him a verdict. At length, his back still towards Bruno, he says, 'The Medicis and the King of Spain, you say?'

'And without doubt there will soon be others, Your Honour,' Bruno assures him, trying not to sound too pushy. 'The French, the Swiss... even, God forbid, the English...'

The Podestà turns back into the room. Being somewhat like-minded, Bruno spots the glow of avarice on his fleshy face even before the turn is complete.

✠

In the parlour of the van der Molens' house, Hella Maas is taking a third helping of Gretie's waterzooi. Nicholas and Bianca can hear the clatter of her spoon as she wolfs down the fish stew, smell its aroma pervading the house, picture her trying to fix the bowl with an intense stare as though she fears it is only a transparent product of her hunger. It is ten o'clock, and beneath the window the canal is a bottomless black chasm.

It has been agreed between them that Hella Maas will accompany them as far as Pavia, on the far side of the Alps. After that, she will join the real pilgrims on the Via Francigena for the journey on to Rome and St Peter's.

'It's a matter of simple Christian charity,' Nicholas says softly. 'Those people by the warehouse, they would have hanged her. And we can't leave her to the mercies of the Spanish – they don't have any. Besides, it will only be until we've crossed the pass of St Bernard. We can put up with her until then, can't we?'

'The Apocalypse for breakfast... Armageddon for supper: we might as well be locked in a room with the worst sort of Puritan for a month.'

'Bianca! Where's your compassion?'

'It's my ears I'm worried about. And my sanity.'

But Nicholas isn't about to let her off so easily. 'We know she's witnessed two terrible murders, and that she isn't safe here. And you're not the woman to leave a pious young maid to a cruel fate. It is not in your humour.'

'I suppose so,' Bianca says reluctantly. 'Anyway, we won't have to spend much time in conversation with her.'

'Why not? We can hardly ignore her.'

'Because the journey will be the perfect opportunity for me to turn your questionable Italian into a semblance of a language that a Paduan can understand. If you're not halfway to being conversant by the time we get there, you're not the clever man I thought I'd married.'

She's right, he thinks – apart from the Italian. Den Bosch has become unsafe for all three of them. It is only because the captain of the garrison is a particularly unimaginative fellow – and Father Albani so persuasive – that any of them are at liberty at all. When the Spanish investigators arrive from Antwerp, the girl is almost certain to face brutal questioning and, judging by what he's seen so far, the citizens of Den Bosch are unlikely to prove any gentler with her.

Nicholas has already planned their departure, enlisting the help of Jan van der Molen. At dawn they will climb aboard the little skiff he keeps tied up in the canal behind the house. They will leave Den Bosch by the Grote Hekel, the double water-gate that brings light shipping on the Dommel into the city. Jan has assured him that the two heavy spiked wooden beams that serve as barriers are still raised, despite the doubling of the guard. The Spanish will be on the lookout for an unfamiliar Dutch male trying to leave, a rebel from the northern states who has slipped into the town to carry out his murderous act. Jan's familiar face will ensure an unquestioned departure. Once clear of the town, they will strike south through Brabant to the French border, joining the Via Francigena at Reims.

Nicholas reckons it will take them a fortnight to reach that cathedral city.

Thanks to Gretie's help, and with assistance from Bianca, Hella Maas has been turned from a wild-eyed stray into something almost human, though the fiery glint in those impenetrably dark eyes has not dimmed for a single moment throughout. To Nicholas, it is as if something inside her is alight, the still-molten core of a furnace whose outside walls have cooled. In such company, he fears the Via Francigena might prove to be a very long road indeed. But at least he knows where that road will end. The weight on his conscience, were he to leave the maid to her fate, might never lift.

When he and Bianca settle down to snatch a few hours' rest before their departure, he finds the images of the day's events are too raw in his mind for sleep to come. Bloodstained bodies – trying to stop a man bleeding to death and failing – are nothing new to him. During his summer as a surgeon with the army of the House of Orange he dealt with more than his share. It is the triptych that sets his thoughts reeling once more. The memory of those monstrous images makes him fear that sleep will carry him to a hellish landscape where demons in the shape of lizards torment his naked body; where a toad in a nun's habit, and bearing an implausibly benign human face, fries disjointed limbs and heads in a pan; where a creature in the shape of a living blade searches for weak human flesh to stab; and where that awful mill grinds human bodies into a rich juice of sinners.

12

Den Bosch, the Duchy of Brabant, 6th July 1594

Dawn lifts the shape of a window out of the darkness of their chamber. Nicholas makes a final check of their bags while Bianca washes the sleep from her eyes from a bowl and ewer that Gretie has provided. Jan van der Molen's discreet knock on the chamber door announces it is almost time to leave.

Downstairs in the parlour Nicholas forces a few *stuivers* into Jan's reluctant hand. Nothing more remains to be done but bid Gretie and the boys farewell. Then it's out through the rear door and onto a little wooden balcony, barely wide enough for one man to stand side-on. The dank stench of sluggish water hangs in the dawn air, though the canal itself is all but lost in a blanket of mist trapped between the houses on either side.

As startling as a pistol shot, an explosive thrashing of wings causes Nicholas's heart to leap. A brace of waterfowl bursts out of the vapour and climbs away between the walls of the brick canyon. Jan slips down into the skiff and extends a helping hand to Bianca and Hella. Nicholas brings up the rear with the bags. When they are settled, Gretie unties the mooring rope and Jan pushes out one booted foot to propel the little boat away from the balcony. The invisible canal emits a belch of rotting vegetation. When Nicholas looks back over his shoulder, the balcony, Gretie and the whole van der Molen house has already vanished.

The waterway is so narrow that the oars almost scrape the brickwork on either side as they glide through the mist, the walls of the houses seeming to emerge from nothingness around shoulder level. Nicholas has the impression they are descending an incline towards a watery underworld, though he knows it is an illusion of the senses. No one speaks.

After a few moments the canal opens out into a broader stretch of water. The mist is more fibrous here, tendrils lifting off the surface like steam from a cauldron. A yellow wash of latent sunlight brushes the silhouettes of the houses and the steeples of Den Bosch.

Soon the Grote Hekel looms ahead, its twin arches bestriding the canal below a broad gatehouse. Nicholas cannot escape the feeling that the arches are the eyes of a great sea beast, its body all but submerged. They seem to be regarding the approaching skiff far too hungrily for his liking.

The letters of safe-passage and credit from Robert Cecil can be explained away, he thinks. If the boat is stopped, he will stick to the story that he and Bianca are fugitive Catholics, and that Cecil has written the letters in generous recognition of the service his physician has done the family. If the letters are questioned, then Bianca's Petrine cross should convince. But it is time, he thinks, to dispose of the wheel-lock pistol. After the murders in the cathedral, it is more of a liability than a protection. It will be hard to explain away to a Spanish guard on the lookout for an escaping assassin. And so it goes into the black water, silently, leaving not a ripple.

As Jan van der Molen had said, the huge wooden booms are raised inside the twin arches. The skiff enters the left-hand one, plunging immediately into shadow. Two figures stand on a raised stone walkway above the surface of the canal. By his bulk, Nicholas sees that one of them is a Spanish soldier in leather trunk-hose and breastplate. The other is a Brabantian. He calls down to Jan van der Molen to identify himself. Nicholas's heart thumps in his chest. It seems to echo around the interior of the archway, a guilty drumbeat that must surely alert the two guards.

To his relief, he hears Jan return a laugh of recognition. 'Hey, Aldert van Ruys, you old rogue! What are you doing here at this hour? Has your wife turned you out of bed early because she can't abide your farting a moment longer?'

'Better my farts than the stink of your herrings, Jan van der Molen,' comes the reply. 'Do you have any Dutch rebels with you this morning?'

'Why do you ask?'

'Have you not heard? One of them murdered a servant of the Archduke of Austria yesterday. Stabbed him and Father Vermeiren – in the cathedral, of all places. They say a column is on its way from Antwerp.'

'I'd heard something of the sort.'

'The *caballero* here wants to know who's with you.'

'Pilgrims, Aldert. Good Catholic pilgrims. They're on their way to Reims, to join the Via Francigena. They're off to Rome to pray for all our souls at St Peter's.'

'Then tell them to ask the Pope to work a miracle for me.'

'What sort of miracle?'

'Tell the Holy Father to pray every night to make that little baker's daughter on the Choorstraat turn her pretty eyes upon me.'

As the Spaniard waves them through, Jan van der Molen calls out in reply, 'The Holy Father may well be infallible, Aldert. But he's not that infallible.'

With the guard's laughter swallowed by the quiescent morning stillness, the little skiff slips out of the Grote Hekel and into the broader Dommel. The windmills stand black and deathly against the lightening sky. Ahead and to the south, the marshland of southern Brabant stretches away towards Antwerp, Brussels and the border with France. Nicholas is too busy staring out over the flat landscape and wondering how long it will take them to reach Reims to notice a second skiff edge silently into the water-gate behind them.

PART 2

✠

The Pilgrim Road

13

Florence, 8th July 1594

What manner of fellow will this Antonio Santucci be? Bruno Barrani wonders as he waits with all the other petitioners in the courtyard of the Palazzo Vecchio. Full of his own importance, without question. A servant of Duke Ferdinando de' Medici is unlikely to have a single modest bone in his entire body. Especially one who holds the grandiloquent title of the duke's Master of the Spheres.

The air is heavy with the summer heat and the scent of male flesh that no amount of laundered silk or expensive perfume can hide. The long wait for Santucci's appearance is making Bruno drowsy. His two servants, Alonso and Luca, are unquestionably on their second bottle at some nearby *buchetta del vino*, enjoying themselves at his expense. His usually irrepressible good humour is flagging by the minute.

To pass the time while he waits, Bruno reaches into his bag and draws out two small pages of parchment, once crisply folded but now a little crumpled from the rigours of the ride to Florence. It is a letter from cousin Bianca, and it arrived the morning of his departure from Padua – posted, according to the letterhead, at the end of September last. It has been making its laborious and itinerant way towards him ever since, via the hands of any number of nameless travelling merchants, banking couriers and other peripatetic travellers on the long and uncertain road from Bankside in London.

Reading it again now, for what must surely be the tenth time, Bruno can still feel joy in his heart. He imagines there will be a lot of surreptitious masculine tears shed when the gallants of Padua learn that Bianca Merton has wed. But he cannot think of a better husband for her. True, the Englishman has no fortune, no palazzi to inherit, or titles, or estates teeming with boar, no vines whose richness – when pressed out by honest labour – will delight the throat and swell the coffers. He's not even Catholic! But Nicholas Shelby has an honest heart. And he's a fine physician – or else Bruno himself would not be here now to approve of the match. And, *Dominus Iesus in Excelsis*, how he loves Bianca!

Bruno knows he owes a lot to Nicholas Shelby. Without the Englishman's skill, he would never have survived his clandestine visit to London with His Eminence Cardinal Fiorzi. He carries the marks to this day. Sometimes his words are a little slow in coming. He still suffers the occasional headache, for which a Paduan apothecary whom he trusts prescribes various remedies, including a powder made from a new plant that has only recently arrived in the merchants' shops in Venice – from China, it is said, though that may be only to raise the price – *rhubarb*. All in all, he thinks, these minor trials are but weak wine when set against what had been the very real possibility of him dying in a heretic land.

Bruno savours the letter again, kisses it and puts it back in his bag. It will be months before he receives another. A lot could happen in the meantime – for good or ill. He harbours a profound hope that when it comes it will bring news of a child safely delivered. He smiles as he recalls what the thirteen-year-old Bianca had told him, in all seriousness, after recovering from a period of religious rapture. 'I shall bear no sons for any man to preen himself over. I will not spend the rest of my life sewing and getting fat while *he* dallies in the tavern and the whorehouse. I will not!'

'The cloisters of Santa Sofia then?' he had suggested.

'Are you a fool, Bruno?' she had said, glaring at him with those feline amber eyes. 'Can you really see me at a life of prayer and contemplation?'

'But last month that was all you spoke about.'

'That was only because of a boy I'd seen coming out of the seminary. I've changed my mind now. I shall become a professor of medicine at Palazzo Bo instead.'

'You said that when you were eight, after you decided not to marry Cardinal Fiorzi,' he had laughed, instantly regretting his mirth as her jaw hardened with an assassin's determination. 'Besides, that's impossible. You're a girl.'

'Impossible – why? At Bologna, Dorotea Bucca held that position almost two hundred years ago.'

'Yes, but the Bolognese all have marsh wind in their brains. It makes them rash.'

'Signor Barrani... Signor Barrani.... Where is the Paduan?'

The sound of someone calling his name brings Bruno out of his reverie. Looking across the courtyard, he sees a well-dressed man scanning the petitioners from halfway down the flight of grand stone steps.

Like many Italian men of genius, at first sight Antonio Santucci looks like a common labourer in a rich man's gown. Take away the expensive cloth and you might expect to find Duke Ferdinando de' Medici's Master of the Spheres up a ladder laying roof tiles, or turning an axle on a foot-lathe. Bruno wonders if God requires you first to show an artisan's ability with a chisel, mallet, saw or paintbrush, before He sees fit to pour the genius part into the mould.

'A thousand apologies for keeping you waiting, Signor Barrani,' Santucci says as they meet at the foot of the stairway.

Santucci is a short man, only four fingers' width taller than Bruno. He has a boxer's shoulders, but his hands are as light and mobile as a painter's, the fingers almost femininely graceful. Bruno puts him in his middle forties, though the dense black beard makes him look older. If he is from humble stock – as Bruno suspects – then commissions from the Medici court and Philip of Spain have put a superiority in his gaze that could match that of a Michelangelo or a Brunelleschi. Or there again, perhaps disdain comes in the milk from a Florentine mother's tit. Either way, Bruno makes a grand bend of the knee, to show that while the Serene Republic might not be quite the power she once was, Venice – and her attendant moon, Padua – can still remember their manners.

'An uneventful journey, I trust,' Santucci says, making an even deeper obeisance. 'I hear there are still brigands in the Veneto.'

'We expelled them some time ago,' says Bruno, smiling diplomatically. *Along with their cousins, the Florentines.* 'And yes, thank you, the journey was good – though the road through Fiesole was surprisingly untended for such a prosperous place.'

'My secretary tells me you are here on a commission from the Doge of Venice himself. I understand you wish to discuss the cosmological sphere I constructed for His Highness, Duke Ferdinando de' Medici.' Santucci raises a quizzical eyebrow. 'You are a man of the new science, perhaps? An astronomer, or a mathematician?'

Bruno must admit to himself that he isn't a man of any science, new or old – except perhaps the science of trying to make a living in an uncharitable world. It is of no interest to him whether the stars move about in crystal spheres or are immutably fixed in the heavens; it is enough that they shine. Neither does he particularly care if the earth sits motionless at the centre of the cosmos, or if it spins around like a peasant dancing the *tarantella*. If he knows anything about anything, it is how to spot an opportunity for profit. And of one thing he is certain: Pasquale Cicogna, the Doge of Venice, is that most useful of sales prospects: a man who doesn't know he has need of a thing until you tell him what he's missing.

'I confess I am neither,' he says sadly, 'merely a humble emissary from His—' He pauses momentarily, remembering how Santucci had described Duke Ferdinando only as 'His Highness'. Not to be bettered by a Florentine, he continues, 'His *Serene* Highness. As for the new science, that I leave to greater minds than mine – the professors at Padua University. I am, shall we say, merely the oil that will aid the mechanism to turn.'

'How much are we speaking of?'

'Just the one device.'

'Ducats, I mean.'

Bruno thinks: trust a Florentine to get straight down to the money.

'His Serene Highness is a generous man,' he says reassuringly, 'I am sure he will make it worth your labour, Master Santucci.'

'Labour? Are you under the impression I build the apparatus with my own hands?'

Is that amusement Bruno can see in the Florentine's eyes? Is the Medici Master of the Spheres laughing at him?

'I assumed—'

Santucci lifts a delicate hand. 'It will require a host of skilled workmen: clockmakers, engravers, carpenters, experts in the application of gilt and gold leaf, forgers of iron...'

Now it is Bruno's turn to be supercilious. 'Of which we have a great number in Venice, Master Santucci. The ships that bettered the Turk did not build themselves. Nor did the clever instruments by which they navigate. The artisans who work in the Arsenale are amongst the finest in the world.'

'Would you expect me to come to Venice? I hear there are more mosquitoes there than there are beggars.'

Bruno places one gloved hand before his mouth and coughs. *But not nearly so many Florentine fleas.*

'Do not fear, Signor Santucci,' he says brightly. 'We bring in the finest muslin from the Orient, to make the nets. The mosquitoes die of a surfeit of admiration before they can find a way through.'

The tightness of Santucci's answering smile makes the extremities of his beard flick upwards. 'I suppose you would like to see the apparatus, having come all this way.'

'If that is not an inconvenience.'

'You are fortunate, Master Barrani,' says Santucci. 'His...' A pause, followed by an expression of superiority that Bruno has difficulty not punching, 'His Most *Gracious* and Mighty Highness, Duke Ferdinando, is inspecting the new work on the Belvedere bastion today. I can show you to the Hall of Maps without fear of disturbing his private studies.'

Santucci leads him up the broad stone steps, past snow-white statues of ancient heroes and on into the depths of the palace. As they walk, the soles of their shoes clacking on the marble, the Florentine drops names every time they pass a painting or a piece of sculpture: Botticelli... Donatello... Michelangelo... Bruno feigns an air of boredom. He has long ago stopped kneeling before an altar painting or a chapel fresco without wondering how much he could sell it for.

At last Santucci brings him to a great salon where the walls are lined not with priceless work but with maps of every land in the known world. There is even one of England, so cleverly drawn that Bruno thinks that if he were to study it closely enough, he might even see cousin Bianca going about her business on Bankside.

But it is the thing that sits at the very centre of the salon that has Bruno Barrani's jaw resting firmly on his breastbone. Twice the height of a man, a vast globe of thick golden thread seems to be floating in the air before him, an intricate weave of concentric rings that disappear into a hidden core. The glare from the windows reflects off its complex surface in dazzling rays of fire. It is the sun itself, confined in a room, or perhaps it is the burning bush from the Book of Exodus, carried by an angel of the Lord from biblical Mount Horeb and set down here in Florence. For what else can it be but miraculous?

Santucci waves a hand at a servant. The next moment the sphere begins to turn. A deep and resonant rumble reaches Bruno through the floorboards. Within the sphere, the rings begin to move as if by celestial magic. Some turn one way, others against them. Some move elliptically, before reversing their path and retreating. The whole thing seems to be alive, turning, tumbling, writhing with a secret purpose.

'There is no armillary sphere anywhere in Christendom that is its equal,' Santucci is telling him, as though to suggest that there might be is to challenge God's own creation. 'It is perfect in every measure, an exact re-creation of the cosmos as described by the great Ptolemaeus of Alexandria and understood by astronomers, astrologers, philosophers and mathematicians down the centuries since. It can show the exact movement of the sun and the planets as seen from the earth, as they move through the celestial spheres in the heavens above us. It can predict the solstices, the vernal and autumnal equinoxes, the procession of the zodiac, how the sun and the moon will rise and set on each day of the year. With this engine, there is no physician who can fail to cast an accurate horoscope before making a diagnosis; no prince who cannot gauge an auspicious day upon which to embark upon a campaign; no astronomer who need tire his eyes searching out a heavenly body to instruct his pupils.'

At Santucci's invitation, Bruno moves closer to inspect the extraordinary device. It towers over him, its circumference beyond the limit of his sight, its innards visibly processing past his gaze, as though it would reveal its secrets to him alone, if only he could read them.

'That is the equatorial ring,' Santucci tells him as a gilded band engraved with the signs of the zodiac swings merrily past him, through Cancer and Leo and on to Gemini, 'passing through the vernal equinox to the summer and winter solstices... and there is the planetary motion of Saturn, one of the six planetary spheres moving according to the way God has designed them... There the equatorial ring... and there the northern celestial pole...'

'But where is the earth itself?' Bruno asks, transfixed by the slowly turning bands.

'Look deeper into the engine, Master Barrani,' Santucci tells him.

And Bruno does, though he has to peer past the swirling vortex that is Santucci's miraculous contrivance in order to see, deep within, a perfect little globe painted with the lands of the known world.

'You are seeing what God sees, when he looks down upon the cosmos from heaven, Master Barrani. How many men can say they have done *that*?'

Bruno has no answer for him. For the first time in his life, he is lost for words.

✶

While Bruno Barrani looks down upon the world from God's own vantage point, at the same time Ned Monkton is sitting in the lodgings by the Paris Garden on Bankside, wishing he'd had the same advantage. He has visited every water-stairs between Lambeth and Bermondsey, every tavern, every dice-house and stew he can think of that a wherryman or an oarsman from a tilt-boat might frequent. But although he knows by name many of the men who work upon the water, calls many of them friend, it has proved impossible to find the one who brought the stranger across the Thames to Bankside.

Until today. Today everything has changed.

Sitting before him is one Giles Hunte, part owner of a wherry that usually operates from the Falcon stairs. Hunte with an *e*, the strong-armed, broad-backed young man is eager to put on record, in case there might be a lesser Hunt working the river.

'I'd have come earlier, Master Monkton,' he says, savouring the hot spiced wine that Rose has brought him for his troubles, 'but I've been up at Richmond, running timber across the river for my cousin. I hear you was asking after a certain body I brought across from the north bank a while ago.'

'How did you know that was the fellow I was seeking?'

'I was drinking last night with Jack Tomblin in the Good Husband. He mentioned you'd been asking around. This fellow fitted the description you put out. I recall him clearly. He asked me how he might find his way to the Jackdaw – he didn't seem to know it had burned down last summer. When I told him, he still wanted to know where it was. That raised my suspicions. I wondered if he might be one of the Bishop of London's fellows, come over with his snout twitching, to root out sin. You know how they sometimes like to do that in Southwark.'

'Aye,' says Ned with a grin, 'and take their time doing it. You'd think the number of times they come, Bankside would be the most sinless place in Christendom.'

Hunte gives a knowing laugh. 'I did ask him if he wanted the address of a clean bawdy-house. He got on his high horse about that. Told me I was a saucy churl. So I made sure he got his arse soaked, getting out of my wherry.'

Ned slaps his knee with one huge palm. The sound makes Rose turn her head. 'I was right, Wife!' he says joyfully. 'I *knew* that little rogue with the wet arse 'ad come from across the river.' To Giles Hunte, he asks, 'Did he have a name?'

The wherryman returns an apologetic shake of his head. 'He didn't give one, and I didn't ask. But I can tell you where I picked him up, if it's of any help. It was from the Blackfriars water-stairs, and he came from the direction of St Andrew's Hill.'

✳

Bruno Barrani raps his gloved hand imperiously against the little wooden window of the *buchetta*. When it opens, he hands in the empty bottle and waits while an indistinct figure within refills it.

He approves of these little counters where they sell rich Tuscan wine. He thinks he might set up a few in Padua – cheaper to run than a shop or a tavern. That means a more profitable margin. And good for his social standing, too. Who wouldn't want to be on first-name terms with a fellow who owned a magic window?

He carries the bottle to the stools set beneath a shady over-hang. Luca and Alonso, his servants, are covetously guarding their empty cups and making obscene comments about the fashion sense of the Fiorentini from behind their hands.

'The price these robbers charge for a bottle of Artimino!' he growls as he puts the wine down on the bench and resumes his place. 'Is there *no one* in this town who isn't either a thief or a whore?'

'Perhaps you should have offered more money, Master,' Luca says, sensing Bruno's anger.

'More money? For this stuff? It would still be extortion if it was half the price.'

'I didn't mean the wine-seller, Master. I meant Signor Santucci. You should have upped the offer. It is the doge's *scudi* anyway – His Serene Highness can afford it.'

Bruno grunts contemptuously as he refills the glasses. He sticks his little black-hosed legs out onto the cobbles. 'Who needs a creep like Santucci anyway? Master of the Spheres! Pompous Florentine ass, more like it. Santucci isn't even master of his own sphincter. I told him so to his face.'

'Maybe that's why he won't play,' Alonso suggests.

'I only told him that *after* he'd turned me down. I'm not stupid, Alonso.' Bruno sips at his Artimino. He runs a hand through his black ringlets. He scowls, which on such a small face gives him the looks of a slapped child. 'All this way, and he turns me down just so that his master, the fucking Grand Duke of fucking Tuscany – Ferdinando de' fucking Medici – can thumb his nose at Venice!' He spits onto the cobbles in disgust. 'They hate us. A pox on them all!'

Alonso looks horrified. 'Hush, Master. Keep your voice down. You'll get us a hard floor in the Bargello – or worse. A brand on my forehead is not the sort of souvenir I'd planned on taking home from Florence, if it's all the same to you.'

'I still don't understand what's so important about this great sphere of his, anyway,' says Luca.

Bruno favours his servants with a condescending smile. 'It's a wondrous engine of science. The cosmos, laid out in brass and gold leaf. You have to hand it to Santucci: it's more than clever. I'd wager even the great Leonardo would have struggled to contrive such a thing. More important, it was going to open the door to the doge's treasury and a hefty commission!'

'Yes, but what does it *do*?' Luca asks. 'I still don't understand.'

'That's because you Veronese have dust for brains.'

'Alright, Master – explain it in terms that a Veronese dust-for-brains can understand.'

'Well, I'm not versed in natural philosophy,' Bruno begins, 'so I cannot rightly explain *how* he's done it, but somehow Santucci has contrived to construct a moving model of the cosmos – one that enables a man to see where the heavenly bodies will lie at any given hour of any day. It's twice the height of a man and, when you look at it turning, you see what God sees when he looks down from heaven. At least, that's what Santucci claims.'

'Trust a Florentine to think he has the same viewpoint as God,' says Alonso, belching a mist of wine into the air.

'But what *use* is it?' asks Luca.

'It can tell you things before they happen.'

'What, like if Alonso gets drunk, they'll ban him from Signora Volante's whorehouse? Who needs a giant golden sphere to tell you *that*?'

'It's the new science, Luca,' Bruno says airily. 'I wouldn't expect a pair of numbskulls like you two to understand.'

'You don't really know what it does any more than we do,' Alonso says under his breath.

Bruno puffs up his little chest in indignation. 'It's the latest thing in astronomical calculation – an engine that can see into the future,' he says laboriously, as though reading a set of instructions. 'It can tell you where the stars and the moon and the planets will be on any given night or day, in any given latitude. It can tell a mariner where the north star will be; allow the astrologer to cast more accurate charts so that he can advise his prince when to start a war, or when to sire an heir. That's what Santucci says. For all I care, it can predict the Day of Judgement. What sticks in my gut is that the Doge of Venice was going to shower us in ducats to build him one of his own.'

'This engine – can it predict when you're going to pay us, Master?' Luca says with an air of fragile innocence.

Bruno nails his servant to his stool with the eyes of death. 'Only after it tells *me* when you two are finally going to get off your lazy backsides and clean my trunk-hose and polish my boots like proper servants.'

Alonso frowns. 'But that's blasphemy.'

'What? You doing an hour's honest work? I should say so.'

'I mean, putting yourself in God's place, Master.'

Bruno licks the wine off his lips. 'Maybe. But Antonio Santucci doesn't mind making these engines for the King of Spain and these Medici bastards. But Venice... Where Venice is concerned, apparently the Master of the Spheres is not for sale.'

'Must be the only Florentine who isn't,' Luca growls softly.

The little Paduan cockerel slowly lowers his cup. He leans forward towards Luca. 'Say that again.'

For a moment, Luca thinks he might have overstepped the mark. Bruno Barrani is a small enough cockerel, but he can deliver a mighty peck when he's roused. 'I meant that Santucci must be the only Florentine you can't buy – that's all, Master.'

Bruno jumps from his stool, sending his glass tottering across the table. 'Luca,' he says, 'if you weren't so pig-ugly, I'd kiss you!'

'Why, what have I said?'

Bruno reaches forward and waggles the lobe of Luca's left ear. 'When I said "The Master of the Spheres is not for sale", you answered, "Must be the only Florentine who isn't".'

'So, Master?'

'"Well, Santucci didn't make that thing on his own, did he?'

'I don't know, Master. I didn't see it, did I?'

'Take it from me, he had help: carpenters, clocksmiths, any number of artisans. They must have drawings, plans... And just as you said, friend Luca, they can be *bought*.'

Luca puts out his cup for a refill – the way only a servant who knows all of his master's foibles and indiscretions may do. 'You mean you intend to make one of these things yourself, Master? Saving your pardon, you can't even fit a door hinge straight.'

Bruno seems quite untroubled by this insult. He sits down again, without his eyes ever leaving Luca's. 'Florence isn't the only place with its own tame genius, my lad,' he says knowingly.

'Do you have someone in mind, Master?' Alonso asks.

'As a matter of fact, I do.'

'Who?' Luca demands to know, leaning inwards as he catches a sniff of conspiracy.

'I was thinking of the new professor of mathematics at Padua University. He'd be the very man to oversee the project.'

'How can you be sure he'll do it?' Luca enquires.

'Because we're friends, and I happen to know he gets paid half of what the other professors get paid, on account of the Palazzo Bo esteeming mathematicians well below physicians and lawyers, and only just above the night-shit removers. I also happen to know he's in need of coin. If we can get a plan and show it to him, and he agrees, then the professor gets to pay off his debts, His Serene Highness gets his toy, *we* get our commission and Master of the Spheres Santucci gets a length of good Venetian *sopressa* up his backside.'

Luca and Alonso digest this in much the same way they digest any other of their master's get-rich-quick plans.

'But if the mathematician isn't to eat up most of the profit, what exactly do you intend to offer him?' Luca asks.

Bruno grins. 'I'd have thought that was obvious. You know how jealous those professors are of their reputation. My good friend Signor Galileo Galilei will get to have his name lauded down the ages as the man who built the doge's great golden sphere.'

14

The Duchy of Brabant, between Antwerp and Brussels, 10th July 1594

In the light of a blood-red dawn, Hella Maas stops at the crest of the little wooden bridge and turns in a slow circle, looking out over the barren, empty polder. Apart from Nicholas and Bianca, there is not another living soul to be seen. All that breaks the horizon is a single skeletal tree shattered by lightning, and a windmill, its sails motionless in the early-morning stillness, pulling the eye towards it like a distant crucifixion. Nicholas cannot help but remember the right-hand panel of the Den Bosch triptych, with its hellish fires glowing in a darkened, satanic landscape. He can see by the look on the maid's face that she is seeing it, too. Her words confirm it.

'Do you not smell what I smell?' she asks, a slight smile of superiority on her lips.

'Smell what?' asks Bianca, wondering if she means the marshy odour of the polder.

'The smell of the flames.'

'There's nothing here to burn,' Nicholas says quickly.

'I speak of the flames of eternal judgement,' Hella announces. 'And it is we who have opened the door to let them enter.'

In the four days since leaving Den Bosch they have grown used to these sudden doom-laden pronouncements. They seem to come out of nowhere. Usually Hella does not even pause when delivering one, as she has now, but keeps up her relentless pace, jabbing at the path with a length of willow held in her right hand, as though every step forward must be won in battle. But they leave Bianca with a sense of foreboding. In her life till now she has had her own moments of uncanny foresight – usually not for the better. Precognition is not something she takes lightly.

'Is this about the painting, Hella – the painting in the Den Bosch cathedral?' she asks gently.

Nicholas closes his eyes in resignation. By now he knows not to ask such a question.

'I tried to warn them,' the maid answers, stabbing at the planks of the bridge with the tip of the willow cane. 'I told Father Vermeiren that he was inviting those same horrors to come to pass, if he let it remain on public view. But he said it was just a painting, and that praying hard would ensure such things were never visited upon us. Now he's dead, and the Spanish will treat the people of his town harshly.' She gives the bridge a final, sharp jab with the willow, as if to put it out of its misery. 'Why won't people listen to me?'

Without waiting for an answer, she resumes her determined march.

Bianca can see only her back, but she knows that on the maid's face will be that sad, ethereal look of almost-tearful foreboding she has become accustomed to. She whispers to Nicholas, 'We're not even in France yet, and it is a *very* long way to the St Bernard Pass.'

'Give her time,' he says quietly, his mouth close to her ear. 'She's witnessed two brutal murders at close hand, and you saw what the townspeople were capable of doing to her.'

'You are right, of course. I should be more charitable,' Bianca says, hoisting her pack into a more comfortable position to ease the blisters forming on her shoulders. She sets off again after the figure pacing so determinedly ahead, leaving Nicholas to follow.

She would prefer to put Hella Maas out of her thoughts, but in the empty polder there is little to distract her. If even half of what Hella claims is true, then she is a most unusual young woman. When Nicholas had asked again how she came to speak such good English, this time she had answered him: Leiden University.

'You have studied at a *university*?' Bianca had said in awe, recalling how the professors at the Palazzo Bo in Padua had laughed at her own demand to study medicine there. She had tried to keep the envy from her voice, telling herself that she had, after all, been only eight years old at the time.

'I learned English, Latin and Italian,' Hella had told her. 'I served the learned men there, and I listened closely to them. They let me read their books. But they would not let me graduate, because God made me out of the rib of Adam. They said it was not proper for one of my sex.'

Bianca had immediately felt a measure of sympathy, bolstered by the fact that there had been not the slightest hubris in the maid's voice. She might have been laying claim to nothing more than a minor talent with bodkin and thimble.

Apart from her command of several languages, it also seems that Hella Maas can recite from Euclid's *Elements*, name the attendants of the North Star, knows the magic contained in certain numbers and can discourse with confidence on the subject of Master Copernicus and his theory of the cosmos. 'God blessed the women of my family with great gifts,' she had announced.

Watching her now, a driven zealot in a borrowed gown striding through the empty landscape as though in flight from an unseen enemy, it occurs to Bianca that at some point God changed his mind. He turned benevolence into punishment. Though how and for what sin, Hella Maas has yet to tell them.

✠

On Bankside, a new Jackdaw tavern is rising from the ashes of the old. The oak frame is up, the brick walls are complete, glaziers are busy setting the lozenges of glass into the lead frames, thatchers scramble over the joists with the confidence of mariners aloft in the rigging of a ship at sea.

It is not the Jackdaw of old. How could it be? For a start, the walls are too straight. They do not sag under the weight of centuries of collected insobriety. Where the timbers were once smooth and darkened with the smoky patina of age, now they are new and honey-coloured, bearing the rough marks of saw-tooth, chisel and adze. The only survivors from the original are the chimneys, the brewhouse in the yard where the mad-dog was made and the tavern's painted sign, which once hung over the lane. True, it is a little scorched. But it survives. Rose and Ned have sworn not to hang it in place again until Bianca and Nicholas have returned from wherever it is they are now.

The steady progress has enabled Ned to pursue the lead given to him by the wherryman, Giles Hunte. He has taken several trips across the river to the Blackfriars water-stairs. For hours at a time he has hung around the jetty, wandered up St Andrew's Hill or into Thames Street, or through the lanes around Baynard's Castle, ostensibly just another citizen fortunate to have time on his hands. But so far, he has caught not so much as a glimpse of his quarry.

At first there were numerous occasions when his imagination toyed with him, causing his huge frame to stiffen momentarily as he noticed a bald man, a thin man, a patched jerkin, a pair of cheap woollen hose… But always the fellow he saw was *too* bald, or not bald enough; too thin, too fat, too young, too old. Now he has managed to chain his impetuosity a little.

He has thought about giving up. Rose is uncomfortable with these journeys across the river. He knows how much she fears he will revert to his old ways, when he knew no other way of handling the world's objection to him than prodigious quantities of ale and the use of his fists. But why, he wonders, would she think he might risk going back there? Especially now that Rose is sure she is with child.

That in itself is miracle enough for him. There had been a time when Ned had only the dead for company, his only home the mortuary crypt at St Tom's – where he worked for pennies as a porter. He had almost come to believe that God intended him to dwell apart from the living, that he should have no place in the world above ground. There is nothing he intends to do that will risk him being buried a second time.

Just a few more visits, he tells himself as he walks back towards the Blackfriars water-stairs. Two... maybe three. Four at the outside. After all, the little arseworm can't stay hidden for ever.

15

Reims, Northern France, 20th July 1594

The flat marshes of Brabant have given way to the rolling verdancy of the Champagne. Two weeks have passed since Nicholas, Bianca and Hella Maas left Den Bosch. Two weeks of steady march, the long miles of chalky road and meadow path taken yard-by-yard. Two weeks of sleeping in the barns of farmers who think the door to heaven may open a little easier for them if they offer clean straw to the pilgrim, or in the cellars of the pious. They avoid the taverns. Nicholas doesn't want to make it too easy for any Privy Council searcher already on their tail.

Muscles are stronger now. Blisters are a weakness of the past to be laughed at. Feet have hardened, tendons toughened. Nicholas's Italian is growing ever more confident, less needful of Bianca's correction. He is a quick learner. She puts it down to his command of Latin, learned at school and honed during his medical studies at Cambridge, where it had been the predominant form of exchange. She must still speak slowly if he is to catch the full meaning of what she says, but her hardest task is not letting him see her smile when she hears her own tongue spoken with a Suffolk burr.

They hear the bells of the cathedral of Our Lady long before they see the city walls. The slow reverence of their tolling echoes through the gentle valley. It is the accompaniment to the crowning of French kings, and a call to the weary pilgrim to rest awhile in shady cloisters. For Nicholas, the sound provides a welcome respite from a particularly difficult exercise in Italian pronunciation. Out ahead, Hella does not slow her march for an instant.

They follow her at a distance, their boots and ankles floured with chalk dust. They are walking a path between endless rows of vines, the sky lapis-blue above them, the sun's hot touch brushing their shoulders.

'It's as if she's compelled to reach God before anyone else does,' Bianca says, looking ahead to where their companion strides out in determined fashion towards the soft rise that will afford them their first sight of Reims.

'Does she walk with such determination because she's in a hurry to arrive,' asks Nicholas, putting voice to a question he has often asked himself since they left Den Bosch, 'or because she is trying to escape?'

It is a puzzle both of them have yet to solve.

✠

Taciturn she might be, dourly pious without a doubt, but when they enter Reims, Hella also proves herself invaluable. With passable French being just one of her professed accomplishments, she finds them good lodgings, even negotiates a fair price – no mean achievement in a town where to tell someone you're a pilgrim doubles the cost of anything.

The chamber she finds them lies above a hostelry. It has three straw mattresses, each with a freshly washed sheet embroidered with images of the saints to inspire the weary pilgrim. There is a night-soil pot discreetly hidden behind a similarly embellished hanging. They may empty it themselves – free of charge – on the midden behind the house, or pay a sou to the owner's grandmother to dispose of it for them. When the shutters are thrown back, there is a fine view from the window, across the busy square to the great cathedral of Notre-Dame de Reims.

'I must offer my heart to the Lord,' Hella announces, gazing rapturously at the two blunted spires and the gallery of stone kings who gaze down on the people below with a hauteur that only French monarchs could contrive.

'I've no doubt He'll be expecting it,' mutters Bianca as the door closes, leaving her and Nicholas alone. 'You haven't given Him a moment's rest since we left Den Bosch.'

Knowing their journey along the Via Francigena will be long and full of peril, Nicholas decides it would be wise to seek advice. He knows exactly where to find it, even though he has never visited Reims before – the local office of the English College of Douai. Just to set foot in the place could be considered treason. The seminary trains English Catholic priests to infiltrate their homeland and spread the papist heresy. Robert Cecil will expect him to remember faces and names. The next morning, following the directions the landlord of the hostelry has provided, he and Bianca make the short walk to the Basilica of Saint-Remi.

The air in the cloisters is heavy with the scent of wild flowers and the murmuring of summer insects at their prayers. After a short wait, the stillness is broken by the soft slap of sandal leather on flagstones. A rotund little fellow with a tonsure comes pattering towards them like an exuberant puppy.

'Father Reginald Peacham,' he announces. 'What a joy to meet you. English pilgrims are rare these days. Is it true? Is the persecution of the faithful really as bad as we hear?'

'In June they executed the queen's physician,' Nicholas tells him, deciding, somewhat uncomfortably, that Lopez's death is as good a means as any of establishing his trustworthiness. 'That was when we decided we could suffer there no longer.'

A nod of commiseration from Father Peacham, a momentary shadow cast across his otherwise-bright disposition. 'Of course I shall do all in my power to help you. We wouldn't want you taking a wrong turn and ending up in Muscovy, or Constantinople, would we?' He beams at Bianca. 'Lost souls, and all that.'

Pleased with his little joke, Father Peacham sets off on a circuit of the cloisters, moving in joyous bounds and clapping his fleshy hands together when a smile isn't up to the job. Every now and then he pauses in his monologue of directions, warnings and general advice to sniff the flowers. Try as he might, Nicholas can see not the slightest trace of a seditious agent of the Antichrist anywhere in the man. But that is how Robert Cecil and the Privy Council would view him. They would send this little packet of good-natured piety to the scaffold without a second thought.

From Reims, Father Peacham explains, they will follow the road to Clairvaux Abbey, to the east of Troyes, then on to Besançon on the River Doubs. From there they will ascend into the hills and forests, before dropping again to the shore of Lake Geneva at Montreux. The greatest challenge will be the St Bernard Pass through the mountains – as high as the birds fly, says Father Peacham. From there they will descend into the valley of the River Po. Weariness and blisters will be the least of it, he warns. Two hundred leagues to St Peter's – some eight hundred miles. There will be brigands and thieves, wolves and bears; high mountains where the weak may stumble or fall, where even the fit can be broken. But worst of all, says Father Peacham with a sudden wide smile, there may be other pilgrims who may prove to be tedious companions. *We've already got one of those*, Bianca wants to say. But she keeps her counsel.

At this point Nicholas shuts his ears to Father Peacham's trilling voice as he lists the Italian towns they must pass. Rome is of no concern to him. They're not going there. But Bianca listens. She lets the names of the towns swirl around inside her head, familiar little echoes of her childhood, even though she hasn't visited a single one of them: *Aosta... Pavia... Lucca... Siena...*

'When do you plan to leave?' Peacham asks when he's offered up the last of his wisdom.

'Tomorrow morning, at first light,' Nicholas says.

'So soon?'

'It is a long journey. The sooner we start—'

'Indeed,' Father Peacham sighs, 'but I confess it would have been good to hear a little news of home.'

Nicholas gives a regretful smile. His desire to be away so swiftly has an ulterior motive. For all his bonhomie, Father Peacham cannot be unaware that the queen's Privy Council sometimes sends agents to spy upon the priests of the English College, agents who pass themselves off as Catholics fleeing persecution. A spy would say he intended to stay awhile. A spy would seek to insinuate himself into one's confidence, ferret out names, make a note of appearances, tease out intentions.

'It is true that you have a long, hard road ahead of you,' the Jesuit says. 'I will pray that God finds time to smooth it a little.'

'Thank you, Father,' Bianca says softly.

Peacham looks up at Nicholas, his face suddenly full of sadness. 'The queen's physician, you say – executed?'

'Yes. There was a crowd.'

He sighs again, this one a little more protracted, a little more heartfelt. 'Even when we seek to give them bodily succour, they turn on us. It is a sign of just how much they have need of us to open their eyes.'

Nicholas suddenly has the awful suspicion that Peacham intends to make the journey to England, to follow in the doomed footsteps of so many of his fellows. 'I wouldn't go over, if I were you,' he says, before the words have even formed in his mind. 'They have watchers at all the ports now. You'd be caught before you stepped ashore.'

'If God calls, my son, we cannot refuse Him simply because the path might be rocky and sown with thorn bushes.'

Nicholas has the sudden urge to shout at this gentle little man, 'Don't go! There is nothing for you in England but an agonizing and humiliating death. It's not worth it.' But he suspects Father Peacham has a martyr's steeliness beneath his merry carapace.

When Nicholas and Bianca come away from the Basilica of Saint-Remi, each has a map in their mind of the journey ahead. But it is not the same map. Each has a different destination. Bianca is heading home. Nicholas feels that he is walking further into exile.

✠

Returning to their lodgings, they see a group of pilgrims in plain smocks and broad-brimmed straw hats preparing to depart. Their faces glow with expectation. Most are of middling age, fleshy, prosperous men, the sort who've decided it might be time to gain a little favour with the Almighty before it's too late and think the Via Francigena is the way to do it. They remind Nicholas of the churchwardens and sidemen at St Saviour's, paragons of comfortable piety.

Close by are two younger men, talking to the owner of the hostelry. Their heads turn as Nicholas and Bianca pass, their gaze more penetrating than merely curious. At once Nicholas feels a prickle of concern crawl over his skin. Are they pilgrims? Or something else? Why have they suddenly taken an interest in him?

He considers the possibilities. Perhaps they're from Father Peacham's seminary, keeping an eye on the English pilgrims to make sure they are who they claim to be. Perhaps the ebullient little priest wasn't as trusting as he appeared. There again, they could be agents of the Privy Council. The English Crown is bound to have its watchers in the city, because for every pilgrim Peacham sends along the Via Francigena, there will be several more being prepared to make a different pilgrimage: into England, carrying with them papist sedition. If that's who they are, then news of an unknown Englishman and his wife appearing in Reims could reach Whitehall in a matter of days.

Reaching the hostelry door, Nicholas nods to the owner. He confines his greeting to a mumbled grunt; no point in advertising his Englishness. Once inside, he positions himself behind Bianca and glances back. As he does so, he catches the pair in a clearly ribald exchange, their eyes firmly on Bianca's back as she begins to climb the stairs. They hurriedly look away, but not before Nicholas spots the sudden blushing of their cheeks. Not spies then, merely two young fellows who've seen a comely woman walk past.

'He was a sweet old fellow,' says Bianca, climbing a few steps ahead of him.

'Who, Peacham?'

'I'd be happy if he were my priest. He seemed a goodly man.'

'I just pray he doesn't take it into his head to try to slip into England. He must know what will happen to him if he does. They're bound to catch him eventually.'

'Martyrs come in all shapes and sizes, Nicholas. But they share the same courage.'

'He'd be throwing his life away, and for what end?'

Bianca reaches the landing. She lifts the latch and opens the door to their chamber. 'You're of the queen's faith, Husband,' she says. 'You've never had to—'

On the far side of the room – not directly in her line of sight, for the ancient floor slopes unevenly, so that Bianca must drop her gaze a little – Hella Maas is on her knees by the window, gazing rapturously towards the cathedral.

In the two weeks they have spent together on the road, Bianca has grown accustomed to the maid's displays of relentless, doom-laden piety. She seems to fear that God will take it into His head to announce that today is Judgement Day unless she intercedes on humanity's behalf every couple of hours. So it is not the sight of a penitent deep in prayer that stops Bianca in her tracks, it is what she holds in her hand: a silver crucifix of St Peter, raised to the window so that it gleams in the light, the upside-down torso offered to the cathedral across the square.

It is Bianca's Petrine cross.

'What are you doing with that?' Bianca asks, too startled at first to be really angry. Then the realization strikes. 'You've gone through my bags. Why?'

Hella turns to her. She lowers her hands so that the saint's nailed feet are pointing towards her, the transverse beam like a crossbow aimed at her heart.

'I am praying for you, Bianca,' she says, her face suffused with a frightening intensity. 'You must be grateful. It is necessary.'

Bianca is speechless. The cross is one of her most intimate possessions. It is her late father's cross, one of the few remembrances she has of him. It is on its way home. And now it has been taken from its hiding place without so much as a *please*. She feels as though she has been robbed.

'Of course it's necessary to pray,' she replies, almost biting her tongue. 'But... but I can do it for myself, thank you.' She walks forward and reaches out to take the cross from the kneeling girl.

'It won't be enough. You do know that, don't you?'

The statement has a coldness about it that chills Bianca to the bone.

167

'If this is another of your warnings about the end of days, Hella, I think we have had one too many of them. It's going to be a long enough journey, as it is. So from now on, Nicholas and I would be grateful if you would keep your peace on the matter. Now give me the cross.'

Hella rises to her feet and holds out the Petrine cross. But she continues smiling the beatific smile of a martyred saint. And it has none of the warmth in it that Father Peacham's smile had.

'I have been speaking with my sister, Hannie,' she says. 'Hannie has seen something she wants me to relay to you.'

'You have a sister – in Reims?' Nicholas says.

'No, not in Reims; in heaven. Hannie is dead. All my family are dead, save for me and one other.'

'And what exactly has this sister Hannie of yours seen that concerns *us*?' Bianca asks, an icy knot of disquiet suddenly forming in her stomach. She stays the hand reaching out for the cross, her fingers closing on empty air.

'A dead child,' Hella says. 'That is why I was praying for you. Hannie senses the presence of a dead child. I sense it, too. We could always sense things together, Hannie and I.'

'This is an old building, Hella,' Bianca says. 'Many people – including children – may have died in this room over the centuries.'

But like someone unburdening herself of an unwanted secret, Hella Maas seems unable to stop.

'We see a dead child... a dead parent – or perhaps it is a dead womb...'

Are these statements? Or questions? Is the maid in some form of trance? Bianca wonders. Is she, perhaps, even possessed?

It is Nicholas's sharp intake of breath that makes her turn.

He is standing in the doorway, a look of terrible vulnerability on his face. Bianca knows at once what he's thinking, and the pain goes through her so sharply that for a moment she thinks it is a knife that Hella Maas has thrust towards her, rather than a silver cross.

He's thinking of his first wife, Eleanor, and the child his physic couldn't save.

16

'It was a guess, nothing more. It just happened to strike the mark,' Bianca says, taking Nicholas's hands in hers. 'It's the same sort of trick the old vagabond women play on Bankside. They say something imprecise, but portentous. That's how they convince the gullible they can foresee the future. There was nothing mystical about it. She's a charlatan. I'm surprised she didn't ask for money.'

The object of her anger is at this moment topping up the well of her piety in the cathedral of Notre-Dame de Reims, making a last-minute personal appeal to God to delay Judgement Day long enough for them to reach Clairvaux Abbey, their next hope of proper rest on the Via Francigena.

'Of all the guesses she could have made, why that one?' Nicholas asks. 'And how did she know there was a cross among your belongings?'

'She didn't. It was chance.'

It is the first time they have been alone and able to speak openly since Hella threw her handful of black powder onto an open fire the previous day. The resulting explosion is still ringing in their ears.

Nicholas says, 'Yet the words she spoke: it was as if she *knew* about Eleanor.'

'That is how it was *meant* to be – to convince,' Bianca tells him. 'Though for what purpose, other than to shock or to cause mischief between us—' She spreads her hands in mystification.

Nicholas knows he should believe her. He is the least super-stitious physician in London, a man of the new learning. Why, he even refuses to cast a patient's horoscope before he makes a diagnosis, a practice that most in his profession believe essen-tial. And yet the maid had sounded so certain, as if she really was seeing the things she spoke of: a dead child... and a parent. At the time, he had felt as though she was looking deep inside his heart, unearthing memories he had thought stilled for ever.

Bianca kisses him lightly on the cheek. 'Do not feel ashamed, Nicholas. Eleanor and your child will always be in your heart,' she says, as though she too can read his thoughts. 'I make no complaint. That is as it should be.' She smiles. 'Perhaps Hella really does believe what she says: that she can see into the future, see something dreadful coming. She wouldn't be the first. We've had maids like that in Italy for centuries. They start off seeing visions, and the next thing you know they're made into saints.'

'We've weeks of this ahead,' he says. 'Couldn't we just slip away before she gets back?'

'Nicholas!'

'I know.'

He takes his wife in his arms, wondering how long they might have before Hella returns from her prayers.

Bianca – eyes closed – feels the warmth of him against her cheek. Feels again the sense of safety she always experiences in his embrace. And then the hairs on the nape of her neck begin to rise. What if the child Hella had spoken of was not the one her husband had conceived with his late wife? What if it was a child as yet unborn?

For some reason Bianca dares not explore, a line from her last letter to her cousin Bruno jumps into her head: *as yet, no sign of our hoped-for bounty...*

✴

On the advice of Father Peacham, further preparations are made. Boots are re-soled. Wide-brimmed straw hats are purchased, to protect against sun and rain. Coins are sewn into linings and hems to make it harder for spur-of-the-moment thieves.

If Nicholas were a true pilgrim and not simply a fugitive, he thinks he might be more inclined to walk the Via Francigena. But the two weeks it has taken them to reach Reims has convinced him that authenticity of cover has its limits. With the help of Hella Maas, he finds a muleteer who caters for the wealthier travellers on the road to Rome. The man has a business partner at a town called Mouthier-Haute-Pierre, where the Via Francigena rises into the crests and gorges of the Haut Jura guarding the way into Switzerland. Monsieur Boiseaux makes his profit sending the mules down, and Monsieur Perrault makes his profit sending them back. And just in case the Englishman is thinking of making off with them somewhere in between, he points out that there is not a pilgrim hostelry between either place that does not recognize one of the Boiseaux–Perrault mules almost as well as an old and well-respected friend, even if the colour of its coat has been artfully changed with soot or flour.

Nicholas rents four of the sturdy little beasts – the fourth to allow periods of unburdened rest. On a mischievous whim, he names them Cecil, Essex, Coke and Popham.

They choose to leave on the feast day of Mary Magdalene, the twenty-second day of July. The day dawns clear and cloudless, the early-morning shadows streaked across the cathedral square like inky lines drawn on parchment. Father Peacham has told them it is the perfect day on which to begin a pilgrimage, particularly if you'd rather trust in the safety of numbers over divine providence. And indeed, looking down from the window of their lodgings, Nicholas can see a crowd gathering. The pilgrims are easily identifiable by their plain brown tunics, broad sunhats and faces flushed with the anticipation of spiritual ecstasy. When they've been on the road a week or more, Nicholas recalls Father Peacham saying sadly, they'll be looking like any other weary, footsore traveller and wondering if it is really worth the effort.

Across the square, the great doors to the cathedral are open. A battle for supremacy is taking place between the eager pilgrims, the city's roosters and the priests chanting Lauds. Nicholas leans out of the window and fills his lungs with clean morning air. It feels cool and refreshing, though if Cecil and the others are right, it should by rights have a whiff of sulphur hanging in it. How, he wonders, can his soul be damned, simply by listening to Roman prayers in Reims? The people beginning to go about their business below – the bakers with their baskets of still-warm loaves, the farmers coming in from the outlying villages with their produce, the washerwomen carrying their bundles down to the Vesle – look much like the people of Southwark, more or less. Is this, he wonders, the enemy that his own queen fears so much she would have her Privy Council make bloody carrion of decent men like Father Peacham and Dr Roderigo Lopez?

He spots Hella crossing the square towards the lodgings, returning from a last-minute dose of spiritual fortification for the long journey ahead. He makes a promise to himself to be charitable. She cannot possibly know about Eleanor and the child she was carrying. That was four years ago, in another land, in another time. Bianca is right: it was just a guess, a cheap street trick, though what Hella thought she might win by it is anyone's guess.

She is walking with her head down, he notices. She moves at the same driven pace that hasn't flagged since Den Bosch. He is sure now that it's a moving away from something, rather than a striding towards it. Perhaps on the road to Clairvaux Abbey she might be persuaded to tell them what it is she is really fleeing from. Perhaps it has to do with what she has already partially revealed: a dead family and a sister who apparently speaks to her from heaven.

Hella is halfway across the square when Nicholas notices someone in the growing crowd of busy citizens step directly into her path, bringing her to a halt. It is a tall man in a grey half-coat, trunk-hose and wide-rimmed boots. He wears a floppy black cloth cap that almost covers his ears. By his posture and the deftness of the way he slips casually in front of her, Nicholas judges he is young, perhaps no older than Hella herself. He can see little of the man but his back. However, he gets the distinct impression they are not strangers to each other.

How can that be? he wonders. The man is clearly neither the muleteer nor Father Peacham, and they have not been in Reims long enough to make other acquaintances. Nicholas senses the same jolt of disquiet he'd felt when he'd seen the two young pilgrims talking to the owner of the hostelry earlier and had mistaken them for Privy Council watchers.

And then the man darts away amongst the throng, leaving Nicholas to think he might have read a great deal more into the encounter than was really called for. He ducks back into the room, a spy embarrassed by his own prying.

✠

In Florence, it has cost Bruno Barrani more *scudi* than he would have liked and taken longer than he had hoped, but the effort – admittedly made mostly by Luca and Alonso – has been worth it. July is not yet out and already a goodly number of Florentine artisans have proved venal enough to sell their secrets. A clockmaker near the Santa Maria Novella has boasted loudly about how he made the equatorial ring for Master Santucci's great labour of science. A metalworker with a shop in one of the lanes off the Piazza Santa Croce would have kept them all afternoon, had not Luca said there really was nothing more he needed to know about the manufacture of planetary gear-chains. An expert engraver by the Ponte Santa Trinità has been adamant there was no one else in all Italy who could have overlain the signs of the zodiac with a matrix of hours, days, weeks and months and not have turned it into an indecipherable jumble. He even showed Bruno his own working drawings, several of which Luca and Alonso had later managed to steal while Bruno was getting him drunk at another *buchetta*.

Bruno himself has spent many hours drawing from memory. While he is no Leonardo – as he would be the first to admit – he has contrived his own representation of Santucci's great sphere. In his rendering, the sphere is not a sphere at all but a misshapen bladder, and anyone relying upon it to tell them where in the sky Capricorn will be tomorrow night is as likely to end up searching the ground beneath his feet as the sky above his head. But it is not a picture of the true mechanics of the machine that Bruno is hoping to carry back to Padua. It is more an impression – an ability to describe with some accuracy to the professor of mathematics at the university how Santucci has been able to construct it. Master Galileo will surely bring his own genius to the enterprise. It is just that the more Bruno understands about the great sphere, the less Galileo Galilei will be able to browbeat him out of his rightful share of the profit.

Bruno has no need of a cosmological engine to tell him his future. He has already mapped it out. It is but a natural progression from the doge's first Master of the Spheres to His Serene Highness's Superintendent of the *Arsenale*, responsible for the construction of a new fleet of state-of-the-art galleys – at 1 per cent commission on the total spend – with perhaps a stint or two as an elected member of the city council to replenish the coffers thinned by his great public works. He can even imagine himself occupying the doge's throne itself, the heartfelt reward of a grateful Republic. At the risk of tempting fate, he thinks he might drop a casual mention into his next letter to cousin Bianca. *Most beloved cousin*, he imagines himself writing, in the privacy of his study back in Padua, *rejoice! You are with child, and my fortunes are about to take a turn for the better...*

✠

The rutted road to Clairvaux Abbey runs south across the valley of the Marne river, through rolling vineyards, pasture and little fields where peasants with downcast faces tend the chalky soil. When Nicholas comments on the poor state of the crops, recalling the storms that had battered Barnthorpe in the spring, Hella Maas announces that the increased prevalence of storms is a sign that a far greater hurricane is on its way, perhaps even a second Flood. Bianca says she hopes it holds off until they reach shelter, because when she walks her feet kill her, and when she rides her backside feels as though the Sisters at her old school in Padua have taken turns applying a cane to it.

'There will be great fires, too,' the maid says. 'Do you not remember them? They were shown in the painting at Den Bosch, glowing in the darkness of hell.'

'Oh, look,' Bianca counters, pointing at the roadside, 'there's a bank of poppies. Aren't they lovely?'

Early in the afternoon of the fourth day after leaving Reims they rest on the fringe of a great forest to the east of Troyes. Another group of pilgrims is encamped nearby, awaiting a local guide who will take them through to the Benedictine abbey of

Clairvaux. Cecil, Essex, Coke and Popham are tethered close to where Nicholas is sitting dozing against a tree trunk, the dappled sunlight sending patterns dancing across his shirt. Bianca is gathering forest flowers and herbs, makeshift remedies for aches and ailments they have yet to suffer.

'What will you do when you get to Padua?'

Hella's question as she eases herself down beside him brings Nicholas out of his torpor.

'I have scarcely dwelt upon it. They have a fine medical school there. I might return to studying – for a while.'

'But you must have a plan. It is a great distance for an Englishman to put between himself and his home.'

'Yes, it is. Further than I had thought to go.'

'Why Padua?'

'Bianca was born there.'

'I thought she was English, like you.'

'Her father was English, her mother Paduan.'

And then the maid says something that jars like a sudden thunderclap out of the clear summer sky.

'Why were you hiding in the chamber of St John's?'

Nicholas sees again the two bloodied bodies lying on the flagstones. For a moment he doesn't answer. Then, simply: 'I wasn't hiding.'

'But you were not there when I entered,' Hella says, as though she has finally caught him out after a long deception. 'You were not there when the rebel came in and stabbed the Spaniard. Then all of a sudden you *were* there. So you must have been hiding.'

'You were there, when I told Bianca. The images compelled me to enter. Then I heard voices. I don't know, I suppose I didn't want to be found gawping at that painting like a superstitious peasant.'

Having said it, Nicholas thinks it a better answer than the truth: that for an instant he had feared some bounty-hunter sent by the Privy Council was about to discover him in a little disused chapel with no way out.

'Are you superstitious, Dr Shelby?' she asks.

'I like to think not. I favour the new learning: observation, using our eyes to witness and record, not relying on what the ancients have written, or what the Church demands.'

'Then are you not obedient to God, Dr Shelby?'

'I am not sure I should be obedient, not when prayers sometimes fail to cure my patients, Mistress Hella. They didn't save my first wife and the child she was carrying, any more than the physic I learned from Galen, Hippocrates and the other ancients did. Therefore, being of a somewhat contrary disposition, I have to ask myself why that is.'

'And do you hear an answer?'

'If there is one, I believe it will be found by adopting the practices of the new science, not by praying harder or casting a more accurate horoscope.'

Her face darkens. She says, as if to warn him, 'In the end, the answer will be the same for both of us.'

He can almost see the images on the Den Bosch painting dancing in her eyes. Hurriedly he changes the subject. 'We still have much to learn about you, Mistress Hella. A young maid who says she attended Leiden University, speaks five languages and can discourse on the writings of Master Copernicus – any one of those achievements would make you a rarity in this world.'

'I have told you, God gave my family unusual gifts.'

'All of them? That was generous of Him.'

'Please don't laugh at me.'

'Forgive me, I didn't mean to,' he says, colouring.

'It was Hannie, my sister, who received most of his bounty. She was cleverer by far.'

'And Hannie is dead?' he says, tiptoeing around the subject as gently as he can.

'They are all dead. Breda is dead.'

For a moment he wonders if Breda is another sister. Then he remembers the name. It belongs to a dark litany he had learned by heart during his summer as a physician to an English company of pistoleers serving with the Dutch Protestant army: Antwerp... Naarden... Haarlem... Breda: any one of them could stand as a monument to the frenzied brutality of Spanish troops when they slip the leash. Breda had been the least bloody – only some six hundred of the population dead. At the others, the butcher's bill could be counted in the thousands. Now he understands why Hella Maas holds conversations with a dead sibling.

'You lost all your family at Breda?'

'Almost all. Hannie, my father, one of my two brothers... My mother had already gone before them – giving life to me. At least *she* was spared what happened later.'

He gives her silence and waits while she decides what to do with it. To his surprise, Hella chooses to reveal more.

'The day of the massacre I was with my twin brother, Ruben. We were with a learned priest who taught mathematics – my father wanted his girls to learn as boys learn, so he paid for me to study with this man. I remember it well. Ruben was terrible at mathematics, but the priest was pleased at how easily I was able to understand what he was teaching me. Then we heard shouting, screaming. The priest had a hiding place, but by luck his house was one of the few spared. I have always wished that it hadn't been. I also wished that God had not given Hannie and me such gifts, that I had been like the other girls – content to sew, content to grow up and marry, to be a wife; then I would have been with my family when the Spanish came. We would have been together.'

Nicholas shakes his head in sympathy. He is no stranger to such a story. Three years ago, at the Mitre in Gravesend, he and Bianca had listened to Porter Bell telling them how he, too, had survived a Spanish fury, at Naarden. How can it be, he wonders, that the same faith burns as brightly in Father Peacham's heart as it does in that of a Spanish soldier fired up on drink and hatred of the heretic? Applying the observational rigour of the new science would tell him the fault must lie in the man, not in the faith.

He listens in the shade beneath the tree as Hella tells him how, alone and orphaned, she and her brother sought shelter. 'Ruben asked me to follow him to the Protestant rebel states. He refused to countenance that God could be a Catholic, like the Spanish who had murdered our family. I wouldn't go with him. I didn't want to leave the place where we had all been so happy. I was too young for the convent and, with my father dead, no dowry to pay for admittance. So the priest found me refuge with the Beguines, an order of pious women who live together but have not taken vows or entered a holy order.'

'What happened to Ruben?'

'He stayed in the rebel provinces. I didn't see him more than once or twice after that. He became a priest, but that was much later.'

The Beguines, she explains, had quickly discovered they had taken in a child with unusual abilities. Within months, the Bishop of Antwerp was proclaiming Hella rare amongst her sex, if not actually unheard of. With the help of the mathematical priest, she had continued her studies. She had flourished. At fifteen she had walked all the way to Leiden, twenty leagues or more, to ask the professors at the university there to let her in. They set her tests – each harder than the one before – to show her how presumptuous she was to think she could enter the masculine world of learning. To their amazement, Hella passed them all.

For eight years the professors allowed her to remain at the university, treating her as though she were part servant, part curiosity. Some even tutored her, though always in secret. Her iron piety had protected her from the few who thought she might have other gifts they could exploit.

By twenty-one Hella could speak five languages, cast horoscopes and solve any complex mathematical problem they cared to set her. So when she asked if she might graduate, they threw her out.

As Nicholas listens, he thinks how Bianca had told him of her longing to study at the medical school at Padua, and how the professors there had laughed at her. He cannot help but think Hella might now be a less troubled young woman if she had done what Bianca had done: thumbed her nose at them, travelled to a different country and purchased a tavern. But the thought is no sooner in his head than he chides himself for being flippant. This young woman has known little but suffering. It does not become him, he thinks, to make light of it.

'What did you hope Father Vermeiren might do, when you went to see him?' he asks.

'I wanted to convince him to burn the painting. At the very least, I wanted to stop him giving it to the Spanish.'

'Burn it – why?'

'Because its fame was spreading. When I returned to Antwerp, even the Beguines there knew of it. If it were to leave Den Bosch, copies might be made. Before long, the whole world might know what it contained.'

'Is that such a bad thing?'

'Bad? Of course it's bad. It shows what is in store for us sinners, and to know *that* is dangerous. If people realize there is nothing after death but everlasting torment, think of the ills that would surely follow. Why would any man or woman live a godly life? There will be murder and sinfulness that will make what happened at Breda seem trivial. Who would obey his master, his prince, even the Holy Father, if they knew that the promise of God's mercy was a lie, that most of us will face nothing but eternal suffering at the end?'

'But that painting was just one man's vision. And not all knowledge is bad, surely.'

Hella considers this in silence, the shadows of the forest's edge casting her face into darkness, so that Nicholas cannot see what is in her eyes. But he can feel the fear in her, as if he had wrapped his hand around a mortally injured bird.

'Sometimes, Dr Shelby,' she says, 'when you unwrap a gift you discover it is not a gift at all – but a curse.'

✠

Clairvaux Abbey is a sprawling complex of buildings set beside the River Aube and protected by densely wooded hills. To Nicholas, it seems preternaturally still. He can hear hens bickering in a garden somewhere, but not a single human voice. And then a chapel bell begins to ring, echoing out across the valley. It sounds to him like a strong heartbeat in a patient who's just been brought back to life.

Clairvaux has sheltered pilgrims on the Via Francigena for centuries. There are guest lodgings, a dormitory for single men, another for unmarried women. There are kitchens to prepare nourishing food from the abbey farm and – for a price – monks skilled at leatherwork to restore shoes and boots worn down by long hours treading the road. There is even a paddock, where Cecil, Essex, Coke and Popham can graze. Nicholas takes a wicked delight in the thought of four such resolute Protestants gorging on succulent Catholic forage.

That evening, as a summer storm hurls itself against the gentle white walls of Clairvaux, Nicholas plays the part of a pilgrim to its fullest. He joins Bianca and Hella at Mass. Like an explorer stepping onto a foreign shore, he stares around in wonder while trying to maintain the fiction that he's done this a thousand times before. Taking his lead from Bianca, he does his best to look practised. If all that he has learned from childhood is true, he should be able to feel the fiery hand of damnation taking hold of his soul. He should, by rights, feel revulsion at the well-known excesses and corruption of papist priests. But he feels nothing, save for a lifting of the spirit as he listens to the Kyrie eleison and the Sanctus. A doubting Protestant pretending to be a Catholic, he thinks. I am not sure *what* I am – I think I may be a heretic to either faith... He wonders what he will do when he returns to England. He can have no future as the queen's physician, not when he has heard the Mass delivered by a priest whose faith proclaims her the Antichrist and calls for her overthrow. And what use will Robert Cecil have for an intelligencer who no longer sees the enemy as the enemy?

✳

They leave the chapel in the twilight, taking the gravel path back to the guest lodgings. If damnation awaits, thinks Nicholas, it is presenting a surprisingly benign face: nothing more menacing than a few black clouds left as an afterthought by the storm in an otherwise clear evening sky. Over the wooded hills, the stars are coming out.

Tomorrow they will take the road to Langres and on to Besançon. From there, according to the monks of Clairvaux, the going will become more difficult as the land begins to fracture. They will face deep gorges; mountain meltwater that can carry away unwary travellers, drowning them or smashing their bodies against boulders; dense woodland where wild boar and bears rule, and an English physician, his wife and a maid from Brabant count for very little.

'You look remarkably untroubled for a man who has just thrown his soul into the balance,' Bianca says, only half in jest, as they walk, Hella trailing a few paces behind.

Nicholas replies with nothing more than a gruff laugh, to show he's heard her. But he understands now how much it must have cost her to keep her own faith hidden during the years she's been in England.

When they reach the door of the guest lodge, something makes Nicholas look back over his shoulder. Hella is standing on the gravel path, staring in the dusk towards the darkening hills, to the track they descended earlier in the day.

What has drawn her eye? he wonders. What is she searching for?

For an instant he thinks he sees – just as he'd seen from the window of their lodgings in Reims – a tall man in a grey half-coat, trunk-hose and wide-rimmed boots, a floppy black cloth cap almost covering his ears. He is making his way down towards the abbey.

But when he rubs his eyes, Nicholas sees it is nothing other than the evening shadows thrown across the path by the setting sun.

17

Padua, the Veneto, 31st July 1594

'What else do you expect from the Fiorentini? Thieves and numbskulls, to a man. Why do you think my father made sure he was safely in Pisa before he sired me?'

Galileo Galilei fits Bruno Barrani's model of an Italian man of genius to perfection – a rough artisan with a mind of quicksilver. He's young for a professor of mathematics: turned thirty in February; a carouser who can think five times as fast as any other man, even when he's in his cups. Bruno has the wild idea that if you got into a fight with him and landed a blow to his head, it would shower bright sparks instead of blood.

But driving the intellect is a labourer's canny gauge of how much his toil is worth, calculated to the nearest *giustina*. And that gauge – as Bruno knows only too well from their frequent drunken sessions when together he and Galileo put the world to rights – shows clearly that Master Galileo is persistently broke. Which is why Bruno is certain that the august professor of mathematics and astronomy at Padua University in the Palazzo Bo is the perfect man for the task.

They are sitting in the sunshine outside Galileo's lodgings in the Borgo dei Vignali. Bruno, still dusty from the ride from Florence, has brought a skin of wine to celebrate. Galileo has just listened intently to his friend's denunciation of Antonio Santucci.

Bruno remembers well the day they first met: the Feast of St Anthony, the June before last. A mutual acquaintance had introduced them. They had hit it off immediately: the quick-witted little Paduan cockerel, always on the search for a commercial opportunity, and the new professor recently arrived from Pisa, searching for heaven-knew-what – for Bruno could barely understand one sentence in five, if the subject turned to the intellectual.

Galileo had told him he was working on a new military compass-rule, a folding device made of etched brass that could calculate just about everything, from how much gunpowder you would need for a given weight of shot, to the required angle of the cannon's barrel when you came to fire it at your enemy. They were commonplace enough, but Galileo had boasted that he could make one smaller, more accurate and easier to use than any yet available. Bruno had advised him on the mercantile considerations of selling it to a wider market abroad: how to beat down the middlemen, or how much it might cost to keep a customs official sweet. By the end of the evening they were pleasantly drunk and the very best of friends. Each had bestowed upon the other an affectionate nickname: Bruno was Signor Purse; Galileo was Signor Compass.

'The question is, Signor Compass,' Bruno says now, to the accompaniment of snoring from the open doorway where one of Galileo's students, Matteo Fedele, is slumbering off the effects of a discourse on Euclidian postulates, 'can you make the calculations?'

'Based upon the drawings you've brought me, Signor Purse?'

'Based upon the drawings.'

'It's possible. The internal workings look clear enough. Who drew the picture of the sphere as a whole? The one that looks like a half-rotten lemon?'

Bruno winces, but presses on regardless. 'Because if you *can*, and we can build a better sphere than that neutered monkey Santucci, then His Serenity the doge will shower us with a weight of ducats heavier than even your clever little gauge can calculate.'

Galileo leans back against the warm mortar of the wall. He tilts his head at the sky and closes his eyes. His eyebrows, bushy arches below a broad, high forehead, make Bruno think of the vaulted roof of a deep cistern where numbers and symbols tumble like cascading water. Bruno takes another mouthful of wine while he waits for the brilliant mind to reach its conclusion.

Then Signor Compass opens one eye. He fixes Bruno with the penetrating gaze of a Pythagoras or an Aristotle. 'My brother-in-law,' he announces cryptically.

'What about him? Is he a mathematician, too?'

'No. He's suing me for my sister's dowry – the one my father forgot to pay before he died,' Galileo growls. 'I've had to ask the university for a year's salary in advance to buy him off. If the doge is paying well, Signor Purse, he can have more spheres than a Florentine bitch has teats. Now pass me the wine.'

✠

'This will be the last time I go across the river, I promise you,' says Ned Monkton. 'I'd stay to comfort you, but—'

'*Go!* Just go,' groans Rose. She is slumped across the side of the bed, her head over the bowl she keeps there, because these days – whenever she wakes – there are always demons stirring paddles in her stomach. She is beginning to wonder if, when she finally gives birth, the little rogue might not have cloven hooves instead of little pink toes.

'Are you *sure*, Wife?' asks Ned uncomfortably. Until he fell in love with Rose, he had never encountered intimate female frailty at close hand. His instinct is to stay and comfort her; but this seems to be the very last thing she wants. He is confused. 'I can bring you some oysters from Ralph Stout's shop, if it might please you.'

'For Jesu's sake, go!'

At the Mutton Lane stairs he waits in the sunshine until a wherry arrives. Sitting silently in the stern during the crossing to Blackfriars, he looks downriver to London Bridge, lying like a street full of tall houses dropped into the water by mistake. It holds dark memories for him. Two men have died beneath those arches – at his hands. They died because they intended to murder Nicholas Shelby, and he and Mistress Bianca had refused to let that happen. He wonders what Rose would think of him if she knew. Knowing her loyalty to Mistress Bianca and Master Nicholas – as strong as his own – he trusts she would approve and forgive him.

At the Blackfriars stairs he bids a curt thank-you to the wherryman and saunters – if a man of his size can ever be said to saunter – up Water Lane towards Ludgate. All the while he stays on the lookout for a small, bald fellow with perpetually hard-done-by features. He knows it would be far easier to ask after him in the shops and taverns, but that would only advertise his interest. This, he knows, has always been a game of stealth.

But today Ned is ready to take the chance. He has promised Rose that he will make no more forays into this part of the city, so the risk has been made acceptable by desperation.

At the top of Water Lane the old buildings of the order of the Black Friars have been pulled down or turned over to more secular use. Now it is full of shops, tenements and private dwellings. Maintaining a determined pace, Ned suddenly has to hurl himself into a shadowed cut between a skinner's shop festooned with hides and a pouchmaker's stall. To his consternation, the very quarry he has hunted so fruitlessly for so long has just stepped out from beneath a lurid sign of a blade dripping blood – the entrance to the Hanging Sword tavern. Balanced on his shoulder is a large stone jug, which he steadies with his left hand.

The pouchmaker opens his mouth to protest at Ned's sudden intrusion. He swiftly shuts it again as he digests the interloper's true size. He goes back to his seat without a word.

Ned is almost certain the fellow with the jug has seen him. But when he sneaks another glance, he sees that the man's heavy load forces him to walk with his head at an angle, limiting his view. Ned turns his face towards the pelts hanging from the wall and waits for the fellow to pass by. When he's sure it's safe to move, he mumbles an apology to the pouchmaker and slips out into Water Lane.

The fellow with the jar is some twenty yards ahead. He walks stiffly under his burden. Ned hangs back. He knows that if his prize so much as shifts the heavy jar on his shoulder, he could be seen.

Following him in the direction of the Blackfriars water-stairs, Ned sees the man turn left into a narrow alley connecting Water Lane with St Andrew's Hill. He hangs back, only daring to enter when he's sure the coast is clear. Reaching the end of the now-empty cut, he looks to his right towards the river. He sees no sign of the fluted top of a stone jar swaying above the other heads. He looks left, up St Andrew's Hill. Within a moment he has the man in sight again. Ned resumes his quiet pursuit.

He knows he sticks out like a performing bear. If the man spots him, his only hope will be to catch him before he drops the jar and runs. And a shattered jar spilling its contents over the street and around everyone's feet will be an effective barrier, even to legs as sturdy as Ned Monkton's.

After barely a hundred yards the man stops outside a narrow, unremarkable timbered house in a row of five, set between the church of St Andrew of the Wardrobe and Carter Lane. Ned steps briskly into the shade of the overhang of the building opposite. He has nothing to rely on for cover, other than the people passing by. Wishing for once he was half the man that God had chosen to make him, he gets glimpses of the fellow hoisting the jar into a more comfortable position and rummaging in the pocket of his jerkin with his free hand for a key. A cart piled high with thatcher's reeds rumbles past. When it has gone, the man with the jar has vanished inside.

His heart pounding, Ned Monkton makes a careful study of the lane, so that he can identify the correct house on his return. Then he goes back to the Hanging Sword.

When he walks in, he gets the reaction he's become accustomed to whenever he enters an unfamiliar tavern: some customers turn their glances hurriedly away, while others – he can see it in their eyes – weigh up the odds of making their reputation as a slayer of giants.

'There was a little bald fellow in 'ere a moment ago – I believe you sold him a flagon,' he says as peaceably as he can to the young taproom boy who stares at his bulk with ill-disguised fear. Then, seizing on the first thing that comes into his head, 'I 'ave a message for him, but I don't know his name.'

The taproom lad – too scared of the fiery countenance glaring down at him to wonder why someone would tell you to deliver a message, but fail to give you the name of the recipient – says, 'You're speaking of Master Ditworth? Is the message for him or his master?'

'His *master*?' Ned says, sensing a veil being lifted.

'Aye, Sir Fulke Vaesy,' the taproom lad says, gaining a little courage, now that it appears this newcomer isn't planning to crush the life out of him with one immense hand. 'But if it's physic you're after, I'd take your message elsewhere. No one around here would trust that rogue to cure a flitch of bacon.'

✠

'Vaesy... Vaesy?' says Rose, looking up. She has spent Ned's absence checking the accounts for the rebuilding of the Jackdaw. 'Wasn't he that professor of anatomy Master Nicholas 'ad a run-in with, a few years back?'

'The very same,' Ned tells her, unlacing his boots. He can smell pottage stewing in the hearth. What good fortune to have such a wife as this, he thinks. There cannot be many husbands on Bankside whose women can cook *and* read. He wonders if he dares ask her to teach him how to make sense of all the incomprehensible scrawls on the papers laid out before her. 'It was the year we had all those murders,' he adds. 'I remember Master Nicholas telling me he'd studied under Vaesy – that Vaesy had lost his place with the College of Physicians because he hadn't seen the signs of foul play on the bodies that Nicholas had. An' there was that scandal with his wife, as well. From what they told me at the Hanging Sword, Vacsy's been reduced to little better than a pox doctor.'

'An' you think he was the author of the false letters?'

'Why else would hc 'ave sent his little arseworm over here to see what had happened to Master Nicholas? Looks to me like Vaesy has finally decided to be revenged for his fall.'

'But how can you be sure?'

'I'll 'ave to ask him, won't I?'

To Ned Monkton, Rose has always shone with a bucolic light. If verdant fields and plump rolling hills bathed in sunlight could ever be made flesh, his wife's face is the very model. But now, as he looks at her proudly, he sees the warmth drain out and the fear rush in.

'Oh, Ned, be careful,' she says, reaching out to take his hand. 'Vaesy might have fallen, but he's still a sir – a knight. Knights don't take kindly to our sort calling them out. I don't want our child to know his father only by what I have to tell him – after he was 'anged.'

'Don't you fear about that, Wife,' Ned says reassuringly as he enfolds his wife's hand with his huge fingers. 'It'll be the new Ned Monkton what does the asking, not the old.'

✠

Besançon lies in the foothills of the Jura Mountains, at the fringes of the long shadows cast by the Alps. Its castle, set high on a precipitous hill on a wooded bend of the River Doubs, guards the way from France into the Protestant Swiss cantons. According to its people, Besançon's ruler is French, Swiss, Spanish or Burgundian, depending upon the season. There are more clock-makers in the town than anywhere else in France. Counting off the hours accurately can be wise, if word comes of an army getting ready to march.

It is Lammas Day, the first day of August, and Hella Maas is waiting for Nicholas and Bianca at the town gate. She has walked ahead, outpacing the mules, and looks like the winner of a sprint, hands on hips, breathing deeply, her faced streaked with dusty sweat. But she has proved a useful lodestar, because by now Nicholas feels so cast adrift from anything even remotely familiar that he's convinced himself it is only a matter of time before he and Bianca get hopelessly lost amidst the swelling hills, eaten by bears or murdered by brigands. Only Hella seems certain of the route. Given that none of them has walked it before, he attributes this to either blind faith or delusional self-confidence.

He has taken care not to press her further on the story of her family. And she has chosen not to expand upon it. He knows only that her ferocious piety, and her need to warn everyone she meets about what she believes lies in store for them, is the hard adult scab that has formed over childhood wounds. It has, he thinks, given her a soul that no amount of sympathy can soften, sentenced her to a life of cold, self-inflicted solitude.

To look at her now, though, you would not think it. The liberating discipline of the march seems to suit that iron determination in her. Her pale skin is now sunburnt. Her dark hair, once butchered, now hangs about her cheeks in a dark ragged bob. She would be a beauty, he thinks, were it not for the fact that laughter seems to have bled out of her. But who with a heart could blame her for that, after what she has told him about her past?

They find a pilgrims' hostelry that offers comfortable straw mattresses and the facilities to wash dirty linen. Nicholas is all for resting up for a few days, but Bianca is impatient to leave tomorrow. She can imagine that Padua is just over the next forested hill, even though she knows that in reality it is weeks away. There is still the great pass of St Bernard to negotiate before they descend into the green valley of the River Po.

'What will you do when you reach Rome?' Bianca asks Hella as they sit in the shadows of the Porte Rivotte, eating bread and cheese.

'I will go to see the Holy Father,' she says seriously. 'I will tell him he needs to pray more.'

'I'm sure he'll be grateful for the advice,' Nicholas says, chewing on his bread and flexing his aching toes inside his boots.

Bianca jams a stealthy elbow into his side. 'Does he not pray for his flock enough?' she asks innocently.

'Why do you not take what I say seriously?' Hella asks, her eyes narrowing. 'Dr Nicholas saw the painting. He knows how the Day of Judgement will unfold. Can either of you face such a thing without fear?'

'I've said it before: it was nothing more than the creation of one skilful, imaginative, but otherwise ordinary man,' Nicholas says, trying to reassure both of them, because he knows how much these statements of Hella's unsettle his wife. 'The painter had no special window that gave him a view of the future. He invented it.'

'But that invention was put into the painter's head by God,' Hella says, giving him a look of pity that Nicholas would find insulting, were he unaware of the tragedy that overtook her when she was young. 'And He did so because the painter sought to know more than a man should know. He sought a truth it would have been wiser not to seek.'

'I thought we *all* sought the truth,' Bianca replies. 'Why would we want to know nothing but lies?'

'But sometimes the truth is more than we can bear to know. In that case, it is better not to seek it in the first place.'

'And live in ignorance?' Bianca counters.

'If you knew the Devil was waiting for you behind a locked door, why would you go in search of the key?' Hella asks. She gestures towards the surrounding lanes. 'Look at all the clock-makers in this town. All their clever artistry devoted to making machines that turn and tick and chime – and all for what? What is the point of counting hours, when you know the only thing waiting for you at the end of them is death?'

Bianca chews the last of her bread. 'I don't mean to be uncivil, but I've had enough of melancholy. I'm going down to the river to wash my feet. They're on fire.' She looks at Hella. 'That doesn't mean I'm being toasted in brimstone, by the way.'

She rises, hitches her gown into her belt to let the air get to her ankles, and sets off towards the riverbank. Nicholas makes to follow her.

'Let her go,' Hella says, reaching out to seize his arm. 'You understand me, don't you? You know the danger that lurks in seeking knowledge, I know you do. I can sense it in you.' She tugs at his shirt sleeve.

Why does he not resist as she pulls him back to sit beside her? Perhaps it is because she intrigues him. Perhaps because – deep down inside – he fears there may be an element of truth in what she says. His own search for knowledge has sometimes brought tragedy in its wake. 'You're wrong,' he says, though he feels far from certain.

'I don't believe I am.'

'Alright, I will admit there was once a time when I would have opened that door and welcomed in the Devil with open arms. I would have sold my soul for the knowledge to save my first wife and the child she was carrying. I would have done it without a moment's hesitation.'

'And you would make the same pact tomorrow, if you thought it would save Mistress Bianca, wouldn't you?'

'It was a *lack* of knowledge that brought me misery, not a surfeit of it.'

'But that merely proves my point,' Hella says. 'When we seek, we also *invite*. That's what I am warning people about. I knew what was going to happen in Breda. I should have seen the signs. I should have stopped asking so many questions. I invited the Devil in through my own front door.'

✠

That evening Nicholas and Bianca lie on the mattresses in their chamber. Hella is at Besançon cathedral, repairing the rents in her piety that several days on the road without benediction have torn.

'She's a contradiction,' Nicholas says. 'An educated young woman who thinks learning is dangerous. More than danger-ous – possibly fatal to the soul as well as the body. She told me she knew in advance what was going to happen to her family in Breda.'

'Like that day in Reims, when she said she knew about "a dead child" and you instantly decided it was yours and Eleanor's.'

'I accept it – her convictions are not always easy to hear.'

'*Convictions?* All that gloom about there being no point in making a clock because all it does is count away the hours of your life?'

'She has a point there,' he says, trying to sound light-hearted.

Bianca rolls into him, sliding one thigh over his. 'Well, I think clocks are a wonder.'

'That's not what you told Robert Cecil, in his study. I seem to recall you disapproved of his. Why have you changed your mind?'

'Because I need to be lightened, after all this talk of inevitability. And by the chimes I've just heard, I'd say we have an hour before she comes back.'

18

'You expect Galileo Galilei to help you build the thing?' says the Podestà doubtfully. 'Seriously?'

The air in the palazzo is sullen with heat. Patches of sweat darken the governor's crimson robe and bead his fleshy upper lip. He wears an expression of overheated disbelief.

'The Fiorentini showed me nothing but contempt, Your Honour,' Bruno says, feigning outrage. 'They are jealous to a man. They could not abide the idea of the Serene Republic matching them in this field of new discovery. Fortunately, I have convinced Maestro Galileo to make the required calculations – solely in honour of His Serene Highness.'

'Professor Galileo is an argumentative rogue who demands his salary be paid in advance, because the one thing he apparently can't count properly is money.'

'But, sir, who else is better qualified than he?' Bruno insists, suddenly afraid the Podestà's apparent dislike of the young mathematician from Pisa might jeopardize his plan. 'Men of great intellect often find the everyday chores of life too insignificant to consider. Is that not why Your Honour must employ his own servants? A man of your standing could not possibly be expected to do his own laundry; and so it is with Signor Galileo.'

'But I don't walk about the streets dressed as a common artisan,' the Podestà wheezes. 'They say he refuses to wear his professorial tóga – that he prefers to go about in the garb of a common labourer.'

'He is a modest man, it is true.'

'I can't say I've heard him described as *modest*, Signor Barrani. I find him somewhat full of himself.'

'He is a man of ordinary pleasures, Your Honour. He likes to dress as such.'

'And he argues a lot.'

'Dispute is the air that all the finest natural philosophers breathe,' Bruno says, wondering if he might have a career as a lawyer if this project is rejected.

'The question is, Signor Barrani: can Professor Galileo be relied upon to fulfil the commission, or will we have to trawl the taverns to find out what progress he's making?'

'With the honour of the Serene Republic as his lodestar, I have the utmost confidence he will be diligent.'

'The honour of Pisa didn't stop him turning his back on that city for one hundred and eighty ducats per annum, I seem to recall.'

Bruno draws himself up to his full height, still a head shorter than the Podestà, and opens his palms to demonstrate an inescapable fact of life. 'Genius must seek its own reward, Your Honour. You can't expect to wear silken hose if you're only prepared to pay for country wool.'

A slow, sibilant intake of breath as the Podestà considers Bruno's assurances.

'Do we have artisans of the required skill to build this sphere here in Padua?'

'Undoubtedly, Your Honour,' Bruno assures him, though at this precise moment the *Arte dei Astronomi*, Padua's newest trade guild (so new in fact that it has yet to be officially entered into the approved list) boasts only three enrolled members: Bruno Barrani himself and his servants Luca and Alonso.

Is that doubt making the heavy jowls tremble, Bruno wonders, or was it the fly that only an instant ago brushed the Podestà's official cheek? He is known to be a man who likes to cover his back. He might be the doge's representative in Padua, but he's not a man to put himself at risk of the doge's displeasure. There again, his avarice is well known amongst those who come to him seeking his official blessing for this project or that. Bruno watches helplessly while the struggle rages across the corpulent battleground of the Podestà's face.

And then, suddenly, all is light and joy.

'I shall write to His Serenity immediately and recommend we go ahead,' the Podestà proclaims with a happy tremor. 'After all, God has set Venice above Florence on the map. How then can we allow her to be below Florence in matters of the new science?'

'That is all that has ever driven me, Your Honour,' Bruno says, contriving the studied modesty of a plaster saint.

The Podestà returns to his desk. He sits down and adjusts the crimson folds of his gown over the arms of his chair, as if Bruno were a painter and he the subject preparing for a sitting. 'I will need a full tally of the proposed cost of the project, of course. His Serenity's purse is not limitless.'

'Of course. I have already prepared one,' Bruno says, producing a document from his doublet.

The Podestà takes it, scans it in a cursory manner and frowns. 'There appears to be an entry missing.'

'Surely not. I have been most diligent in the accounting,' Bruno assures him. 'To the last *scudo*.'

With a smile that says, *Come now, we're both men of the world*, the Podestà leans forward, tapping Bruno's estimate with the tip of one fleshy fingertip. 'It can go... *here*.'

'What can, Your Honour?' Bruno asks, noticing that the official digit seems to have alighted upon blank parchment.

'The cost of my favour,' he says. 'Four per cent of the gross. Shall we call it... "supplementary reckonings"?'

✠

The street door of Sir Fulke Vaesy's house on St Andrew's Hill lies beneath the overhang of the upper storey. Rose and Ned have timed their arrival carefully. It is late afternoon, and this side of the lane is now in deep shadow. As a further precaution they linger until it is almost empty. Then, with Ned flattening himself as best he can beside the door, Rose announces her presence with a determined hammering on the little iron grille set into its face. Almost at once she hears footsteps beyond. The grille slides open and she sees a pair of anxious eyes peering out.

'I bear a message for Sir Fulke Vaesy,' she says in the authoritative voice she uses for Bankside tradesmen whenever they try to deliver a skimmed order to the Jackdaw. 'My mistress has need of a physician. She is ill, and rich. Very rich.'

As the door opens, Ned moves with a speed not even Rose expects of him. He barges inside, driving Ditworth before him and sending him stumbling backwards onto the floor rushes. Rose slips in behind, closing the door after her.

'Where is the rogue?' Ned growls, hauling Ditworth to his feet and holding him up by the neck of his jerkin like a child's rag doll.

'Have mercy on me, Master,' Ditworth pleads, trying to make his head disappear into his tunic on the presumption Ned is about to decapitate him. 'There's nothing in the house worth stealing.'

Ned, who for all his faults has never stolen so much as a button, drops him like a hot coal. 'I'm no house-diver, you scoundrel! I'm an honest man.'

200

'God's wounds!' Ditworth cries, getting his first proper look at the intruders. 'It's *you* – from Bankside.'

Rose demands, 'Where is your master?'

Like a cornered fox, Ditworth seems reluctant to take his eyes off Ned. His head gives a twitchy little jerk over his shoulder, towards a door set into a wall covered from floor to ceiling in cheap wainscoting. Silently, Ned motions for him to open it. Rose pushes the servant through and follows. She hopes that by placing herself in front of her husband she can prevent any inclination he might have towards murder, though the anger burns so hotly in her that she fears *she* may be the one to lose all control.

She finds herself glaring at a shabby-looking man in his fifties, frozen in the act of rising from behind a desk cluttered with astrological charts, leather-bound medical books, pots and vials, and a scattering of knives and lancets that makes her think of a meal table after the plates have been cleaned away. Clad in the dark gown of a doctor of medicine, with a tangled grey beard framing an aggressive jaw, Vaesy waves a quill at the intruders as though he intends to defend himself with it. 'What is this rank discourtesy?' he demands to know, almost knocking over a flask of straw-coloured liquid that looks to Rose suspiciously like urine. 'Who makes such ungovernable sport with my privacy?'

Ned leaves the talking to his wife. She has a better way with words.

'Tell us the truth, you vile arseworm,' Rose snarls, her face turning crimson. 'Was it you who made the false denunciation against Dr Nicholas Shelby? Admit it, as God is your judge!'

Vaesy stares at her as though he cannot quite believe what he is hearing. He has never been spoken to in such a manner, certainly not by a female of the lower orders. 'Christ's holy nails – you're a *woman*!' he says in bewilderment.

Rose glances at her husband. 'See, Ned? He 'asn't forgotten his 'natomy. That's proper university learnin' for you, that is.'

Ned can almost hear Mistress Bianca in her voice. Knowing it would ruin their advantage, he struggles not to laugh.

Vaesy says contemptuously, 'What is this insult? I am Sir Fulke Vaesy. I have no cause to make an account of myself to some bawd's moll.'

Rose has to put out a hand to stay her husband. She says, 'You'll answer plainly, if you know what's good for you. Otherwise I shall be 'ard-pressed to stop my Ned here from giving you a private lecture in dissection.' She nods towards Vaesy's groin. 'Startin' with your pizzle!'

Vaesy waves his quill at the hapless Ditworth. 'Go – fetch the constable!'

The servant looks up at Ned in despair. 'May I go, sir, as my master commands?'

Ned says, 'By all means, Master Ditworth. I 'ave no quarrel with you. Go, fetch the constable.' Then, to Vaesy: 'But by the time he gets here, you won't be in any state to tell him why your blood's splashed all over the wainscoting. Now sit down, an' if you're truly the gentleman you seem to think you are, answer my wife properly when she asks you a civil question.'

Less than an hour later Ned and Rose sit in the stern of a wherry as the boatman pushes with one oar against the Blackfriars stairs to point them in the direction of Bankside. The wind has risen. The wherry jolts to the slap of spiteful little waves. Ned leans over to shield Rose from the spray. Their mood is as grey as the river. 'You should 'ave let me throttle him,' he says. 'What use is a confession, if he won't put right what he's done?'

'Because I don't want our child to grow up knowing his father was a felon 'anged for murder, that's why.'

Rose lays her head against the breast of Ned's jerkin. She is prouder of him than he will ever know. But the greater emotion she feels is relief.

Vaesy has admitted to them that he was the author of Master Nicholas's misfortune. He even appeared proud of it. But with pride had come a return of his former patrician self. He had called their bluff. He had refused to commit to paper any statement that his claims were baseless.

For a terrible instant Rose had feared Ned was going to smash him to a pulp. She could see the inner battle he was fighting, as clear as day: a terrible stillness had come over him, save for his breathing, which was deep, slow and rasping, like a man close to expiring from flux in the lungs. To her joy, the better Ned had won.

'I could 'ave made him write a letter of retraction. I know I could,' Ned says angrily as the wherry rolls alarmingly with the waves. 'You could 'ave read it to me, so that I could know it was proper.'

'Vaesy is a serpent, Ned,' she says. 'Even if he'd written a letter, he'd 'ave told the magistrates we forced him to it.'

Ned knows his wife is speaking the truth. The way Vaesy had so contemptuously refused to put right the wrong he had done has set a bitter fire raging inside him. Vaesy had called him a churl, a vagabond, a low-born of no consequence – told him there was not a law officer in the land who would believe a person such as him, over a knight of the realm. Ned had kept his fists by his side throughout, knowing in his heart that Vaesy was right. If he went to the Privy Council, they wouldn't believe him. He wouldn't even get a hearing.

'What do we do, Wife? There must be *something*.'

But Rose has no answer for him, which only adds to his despair. As the wherry fights its way towards Bankside, the knowledge of his own impotency stings Ned Monkton far more than any of Sir Fulke Vaesy's insults.

19

The road is rising. The hills grow ever steeper. To ease the burden on the mules, the pace has slowed and only Bianca and Hella ride. Even though Nicholas feels as fit as he ever did on his father's farm at Barnthorpe, his calves ache at the end of each day when they rest in a pilgrims' hostelry, or in a barn, or even beneath a hedge – something he has only vague memories of doing after Eleanor's death, when grief and drink had made a deranged vagrant out of him.

They cross little stone bridges over torrents of mountain melt-water tumbling through narrow defiles. Knuckles of granite thrust out of wooded inclines like the tips of a reef breaking the surface of a dark-green ocean. They have almost reached the village of Mouthier-Haut-Pierre, where they will surrender the mules. Nicholas has walked ahead a little, to check the way from the next crest. Bianca can see him in the distance, silhouetted against the sky where the path leads between dense stands of fir trees.

'Nicholas tells me that you have a brother still living,' she says to Hella, suddenly weary of the silence.

'Did I tell him that?' she replies distractedly.

'When we were resting in that forest near Troyes, you told him what had happened to your family, at Breda.'

'If you say so, I must have done.'

'I don't mean to pry—'

Hella looks down at her dust-covered leather overshoes. 'I haven't seen him for some time. He is a priest – *was* a priest. I think he lost his faith in God, after what happened.'

'So too did Nicholas, when he suffered a great loss. When we are in pain it is easy to rail against His plan for us. But the pain passes – eventually.'

Hella lifts her gaze to meet Bianca's. There is a frightening coldness in it, which makes Bianca think she has intruded too deeply, struck some deep vein of suffering that runs through the maid's memory and that she would prefer were not mined.

'It will break his heart when he finds out,' Hella says.

'Your brother's heart?'

'No – your husband's.'

'I don't understand what you mean.'

For what seems like an age, Hella studies Bianca's face, as though trying to recognize someone she remembers only from her childhood. Then she says, 'It will break his heart when the child you are carrying is stillborn.'

The heat goes out of the air with a rush. On either side of the track the forest turns from summer to winter in the passing of a single breath. Bianca almost reels at the cold cruelty in the maid's voice. For a moment she is speechless. Then, through a jaw that seems to have fused itself to the rest of her skull, she says, slowly and with great resolve so that her voice does not falter, 'I am not with child, Hella. I am sure I would know. And even if I was, why would you say such a vile and hurtful thing? Do you get pleasure from it?'

But in Hella eyes there is no regret, only an intolerable pity.

'It is right to speak the truth,' she says. 'I gain no pleasure from it. But once knowledge is let loose into the world, it must be accepted. Not denied.'

With great effort, Bianca keeps her voice low – in case Nicholas, even at this distance, catches a hint of the tension between the two women.

'Well, I think this *knowledge* of yours is nothing but a hateful trick, played only so that you can see the pain it causes people. You may have suffered in the past, Hella, but that is no reason to hurt people who wish only to help you. We didn't have to let you come with us, you know. And to speak plainly, I rather wish we hadn't.'

But the maid seems not to have heard her. Or if she has, Bianca's statement is lost on her. 'How much of a disappointment will you be to him – barren after a stillbirth?' she asks in a monotone voice. 'How will he survive the loss of a wife and *two* children?'

Suddenly the words Hella spoke in the chamber at Reims seem to fall out of the sky around Bianca like the cast-out angels in the Den Bosch painting: heralds of torment to come. *We see a dead child... a dead parent – or perhaps it is a dead womb...* And then an even greater sense of dread seizes her. Then, Hella had spoken only of *one* child.

'You said "a wife and *two* children". Even if I *was* pregnant, how do you know about his Eleanor and the child she was carrying?'

Hella smiles. 'He told me.'

For Bianca, this is even worse than Hella being able to see inside her husband's mind, or her own for that matter.

'He *told* you? When?'

'At Besançon. When you went down to the river. We understand each other. You should let him go. Let *me* have him. He does not deserve more pain.'

There is only so much a woman with blisters on her feet, who's sure she stinks of mule, and has a mountain range ahead of her to cross, can suffer with equanimity. Bianca drops the reins of the mule she is leading. The beast immediately begins grazing at the roadside.

'Listen to me, girl,' Bianca hisses in a voice that would have silenced the entire taproom of the Jackdaw in an instant. 'I don't know what manner of sport you think you're playing, but I am having *none* of it. I've spent too long on Bankside not to know a gulling when it's in the offing. And I don't fall for any of them. Whatever you *think* you're achieving by this manner of talk, I can tell you it won't work. You're wasting your time. Nicholas and I have been through too much together to be sundered by a trickster, however sad her story. I'm not with child, do you hear? And when I am, it will be born to us *healthy*.'

In that instant Bianca knows she has made herself a terrible hostage to fortune. In her mind she whispers the phrase Nicholas brought back from his journey last summer to the Barbary shore: *inshā Allāh* – if God wills it.

But the cold pity in the other woman's eyes is merciless.

'I am sorry, Mistress Bianca, if you find what I have to say upsetting,' Hella says. 'All I know is that when the knowledge of something is out, it cannot then be erased. And to deny its existence would be a sin. Measure the hours how you will, the darkness will always come eventually.'

✠

'You've hardly spoken a word to Hella all day,' Nicholas says. 'Has some dispute passed between you?'

They are in their lodgings at Mouthier-Haut-Pierre, in a house owned by Perrault the muleteer, business partner of Monsieur Boiseaux in Reims. Freed from their temporary Protestant identities, the former Cecil, Essex, Coke and Popham are now grazing contentedly on good Catholic grass in a nearby field.

A dispute? Bianca says inside her head. *A dispute between Hella Maas and me? Do you think that while you were spying out the way ahead from the crest of that hill, we had a mild disagreement over my ability to bear a child with you?* She clenches her jaw to stop her thoughts tumbling out and becoming words.

'Hella speaks as if she likes to wound,' she says. 'I've borne it about as long as I can.'

Nicholas is gathering a pile of laundry. Amongst the other services Perrault provides for weary pilgrims is the chance to wash their dusty, sweat-stained clothes in a nearby stream, or – for a single *denier* – have a washerwoman do it for them. Nicholas's motive in discovering this has not been entirely domestic; his exploration of the town has enabled him to scan the approaches for a man in a grey coat, or any number of imaginary Privy Council watchers, all pointing their fingers in his direction and scribbling down messages to send to Attorney General Coke and Chief Justice Popham, messages that begin with the phase *We have found him...*

Hella is out buying food from the town market, leaving the two of them alone for the first time in days. Bianca would prefer it if she never returned.

'I don't think she realizes,' Nicholas says casually. 'It's as if other people's sensitivities don't exist for her. Don't let it trouble you. We're getting closer to leaving her every day.'

Don't let it trouble you. Bianca longs to have Nicholas take her hand – the way he does when he knows instinctively that she is in need of comfort. She wants his physician's cure for her present malady: kissing her fingers one by one, then the tautness of the skin below the knuckles, then her palm, then her wrist, until the tension has gone out of her. But at this precise moment she fears that if he does, it will serve only to tear open the fragile net that holds in her rage.

'Did she say something particular that's brought on this distemper?' he adds.

'It doesn't matter, Husband.'

'It matters to me. What was it?'

'Women's talk, that's all.'

'Nothing about how we sinners are all going to burn in hell before the month is out?'

His clumsy attempt at parody is designed to make her smile. It almost succeeds.

'I think she's grown weary of that song, now that it no longer makes us shiver,' Bianca says.

'Then what is it?'

Bianca takes a deep breath. 'You told her about Eleanor and your child.' It is said without recrimination. Just a bald statement of fact. And even before the words are out of her mouth, Bianca wishes she'd never spoken them. But it's too late to take them back now. 'You allowed her to see into one of the most important places in your heart. Why would you do that?'

For a moment he's flustered, unable to answer. He simply stands there, holding her dirty linen under-smock as though he's been caught with a weapon at the scene of a killing.

'It was at Besançon... when you went to wash your feet in the river. Hella was speaking of how searching after knowledge can lead to evil things happening.'

Bianca frowns. 'Well, we both know how true that is.'

'What do you mean?'

'Our life on Bankside has not been exactly what one might call tranquil, has it?'

Nicholas fumbles for words that won't make things worse.

'Those events – the ones that happened to you and me in the past – nothing we did was ever with evil intent. You know that. God knows it.'

'We are damned if He doesn't,' she says softly. 'Just as Hella says.'

He pretends he hasn't heard; the same thought has occurred

to him more than once. But the past they share cannot be undone.

'When Hella and I spoke,' he says, 'I chose Eleanor as an example of how it was my lack of knowledge that brought ill upon us, not my searching after it.'

'Nevertheless, I wish you had not spoken of Eleanor and your unborn child to that woman – even if it is not my place to say it. The more she knows about us, the less comfortable I feel. I don't trust her.'

Nicholas tries to set her mind at rest. 'She's merely a young maid who has suffered great hurt in her life: all her family dead – for which she blames herself. Her home is denied to her... she is an outcast... We must excuse her if she says things that provoke. It's probably because she's testing providence. When people spurn her, she takes it as proof that she's right. It's self-fulfilling.'

'Excuse her? Why must I excuse her when she says hurtful things to me? Worse than hurtful! More to the point, why do you excuse her?'

Bianca's cheeks are flushed now. The anger has returned. It is threatening to boil over. She can hear Hella's voice echoing around a dusty mountain track: *How much of a disappointment will you be to him – barren after a stillbirth?*

She stands to her full height, throws her shoulders back, arches her neck. She thrusts her chin purposefully towards her infuriatingly compassionate husband. Sometimes she wishes he wasn't so damnably considerate – of other people's faults.

She unties the string of her kirtle and lets it fall. As he stares at her nakedness she can think only of her poor blistered feet, and whether the sight of them will douse the fire the rest of her body lights in him. But the kirtle has somehow absorbed a little of her fury and coiled itself around her ankles to hide the blisters from his sight.

'*Knowledge*, Husband?' she says huskily. 'Have all the knowledge of *me* you want – and then tell me to my face if it leads to evil.'

✠

Beyond the riverside town of Pontarlier the path rises into forested hills on the northern edge of Lake Geneva. The country is wild here. Boars grub noisily amid the trees. It is late afternoon and the three travellers are alone on the track. The air is close and threatening. Overhead, towers of grey, roiling thunderclouds billow upwards like smoke from the Devil's fires. Shortly before the heavens open and wash them from the face of the earth, Hella – in the lead as usual – calls out that there is shelter ahead.

The hamlet of mean houses and a single barn is scattered around an ancient bridge, a single arch thrown across a fast-flowing, deep-cut stream. Where the water surges over the rocks it is as white as bleached bone; in the depths, as black as sin. There is no one about, and the barn has holes in the roof. But there is a tavern, a sprawling, broken-backed place of slate and stone draped over a rise just above the bridge. Above the door is a painted sign of a bunch of grapes. But the real clue to the building's existence lies in a little niche set into the wall, home to a carved effigy of St James, patron saint of pilgrims. In his weather-worn hand he holds his staff, while his blunted feet stand on scallop shells. Nicholas realizes the place is a former religious house turned over to earthier indulgences.

They have had mixed fortune with their choice of places in which to lay their heads. When Bianca ducks below the crooked stone lintel, the tavern-mistress in her sounds a warning note about this one.

She studies the dark interior with a professional eye while

Nicholas pays for a room. It seems on the surface like any humble country establishment: low, smoke-blackened beams; rustic benches; foresters in leather jerkins and plain broadcloth, playing dice. None look to her like pilgrims, but then they haven't seen any on the road for days. A hound lies close to the hearth, gnawing on a bone that still has a scrap of flesh left on it and eyeing them with suspicion. The customers glance at the three strangers with sullen curiosity. There seems to Bianca to be a sense of unspoken anticipation in the air. It is only when a plump, white-haired, flush-faced man wearing a threadbare black cassock comes down the stairs, pauses on the last step to tug his gown straight and lace one shoe, that she realizes the truth.

'It's a bawdy-house,' she whispers to Nicholas when he re-joins her, just as the first crack of thunder sounds and rain begins to stream down the windows. A moment later a stocky peasant woman of indeterminate years with a carnivorous eye and fists like a farrier's clumps down into the taproom. She gesturers impatiently to a little bald fellow who nervously cradles his felt cap in his lap. As he rises to his feet, she turns imperiously and ascends once more to the upper floor. He follows, like a man going to be bled by the barber-surgeon.

'Do you see? I was right.'

Nicholas says, 'We've passed nowhere else on the road since Pontarlier. It has a fire, and we've paid for a chamber. If we go outside, we'll likely drown.'

'Come, Husband – you cannot think me too precious to abide a jumping-house. I've lived on Bankside longer than you have, remember?' Bianca tells him, as the sound of hail striking the shutters intensifies. She glances at Hella, who is questioning the landlord in serviceable French about the state of the road through the hills and onwards to the lake. 'But what about her?' These don't seem like the sort of clients who'll take kindly to being chastised loudly for loose morals.'

'I'll suggest to her that we rest until supper,' Nicholas says, rolling his eyes. 'If she's asleep, perhaps she won't notice.'

In the event, their chamber is not conducive to rest. It smells of unwashed bodies and the mattresses feel as though they haven't been aired in a year. Within the hour there is little to see from the window but intermittent torrents of grey rain, which thrash the branches of the trees and send dirty rivulets coursing down the steep street of the little hamlet. They fill the time as best they can, accepting their confinement, welcoming the opportunity to rest. Hella spends much of it mouthing silent prayers. Nicholas wonders if she can smell the sin.

Supper is a tolerable stew of boar meat, better than the surroundings might suggest, though the table they eat at is as sticky as a honey jar. As the evening draws on, the inn begins to drop the thin veneer of propriety it had shown in daylight. Whenever the rain eases, men scuttle in to dry themselves by the fire: local foresters, poachers, hunters, even a few gentlemen, judging by the quality of their clothes. Where they come from is anyone's guess; there aren't enough houses in the hamlet to home them. The swelling crowd plays dice and cards, chalking the scores on a slate as they down flasks of sweet wine and a spirit that smells of fermented pears. At some invisible sign, a procession of young women comes down the stairs and passes amongst them, alighting first on the better-dressed customers. Their smiles are flat and sickly, their eyes dead. These are not local drabs, Bianca guesses. They have dark, almost Moorish faces, and weals on the back of their wrists where they've been branded with a hot iron. From her place beside the landlord, the bawd with the farrier's fists keeps a beady eye on her stock, while a youth with one empty eye socket plays angry little galliard tunes, though no one is dancing.

'It's worse than the Tabard on a feast day,' Bianca says under her breath. 'I wouldn't have this crowd in the Jackdaw if they offered me all the gold in the queen's mint.'

A sudden double boom of thunder, seemingly overhead, makes her wonder if Hella Maas has somehow brought the storm down upon the hamlet as a warning. But the maid merely observes the scene with detached interest, just as she might watch an ants' nest she'd poked with a stick.

By the time the rain eases a little, it is dark outside. The taproom is now full of revellers sprawled in the alcoves and on the floor, the drabs pouring wine and spirits into their open mouths, or relieving other appetites with a not very discreet hand beneath gown and jerkin. When copulation seems imminent, the bawd demands her money, before shooing the couple upstairs.

'Never mind the Tabard,' Nicholas says, 'it could be a gathering of the Privy Council at Whitehall.'

'Or a meeting of the Bishop of London's ecclesiastical court,' Bianca counters, adopting a wholly uncharacteristic primness.

'Laugh if you will,' says Hella with a quiet sadness. 'But remember the painting. There will be a judgement for these sinners. And it will come soon enough.'

'Do you want to tell them, or shall I?' Nicholas mutters.

As he speaks, the plump white-haired man in the threadbare cassock that Bianca had seen earlier stumbles into their table, as his friend – a sallow-faced reed with a goitre on his neck and no teeth in his upper jaw – tries to steer him to the exit. The man is around seventy. He has a veined face flushed with drink, and a nose pocked with tiny boils. Bracing himself with one hand on the tabletop, he leers at Bianca and gurgles something in French through fumes of fermented peach spirit.

She wonders if stabbing him in the hand with her food knife would be worth the uproar. She decides against it. His companion

215

mutters an apology, regains control of his charge and makes it to the door without further incident.

'He was wearing a cassock – do you think he was a priest?' she asks Nicholas.

'With manners like that? Probably an archbishop,' Nicholas replies. 'The question is: Lutheran or Catholic?'

'Definitely Lutheran.'

'On what grounds? The fact we're nearing Switzerland?'

'No,' Bianca says with a shake of her head. 'A Catholic archbishop wouldn't be seen dead in clothes like that.'

They sit a little longer, neither wanting to return to the uninviting chamber, trying to sustain an air of world-weary nonchalance, until the door flies open as if blown in by a sudden return of the storm. The thin fellow with the goitre stands against the black night, yelling wildly and pointing repeatedly out into the darkness.

'What does he say?' Nicholas asks Hella, even as he guesses the truth.

'There has been some manner of calamity – the stream, by the bridge,' Hella confirms.

Barely half a dozen customers are in a fit state to help. The landlord lights a thick rush taper in the fire and leads them out into the night. Nicholas and Bianca follow, Hella taking up the rear.

There is nothing to see beyond the meagre pool of light from the tavern windows. The night is all noise: the roaring of the wind through the trees and the rushing of hidden water. The air is heavy with moisture. For Bianca, it clings to the skin like the cold, wet winding sheet of someone who has just died from the sweating sickness. A flash of lightning further into the hills gives a momentary grey glimpse of the tumbling stream pouring through the rocky cut below the bridge.

The men are calling out a name: *Donadieu!... Donadieu!...* But the night will not receive it. It hurls Donadieu back at them in angry gusts. Bianca can see only the rush taper some way ahead of her. She senses Nicholas close by, reaching out to her lest they get separated in the darkness.

And then a sudden flurry of rain blinds her. She gropes for Nicholas's outstretched hand. Her fingers claw at the place she expects it to be. They grasp only empty night. When she opens her eyes again, she can see nothing at all. The wind has torn the flames from the rush taper and buried them.

She turns about, the panic rising in her. Even the pool of light from the tavern windows has gone now. Utterly disorientated, she calls out to Nicholas. She hears him answer, so close that his voice is clear above the roar of the wind. But when she tries to move towards the sound, she has the sensation she's stepping over a cliff. Her legs lose their strength. Her feet no longer trust the pressure of the ground against them. She can't tell if she's standing still, turning in a circle, putting one foot in front of the other – or falling.

Then she feels herself begin to slide. She hears the scattering of earth and rock clearly above the wind as the bank crumbles under her feet. She catches the hungry howl of the racing torrent, so close now that it freezes the unborn scream in her mouth. Flailing with outstretched arms, she knows – even before her mind can set it out in thought – that she has made the same awful error as the man called Donadieu. And then a second ripple of lightning illuminates the rocky bank inches away from her face.

Hella Maas is looking down at her, her face white like that of a plaster saint, a martyr caught in the moment of heavenly release from pain. Bianca stabs her open fingers towards the image, calling Hella's name in desperation. Waiting to feel the warmth, the strength, of human flesh seizing her own.

But Hella does not move.

Perhaps it is the lightning flash that robs her of all movement. It certainly slows Bianca's own thoughts almost to a standstill, for she is too stunned for the real fear to bite yet. She is staring straight into the maid's face.

Is that really murderous intent she sees reflected in her eyes? Or is it just a beatific certainty – an unbending belief that this one event is merely another step along a preordained path. Either way, the intent is the same.

Hella Maas is going to let me fall.

Then the darkness returns as quickly as it was parted. And Bianca feels the maid's hands around her wrists, gripping her with surprising strength, catching her in the instant before the soil beneath her feet gives way entirely.

✠

In the morning Bianca stands with Nicholas on the bank of the raging stream, not far from the place where deep gouges in the earth bear witness to her brief struggle the night before. Nicholas has treated the gazes on her arms and shins with the balm of woundwort and sea-holly that she packed for just such mishaps. Though cleaned, the abrasions still sting.

Together, they watch in silence while the white, bloated body of the man named Donadieu is hauled from under the bridge where the torrent has lodged it. The threadbare cassock has been torn off, leaving him naked. As the men from the hamlet drag him out, a large dark-brown toad skips down off one plump hairless thigh and jumps back into the shadows under the stonework.

'Do you see *now?*' Bianca hears Hella say at her shoulder. 'I foretold there would be a reckoning. He was a lascivious sinner, his body bloated by drink. Now he has drowned in his own sinfulness. The toad is Satan's familiar. He sends the toad to guide to him all those with lust and deceit in their hearts. It was all shown to you in the painting. Now will you believe me when I say I know what is coming?'

20

Padua, 7th August 1594

The summons comes sooner than Bruno could have hoped for. As he returns to the Palazzo del Podestà in the crushing afternoon heat, he finds it difficult to maintain his cockerel's strut. He is too short to run with any expectation of dignity, too impatient to saunter. His mood swings wildly between opposing poles. At one pole lies success: envy of the Medici has driven His Serenity the doge into a burst of uncharacteristic ardour. Yes, build me a sphere to humble the Fiorentini, and start at once! At the other, failure: the doge has dismissed his scheme out of hand. Are the Paduans all mad? Do they think I'm made of ducats?

When at last he stands expectantly before the city governor – his forehead gleaming with sweat from taking the stairs two at a time – Bruno has to force himself to slow his formal bow and bend of the knee so that he doesn't look like someone doubling up with colic.

Unable to penetrate the Podestà's inscrutably aloof expression, he takes the sheet of expensive velum offered to him. The heavy wax seal hanging from its braided ribbon swings listlessly in the stifling air. It bears the imprint of a winged lion – the symbol of the Serene Republic. As he reads the document, his eyes move too fast, too hungrily, to notice that the drops of perspiration falling from his brow are spotting the neat, official hand.

... unthinkable that Venice should stand reduced behind the city of Florence... her rightful place as a hearth wherein the new learning may blaze... bringing rightful honour and prestige to the republic most deserving of it in all Christendom.

His eyes only settle when he reaches the sum that His Serene Highness has approved for the project. Bruno tries not to grin. It's everything he asked for.

'This is a great honour for the city of Padua, Signor Barrani,' the Podestà says loftily. 'Do not give anyone the opportunity to hold us up to ridicule, especially the Medici and the rest of those thieving Fiorentini.'

It is all Bruno can do to stop himself singing. 'That shall be my only guiding star, Your Honour,' he proclaims. 'I do this solely out of love for the reputation of the Veneto and the Serene Republic.'

'Really?' says the Podestà, lifting one bushy white eyebrow.

'But of course,' Bruno protests, as though to suggest otherwise would be the gravest of blasphemies. He draws himself up to his full but modest height. 'I will slay with my bare hands the first man who says it was ever only about the money.'

✳

His neighbours in the Borgo dei Vignali will tell you that you don't need a cockerel to know when it's sunrise at Signor Galileo's lodgings: the sound of heated discourse will wake you soon enough. It goes on all day, and for far too much of the night. The only relief comes when the sun is too fierce even for argument in the shade, or when the young professor of mathematics is at the Palazzo Bo delivering a lecture, or in the tavern.

The raised voices are not always unwelcome. The students who rent rooms in his house, his drinking friends, his creditors (if they dare to risk his temper) – even dapper little merchants who have dropped by with a shiny new commission from His Serenity the doge in Venice – will tell you that you'll learn more in ten minutes in Signor Galileo's house than most men might hope to learn in ten lifetimes.

This afternoon is no different. A pupil is debating with the maestro why the water in a leaky rowing boat suddenly surges forward if you accidentally ram the bank whilst seeking out a shady spot on the Bacchiglione where you and your mistress might spend a while unobserved.

'It is because the earth is in motion, carrying the water along with it,' says the pupil, Matteo Fedele, as he tries to remember Galileo's explanation, made before the wine started to flow. 'If you are on its surface and come to a sudden stop, the water in the boat will seek to maintain its velocity.'

Galileo swigs at his wine jug, belches loudly and counters, 'You don't think, young Matteo, that it might be because you were too busy ogling her tits to notice the bank approaching, and that it's God's way of telling you you're an unobservant little self-abuser?'

'You can't speak to me like that, Maestro,' the pupil says with good-natured defiance. 'I pay rent, and my father pays you to teach me.'

'You don't think I'd bother with a brain like yours if he didn't, do you?' Galileo tells him.

'I should have studied medicine under Professor Fabrici,' Matteo laments. 'At least he wouldn't make me climb the bell tower with a sodding cannonball on my shoulders to see if it fell faster than an apple. How come Girolamo always gets to carry the lighter objects?'

'Because Girolamo pays more rent. That's how shit at mathematics you are, Matteo.'

Bruno Barrani listens to these exchanges with a rictal smile on his face, as though he understands everything that is said about who is right on matters of natural motion: Aristotle or Archimedes, or whether Master Copernicus is a genius or a heretic, and just how large the heavens must be if his cosmos is to be realistically contained within them. At Signor Compass's house, Signor Purse does a lot of nodding. Not to mention nodding off.

Diverted by a discreet cough from the doorway, all three men look up.

'Signor Galileo, if I might be permitted a word with Your Honour... about your account?'

The man standing in the street entrance is a lanky fellow who looks like a loosely draped sculptor's armature, all rods and angles. His moist, bulbous eyes peer out timidly from beneath a mop of pure-white hair.

'Ah, good morrow, Signor Clockmaker,' Galileo says pleasantly, offering the man a slice of pork sausage with one hand while wiping the grease from his own mouth with the other. 'Far too early in the day to speak of something as profane as money. We're not finished debating the new learning here. Have some of this fine Bondola.'

The newcomer declines as gracefully as his unpaid bill allows. 'Very kind, Signor Galileo, but no, thank you. I've come about the outstanding—'

The professor cuts him off with an airy wave of his hand and turns to Bruno. 'Signor Purse, in the matter of the doge's new sphere, we will need someone with a clockmaker's skills, will we not?'

'Most certainly we will, Master Compass,' Bruno agrees. It's the first question he's been able to answer since he dropped by to tell the professor that His Serene Highness has approved the plan.

'What excellent fortune, Signor Mirandola!' Galileo says happily, slamming the jug of Bondola onto the table for emphasis. 'How would you like to count yourself amongst those who hold a warrant of approval from the Doge of Venice?'

'The *doge?*' says Mirandola the clockmaker, interest and suspicion wrestling in his eyes. Interest wins by a throw. '*Me*, working for His Serene Highness? How? Does he have need of a clock?'

Galileo looks at Bruno and gives him a theatrical wink.

'Oh, Signor Mirandola,' he says, reaching for the wine again, 'he will have need of *much* more than that. Tell us: what's the biggest clock you've ever built?'

✠

Six weeks since leaving Bankside, and Nicholas has given himself up to exile because exile has an allure all of its own. Here, on the path down to the northern shore of Lake Geneva, the air is sharper, more bracing even than a tub of cold Thames water, more cleansing than the stinking fug he breathes in the narrow lanes of London. Here, you cannot breathe without inhaling dreams of high peaks and eagles wheeling in the glare of the sun. The horizon – at least when he views it from a craggy rim of granite – is wider than any he has ever seen, including the marshy wastes of Suffolk. England seems like a half-forgotten memory from his early childhood, a place he thinks he may have read about once, like Avalon or Troy. Cecil is the name of a mule he rode until a short while ago – not a man made of flesh and blood. The only Essex he has ever known had a coat of coarse grey-brown hair, and would only think of following him in order to receive a handful of freshly torn grass.

They reach the town of Montreux the day after the Feast of the Transfiguration. He knows this because Bianca tells him so. In

England feasting the saints has long since been ruled a dangerous superstition, an offence against the queen's religion. Now Bianca takes great delight in acknowledging these holy days, something she has previously had to do in secret.

Montreux itself is staunchly Protestant, governed by the Swiss and full of Huguenot exiles from Italy. Yet still Nicholas does not feel safe. He cannot shake the sense of being watched. In the street, every eye that turns his way – no matter how casually – heightens his conviction that they are being followed. When he tracks down a merchant who trades with England, in order to top up his purse on Robert Cecil's letter of credit, he comes away with the nagging feeling that he's fixed his presence here for everyone to see.

But there is an even greater concern now occupying his mind: crossing the mountains. From their rented room in a hostelry on the lakeside, they have a breathtaking view of the snow-clad peaks across the water, jagged rents in the sky capped by a tumult of white cloud.

'How in the name of Jesu are we going to cross those?' he asks the owner of the hostelry, an Italian Protestant refugee from Lombardy. After Bianca's tuition over so many weeks, he finds he can converse adequately in the man's tongue, even if his accent raises a smile.

'Bravely, or not at all,' the man replies. 'There are more bones up there than rocks.'

But it turns out that he's only having a joke at the Englishman's expense. The great pass of St Bernard is open. And there is a hospice in the monastery at the highest point, where pilgrims can rest after the ascent.

'We ought to buy warm coats,' Bianca suggests. 'Even at its best, it will be no warmer than a winter's day in Milan.'

'How distant from here?' Nicholas asks.

'Four days to the pass. One to cross. We could be in Italy by the twelfth, Pavia six days later.'

'Is there a saint's day for that?' Nicholas asks mischievously.

'There's bound to be,' Bianca replies. 'There's a saint's day for everything.'

And if there isn't, there ought to be, she thinks. It should be called *St Bianca's Day*. Because, at Pavia, Hella Maas will continue on to Rome. And if I don't merit sainthood by then, I never will.

✠

In fact Montreux holds them for three days. There is no dissent. Foot leather needs repairing or replacing, tired joints need resting, and even Hella Maas accepts that you cannot march resolutely towards Judgement Day and expect to get there promptly on blistered feet.

When Bianca wakes on the third morning she leaves Nicholas asleep and goes down to the lake. She walks along the shore, marvelling at the view. The mountains wear two faces: one stark against the sky, the other reflected in the shimmering water. Their cold, magnificent mystery makes her think back to the night when Hella stood over her on the bank of the raging torrent, her face frozen in the lightning flash. It had the same unfathomable indifference in it, the same age-old disregard for the petty trials of mere mortals.

Did she intend to let me fall? Bianca wonders. Or was I so frightened that my mind saw danger everywhere? Hella could have done it, had she wished; no one would have been any the wiser. So if she has ever really intended me harm, she could have taken her chance at that moment. There would have been none better.

The thought only partly reassures. There is still the matter of the maid's claimed precognition. Bianca remembers the images of the bloated sinners in the painting at Den Bosch and the torments they were suffering, each dependent upon the sin committed. Then she thinks of the naked drowned corpse of the man called Donadieu, and the malevolent-looking toad squatting on his dead white flesh. She shivers. What if their strange companion is right?

She walks on, gauging how much longer she must suffer Hella's presence. She has often considered abandoning her. But Nicholas is right: a maid alone on the road would have enough real life-threatening dangers to face without considering supernatural ones. They made a promise to her in Den Bosch, and neither of them is the sort to break promises. *Once we have passed through the mountains...* Bianca repeats to herself as she walks.

And the mountains give her pause enough. Overawed by their majesty, she wonders how it will be possible to cross such a barrier and emerge safely into the lush valley of the Po river. She knows she has the determination. But has she the courage? Has she the strength? From where she stands, the peaks look impassable. But then she thinks of the warm cobbles and the shady arcades of the Palazzo delle Erbe, of the handsome young Paduan gallants in their bright satin doublets, hose and half-capes strutting about like fighting cocks, and the maidens as chaste as nuns on the outside but still contriving to smoulder even under the chaperone's watchful scowl. She will find a way.

Turning reluctantly away from the breathtaking view across the lake, she sets off on the short walk back to their lodgings.

When Bianca opens the door of the chamber she is expecting Nicholas to be up and about. He is not. And once again – just as in Reims – she is unable to fully comprehend what she sees before her.

The shutters are drawn. Shafts of sunlight slice into the shadowy interior, falling across the bed like molten steel running in the mould.

She left Nicholas dozing. And he is still there in the bed, his head turned sideways on the pillow, his wiry black hair tousled, his close-cut beard making a dark archipelago of his chin. But he is not alone.

Lying against him, one arm thrown casually like a lover's across his chest, is Hella Maas.

21

Standing in the doorway of their chamber, Bianca can only stare in disbelief at the bed, and at her husband sleeping the slumber of the innocent, while a young maid – whose own innocence she is rapidly beginning to question – lies next to him in a pose of stomach-churning familiarity.

Hella lifts her head a little from the coverlet. 'Quiet, Mistress Bianca. You'll disturb him,' she whispers without the slightest edge of guilt in her voice, and so close to the nape of Nicholas's neck that in her own mind Bianca can smell his hair, imagine her own breath ruffling the thin black curls of down that disappear between his shoulders.

Bianca counts slowly to three, partly to stop herself flying at the audacious little drab, partly to savour the sudden image of her mother in the kitchen at Padua mixing her poisons: *This one for giving a rival in love the breath of a diseased dog... this one for making her wind intolerable in polite company... and this one for when all else fails, and you want to do away with her entirely.*

On three, Bianca slams the door behind her loudly enough to wake the sacred dead in every churchyard in Montreux.

Nicholas sits up so quickly his left shoulder sends Hella's body rolling across the bed. Blinking, he stares at Bianca, then at Hella, who is trying to make herself prim by folding her legs under herself and clasping her hands in her lap, like a novice awaiting a lecture from her abbess.

'*Jesu!* Bianca, what are you...? What's...?'

'If you are about to ask me what's happening, Husband,' Bianca says coldly, 'I suggest you ask Mistress Doomsday here. I'd rather care to know myself.' She fixes the woman she is now convinced is her rival with a gaze bordering on murderous.

'You were not here to comfort him,' Hella says, as though she's been poorly rewarded for performing a necessary service. 'He was dreaming – a bad dream. I meant only to comfort him.'

'*Were* you dreaming, Husband?'

Nicholas shakes the sleep from his eyes. 'In truth, I was. A demon – like one of those on the altarpiece at Den Bosch. It was half-human, half-mule, and it was pushing us up a mountain, jabbing at us with a fiery trident. When we reached the top there was nowhere to go, other than to plunge down into a great machine in the valley below that was grinding people into dust.' He gives a tentative, self-deprecating laugh. 'It must have been something I ate last night.'

'You see,' says Hella triumphantly, 'even in sleep we cannot escape the warnings of what lies ahead.'

'Oh, spare me the false necromancy,' Bianca snarls. 'Come with me!'

She seizes the younger woman by the sleeve and drags her out of the lodgings and into the early-morning air. On the shore, fishermen are preparing their nets. They give the two women not a single glance.

'Let go of my arm, Mistress Bianca,' Hella pleads. 'You're hurting me. Why are you so angered?'

'Why am I... *angered?* Why does the sun rise every morning?' Bianca looks around at the mountains as though seeking inspiration from them. 'Shall we begin with the intimacy I've just this moment witnessed in our chamber?'

'I told you: I was only comforting Nicholas.'

'It is not your place to comfort my husband.'

Hella gives her a sullen look. 'And as such, he deserves obedience.'

Bianca considers slapping her. She decides against it, if only because she thinks it would be a shame to sully the pristine landscape with an act of violence.

'I know you think you owe Nicholas your life,' she says, trying to calm herself by slowing her speech, 'but it was I who wielded that bale-hook in Den Bosch, and don't you forget it. This has gone far enough.'

'I don't know what you mean,' Hella protests.

'Do you really think I don't know what you're about? I can see through you like the very cheapest Bankside drab.' Bianca forcibly turns the maid to look out across the shining water. 'Do you see those mountains? We have to cross those, if Nicholas and I are to reach Padua and you are to reach Rome. After all your mischief since Reims, I have tolerated your presence only because my husband is too much of a decent man to abandon you to the dangers of a solitary journey. If you want our continued protection, then you will make no further sport with him. If you do, I can promise you this: that dream Nicholas said he was having will come true – but the demon with the fiery trident will be me, and the one plunging off the summit to be ground into dust will be you. In Southwark they call me the one witch no one dares hang. So if it's to be a contest over whose enchantments are the more powerful, I can predict this with absolute certainty: you, Mistress, will be the loser.'

Her anger spent, Bianca lets go of Hella's sleeve. She steadies her breathing.

The maid rubs her arm where Bianca's fingers have driven into the flesh. Still gazing at the mountains across the lake, the sunlight turning the snow to gold, she says, with a studied compassion that turns Bianca stomach to ice: 'I understand why you're distraught, Mistress. But I am the last person you should blame... now that you are with child.'

22

Bankside, 10th August 1594

Ned Monkton sits in the stern of Giles Hunte's wherry, wringing his huge hands as though trying to rub a stain out of his flesh. The good weather has broken. Across the river, ragged grey clouds drift over the stunted spire of St Paul's church. He wonders if he should stop there first, to pray for God's guidance in what he knows he must do.

'Something amiss, Master Ned?' Hunte asks as he leans into his oars. 'You look ill at ease.'

What to tell him? Ned wonders. That I feel guilty at having lied to Rose about where I'm going? Or that I fear what I may do when I get there?

So Ned just grunts and, as Hunte knows – if only from what he's heard, rather than from personal experience – if Ned Monkton grunts when you ask him a question, don't press him for an answer.

As the wherry makes its way across the river, Ned thinks of how much he owes to the man whose future he is on his way to protect. When he considers his former life, spent in the mortuary for the deserving poor at St Tom's, with only the dead and the bottle for company, an angry demon that most decent folk feared to be around, he knows that were it not for Nicholas Shelby he would still be wrapping those corpses in their winding sheets, bundling them into the single reuseable coffin that served as their means of transport between the mortuary and the graveside, and unceremoniously tipping them out into the waiting earth. As a consequence, he is loyal beyond measure to his friend. He would kill for him. *Has* killed for him, though only in defence of Nicholas's own life. And one way or the other – regardless of what he has promised Rose – he is determined to make Fulke Vaesy publicly confess his treacherous slanders.

Bidding curt thanks to Hunte at the water-stairs and walking – briskly for such a large man – up St Andrew's Hill, Ned is not surprised when Ditworth refuses him entry to Vaesy's house.

'Go away. I shall call the constable,' the servant says, staring in terror at him from behind the little grille. 'You've no cause to be troubling a gentleman of Sir Fulke's station.'

'But he's not a gentleman, is he?' rumbles Ned, peering in like an ogre in a story told to frighten children. 'An' you an' I both know he treats you no better than a ship's master may treat a blackamoor.'

'I *can't* open the door,' says Ditworth wretchedly. 'Sir Fulke will make free with his cane, and I may not leave him 'cause I'm indentured.'

'Then I'll sit outside his door for as long as it takes to scare away those last few clod-pates who've yet to see 'im for the charlatan he is. How will he feed his indentured servant then, Master Ditworth? Do you want to starve with him? Go, tell him that.'

A short while later, Ned is standing in Vaesy's study. The once-great anatomist eyes him warily.

'I thought I'd seen the last of you,' he says, his patrician face showing no sign of fear.

'You would 'ave – if you'd done what I asked the last time I was here: recant your charge 'gainst Dr Shelby.'

'And do you really believe I'm going to do that now, just because you've barged into my home like the worst sort of Bankside house-diver?'

Ned can feel the old rage rising in him. He tries to calm it by imagining his Rose a few months in the future, their newborn infant at her generous breast. 'I told your fellow, Ditworth, that I would sit outside your door for as long as it took to scare away every patient you still 'ave,' he says. 'Look at me, Vaesy. Do you really believe they'll chance it with someone of my size? You'll be trying to trap the local cats inside a week. When they've gone, you'll either 'ave to eat poor Ditworth or throw yourself on church charity – you, a knight of the realm.'

'Linger on my doorstep and I'll have you taken up for a vagrant.'

'I'll come back.'

'Then I'll raise a suit against you.'

'You 'aven't the money.'

Vaesy stares at him uncomprehendingly. 'Why is this so important to a common rogue like you?'

'Because Dr Shelby turned me from a common rogue into a man who knows 'is right from wrong. Unlike some *gentlemen* I could name.' Ned tries to make himself smaller, less threatening. 'Look,' he says, gentling his great voice, 'there is a course that could serve us both.'

'And what is that?'

'Write the letter an' sign it. But put in something about you hearing the accusation from some other fellow, who mistook Dr Shelby for a different man entirely. A simple mistake. You was only doing what you thought at the time was your duty. The Privy Council can't blame you for that, can they? That way Master Nicholas is cleared, an' you get to look like an honourable man with a conscience.'

Vaesy comes round his desk. He moves stiffly, as though even the air he walks through is an adversary. Looking down on him, Ned can see just how threadbare he looks, his once-smart doublet patched and poorly washed. One of the ribbons around the knees of his hose has a tear in it. His severe face is deeply lined, the eyes tired. But there is still defiance in them, and the bitter anger of a once-powerful man reduced to an insignificant shadow.

'Why should I consider, for so long as a single breath, doing what you demand?' he asks.

'Because it's better than losing even the little that remains. There can't be many fools left in London still willing to shell out for your quackery, Vaesy. But there'll be none at all once the word gets around that you've an enemy like me haunting your doorstep. An' on the chance there is still a clod-pate or two sick enough – foolish enough – to call on you for physic in their time of need, well, you won't be able to visit their sickbed, will you? Especially when it's dark.'

'What do you mean?'

'You claim to be a learned man. Work it out for yourself.'

'Are you threatening me with harm, Monkton? Me, a knight of the realm – a gentleman?'

'Let's just say the night-watch can't be everywhere at once.'

Vaesy sneers. 'If any harm comes to me, if my body is found slain, where do you think the magistrates will look for the culprit? Ditworth will lead them straight to the door of whatever hovel you hail from. Have you thought of that, you oversized cock-pimp?'

To his astonishment, Ned lets the insult wash over him. He imagines a terrible silence must be falling upon Southwark at this moment; if anyone there had dared to call him the husband of a whore, blood would be about to flow. Perhaps Rose is right, he thinks. Perhaps I really am a new Ned. He leans over Vaesy and whispers, in a very civil voice, 'There won't be a body, Sir Fulke. I'm a Banksider – I know where to put one into the river so as it never comes out again.'

For a moment Vaesy does nothing. He does not look up at Ned; and Rose, if she were here, would put his stillness down to the once-great anatomist finally accepting that he's been bested by the better man. Ned himself simply waits, not too sure what he will do if Vaesy calls his bluff.

Then Vaesy gives a very small sigh of resignation. He goes back to the desk, takes up a sheet of paper and a quill from the inkpot and begins to write. 'Who shall we call this fellow, the one who told me about Shelby?' he asks after he's written a few words.

'Call 'im what you like,' says Ned. 'Call 'im Tom-o-Bedlam. Call 'im nothing at all. Just so long as you write that you're sure now that he was talkin' about someone other than Dr Nicholas Shelby.'

Vaesy writes on. He signs with a flourish and hands Ned the sheet of paper.

Ned stares at the words. He lets his eyes run over them, back and forth in a random sweep. Though they mean nothing to him, he understands how crucial they are to Master Nicholas, and so he sees every stroke of the nib, the ink still gleaming, as a man dying of thirst might see the opening raindrops of a sudden and unexpected shower. He barely hears Vaesy give a sharp, contemptuous laugh.

'You can't read it, can you? You haven't the skill with letters.'

Ned looks down at Vaesy across the slope of the letter. Even now he doesn't take the bait. He turns surprisingly lightly on his heels and heads towards the door, calling over his shoulder, 'My Rose will tell me if you've played me false. In which case, I will see you again.'

Vaesy allows him three paces before he says coldly, 'You're as ignorant as a beast from the bear-garden, Monkton. You just dance tricks, to impress with your strength.'

Without breaking stride, Ned replies, 'An' I remember what Dr Shelby said about you not being able to tell an 'amstring from an 'ernia. Master Nicholas would be ten times the physician you are, even if he'd never studied medicine at all, Sir Fulke Vaesy.'

The 'sir' is delivered with as much thick sauce of contempt as Ned can ladle. He doesn't consider the effect it will have on Vaesy, because inside he is glowing with satisfaction. He's thinking there's no need to trouble Rose with reading the letter to ensure Vaesy hasn't gulled him – he can take it straight to Lord Lumley's town house on Woodroffe Lane for forwarding to the Privy Council. If Lumley is at Nonsuch, his London steward can authenticate it. With luck and a following wind, he could be back on Bankside within two hours. He pictures Rose's smile when he tells her what he's accomplished.

He is almost at the door when it opens of its own accord. Ned pauses, one hand out for the latch, the other holding tight to the letter that will bring Master Nicholas and Mistress Bianca back home. Ditworth is standing on the other side of the frame, his face full of relieved expectation that this huge intruder is on his way out, hopefully never to be seen again. He lets his hand fall from the latch, flattens himself against the wall in case Ned thinks he might try to stop him leaving.

And then his expression changes from meekness to one of astonished fear.

In the same instant Ned hears movement in the study behind him. He wonders if Vaesy has changed his mind and is about to try to snatch the letter from him. He turns, ready to flick the man away as easily as he might a persistent fly.

Vaesy is already halfway across the space between the desk and the spot where Ned is standing, and if Ned were a man given to philosophical contemplation, he would see that in those eyes the bitterness, the blame, the resentment at all the lowly, worthless fools who have helped topple his once-great edifice of self-importance have spilled over.

In their place is murderous revenge. In Vaesy's hand, a gleaming stiletto – the sort a rich and successful knight of the realm might wear at his belt in a happier life.

23

The Valais, Switzerland, 13th August 1594

They are climbing into the heavens. Bianca thinks there should be cherubs up here, blowing golden trumpets. If she raises her hand, she will surely touch God's fingers. Yet in all the hours they have been travelling the mountain tops seem not to have come one inch closer. Not that they can see them now, the darkening clouds have bitten off the peaks. Behind them, the ragged track curves away into the purple shadows of the valley. To look down makes her stomach lurch and her head spin. Down there, the chiming of steeple bells marks the hours with distant voices barely heard over the sighing of the wind. But up here time seems an inconsequential thing, humbled by the vast emptiness. Great hunks of grey stone jut fiercely on either side of the worn path, like the tumbled ruins of ancient temples smashed down by a spiteful god.

Nicholas has found three new mules to rent, from the village of Martigny. The animals must remain unnamed (no more a Cecil or an Essex, a Coke or a Popham) because levity belongs to the past. Laughter has no place amongst the mountains. A silent determination is required here. Besides, Nicholas is too aware of the tension between his wife and Hella Maas – still striding out a hundred yards ahead – to suggest anything so flippant as naming the mules.

What Bianca said to Hella when she dragged her outside that morning in Montreux is still unknown to him. She has resolutely refused to answer his questions. From watching her rule over the Jackdaw tavern on Bankside, he suspects it will have been blood-curdling. He admires that resolve in her – her determination to protect those she loves. He thinks that to be on the receiving end of it would be terrifying.

The last exchange between them on the matter occurred during a rest halt earlier in the day. While strange, matted beasts with curving horns watched them with disinterest from the crags, and Hella was picking mountain flowers some way off, Nicholas had said, out of the blue, 'That morning – when I was abed – I'm sure she meant nothing improper. It was sisterly, that's all. I think, underneath, she is frightened. She has no one else to turn to but us.'

Bianca had refused to meet his eye. Instead she had replied tautly, 'Why is it men can be so blind, even when the sun shines brightly?' Then she had turned away from him, to tell him she had no need of any answer he might think of making.

The chill between Bianca and Hella is now mirrored by the cold air of the mountains. For weeks they have been travelling under a hot sun, always grateful for a summer shower to wash the dust from their faces and refresh their parched throats. Now they could be back on Bankside in the chill of a late-autumn day. Nicholas is thankful that he took advice and purchased cloaks of coarsely woven kersey before leaving Montreux.

For Bianca, the low moaning of the wind is a permanent accompaniment to a voice she seems unable to banish from her head for longer than an hour or so. *I understand why you're distraught, Mistress. But I am the last person you should blame... now that you are with child.*

How can the maid possibly know? Is it another of the tricks she plays – nothing but a wild guess aimed at unsettling the mind? Bianca does not feel as though she is pregnant. She has been called upon enough times – to mix the distillations, syrups and tinctures that ease the travails that come with pregnancy – to know the signs. And even if Hella is correct, her longing for a child with Nicholas has somehow suddenly faltered. What manner of creature would it be, if it has been conjured by someone else's will, someone with a longing for death and judgement? The idea that Hella can influence her body fills Bianca with dread. She reminds herself that the maid is a fraud. She cannot allow herself to think otherwise. But when she glances at Hella driving herself ever onwards, the mountain chill is not the only thing that threatens to freeze her blood.

Bianca Merton is not alone in trying to read another's face at this moment. Because her Ned was born with a face to put the fear of God into his enemies – Rose sometimes likes to imagine that he popped out of the womb complete with his scowling, fiery complexion and bushy auburn beard – it has taken her a while to learn how to read its more complex emotions. But she is adept at it now, and she knows Ned is keeping something from her. Witness the way he changes the subject about what occurred between him and Sir Fulke Vaesy, when he went across the river without telling her and procured the treasured letter exonerating Master Nicholas.

Where, she wonders, is the joy in him now? Why isn't he dancing a happy measure at the prospect of Master Nicholas's and Mistress Bianca's return? Why did he sound so low-key when she finally prised out of him the few details he seemed prepared to vouchsafe to her? Yes, Vaesy had written the letter voluntarily. No, Ned hadn't forced the quill into his trembling hand after beating him half-senseless. The letter is obtained. It is what they needed. It has been passed to Lord Lumley for presentation to the Privy Council, and if they won't act upon it, then to the queen herself. There's little more to be said.

So why does he lie so still when he rolls over in their bed at night? Why does he wake in the small hours and pace their chamber like a caged bear when he thinks she's still asleep?

✳

Where the track levels a little, close to a tumbling stream that fills a black rockpool, Nicholas calls a halt. While Bianca wraps her cloak about her for warmth and seeks a little slumber on a bed of moss, Nicholas leads the mules to drink. He waits while they take their fill, staring tiredly into the mirror of the pool.

'Why are you letting her lead you somewhere you don't want to go?' Hella Maas's reflection says.

Torn from his musings, he turns to her. 'When have I said I did not wish to go to Padua?'

'You haven't. But I have sensed for some time that you are not sure in your heart it is truly what you want.'

'It is not my home; that, I confess. And Bianca fled it several years past. But I have always thought the day might come when she would wish to return. And why should I not follow her? She is my wife and, for the present, Padua is as safe for us as anywhere.'

'My sister Hannie thought Breda was safe. But I knew differently. I was warned. I should have spoken louder.'

'Are you trying to warn me that Padua is unsafe?'

'Nowhere is safe, Nicholas; Breda, Padua, this very spot...'

He gives a sad, compassionate shake of his head. 'You couldn't have known what was to happen in Breda, Hella. You are not to blame for what the Spanish did there, any more than these mountains are.'

In the mirror-glass of the pool, her face contorts into ugliness. 'But I am. I *knew*.'

'How?'

'Because I can read the signs. Remember, I was born when a new, bright star blazed in the night sky and men of learning scratched their heads in wonder at it. Many said it was a portent. And ever since I can remember, I have known when bad things were about to happen. I could see it in the fall of the numbers when my father played cards with my mother; in the harvests that failed; in the villages that emptied when the wool trade with England fell off; when the great winds came, when the rivers flooded, when the stars with long tails appeared in the sky. All these things are God's warnings to us. Why will some people not see what is so clearly visible?'

'If Padua is unsafe, Hella, then so is Rome. So is anywhere you choose to go. In which case, why did you come with us? Why not stay in Brabant?'

'You know why – because eventually they would have burned me as a sorceress. And because I wanted to be with *you*, Nicholas.'

He glances to where Bianca is sleeping on the moss, then back to Hella. A stab of alarm courses through him. 'Me? Why me?'

'Because we are the two poles of the same star. We have been in company a long time now, and I have heard you say how you mistrust the knowledge of medicine that you learned from ancient books and old professors – how it may harm as well as cure. I know you blame it for the death of your first wife and her child.'

Nicholas has to stop himself from shouting, lest he wakes Bianca. 'You're wrong! I seek *better* knowledge – knowledge that can be trusted to save lives. You believe only that it will end them. I am not the other pole on this meridian of death you have set around yourself, Hella. I want no part of it. Unlike you, I have no idea what the future will hold. I don't much care – just as long as it has Bianca in it.'

Hella's face is as cold as the mountains now, twisted half in fear, half in unbearable sorrow. 'But you saw what was coming, in the painting of the Day of Judgement. How can you deny it?'

'It was one man's imagination! It was nothing but a nightmare retold in paint and pigment.'

She grabs his arm. Nicholas almost gasps at the strength of her grip, at the alarming fervour in her eyes. 'Take me to Padua. When the endtime comes, I don't want to face it alone.'

Nicholas pulls away. 'Hella – go to Rome with the other pilgrims. You'll be safe there. If the Pope and all his cardinals can't give you peace, no one can.'

And then he is looking into the crumpled, tearful face of a small girl, the survivor of a slaughtered family, a child who's convinced herself that if she had tried, *really* tried, then she could perhaps have moved the world off its axis. She could have turned it, so that the day that brought her such pain had not dawned.

'Please let me tell you one more truth, Nicholas,' she says, fighting back the tears. 'About Bianca. Did you know she is preg—'

But he stops her dead, raising a hand as if to ward off a blow. 'No! Enough! I will hear no more of this.'

And he turns away, leaving Hella and her reflection in the rock-pool to the judgement of the mountains.

✠

Later, as darkness falls, they see ahead of them torches burning like beacons from the walls of the monastery of St Bernard, signalling to the exhausted pilgrim that safety lies just a short distance ahead. Set beside a lake of meltwater at the highest point on the pass, it seems to carry the cold solitude of the mountains in its stones. They are welcomed by an ancient Augustinian monk who appears to make no gesture, speak no word that is not glacial.

The mules are stabled; they will carry their riders no further. From here the journey will continue on foot. But at least it will be downhill.

Inside the hospice the furnishings have a competitive frugality: pious restraint set against rustic simplicity. Meals are taken communally: men in one room, women in another. The fare is plain and limited, but Nicholas hears no complaint. If a traveller reaches here and thinks he's had an easy journey, he's either in the grip of a religious delirium or he's been born without feeling in his legs.

The dormitories are austere, but weary bones take comfort where they can. There is no provision for married couples, so Nicholas and Bianca must sleep apart. Instead of the reassuring sound of her breathing, he must endure the murmured prayers of the other pilgrims, their echoing flatulence and the occasional agonized grunt as cramp bites stiffening muscles.

Matins is sung against the crashing of a violent summer storm. Lightning blazes in the darkness beyond the narrow windows of the dormitory. Nicholas shivers miserably under a thin blanket while he waits for sleep to claim him.

He is troubled by what Hella said to him earlier. No matter how often he reminds himself of what Bianca believes – that she's driven by the need to provoke, that her wild claims of precognition are nothing but the sleights of the street-trickster – he cannot now help but wonder if her performance by the rockpool really was just a masque. Could it be that there was truth in it? Occasionally he laughs at himself, the believer in the methods of the new learning losing his critical faculties to a young maid's play-acting. But whether she can see the future or is merely deluding herself, in his heart Nicholas feels a deep sadness at the damage fate has inflicted on her, robbing her of even the slightest warmth of hope.

Alone in her own darkness, Bianca lies awake and thinks of Hella's unfathomable face caught in the lightning flash of another storm, and wonders if she is now – finally – rid of her malign influence.

✠

The monks rise before dawn. The stillness is oppressive after the thunder of the night. It is broken only by the murmur of prayer. Nicholas takes a plain breakfast of bread and water, the liquid like cold fire on his tongue. He sits apart from the other pilgrims, the only Englishman present. They are an unremarkable crew. Some have faces made rosy by a surfeit of holy fervour, others scowl with the intensity of the overtly pious or the thought of how many leagues remain between the mountains and St Peter's in Rome. He would pay them little heed – were it not for one of their number who draws his attention like a beacon blazing on a dark shore.

Alone, he sits stooped at his bench while he chews his bread, head lowered, his face almost hidden by his steepled hands. He wears a grey half-coat. His legs, clad in trunk-hose, fold back under the bench, the toes of his leather half-boots flexed against the flagstones as though ready for flight at the first sign of danger. And on his head is a floppy black cap that almost covers his ears. All in all – though a little dustier, a little wearier in the face – a man almost unchanged from the morning he stepped out in front of Hella Maas in the cathedral square at Reims, one hundred leagues and almost as many years ago.

24

The storm during the night has left the mountains so sharp that just looking at them pricks the eyes. From the hospice of St Bernard, the path descends in giddying coils like a serpent basking in the morning sunshine, down towards the valley of Aosta. From the flat ground beside the lake, Nicholas watches a group of pilgrims moving amongst the scree, making their way into Italy.

'I must hurry if I am to catch them,' Hella says. 'You have been kind. I would have died in Den Bosch, had you not saved me.' She turns to Bianca. 'I am sorry if neither of you wanted to hear what I have say. I do not seek these revelations that come to me. I mean only to tell the truth of what I know.'

Bianca, who has informed her husband that the maid has decided to attach herself to the group in the distance rather than wait until they reach Pavia and the road to Rome, affects an expression that says, *It's not my doing, if that's what you think.*

Nicholas says, 'Before you leave us, will you answer me one question? There was a man sheltering here last night. A man wearing a grey coat, black cap. Tall and thin, a little younger than I am. Did you see him, perhaps?'

The look Hella gives him is as empty as the surrounding mountains, and as icy. 'I was in the women's dormitory. How could I have seen *any* man, let alone the one you describe.'

'Are you sure? Only I thought I had seen him before – in the cathedral square at Reims. I thought I saw him speak to you then.'

But it seems that Hella's ability to see what others do not see fails to extend to young men in grey coats and black caps. 'I'm sorry, but you must be mistaken,' she says. 'I saw no such man here, and I know of no one in Reims. I cannot help you.'

And, with that, she hoists her pack across her shoulder and sets off after the pilgrims, as though she and Nicholas had met barely a moment ago, and the long days spent treading the dusty miles from Den Bosch live only in his imagination.

✳

'I really cannot tell whether she was lying or not,' Nicholas says as he extends a hand to help Bianca cross a little stone bridge over a tumbling stream. Below them a tiny cluster of stone houses lies cupped in a valley close to the border with Italy. The hills are clad with pine, bearding the mountains with a dense green. But in the open the going is soft and grassy. He is warm again, after the night spent in the pass.

'Why did you not tell me about this man when we were in Reims?' Bianca asks.

'I wasn't sure I'd seen anything other than a chance encounter. They were face-to-face only briefly.'

'Perhaps he thought – mistakenly – that Hella was someone he knew,' Bianca says.

'That is what I told myself. But there is another possibility, of course.'

'Which is?'

'That it's us he's following, not her.'

'You think he might be a Privy Council man? One of Essex's, maybe?'

'We may have laughed at them when we gave their names to our mules, but they have their people in all the major cities.'

He watches a single buzzard launch itself from a high crag and go sweeping above the trees down the valley in search of prey. 'Especially in Catholic ones like Reims.'

'You think he might have stopped Hella to ask her where we were staying?'

'Perhaps. If so, she doesn't remember him – if she's telling us the truth.'

'But if you're right, how did he know who we were? How did he know he was supposed to follow us?'

'Remember when the searchers arrived at Woodbridge?'

'Of course. I could hardly forget.'

'I had to show Robert Cecil's letter of safe-passage to stop them going through your bag and finding your Petrine cross. They could have reported to the Privy Council that we'd been spotted leaving on a vessel for Den Bosch.'

'Do you think he's been following us all the way from Brabant?'

'Again, perhaps.'

Bianca looks unconvinced. 'But we were in Den Bosch only a few days. He couldn't possibly have received a command to follow us in such a short time.'

'I know the Privy Council is a ponderous beast,' Nicholas says. 'It takes them weeks to agree whose signatures to place at the foot of a sentence of execution. But not Essex. Essex is a man of hot temper and swift action. With a fast rider and a speedy ship, he could have sent the order quickly enough.'

Bianca scoffs. 'But we were in Den Bosch, not Antwerp. Even Robert Devereux cannot have spies *everywhere*.' A thought occurs to her. 'Why didn't you simply ask this fellow to his face, when you saw him?'

'I wanted to speak to Hella first, lest I was jumping to a false conclusion.'

'Where is he now?'

'I don't know. After he'd taken breakfast, I tried to follow him, but I was stopped by two of the monks. By the time I'd worked out travellers aren't allowed in that part of the hospice, he'd vanished.'

'I think you're making too much of this, Nicholas,' Bianca says, giving him a smile of reassurance. 'He's probably just an innocent pilgrim. But if we see him again, I'll stand in his way and say, "Why are you following my husband, you saucy rogue? Away with you, or I shall fetch Hella Maas back, to drive you mad with her pious warnings of the apocalypse."'

It does Nicholas good to hear his wife laugh again. With the maid gone, a weight seems to have been lifted from her shoulders.

'Tell me – now that she is safely gone away – what caused the coldness between you? Surely you must know that nothing happened between us that morning in Besançon.'

For the briefest instant Bianca's smile falters. Then it strengthens again, which Nicholas puts down to their closeness to Italy.

'It is of no matter, Nicholas. She's gone. Let any enmity I felt go with her.'

But inside Bianca is thinking again of the words Hella had spoken on the lakeside at Montreux: *I am the last person you should blame... now that you are with child.* Angrily she imagines herself stamping on the words, crushing them underfoot. Words are nothing, she tells herself. A few words in French do not prove fluency in five languages. Simple tricks with numbers do not make a person a mathematician. Naming a few stars in the night sky does not prove the ability to discourse on the merits of Master Copernicus's model of the heavens. And telling me I am pregnant does not make it so.

And yet...

And yet.

Below them the bell tower in the village of Saint-Rhémy signals the way down into the fold of the valley and the track on into

Italy. As Bianca walks beside her husband she cannot escape the alternative possibility: that Hella Maas was speaking the truth.

That Hella Maas *can* do all these things, and more.

That Bianca *is* pregnant.

That there will be a death.

Echoing between the granite peaks, the sudden ringing of the Saint-Rhémy bell sends a jolt through her body. And in its wake come more of the maid's words, as though all it was ever going to take to breach the dam was this single, sudden shock: *It will break his heart when the child you are carrying is stillborn... How much of a disappointment will you be to him – barren after a stillbirth?*

✠

The mist hangs in the valley of the Po like a pale banner discarded after a saint's day parade. It hugs the hem of Pavia's city walls, lies as still as death on the surface of the Fossa Bastioni that guards the western gate. In the calm morning air the smoke rising from countless chimneys looks like pale strings suspending the city from a crystalline heaven. Almost a week has passed since they left the mountains, and Bianca and Nicholas are footsore and hungry. But before they seek out somewhere to breakfast, there is first a task Bianca has been anticipating with growing pleasure. She finds a scrivener's shop near the Porta Santa Croce. The message she writes there with a borrowed quill is brief:

> *Most beloved cousin, we are in Pavia. God willing, we shall rest in Padua by the end of August. We come by way of Verona, and each step fills me with a greater joy at the prospect of our meeting again.*
>
> *May God's kindness and mercy carry these words to you on joyous wings.*
>
> *Your cousin,*
> *Bianca*

And having paid the scrivener to seal the letter with wax, she drags Nicholas off in search of one of the many couriers, official and mercantile, whose sweating mounts speed so imperiously between the cities of *La Serenissima*.

✠

On Bankside, serenity is in scant supply. The River Thames lies beneath a sullen sky like a trail of melted pewter after a fire. A penetrating drizzle falls on Southwark, more appropriate to a grey January than late August. And while Bianca entrusts her letter to a messenger, Rose Monkton is answering a sudden, imperious hammering on the door of the Paris Garden lodgings. She finds Constable Hobbes on the step, flanked by two of the Bankside watch, their leather jerkins black with rainwater and their official cudgels dripping like driftwood lifted from the riverbank after the tide's gone out. It is a sight that at any other time would make her laugh out loud. Today, however, she knows intuitively that all her unspoken fears have been realized.

'I pray you, Mistress Rose, counsel your Ned to come peacefully and without anger,' Hobbes says, not entirely confidently. He is still somewhat new to his role, his predecessor having succumbed to the plague that stalked Bankside last year.

'What am I charged with, Constable Hobbes?' Ned asks from behind Rose's shoulder. 'A fellow should know what manner of felony he's being accused of. That's the law, ain't it?'

Ned says this without the slightest animosity, as though he has long been preparing himself for this moment. Rose turns and stares at him in horror.

'Manslaughter, Master Ned,' says Constable Hobbes. 'I am informed by the coroner that Sir Fulke Vaesy died of his injuries last night around nine of the clock, in his bed, following an assault occasioned by you some days ago. You are to be taken to the Marshalsea for examination by the justices, in preparation for arraignment.'

Rose seizes her husband's hands, pulling them towards her as she might tug two large joints of meat across a table. She kisses the knuckles frantically.

'Oh, 'Uusband, what *'ave* you done?' she manages through her tears. 'My dear, dear, foolish Ned.'

He bends down and brushes his lips across the crown of her head. 'I did not murther 'im, Wife. It were not done maliciously, I swear it. 'Twas an accident.'

She looks up at him pleadingly, while Constable Hobbes fidgets uncomfortably in the drizzle. 'Did you not think of this child of ours that I carry in my belly?'

'At every moment on the journey there; through every word of insult that Vaesy threw at me while he wrote down his admission of guilt.'

'And then the old Ned came back to claim you?'

He smiles, his great ruddy face infused with more gentleness than she has ever seen in him. 'When I 'ad the letter from 'im exonerating Master Nicholas, I went to turn my back to leave. He drew a blade. I took it off 'im – pushed 'im away. He went down, struck his head upon the desk.' Ned slaps the back of one huge hand into the palm of the other, causing Constable Hobbes to wince. 'If I am guilty of anything,' Ned continues, 'it's that for a moment, hearin' 'e's dead, I was glad.'

Rose turns to the dripping constable. 'There, Master Hobbes – you see. My 'usband is an innocent man.'

'But he must still come with us to the Marshalsea, Mistress Rose, to answer for the death,' Hobbes says regretfully.

And so Rose Monkton stands in the doorway and watches her husband go, unresisting, a giant figure flanked by the two watchmen and led by Hobbes. She has the image in her mind of a tired old bear being led to a baiting. As the grey drizzle takes him from her, he turns and calls out, 'Do not fret for me, Wife. The servant, Ditworth, will confirm what I say. He was there. He saw it with 'is own eyes. You 'ave no need to fear for me. No need whatever.'

PART 3

The Mathematician

25

Padua, 29th August 1594

The last two days of their long journey have taken them over the vine-clad Berici hills. Sheltering from the sun in the shade of the willows that line the path along the edge of Lake Fimon, they have watched pike and eel slumber in the torpid water. In sight of the hazy, towering Monte Venda, they have marvelled at the fine villas of wealthy Paduans nestling amongst stands of poplars and groves of olive trees, and passed vineyards so bountiful that the gnarled old vines seemed almost too weak to stop the grapes from flying off like plump purple fledglings. Long before she reaches the walls of Padua, Bianca Merton has all but discarded the years she has been away. She leaves the memory of them lying in her footsteps like sloughed-off snakeskin.

She stops beside a little roadside shrine, barely a hundred paces from a moat filled with brackish brown water. On the other side of a stone bridge, the path runs on beneath an imposing square gateway set into the modern brick ramparts. She kisses her fingertips, then touches them to the feet of the crude plaster effigy of the saint, giving thanks for having arrived safely. Today, she recalls, is the Feast of the martyrdom of St John the Baptist. It is sixty-seven days since they left Bankside.

Nicholas leaves her to sit alone by the roadside in contemplation. Sometimes, he notices, she rests her head on her knees, deep in thought. At other times she watches the traffic passing through the Porta Liviana. She does so wistfully, as though she is still an exile viewing the scene only in her imagination. Once or twice she draws the back of one wrist across her eyes, mumbling something about the sun being too bright. At last, when the emotions have quietened in her, Bianca climbs to her feet, goes over to where Nicholas is guarding their bags and says, almost inaudibly, 'Come, it is time.'

Nicholas has lost count of the city walls he has passed through since leaving London, but these are amongst the strongest he has yet seen: modern sloping defences designed by clever military architects to provide enfilade fire from matchlock and crossbow, and to withstand bombardment by stone and iron shot. He is glad of a brief moment of shade as they enter the city through the Porta Liviana. The archway smells of manure and human sweat. It echoes to the sound of haggling, bargaining, complaining and petulant denial, as the traffic passing in and out collides with the two soldiers trying – and failing miserably – to keep an orderly flow.

Once inside the walls, Bianca leads him through pleasant open gardens where smart houses with tiled roofs stand, and to another moat and an older set of high walls encircling the heart of the city. Only when he is through this last barrier does Bianca's birthplace truly show itself to him. At its core, it is little different from the denser parts of London: narrow lanes that seem to lead nowhere, revealing only at the last moment an escape to left or right; cut-throughs and angles that rob him of any sense of progress; dark colonnades with benches piled high with fruit and meat, which attract more flies than customers in the heat; piles of decaying vegetables and cow dung; open sewers that are the last resting places of drowned cats. If it were not for the heat and the din of voices calling out in Italian, Nicholas thinks he could be back on Bankside.

And then they emerge into a wide sunlit square that is anything but Bankside. Beneath the elegant façades, and in shady colonnades, brightly dressed citizens shop at well-stocked stalls and young men in vibrant hose and vivid capes play thrust and parry with their eyes, with maids in full-sleeved gowns. The glances they exchange are as sharp as any of the rapiers carried at such jaunty angles from the belts of the gallants, or the hairpins keeping dark tresses in place. Nicholas is captivated. He understands now where Bianca imbibed her spirit.

Stopping at a pastel-washed corner house of three storeys pierced by narrow shuttered windows, Bianca puts down her bags and bangs twice with her fist on the double door. A moment later there is the rasp of a bolt being slid back, and a thin, dark face peers through the gap in the cautiously opened doors. It takes in the couple standing expectantly in the lane and disappears again.

'If I know Bruno, he's sent his servant to make sure I'm not a creditor,' Bianca says with a laugh.

And as if to prove her right, the twin doors fly open and there he is: all five feet three of him, clad in a fine black jerkin and red-and-white striped hose, his dark curls almost as full and as long as Rose Monkton's: her little cockerel of a cousin, Bruno Barrani.

Nicholas observes the explosion of delight with a smile. First Bruno seizes Bianca by the waist and dances a violent *volta* with her, round and round, lifting her off her feet so that his eyes are at a level with the bottom of her laced blouse. She towers over his head, squealing with happiness, like a little girl being tossed over a father's shoulders. People in the lane stop and smile.

'My cousin!' he tells them. 'Safely returned to us from the clutches of the heretic English!'

Setting her on her feet once more, he grasps Nicholas's arms and reverts to English. 'My new brother!' he exclaims. 'If only I had enough to give you a proper dowry.'

'A dowry?' Nicholas replies.

'I am cousin Bianca's only living male relative. It is up to me to provide a dowry for her new husband.'

'That really won't be necessary.'

Bruno looks relieved. 'But one day – soon – Barrani will make you a grand dowry. Enough to buy you a nice house in South-walk.' He steps back and bends his head, showing Nicholas the crown. He parts his curls to reveal a line of scalp. 'You see? Very good heal. Fortunately there are no bald Barranis. Not even the women.' He is showing the scar of the wound that – three years ago, on Bankside – almost killed him. 'If it was not for your English physic, there would be no Bruno Barrani any more, and the doge in Venice would be a man of no repute.'

Bianca looks at him askance. 'The doge? In Venice? What does his reputation have to do with the healing Nicholas gave you on Bankside?'

Bruno pulls himself up to the limit of his modest height and puffs out his chest. 'Everything – because had I not lived, His Serene Highnesses would have been unable to appoint a Master of the Spheres.'

Bianca throws back her head and closes her eyes. On her mouth is an expression that is half-admiration and half-exasperation. 'Oh, Bruno!' she says, laughter in her voice. 'What wild scheme are you embarked upon now? Wasn't trying to sell Lombardy rice to the English enough to make you see reason and get a proper job?'

For the next two days Nicholas and Bianca take their rest as best they can in Bruno's house in the Borgo dei Argentieri. It is a fitful rest, interspersed with the urge to be up and about. Luca and Alonso hover like damselflies, ever attentive to their needs – especially Bianca's. As for her cousin, he has always brimmed with a confidence that no commercial disappointment has yet dented. Now Bruno seems borne on a wave of almost delirious expectation.

'And the doge is paying for all this?' Bianca asks him when he has given her and Nicholas an account of his visit to Florence and the progress of the grand project of the *Arte dei Astronomi*.

'By the cartload. But it will be the fame and renown attached to the device itself that will make the doge's Master of the Spheres his fortune. The name of Barrani will be known throughout the civilized world. Even in England they will know of me.' He grins at Nicholas. 'Perhaps your heretic queen will invite me to construct one in her palace. The English must have need of a machine to tell them where the constellations will be at any given time – as the skies are always cloudy.'

'But what *exactly* is it for?' Bianca asks.

Bruno contrives a scholarly look. 'Well, it turns... and the wheels and the ellipses and the meridians all move within it – to show when the solstices and the planets...' He wrangles his hands together, the fingers like entwining snakes, to describe what his vocabulary cannot.

'You don't *really* know, do you?' Bianca says with a sigh for the litany of Cousin Bruno's doomed commercial enterprises.

'It's an armillary sphere,' Nicholas says. 'I've seen small ones, when I was at Cambridge. Robert Cecil has one. They show how the heavens move with time. They're much used in the sciences of astronomy and astrology. But I've never heard of one as large or as complex as this one by Master Santucci.'

Bruno snorts an explosive sneer. 'Santucci is a dunderhead! He's a Florentine. I wouldn't trust him to make me a climbing frame for my *fagioli*.'

'But how are you building it, Bruno? You're a man of commerce, not of science,' Bianca points out.

If Bruno is hurt by the implication behind her question, he doesn't show it. 'A great admiral does not climb the mast to set the sail, does he, Cousin?' he says haughtily. 'I have gathered the best men in Padua to assist. My friend, Signor Galileo, is the professor of mathematics at the Palazzo Bo. His student, young Matteo, is making the calculations under his wise and guiding hand. As for the construction, the *Arte dei Astronomi* is already at work. I will show you, tomorrow.'

'But how did you get the plans?' Nicholas asks.

Bruno shrugs and adopts an air of total innocence. 'Let us say they blew off the back of a cart – with the help of a little wind fanned by a few of His Serenity's ducats.'

'But if it's for the doge, why build it in Padua?' Bianca asks.

'Because Signor Galileo is in Padua,' Bruno says, as if even a child would know the answer to her question. 'When it is complete and working, and he is satisfied that it is performing its calculations as it should, we will dismantle it, take it to Venice and reassemble it in the Sala dello Scrutinio. His Serene Highness will then be able to gather his ministers and the citizens about his Serene personage in St Mark's Square, hoist his golden mantle around his Serene waist, bend over and expose his Serene arse in the general direction of Florence and Duke Ferdinando de' Medici. And your cousin Bruno will be there to enjoy the spectacle and watch the ducats flow in.'

'Can he do it? Is it truly possible?' Bianca asks Nicholas that night as they lie abed, bathed in sweat from the oppressive heat, a wash of stars glittering in the ink-black sky above.

'We have never doubted that Cousin Bruno is a man of great determination. And there is no question that Venice would have her reputation much enhanced by the possession of such a machine.'

'But is it even possible to make a device that mirrors the motion of the cosmos?'

'The Florentine seems to have achieved it. And if this professor of mathematics at Padua University is even half as good as the professor of anatomy – Fabricius – then he'll be a man of rare ability. Fabricius is known even amongst medical men in England. I hope to meet them both. I could learn a lot while we're here.'

In the darkness, Bianca frowns. 'I'm worried Bruno has let his flights of fancy run wild. Padua may like to show herself as a city open to new learning, but the Inquisition still exercises much power in the Republic. Free thought is tolerated only so far. Look what happened to my father: he died in a cell here for his ideas and his writings. Do you not recall what my cousin wrote in his last letter to me?'

'About the friar, Giordano Bruno?'

'Arrested when he went to Venice, to speak upon his revolutionary theories. He thought he was safe in the Veneto. But he wasn't. Now he's in Rome, on trial for heresy. I don't want that to happen to my Bruno.'

'The sphere itself is not heretical – not if it conforms to the Church's teachings on the movement of the cosmos,' Nicholas says. 'But judging from the way your cities are fortified against each other, I'd be more worried about Florence sending some rogues here to threaten Bruno or smash the engine to pieces.'

Bianca throws back the single sheet and rolls over, spreading her gleaming limbs in an effort to cool herself. She glances out of the window at the pale rooftops of Padua, then back at her husband.

'Enough of this disagreeable talk. I am more interested in the movement of my own cosmos,' she says.

'It's very hot,' he replies.

'Perhaps. But being an academic man, are you not inclined upon some interesting discovery of your own? You never know what you might find.'

Nicholas props himself on one elbow. He feels a cold rivulet of sweat run down his upper arm and pool in the fold of his elbow. With a husky catch in his voice, he replies, 'Mistress Merton, in the quest for the new learning there is no avenue a man intent on diligent study should be reluctant to explore.'

26

Rose Monkton feels her stomach heave. The smell assaults her nostrils and makes her plump, happy face contort in disgust. She stops in her tracks at the foot of the steps and clutches at her black ringlets, pushing them over her nose and mouth even as she hears the gaoler laugh behind her.

Though Bianca Merton might call her 'Mistress Moonbeam', and newcomers to the Jackdaw – before it burned down – think her not entirely anchored to the practical, and though she might look as if she's just come in from milking cows or gathering fruit in some idyllic pastoral setting, Rose has endured a hard schooling. She grew up in a stew behind the Mutton Lane shambles. The sound she most recalls from her childhood is not the singing of the lark, but the scream of cattle having their throats cut. It takes a lot to make her knees go weak. But the common durance – the public dungeon – of the Marshalsea prison tests her fortitude to the limit.

It is almost too dark to see, which in itself is a mercy, even though it isn't noon yet. The stone stairs she's descended were not reached by a door, but by an iron grille set into the floor. What light there is down here shows a vaulted ceiling too low for a man of moderate height to stand with his head straight, and Ned – she is already casting her gaze around to spot him – is a head taller than most.

Her nose twitches as it objects to the pervading stink of piss-soaked straw, human excrement, sweat and despair. A rat the size of a large hedgehog scurries past her feet, leaving Rose to think she would almost certainly swear on her Bible that it looked up at her and thumbed its nose as it went by. Summoning all her willpower, she steps out into the cellar.

As she skirts the brick pillars holding up the ceiling she expects a cacophony of ribald comments from the men lying or sitting in the straw, but they all seem too weary, too downcast, even to turn their heads. Rose is not used to being invisible amongst male company. She worries that when she finds Ned, he will stare through her as if she wasn't there, as if she was a ghost.

To her immense relief, it doesn't take her long to locate him. She spots what she imagines to be a bear surrounded by its cubs, and realizes the smaller, weaker prisoners have gathered themselves around Ned for protection from the habitual predators of this awful realm.

He tries to get up, but the ankle-irons he is wearing make it difficult. Rose finds the courage to look at where they encircle his limbs, praying the metal hasn't bitten into the flesh too deeply; in the short time it has taken to reach him she's seen ankles bloodied and brimming with pus. To her relief, his skin is unbroken.

'How now, Wife?' he says cheerfully. 'Close your eyes, an' it smells no worse than the Tabard or the Turk's Head after the Midsummer Fair.'

But Rose cannot laugh with him. She would sooner cry for his bravery.

'This is beyond all enduring, 'Usband,' she says. 'I'm going straightway to see the warden.'

He frowns. 'I'll not 'ave you giving of yourself to another, just so as I can 'ave a mattress to sleep upon. Think of the baby...'

Rose puts her hands firmly on the hips of her farthingale. 'I mean to offer him coin, you great clod-pate – not my body! To get you a better cell.'

'Oh. Well, that's alright,' he says. A troubling afterthought shadows its way across his face. ''Cept we don't 'ave coin to spare. I'll not 'ave Rose Monkton go without. I've slept in worse places than this, I can tell you.'

She presumes he means the years he spent working in the mortuary crypt at St Tom's.

'That's as maybe,' she tells him sternly. 'But no husband of mine is going to walk into the lodgings Mistress Bianca loaned us as a free man, if he's smelling like he's been stood under a window while someone emptied a full piss-pot over his 'ead.'

Ned looks downcast. 'Is it that bad?'

She avoids a direct answer. 'I shall take just a little of the purse she left us for the work on the Jackdaw. Not much, mind – only what's needed to get you out of here. Mistress Bianca wouldn't begrudge it for a moment, I know she wouldn't.'

'I wonder where they are,' Ned says, looking around the durance as though he expects to find them hiding behind one of the brick columns.

Again Rose does not answer him. But she dearly wishes Nicholas and Bianca were both back here in Southwark, because frankly the thought of having to face what is approaching her husband fills her with a dread worse than anything the Marshalsea can conjure up, no matter how innocent she knows him to be.

✠

The ranks of the *Arte dei Astronomi* have swelled by two. Nicholas is now the guild's honorary physician. He will be called upon, should any member accidentally trap a finger in his pliers, skewer himself with his burin or inadvertently hammer his knuckles flat on an anvil. Bianca is the *padrona di rimedi*, in charge of mixing what Nicholas prescribes. Hers is a wholly invented position, as a woman is not customarily permitted to hold office in a city guild. Nor, Bruno explains in his most apologetic manner, will she be allowed to march with the *Arte* through the city streets on the Feast of the Holy Rosary in October.

'I had the same trouble with the Grocers' Guild in London,' she sighs, 'when I told them I wanted to practise as an apothecary.'

Nicholas asks to borrow paper, quill, ink and a pounce-pot. He writes a brief note to Robert Cecil, encoding it with the cipher the two men employ for Nicholas's work as Cecil's intelligencer. In it, he informs Lord Burghley's son that he is in Padua and can be reached at the home of Signor Bruno Barrani, merchant of that city. Then he entrusts the letter to Bruno and the network of merchants and go-betweens he used for his correspondence with Bianca when she was living on Bankside. Nicholas knows it will take weeks – if not months – for the letter to arrive in London. When he might expect a reply, and whether it will tell him it is safe to come home, is anyone's guess.

On a cloyingly hot Monday afternoon in the first week in September, he and Bianca are introduced to the other luminaries in Bruno Barrani's bright new cosmos. In a little shop near the Torlonga tower they meet the angular Mirandola, whose spindly limbs seem almost an extension of the rods and bars that make up the skeletal frames of his clock mechanisms. He is supervising an assistant at the little furnace in the back of the shop when they walk in. With a pair of tongs, he proudly holds up what looks like a still-glowing crown with saw-teeth along one rim. 'A better balance wheel than this you'll not find in all Italy,' he tells Bruno as he hands the tongs back to his apprentice. 'I don't suppose there's any sign of His Serenity's coin yet? You still have not paid me for the three foliot balances I made.'

'All in good time, Master Mirandola,' Bruno says engagingly. 'There'll be ducats and glory soon enough. Now, meet my cousin Bianca and the brave Englishman who has consented to be her husband.'

From Mirandola's shop they move on to visit Pasolini the carpenter. He is a sullen chap of forty with only one eye. 'Have you brought me any of the doge's gold yet?' he asks Bruno.

'Patience, I beg you, Signor Pasolini,' Bruno says. 'Meanwhile, we'd ask you kindly to put curves in only where they are signified in young Matteo's drawings.'

Next on Bruno's list are the Corio brothers, whose foundry lies in the Borgo Socco. They are friendly enough, but Bianca comes away with her ears singing from the noise of hammers ringing on anvils and the roaring of bellows – and the older Corio brother's voice shouting above the din, 'Where's our money, Signor Barrani?'

At the premises of Bondoni the goldsmith they meet a jovial old fellow in bright-yellow Venetian hose, his plump arms defiantly white despite the Veneto sun, and his face speckled with gilt dust as though he were a satyr in a masque. 'Are we going to get paid before the Feast of the Holy Rosary, Signor Barrani?' he asks with almost indecent haste, once the introductions have been made.

'When are we to see the sphere itself?' Nicholas asks when they leave.

'Soon enough,' says Bruno. 'We've only the lower part of the cradle constructed as yet. And even then, we have to keep sending back Signor Pasolini's work for his apprentice to put the correct bend in it.'

'Where are we going next?' Bianca asks as they cross an elegant Roman bridge over the hide-coloured waters of the Piovego canal.

'I have saved the best until last,' Bruno says proudly, 'for your husband's sake.'

✠

The house in the Borgo dei Vignali is much like any other in the street: a four-storey façade of stucco, the entrance set back a little within a pillared arcade. When Bruno raps on the door, the answering shout comes not from inside but from above. This requires him to retreat into the lane, to where Nicholas and Bianca are waiting. He cranes his neck towards one of the windows on the third floor.

Leaning out in search of the source of the disturbance are two figures, a man and a woman. Both appear to be naked. The male has a stocky, hirsute torso, topped with the bearded face of a country taverner.

'What do you want, Signor Purse?' the man shouts.

'Busy, Master Compass?' says Bruno doubtfully.

'University business. I'm instructing Signorina Storzzi in the acceleration of an object on an inclined plane. Can you come back in... let's say... October?'

'Isn't he going to ask you for money?' Bianca whispers into her cousin's ear.

'Don't worry. He will,' Bruno replies.

'Who's the pretty maid with you?' Professor Galileo Galilei calls down from the window.

'My cousin, Bianca Merton.'

'I don't suppose she's interested in mathematics lessons?'

'She's married – to this fine gentleman here. He's an English physician.'

Nicholas is looking up at a heavy-featured man about his own age, with dark, receding hair and dissolute brown eyes. He wears an expression of put-upon good humour. 'Surely that's not *him* – the professor of mathematics?' he asks Bianca out of the corner of his mouth.

'It would seem so,' she says, trying to maintain a straight face. 'He's not at all what I expected. I hope Bruno knows what he's about.'

'I thought for a moment we were back on Bankside.'

'Don't be foolish, Nicholas,' Bianca says. 'On Bankside a maid would likely get frostbite leaning out of a window unclothed like that.'

The man and woman vanish back into the room. A short while later the street door opens and the mathematician reappears. He is barefoot, dressed in woollen hose and a shirt that has been hurriedly laced, judging by the apparently random criss-crossing of its points. He is alone.

'Come in, Signor Purse. And bring your friends with you. I don't suppose you've brought—'

Bianca cuts him off with an amused shake of her head.

Inside, the shady courtyard is set around with mulberry bushes in huge earthen pots. The far wall is similar to the street aspect: four rows of windows, only these have narrow little balconies. Stretched across the lowest is a line of sheets, shirts and under-shifts drying in the heat. A manservant brings a jug of wine. The mathematician toasts his visitors' health.

'So, a physician – from England,' Galileo says to Nicholas. 'Would you rather we spoke Latin?'

'I can manage in Italian. If I have trouble, I'll let you know.'

'I too studied medicine, at Pisa,' the mathematician tells him. 'It was my father's wish. Almost sent me mad with boredom. I gave it up and turned to mathematics. Best thing I ever did. Numbers don't get sick and stink, they don't leak pus and they don't complain of bellyache. I can't think of a worse life than spending your days sniffing boils and old men's piss.' His satyr's eyes dart to Bianca and then back to Nicholas. 'And this is your wife?'

'Yes. We were married last summer.'

'How are you with a sword?'

Nicholas looks puzzled. He wonders if this is some coarse Paduan euphemism. 'Dangerous, but not in a competent way. Why?'

With a broad grin, Galileo thrusts a full wine cup at him. 'I make it a strict rule never to launch a sally against another fellow's woman if he can tell one end of a sword from the other.'

Nicholas decides he rather likes the brash young professor of mathematics from Padua University.

When enough wine has been taken to toast the arrival of England's foremost man of medicine and his bride – whom Galileo generously forgives for depriving Padua of her exceptional beauty, to live in godless England – he puts two chubby fingers between his lips and lets loose a whistle that echoes around the courtyard. He shouts, 'Matteo, take your hand off your privy sausage and get out here this moment, and bring the sketches with you. Master Purse is here and he's brought company.'

Matteo Fedele is a gentle-looking lad of about seventeen, lean-hipped, with soft grey eyes and black hair swept back over the crown of his head and tied in a knot at the nape of his neck. The cleft in his upper lip gives him the air of a vulnerable child. Nicholas learns he is Galileo's pupil, one of several who live in the house. Matteo has taken on some of his teacher's rustic earthiness, but it sits uncomfortably on such a diffident character. He spreads the parchments that he brings with him over the bench in the courtyard with a flourish. On one, Nicholas sees clever drawings with Latin annotations: quadrants of cog-wheels;

balances shown from above and from the side; coiled springs and levers; flywheels and drums wrapped with chain; sections of meridians with the lugs and holes intended to connect them – all clearly drawn for the instruction of the artisans who will carve, hammer or forge them. On another sheet he sees diagrams of the constellations shown from different latitudes; pictorial renderings of the zodiac; images of planets and stars, some with fiery tails drawn to show their movement through an imaginary heaven.

Matteo Fedele beams with obvious satisfaction. 'The ability to place the planets and the stars correctly in any quadrant of the heavens, and to show them accurately from any latitude, at any date, will make astrology and astronomy the foremost of all the sciences,' he announces. Nicholas thinks it best not to tell him he hasn't cast a horoscope when making a diagnosis since long before Eleanor died.

'Imagine it, Nicholas,' Bruno says proprietorially, 'to be able to turn the engine through year upon year in a few cranks of a handle, and so be able to look into the future and say which day was auspicious and which was not; to establish if Church doctrine is correct in the matter of the earth's place in the cosmos; perhaps even to foretell great events by the accurate positioning of the planets and the stars. What would a prince not pay for such a window through which to view God's plan?'

'The plan is certainly ambitious,' Nicholas admits.

'That dog Santucci's sphere is astounding enough. But the Barrani sphere will have the men of the new learning beating a path to our door.'

It is said in English. And as Bruno raises his wine cup again in a toast to the project, he does not glance at either Galileo or Matteo Fedele – leaving Nicholas to wonder just how many members of the *Arte dei Astronomi* know it is to be called the *Barrani* sphere.

For the first time since their arrival in Padua, evening brings a cooling north wind that carries away the worst of the heat. Nicholas, Bruno and Bianca walk arm-in-arm back to the house in the Borgo dei Argentieri. Mellowed by wine and good company, Nicholas is in a happy, optimistic mood. Signor Galileo has promised to introduce him to the professor of anatomy at the university, the man the world of medicine knows as Fabricius, but whom the mathematician calls by his Italian name: Girolamo Fabrici.

The offer has given him reason to think his stay in Padua might prove more beneficial than he'd thought. A few months' study under the famous physician would give an insight into the latest advances in surgery. It would improve his Latin no end. And on his return to England it would give him a status that the College of Physicians would be unable to deny. As the trio enters the great square in front of the Basilica of St Anthony, Nicholas feels a sense of peace he hasn't felt in all the long miles since Den Bosch.

Ahead of him, the six domes of the basilica are washed with a pale-saffron light from the setting sun. Across the city, church bells ring out for Vespers. The sound echoes through the narrow streets, rolling around the church towers like a wave breaking against a sturdy harbour pile.

And then Nicholas sees him. *There* – at that counter, the one that spans the narrow front between this lane and the next. The man in the grey coat!

In the time it takes his eyes to settle on the figure inspecting the wares for sale – old lantern frames without the glass in them – Nicholas has already chided himself for being overly suggestible. But then he sees the awkward feigning of interest in the man's exaggerated movements; and the trunk-hose showing above his broad-rimmed boots, and the black cloth hat he wears even though most men in the square are bare-headed in the warm evening air.

'Hey, you!' Nicholas shouts as he sprints towards the counter, leaving Bianca and Bruno to stare after him. 'Hold a moment. I want to speak to you!'

He hasn't gone more than six paces before the man drops the lantern frame he was inspecting so unconvincingly and bolts round the corner into the adjacent lane.

Nicholas reaches the counter in less than two tolls of St Anthony's bell. Taking the corner into the lane the man has just vanished into, he stumbles. He throws out a steadying hand. Lantern frames clatter onto the cobbles. With a muttered apology to the counter owner – who stares at him in anger – Nicholas dives into the shadows after his quarry.

He can see him ahead in the lane, dodging people as he tries to put distance between himself and his pursuer. Nicholas offers more breathless grunts of apology to passers-by as he weaves after him. He doesn't know where the lane goes. But from the way the fellow keeps glancing to cither side, evidently hoping for a crossroads that he can escape down, Grey-coat doesn't know, either.

Nicholas is almost brought to a halt by a matron in a colourful gown and wide-brimmed hat. She's ushering two veiled daughters across the lane to inspect a shoe stall. She regards him with disgust; mutters something in Italian that is clearly not complimentary; shoos her daughters ahead of her to avoid the maniac gasping at her in a foreign tongue. Glancing over his shoulder, Nicholas sees Bruno and Bianca enter the lane, their bemused faces flushed with the effort of trying to catch up with him, frightened he's taken leave of his senses. For an instant he considers abandoning the chase. But only for an instant.

Reaching the spot where his quarry seemed to disappear, he sees the entrance to a narrow side-street. A fleeting glimpse of grey catches his eye. He follows. Within moments he is deep inside an unfamiliar part of the city, uttering breathless apologies – in Italian now – to everyone he barges past. He knows exactly how this would play out on Bankside: a foreigner racing through the lanes and alleys as though all the demons in hell were on his heels. The dangers inherent in what he's doing are not lost on him.

A few more paces and the man in the grey coat glances over his shoulder. Seeing that Nicholas is gaining on him, he sprints on past a small group of young men in bright hose and jerkins, then suddenly makes a dart to one side. Nicholas sees one half of a pair of embossed bronze doors swing open, shielding the man from his sight. When the door swings closed, he has gone.

As Nicholas reaches the place, two of the young gallants pick that moment to step further into the lane. Nicholas cannons into one of them, stumbles, rights himself and once more offers an apology. Oblivious to the angry response he gets, he sees that the doors form the entrance to a small church. He throws yet another muttered apology at the young gallant rubbing his bruised arm, pulls open one of the heavy doors and goes inside.

He has a sudden, unsummoned guilty recollection: of slipping late into one of Parson Olicott's Sunday sermons at Barnthorpe. He'd been fifteen. His excuse, prepared behind the tithe barn even while Yeoman Deary's oldest daughter was letting him insert a hand beneath her kirtle: *It's taken longer than I thought to sharpen the sickles.*

It takes a few moments for his sight to adjust to the darkness. For a while, all he can see is an inky blackness broken by slivers of golden light. What dominate his senses are the smell of incense and the chanting of pious voices.

As his eyes become accustomed to the interior, a small congregation seated in wooden pews emerges from the darkness. At the far end of the church is a gilded altar. Behind it, a garishly pink Jesus hangs from His cross, His bowed wooden head surrounded by golden rays of painted sunlight. A priest in a black robe is pouring the blood of the living Christ into a silver cup. Once again Nicholas feels the shock that comes with proximity to a practice that almost everyone he knows in England would consider amongst the very worst of blasphemies: the consumption of the real blood and flesh of their saviour. Just to be in this place would, for all but recusants like Bianca and John Lumley, put him in danger of damnation. But at this moment the safety of his eternal soul is of secondary importance to finding his quarry.

His sight regained, Nicholas scans the congregation from his place at the back of the church. All he sees are shoulders and the backs of pious heads. None of the shoulders are grey. None of the heads wear a black cloth cap.

He can recall little of the man's features from the sighting at the hospice in St Bernard's pass, but he can hardly demand that everyone turns towards him for inspection. Even less can he stride to the altar, push the priest out of the way and view them from the front. He sinks back against the doors, in the hope that no one will take too much of an interest in his arrival. The man will have to leave eventually.

Unless, of course, there's another way out. He searches the shadows either side of the candlelit altar. The priest's softly spoken Latin sings to him like a dangerous lullaby: *Suscipe, sancte Pater, omnipotens aeterne Deus...*

As sure as he can be that there is no way of leaving the church other than through the doorway he came in by, Nicholas lets his eyes linger on the congregation, looking for someone sitting on his own – someone with a hint of the hunted about him.

Three different men draw his attention. Each wears a jerkin or coat that might be grey. But it is too dark to be certain. If one of them is the fellow Nicholas has chased, he's taken off his cap, out of respect for his surroundings. And there is no way of getting closer to any of them without drawing attention to himself.

He feels the door move at his back. A glint of evening sunlight from the street, and Bianca is beside him. One or two of the congregation in the rear pews turn their heads and tut.

'What in the name of Jesu are you doing?' she whispers. 'Have you taken leave of your senses? You took flight as though the Devil was after you. You've left a trail of destruction and outraged Paduans all the way from St Anthony's!'

'Didn't you see him – the fellow at the lantern stall?'

'What fellow?'

'The one in the grey coat and the black cap. The one from the monastery in the mountains – the one who's been following us all the way from Reims.'

'All I know, Nicholas, is that one moment I was talking to Bruno about finding him a wife, and the next my husband was off like a spaniel after a coney.'

'He's here. I chased him into this church.'

Bianca, having forgotten herself in the heat of the moment, genuflects in the direction of the priest. Then, turning back to Nicholas, she says, 'Are you certain? Are you sure the sun hasn't fried your brains?'

'Of course I'm sure. He's *here*. Or if he isn't, there's another way out of this church that I haven't seen.'

More heads turn towards them. More tutting.

'Then the best thing we can do is to wait out there,' Bianca says, tugging at his sleeve and nodding in the direction of the street, 'before you bring down the wrath of Holy Mother Church upon our heads.'

Reluctantly, Nicholas accepts the wisdom of her advice. Opening the heavy bronze door as quietly as he can, he follows her outside.

Immediately the setting sun low over the rooftops opposite almost dazzles him. Human shapes are momentarily turned into hazy grotesques. He hears squealing and the thwack of cane on hide as someone drives a pig across his path, an indistinct blur of pink teardrops floating just above the cobbles.

And then someone pushes him violently.

As his eyes focus, he sees the young gallant he cannoned into on his way into the church. He has a look about him as sharp as the rapier he wears at his belt. One hand is held below his nose, flicking at his nostrils with a thumb in a gesture of contempt, the other already lifting steel from its scabbard. He lets loose a tirade in Italian too fast for Nicholas to fully catch, though the meaning is clear. Behind him, his companions are lending moral support by jeering and catcalling.

On Bankside – Nicholas knows – fatal street fights can easily begin with an imagined insult, an inadvertent jolt, a misunderstood glance. He has no reason to think Padua is any different. He raises his hands and lowers his head apologetically, trying to defuse the situation.

It doesn't work. He finds himself staring at the rapier's tip hovering barely a foot from his throat, brilliant beads of light reflected in the needle-sharp steel. And when his eyes are drawn along the blade to the youth who holds it, he can see in his eyes not sunlight, but murder. With his attention fixed on the sword point menacing his throat, Nicholas catches only the indistinct impression of movement to his left. One of the youth's companions seems to be offering him something. Then the lad holding the rapier steps back.

Now Nicholas can see that the second fellow is presenting him with the hilt of his own weapon, the curved knuckle-guard and the cross-quillons rising and falling like the head of a flower stirred by a gentle breeze as the supple steel of the blade flexes. *Jesu*, he thinks, they want me to fight a duel.

'Forgive me, it was an accident. I intended no insult,' he says lamely in Italian, knowing that if Padua is anything like London, a foreign accent will only make things worse. He makes a crossing motion of his hands to show he wants nothing to do with the rapier he's being offered. '*Spada... non posso...*' he manages, in a mangled effort to explain that he has little skill at swordplay.

And then little Bruno Barrani is amongst them, roaring like a lion and letting fly a violent reprimand, though it's delivered too speedily for Nicholas to catch more than a few words. He seems quite untroubled that he's outnumbered, unarmed and a head shorter than any of the gallants. But the rapier comes down. The youth looks sullenly at Nicholas, calls him a foreign dog and then leads his companions resentfully to the other side of the street, where he glares at his lost opportunity like an alley cat deprived of its kill.

Nicholas breathes again. 'What did you say?' he asks as Bianca hurries to his side.

'I told them I'm a member of the Podestà's council, and that duelling is forbidden in public. I told them if they persisted, they'd find themselves enjoying a spot of rowing – in the galleys.'

'I think I owe you my life, Bruno,' Nicholas says, realizing his hands are shaking.

'Then my debt is cleared,' Bruno says happily. 'But I think we should go now.'

'I can't. He's still inside that church.'

'Who?'

'The fellow I was chasing. Didn't you see him?'

Bruno looks perplexed. 'All I know is that you set off as though you'd caught sight of a tax collector. Who, in the name of the Holy Mother, were you chasing?'

'Someone who's been following us from Brabant. I think he may be in the pay of the English Privy Council. I have to wait for him to leave, so that I can confront him.'

Bruno's face darkens. 'You've done enough confronting for one day. I don't think you appreciate the situation. If you don't leave now, that fellow with the rapier and his friends will track you down and throw you in the Bacchiglione in a sack weighted with rocks. And I'm not sure he was speaking in jest. If they get their blood hot again, I cannot guarantee I will be able to cool it a second time.'

'He's right,' Bianca says, tugging at Nicholas's sleeve. 'I didn't come all this way only to lose you in a silly street quarrel. *Please.*'

Reluctantly, he turns away. As he follows Bruno back out of the lane he can feel malevolent stares burning into the nape of his neck. Angry gallants, drunk on pride, he can ignore. What troubles Nicholas more is the knowledge that with the appearance of Grey-coat in the city, the destination Bianca has brought him to is no longer the sanctuary either of them had imagined.

✠

'Now we know the truth. It wasn't Hella Maas our friend was following, it was us. Me.'

Nicholas cups the back of his head in his hands, splays his elbows and leans back on the bolster. It is midnight. Their chamber in the house in the Borgo dei Argentieri is in darkness, save for a single oil lamp burning on a clothes chest by the window. Outside in the street, revellers are making their way home to the accompaniment of someone playing a mandolin badly. It almost masks the sounds of Bruno's contented snoring from the adjoining room.

'He could have been following us all the way from Den Bosch,' Bianca says, lying against him while she traces the contours of his shoulder with an index finger. 'Perhaps it's just a matter of chance that we didn't see him until Reims.'

Nicholas considers this awhile in silence. The list of possibilities is a short one. He says, 'Either he's a friend, sent by Robert Cecil to report on our whereabouts. Or he is an enemy, sent by the Privy Council for much the same reason.'

'If he's the former – a friend – why did he not stop when you called him? Why did he run?'

'I cannot tell,' Nicholas says with a shrug, 'He certainly didn't want to be caught.'

'So he must be an enemy?'

Nicholas lets out a long, slow exhalation. 'Very probably.'

'What if he's not alone?' Bianca asks.

It is a question Nicholas has asked himself more than once, from the moment he spotted the man loitering so unconvincingly at the lantern stall. He imagines a dark night in the near future, Alonso or Luca – perhaps both – bribed to leave the street door unbolted. The soft scrape of covert boot-leather on the stairs. A sudden rush taking the sleeping victim before he knows what's happening. Hands tied. Woollen cape thrown over the head to keep the cries of surprise to a minimum. A hurried bundling through the darkened streets to the Brenta canal and a waiting boat. Then the journey to the Venetian lagoon – barely twenty miles away – trussed up and gagged beneath some innocent-looking cargo. An English merchant barque moored there, primed to expect a last-minute addition to its load, an addition

284

that must be carried home with all dispatch. It wouldn't be the first time a perceived enemy of England has been snatched from what he imagined was a safe exile.

As he lies in the darkness, waiting for sleep to come, Nicholas discovers that every sound that issues from the house in the Borgo dei Argentieri – no matter how familiar or previously innocent it had sounded – has suddenly taken on the furtive, threatening nature of a warning.

27

'T his is... an improvement,' Rose says tentatively when
Ned has released her from his embrace. 'Are they treating you well?'

She looks around the grim little chamber that has cost her five
shillings in bribes to the prison warden. She takes in the dirty
straw mattress, the stained privy bowl, the little table without
a chair and the floor-to-ceiling wainscoting carved with names
and messages of despair. It is indeed, she thinks, an improvement over the communal, stinking, low-ceilinged cellar that
was Ned's previous tribulation. The stench, the flesh rubbed raw
by ankle-irons, the whisper of rats wandering with disgusting
disdain amongst the straw, and the overwhelming miasma of
piss, sweat and misery that is the Marshalsea prison's common
durance is going to take some time to cleanse itself from her
mind. But at this moment nothing can dilute the joy she feels at
seeing her husband again.

'I've paid the warden to bring you food and ale,' she continues.
'Has he been true to his word or has the rogue kept them for
'imself?'

'He's fair enough, Wife. Master Nicholas cured his brother of
the flux a while back, so he's matey enough with me. I've good
news for you.'

Hope swells in Rose's heart like a wave. 'They're letting you
go?'

286

'No. The Trinity term for the assizes is running late. I'm to go before a judge inside the week.'

'That's *good* news?'

'If it had been held at the right time, I'd 'ave missed it,' he tells her. 'I'd be 'ere until the next circuit. That'd be after Michaelmas. If you haven't noticed, Wife, there's no hearth. I'd freeze.'

'I've written to Lord Lumley, 'Usband. I've begged him to find us a lawyer.'

'We 'ave no coin to pay some splitter-of-causes who tells you it's coming on to rain and then charges an 'alf-angel for giving you his opinion.'

'But we need someone of learnin' to speak for you.'

'I'm an honest man, Goodwife Monkton,' Ned says proudly. 'The jury will see that clear enough. In his own land an Englishman can be sure of a fair trial and a fair judgement. An' that Ditworth witnessed everything that happened – from Vaesy drawing a blade on me, to when his 'ead hit the desk. He'll confirm my account of what 'appened.'

And with that, he sinks to his knees and places the right side of his huge bearded head against her stomach, the better to sense the presence of the child growing inside her.

✠

It is a sultry September afternoon. In the courtyard of the house in the Borgo dei Argentieri, Nicholas and Bruno Barrani are playing dice in the shade of a mulberry tree to the accompaniment of a chorus of cicadas. The game is close enough to the hazard so beloved of the Jackdaw's customers for Nicholas to play with confidence. Indeed, he is winning. It is his turn to throw.

'Go on – kiss the die and let it fall, Nicholas,' Bruno says, his black ringlets speckled with sunlight filtering through the branches. 'Despite the way your luck's been running, I have the feeling it will be... what do you call the two?'

'We call it *deuce*,' says Nicholas with a smile. Even in defeat, nothing can dent Bruno's natural tendency to believe his luck is on the cusp of changing. He throws. It's a *sink* – a five.

'*Pah*,' Bruno exclaims. 'Why do heretics have all the luck?'

'Bankside gives a man as useful an education as any he'll get from Cambridge or Oxford, and you don't even have to know Latin.'

Bruno raises a cautionary finger to his nose. 'You and my cousin should have been more honest with me from the start.'

'Honest? We have not lied to you, Bruno – I promise it.'

'Honest about the real reason you had to flee England. Honest about why you came to Padua. And honest about the fellow you chased into the church, before you almost got yourself skewered.'

'I'm sorry. We didn't want to cause you concern. We thought it best if we just said Bianca had grown tired of England. And until I saw him at the lantern stall, I couldn't be sure it truly was me he was following.'

'And now you're worried that he might not be alone?'

'If the Privy Council has put a purse on my head, he may have others with him. I don't want to put you in danger too, Bruno.'

Bruno spits on his die and rolls it. It tumbles for a moment, and then – with a snide little quiver – settles with the *deuce* uppermost. Even this can't dent his good humour. 'Don't fret, Nicholas,' he says with a grin. 'This is Padua, remember? Think of Bankside with better fashion sense, but less restraining manners. If you need protection, I can drum up any number of squint-eyed, broken-nosed *omicidi* who'd make that kid you barged into look like a castrato. They'll deter anyone who thinks he can make a few ducats by causing you and my cousin trouble, never fear.'

'Then I'll only feel worse about beating you at dice,' Nicholas says.

Bruno takes up his die and kisses it for luck. He looks Nicholas straight in the eye. 'She's looking very comely, for all that walking you've done and the worry you've put her through.'

For a moment, Nicholas is taken off-guard. 'Bianca?'

'Of course. Who else do you think I'm speaking of – Caterina de' Medici?'

'Is she?' Nicholas asks, wondering if this is some strategy of Bruno's to take his mind off the game.

'Trust an Englishman not to notice that his wife is blooming.'

'Blooming? I hadn't thought of her as blooming.'

Bruno gives him a sly look. 'If the child is born in Padua, I demand you call him Bruno.'

And then he throws a *sise*, and puts himself squarely back in the game.

✶

'Blooming?'

'That's what he said – "blooming".'

They are walking back from the Basilica of St Giustina. Bianca had wanted to show him Veronese's depiction of the saint's martyrdom, and it has taken Nicholas a while to regain the capacity of speech. He has never in his life seen such extraordinary colours and images. For a moment he thought he had been transported to the very moment when the cruel Moor pierced her white flesh with the tip of his knife. He can think of nothing like it in any church in England. The knowledge that Robert Cecil would consider it a dangerous papist icon only added to the thrill. Now they are stepping carefully around a gang of plasterers splashing stucco on the wall of a house fifty yards from Bruno's. Bianca hoists the hem of her gown to avoid the pools of sticky pale soup.

'And do you think I'm *blooming*, Nicholas?'

He squirms. Comes out with a hurried excuse. Knows it's lame even as he delivers it.

'I'm sorry if you think I haven't noticed. It's just that whenever I look at you, it's still as though I'm seeing you for the very first time.'

Her expression changes from disbelief to icy. He thinks: she's hurt that her cousin can see she's with child, but her husband – her stolid *English* husband – is not blessed with such arcane skills.

'Well, is he right? *Are you*—?' he asks clumsily. 'It *is* what we hoped for...'

Bianca shakes her head to dispel the awful feeling that somehow Hella is still with them, still working her sick artifice. But it will not leave her. She recalls the awful sense of helplessness and dread she'd experienced when she'd wondered if the maid could somehow influence the workings of her body. If Bruno is right, then what kind of creature could be growing inside her – if it was somehow under the influence of another person's will?

Nicholas takes the tossing of his wife's head to mean denial. 'It doesn't matter, there's time enough...'

Bianca does not reply, although inside her head her thoughts are shouting at her: Bruno is wrong. Hella was wrong. No one can see inside my womb except God. And no one but He can set life growing there – certainly not a wild-eyed maid who thinks of nothing but death and judgement.

As she steps through the door of her cousin's house and into the courtyard, Bianca Merton wonders how it is that she missed the moment when the thought of bearing her husband a child changed from joyous to terrifying.

✠

The storehouse lies behind the Porta Portello, on the bank of the river. They reach it by crossing a narrow stone bridge capped with the likenesses of leading Paduans got up as Roman emperors. Bruno stands before a set of high wooden doors and rams his fist several times against the planks. Nicholas detects a sequence in his knocking: two in slow time... one on its own... three in a fusillade. He thinks: if that isn't a coded message that it's safe to open up, then I don't know what is. He hears the rasp of a wooden bar being slid past iron hoops, then a prolonged groaning of hinges as one half of the doors is opened. A face peers out, the eyes darting like a kingfisher's. Once satisfied that those waiting outside are not in any way associated with the city's law officers, its customs officials or the Holy Office of the Faith – the Inquisition – the face calls for them to enter.

Inside, Nicholas is surprised to find the place is not as dark as he'd expected. High windows set into the far wall let in a dusty light. A small forge glows in one corner. One of the Corio brothers, clad in a leather apron, is beating still-glowing iron into shape. The ringing of his hammer sings around the plaster walls. In the centre of the space sits a large, circular cradle-like structure of wood. It rests on four splayed feet, carved in the shape of a crouching lion's paws, claws extended. By the chisel marks, Nicholas can see it is a work in progress.

'A nice touch, don't you think?' Bruno asks. 'The emblem of Venice is the winged lion. He'll like that, the doge, when it's all gilded properly. Our goldsmith, Signor Bondoni, says it should be done by the Feast of St Francis. But he has six children by his mistress, who's an ogre, so we have to be flexible in the exact timing.'

Propped against one wall are the quadrants of a huge brass ring, which – when completed – Nicholas judges will be twice the height of a man in diameter.

'That's the equator ring,' Bruno explains. 'It will sit on the rim of the cradle. The sphere will revolve within it. Of course, when I say *sphere*, it's actually concentric rings that move the sun, the stars and the planets in their appropriate motions. The true sphere, the earth itself, is at the very heart of the engine and remains motionless, just as the true earth sits motionless at the centre of the cosmos.'

'You really *can* do this,' Bianca says, smiling in admiration. She embraces her little cousin. 'I'm so proud of you, Bruno. I take back all my doubts.'

Proudly Bruno leads them to a bench where young Matteo Fedele is bent over a spread of papers, making notes and calculations with a quill.

'How goes it, Signor Matteo?' Bruno asks.

Fedele looks up with a start. 'Forgive me, I was miles away. The maestro set me to thinking on how it might be possible to show the flight of meteors through the celestial rings. I told him that everyone with any learning knows meteors emanate from within the earth and glow because they absorb the sun's heat as they travel through the heavens. Therefore they should not be depicted in the orbits of the planets.'

'And the answer Signor Compass gave you?'

Matteo's cleft lip gives a little quiver of indignation. 'He told me I had the imagination of a castrated lapdog.'

'Knowing Signor Compass, I think you escaped lightly.'

Matteo rubs his forehead. 'But I still can't work out how to do it. It would be a lot easier if we were making a sphere based on what Signor Copernicus writes. If the sun were at the centre of the engine instead of the earth, we wouldn't need nearly so many cogs and counter-movements.'

The colour drains from Bruno's face. A nervous tick causes the corner of one eye to tremble. 'I don't want to hear that,

Matteo. We're doing this to make money.' He adds, as an after-thought, 'And for the glory of the Republic, of course. That's a given. I have no intention of getting into the middle of a phil-osophical debate.'

'It does seem a shame not to consider the latest thinking on the matter,' Nicholas observes. 'Seeing how much effort you're putting into this device.'

'I am reliably informed by Signor Galileo that no one in Venice gives any credence to such a demonstrably false idea, Nicholas,' Bruno says. 'If the doge doesn't disagree with Holy Mother Church, I'm not going to be the first one to tell him he ought to. You clever fellows can debate such matters all you like, but I'm a businessman. And I have no interest in being burned alive in the Piazza dei Signori. I have sensitive toes.'

Bianca says gravely, 'Don't joke about such matters, Cousin. Remember what happened to my father, dying alone in a cold cell because he challenged the Church's dogma on how the world is made. It is why I left Padua. Don't give me reason for a second exile.'

Bruno answers her with a dazzling smile. 'Rest easy, Cousin,' he says. 'Not even the Holy Father in Rome and all his cardinals – be they as pious as St Peter – will find a single fault with what your clever cousin and Signor Compass are building here. If Church dogma says the earth is made of custard, then I would happily give His Serenity a custard earth. And I won't risk being burned for heresy by sticking a cherry in it, either.' He points at the high windows of the storehouse. 'Do it any other way and, if I open that, I'll be able to hear that rogue Santucci laughing at me all the way from Florence.'

✠

Bruno has hired a barge for an afternoon on the river. He says it's what all the best people do. He tells them it's in honour of

Bianca's return to Padua and her marriage to Nicholas. Galileo and Matteo Fedele are invited – the professor because he is good company, Matteo in reward for his labour. Luca and Alonso pack sausages of fine Lombardy pork, Lodigiano cheese and a skin full of rich red wine. 'Best make it two,' says Bruno. 'Signor Compass will have had a hard morning trying to unblock the ears of his students.'

The sky is the purest blue, the shade beneath the boat's awning soporific. While Bruno and Bianca doze, Nicholas develops an easy friendship with the professor of mathematics. Both of a similar age, both from relatively humble origins, both harbouring a mistrust of ancient teaching, they find they have much in common. Where Nicholas's Italian fails, they revert to Latin, the professional language they share.

To Nicholas's surprise and delight, he discovers Galileo refuses to wear a professor's toga when out in the city streets. He thinks of the disgust on the faces of the Censors of the College of Physicians when he'd told them he'd thrown his own gown into the Thames, rejecting the false efficacy of so much of his medical training.

Galileo promises to introduce him to the famous Girolamo Fabrici, professor of anatomy and surgery. As the wineskins flatten and the villas on the banks of the Bacchiglione drift by in the hazy afternoon heat, Nicholas begins to think there could be worse places in the world than Padua to be a physician. Beside him, Bianca watches the world drift pass, aware that something is missing. It is the familiar ache that she's been expecting for days now. The one that warns her menses are on the way.

28

The Queen's Bench Prison, 16th September 1594

Ned Monkton is one of twenty prisoners appearing this morning before a justice of the assizes. He is next in the queue, between a permanently soused woman of sixty accused of naming her cats Lucifer and Belial, and a labourer indicted for stealing an awl and a hammer from his employer.

The clerk has already read out the charge, first in Latin, which was meaningless to Ned, and then in English: that he did, in chance medley – that is, in a hot quarrel – kill Sir Fulke Vaesy, knight, a resident of the Castle Baynard Ward of the city, in contravention of the queen's common law.

Ned has submitted his plea: not guilty. The findings of the coroner's jury and his own deposition, written for him by Rose, have been presented to the justice in advance. A jury of residents drawn from nearby Borough High Street has been assembled. A small crowd has gathered to watch the proceedings. Rose stands amongst them, drying her eyes on her sleeve. She doesn't want Ned to see her distressed.

The conversation between the magistrate – imperious in a red gown and a black cloth cap – and the prosecuting sergeant dies on their lips when Ned is brought before them. They stare at him, the magistrate through a pair of slightly opaque spectacles. Then, hurriedly calculating the distance between the accused and their own suddenly vulnerable bodies, they independently wave the two court guards to move closer to the giant standing in the body of the court.

What is to be made of him? the justice wonders, tugging a little nervously at his ruff. Look at that bushy auburn beard. You could hide a whole gang of cut-purses in that thicket. Look at the ruddy complexion – clearly a man drunk from dawn to dusk. Or is he flushed with an inveterate and dangerous anger? And those huge hands. Murderer's hands, without a doubt. This humble show that he is putting on must be intended to deceive. It cannot be his true nature. That is not how God has fashioned the bear.

'You plead not guilty,' the sergeant says, 'yet you look like a man easily roused.'

Rose calls out, 'Oh, he's easily roused, Your Honour. It's a job to stop him being roused. Sometimes I 'as to ask for a night off.'

Guffaws from the assembled spectators.

'Restate your account of what happened, Master Monkton,' the magistrate says, quieting the laughter with a downward wave of his hand.

Intimidated by the majesty of the law, Ned does his best. And it is not at all bad. He has a confidence in him that Rose hasn't seen before. It makes her proud. It makes her weep again.

'Your Honour, Sir Fulke Vaesy wrote a letter to the Privy Council denouncing my friend, Dr Nicholas Shelby, who is physician to the young son of Sir Robert Cecil. I went to his house on St Andrews's Hill to make him retract the calumny.'

'And that's when you murdered him,' the Crown's sergeant interjects helpfully.

'No, sir.'

'Did Sir Fulke agree to your request?'

'He did so agree, yes.'

'By your gentle persuasion, no doubt?' More laughter from the public. 'And then you killed him.'

'I had words with him, yes. But I laid not a hand upon him, sir – not until I went to leave. Then he drew upon me. It was a poniard.' Ned places his two palms a foot apart. 'About this long. He sought to strike me with it. I pushed him. He fell against his desk. His brains was dashed out.'

Rose smiles proudly from the public cordon. She had counselled him to speak simply and plainly, not to try to impress with airs that might only make him risible in the eyes of the court. He has not let her down.

The magistrate shuffles through the written depositions before him. He finds what he is looking for. 'It is written here that the accused cites the manservant of Sir Fulke Vaesy as a witness. Is he here?'

'No, Your Honour,' says the sergeant. 'He is not to be found.'

'The constables have made a proper search for this... Ditworth person?'

'No effort has been spared, Your Honour. All we can ascertain is that he has taken the opportunity of his master's demise to leave the city. It seems that, as Sir Fulke's servant, he was ill used.'

'So we have only *your* word that you did not assault the victim,' the magistrate says, addressing Ned with a doubting eye.

'That is how it passed, Your Honour. I 'ave sworn to it, on the Bible.'

Another ruffle through the documents, a downward jab of the magistrate's thumb as though squashing a woodlouse. 'Ah, *here* it is: an account that tells me you are well known on Bankside as a drunk and a brawler. A Constable Willders reports that on numerous occasions you fought with the watch when leaving taverns in an inebriated state. You were so quarrelsome, in fact, that they paid you money to go quietly to your bed, rather than risk injury to themselves. The warden at St Thomas's Hospital writes that you were frequently to be found intoxicated in the mortuary crypt. How say you?'

Ned finds an unexpected dignity. To Rose, he seems to grow even taller, causing her to make tearful honking noises that draw a frown of irritation from the magistrate.

'That was my place of work, Your Honour,' he says calmly. 'All day an' into the night, amongst the dead. That it made me quarrelsome, I do not deny. But that was before Master Nicholas and Mistress Bianca found me. I was a different man then. I was angry. So might you be, with only the forgotten dead for company.'

'And I would suggest the accused is angry still,' the sergeant says. 'So angry, in fact, that he forced a supposed confession from Sir Fulke Vaesy and then beat him to death.'

'Where is this letter you forced Sir Fulke to make, before you killed him?'

'I didn't kill him, Your Worship,' Ned objects. 'The desk did.'

More guffaws from the public, silenced by a mournful glare from the magistrate.

'*Where* is the letter?'

'It is sent to Lord John Lumley, at Nonsuch Palace. I gave it into the hands of his secretary at his London house on Woodroffe Lane. I have placed my trust in Lord Lumley to lay it before the Privy Council.'

'To what end?'

'So that Dr Shelby can be zonerated.'

'Exonerated of what?' the magistrate asks.

'Seeking to poison our sovereign lady Elizabeth, the queen.'

A single gasp from someone in the crowd. Then almost complete silence, freighted with appalled expectation.

The only sound comes from Rose: a tearful porcine snort. For a moment she is too taken by compassion for her great, dumb, cod's-headed magnificent bear of a husband to comprehend the implication of what he's just said. But not for long. The look on the magistrate's face sees to that. Then she can only watch and listen with mounting horror as everything unravels.

The magistrate says ponderously, 'Are you informing the bench that Sir Fulke Vaesy had denounced this Shelby person for attempting *regicide*?'

Ned looks at him blankly. 'I know not what that means, Your Worship.'

'Killing his queen, man! Killing the anointed sovereign set over him by God.'

'But he *didn't*, Your Worship.'

The sergeant chips in helpfully, 'That is what the papist rogue Lopez claimed when he faced the same charge.'

'Where is this Dr Shelby now?' the magistrate demands to know. 'Is he in the court?'

The clerks look around expectantly. When no answer comes, the magistrate returns his bespectacled gaze to Ned. 'Accused, where is this Shelby now?'

'He has gone abroad, Your Worship.'

'Where?'

'He did not care to tell us, Your Worship.'

Rose is silently screaming at her husband not to say another word. But Ned is still suffering from the deluded belief that telling the truth will save him.

The magistrate leans slowly forward from his chair, the deep trailing cuffs of his gown pooling around his hands as he spreads his fingers on the counter to balance himself. 'So that the jury may be spared any confusion, answer truthfully to the following.'

'Yes, Your Honour.'

'Sir Fulke Vaesy wrote a letter to members of the Privy Council denouncing the physician Shelby for being involved in a plot to poison the queen. True or false?'

'True, Your Honour.'

'The physician Shelby then flees abroad, omitting to tell you, his servant, where he has gone. True or false?'

'I'm not his servant, Your Honour. I'm his friend.'

'The friend of a man who seeks to murder his queen,' the prosecuting sergeant slips in.

'But he didn't—' Ned tries to protest.

'TRUE or FALSE?' shouts the magistrate.

'Well, Your Honour, it is true he went out of the realm without saying where he was bound, but—'

The magistrate cuts him off. 'And following this secretive departure, you go in a hot temper to Sir Fulke Vaesy's house on St Andrew's Hill and there beat from him a retraction, before killing him in an unprovoked fury. Do you see why I might distrust your plea of not guilty?'

When put to him like that, the colour drains from Ned's ruddy face. He raises his hands slightly, as if to add weight to the denial he is about to make. The chains on his wrist-irons jangle loudly around the still chamber.

'It weren't like that, Your Honour. That's not 'ow it was.'

A flick of one hand from the magistrates, and the two guards, who until now have been standing a little way either side of Ned, move even closer.

'I have heard all I need to hear in this particular matter,' the magistrate says. Then to the jury, 'You may begin your deliberations. You will bear in mind that the servant, Ditworth, is not present to lend any credence to the accused's claims that he acted in self-defence. More importantly, the denunciation of a suspected regicide – in these present times of danger – is a duty that lies upon *every* Englishman. If that duty can be hindered by the threat of violence, Her Grace the queen must live every day in peril. The fact that the subject of the denunciation in question has fled abroad speaks for itself. The accused is clearly guilty of the felony with which he is charged.'

It takes all of two minutes for the jury to act upon the justice's direction, two minutes during which Rose has to be restrained by the court clerks. Ned stands there silently, manacled like old Sackerson the bear waiting for the mastiffs to be released for another baiting. Ned Monkton, taverner, resident in the parish of St Saviour's, Bridge Ward Without: guilty of manslaughter as charged.

'I have a number of sentences at my disposal,' the magistrate says in a tone that leaves no doubt he intends to discard all but the severest. 'You should prepare your soul and your conscience for a higher judgement than I can make upon you, Ned Monkton, but execution is inevitable—'

Rose's screaming drowns out much of what follows. Ned doesn't hear it, either, because he's too occupied trying to drag himself towards his wife while the guards and several of the clerks hang onto his chains to prevent him. Thus the magistrate finds himself speaking to a court that isn't listening to him.

'I will, however, postpone formal sentencing,' he continues, 'until the Privy Council has been afforded the opportunity to question the guilty man under hard press. It is true he may have acted out of misguided loyalty to his friend the physician by forcing Sir Fulke to retract his accusations. But he may also have killed him for something more troubling: sympathy for the intended crime for which this Dr Shelby was denounced. In which case they may choose to further arraign the felon for treason. Remove the condemned man to the Marshalsea!'

29

Aman and his wife cannot live on air, certainly not in a city like Padua where a fine coat of silk and damask in broad red-and-black stripes is the very least you need to be taken seriously. Bruno has purchased one on the back of the doge's commission, and Nicholas feels even more of a poor relation, clad in the same worn white canvas doublet he has owned for years. He has noticed, too, how Bianca becomes a little truculent whenever they go out in public, judging herself against the standard set by Paduan women. Bruno steadfastly refuses all offers of payment for food and lodging, but with his purse close to depletion, Nicholas is in need of coinage. Bruno accompanies him to the local house of the Baldesi, a banking family based in Venice. A bill of exchange is drawn up with Robert Cecil's letter of credit as security, to be redeemed one year hence in either London or Padua at an agreed rate. 'You're lucky I'm here with you,' Bruno tells him. 'The Baldesi like to stiff every foreigner in the city if they think they can get away with it.' Nicholas withdraws just enough for their needs and a decent new gown for Bianca.

Walking back to the house on the Borgo dei Argentieri, he keeps a wary eye open. It is not only the possibility of being robbed that concerns him. Somewhere in the city an agent of the English Privy Council might well be prowling, for he can think of no other reason why Grey-coat – as he now calls him – is here.

Bianca has returned to the church, to ask the priest if he knows the man who came in halfway through the Mass and either hid himself amongst the other worshippers or slipped out again through another door. He doesn't. When he is giving the Eucharist he is communing with God, not looking out for people taking inappropriate refuge from a quarrel that is none of his business.

For Nicholas, it is hard not to imagine Grey-coat lurking in the shady lanes, watching him from the shadows. Will it be kidnap? Or a knife in the ribs? To a bounty-hunter sent by the likes of Robert Devereux, Earl of Essex, the latter would be easier work – less effort. Bruno has laughed away his friend's fears. But he's hired three cousins of the Corios – the brothers who are casting the sphere's cogs and gears in their foundry on the Borgo Socco – as temporary bodyguards. Just as a precaution.

With enough coin in his purse to provide a modest but comfortable existence for himself and Bianca, Nicholas considers a return to the life of a student of medicine. He thinks: if I am to be an exile for a while, I would be a fool not to avail myself of the opportunities afforded by one of Europe's foremost medical faculties. Over a jug of wine, he asks Signor Galileo to honour his promise to introduce him to Professor Fabrici at the Palazzo Bo. Bruno asks if might be allowed to accompany them – as leader of the *Arte dei Astronomi*. 'When I am Master of the Spheres to His Serene Highness,' he tells them in all seriousness, 'they'll have my statue there. I should take the opportunity to assess the best place for it. I don't intend to spend eternity on a plinth behind the privy.'

✳

The university is a handsome building in the classical style, with Roman pillars and an airy, colonnaded central courtyard open to the vivid blue sky. Arriving early, they are directed towards an open entrance through which echoes the sound of sawing and hammering. Nicholas wonders if perhaps the august professor of anatomy likes to take his ease repairing the university's tables and pews, or building furniture for the rector. But as he passes through the doorway he is brought up with a jolt of astonishment.

He is standing in the entrance of what appears to be an elliptical playhouse. Lit by stands of tallow candles, tiers of concentric wooden balustrades curve away on either hand, each set back a little from the one below, rising towards the high domed ceiling. Each has its own exterior staircase and a narrow door giving onto a gallery so narrow that only one man may stand between the back wall and the edge without the risk of tumbling into space. The top two tiers are nothing but naked wooden beams, workmen's planks and scaffolding thrown across the void. Nicholas can see labourers perched precariously some thirty feet above the floor, working with mallet, awl and plane. It dawns on him that this whole edifice is indeed a theatre. But no living actor will ever declaim upon the man-sized rectangular platform that is the focal point for those standing in these galleries. There will be no stirring victory speeches given here, no tragedies played out to their tearful end. This, he realizes, is a theatre in which the leading character is already dead. The player who lies here will give a very different performance from any Nicholas has seen at the Rose theatre on Bankside. He will reveal to his audience not emotion, but the inner complexities of his own body. This is an anatomical theatre, designed for dissection.

At once he is taken back to a hot Lammas Day in London. In a stuffy, airless guildhall – quite unlike this magnificent construction – he is attending a lecture given by the holder of the chair of anatomy at the College of Physicians, Sir Fulke Vaesy. He is looking down on the dissecting table as a small, cheery, bald-headed barber-surgeon, working to Vaesy's instructions, pares back the muscles and sinews, the blood vessels, connective tissue and fat around the inner organs of an infant boy, whose name he will not learn until much later. So much of what has happened to Nicholas in the intervening years can be traced back to that one moment. He recalls now what Hella Maas said to him at Besançon: *You know the danger that lurks in seeking knowledge, I know you do. I can sense it in you.* And he remembers his reply, clearly: *It was a lack of knowledge that brought me misery, not a surfeit of it.*

Seeing in his mind the scalpel slice into the dead child's waxy white flesh, he thinks now that even if he had known what was to come, it would have changed nothing. All the knowledge in the world isn't enough to prevent one single hour running inexorably into the next.

An unrestrained rustic cough from Galileo brings Nicholas out of his reverie. In the centre of the theatre Professor Fabrici is in conversation with an architect in a sober gown. They are poring over plans and diagrams. The anatomist is a compact little man of around sixty, with a high round forehead, arched eyebrows and a neatly trimmed iron-grey beard.

'Magister Galileo,' he says, looking up as the mathematician approaches, 'have you come to argue with Signor Sarpi here about his calculations? You're a little late. We can't ask the carpenters to tear it all down and start again.'

'Heaven forefend, Magister Fabrici,' Galileo says. 'I'd hate to delay the opening of the most expensive butcher's shop in Padua. I look forward to buying my sausages and my hams here, just as soon as the Podestà declares it open.' He lays a hand on Nicholas's shoulder. 'May I present to you Signor Nicholas Shelby, from England. He is physician of some reputation there, I understand. He has recently arrived in the city.'

The curiosity gleams in Fabrici's old eyes. 'We have a few of your nation here at the university, Dr Shelby,' he says pleasantly. 'Fewer, of course, since England abjured the true faith and turned to heresy. Some want to learn, but for the most part they tend to prefer the sightseeing – rich fellows with too much time on their hands. Which are you, if I may be so bold as to ask?'

'Definitely the former, Magister,' Nicholas assures him. Then, looking around at the galleries, he says, 'This is remarkable. We have nothing like it in England. Our College of Physicians thinks that getting one's hands bloody is the preserve of a tradesman. They leave it to the barber-surgeons.'

'It was the same here until not so very long ago, young man. As you can see, I have shaken things up a little. Have you any practical experience in surgery?'

'After Cambridge, I served as a physician in the Low Countries—' He stops mid-sentence, conscious that he's about to put his head into a noose. If he admits his ministrations were to the Protestant forces of the House of Orange, he is going to fatally undermine his claim to be a recusant fugitive. 'I was idealistic – I thought I might bring healing to the people of a land ravaged by war. But I learned a lot.' He glances up at the workmen on the scaffolding above. 'For a start, I learned how to saw quickly; how to pull out bits of iron that had been driven into places they weren't meant to be.'

Fabrici looks at him with new respect. 'Nothing to be reticent about, young man. The great Ambroise Paré made his reputation doing that, and we now count him amongst the finest of surgeons. You will be welcome to attend my lectures while you are here, Dr Shelby. With God's will, we might teach each other a thing or two.' He gives Nicholas a friendly tap on the shoulder. 'If you are not pressed for time, I will be conducting a private tutorial on optics. Perhaps you would care to observe?' He glances at Bruno. 'Your friend, too. If he has the stomach for it.'

'I am a son of Padua,' Bruno assures him loftily. 'I have the stomach of a lion.'

'I'm sure you do,' says Fabrici, giving him a knowing smile.

✠

In a small chamber with a ceiling plastered and painted like a chapel, a dozen or so young men are gathered. They are a mix of nationalities, though Nicholas is the only Englishman. He and Bruno make polite small-talk until the professor arrives and calls them to gather around a table draped with a square of embroidered Bergamo linen. Prayers are said in Latin. Then Fabrici claps his hands and two servants enter. Each carries a small walnut chest inlaid with mother-of-pearl. The smaller box is laid in the centre of the table. The larger is set to one side and opened with a discreet little click of its brass lock. Inside is a collection of scalpels, lancets, trocars and probes, all lying on red silk.

'Signori,' Fabrici begins, 'the ancients from whom we take our guidance are wont to consider the human body a singular thing – a man in his entirety.' He places one hand over his heart. 'I believe we can do better. It is not enough to learn how a limb functions. That is not true knowledge. A leg is nothing if it is to be considered only as a collection of bones, sinew and muscle. How can a runner imagine the triumph of victory, if his legs are no more to him than that? Therefore we must look deeper into the structure. We must consider *purpose*... the beauty of the effect... the promise... A man is so much more than the sum of his parts. He is made in the image of God. The purpose of those parts is to give him his godliness.'

Fabrici snaps his fingers. One of the servants steps forward and opens the second box. The students peer closer. Resting upon a bed of chipped ice, like a pair of shiny pickled onions, are two human eyeballs. At his side, Nicholas hears Bruno make a strangled little gasp.

'Plato tells us the human eye is fiery in its humour,' Fabrici runs on, 'and that it mirrors the cosmos, in that – like the earth – it is at the centre of perception, surrounded by crystalline spheres. Galen holds that it is filled with *pneuma*, the life spirit. Aristotle suggests that the humour pertaining to it is aqueous. What are we to make of these conflicting claims?'

The professor takes a trocar from the instrument chest and, with the hollowed tip, straightens the two tails of blood vessel and optic nerve. He likes things neat.

'It is believed by most professors of optics and their students that sight is the manifestation of certain rays, or emanations, that are emitted by the eye,' Fabrici continues. 'These fan out to alight upon what is before them, somehow transmitting the result to our perception. I do not believe that.' He looks around to see if there is any disagreement. There is none, or at least none voiced. 'I believe the eye is a receptacle. It gathers emanations *from* the objects themselves. It does not project them. And those emanations are bound by light. Let us see if we can find anything in the eye that proves I am wrong.'

And so saying, he picks up one eyeball from the box and lays it on the Bergamo linen. He takes a scalpel from the other box and punctures the sclera. A little bubbling dribble spills out around the incision. The chamber is silent – save for the sound of Bruno Barrani's body hitting the floor.

'I will see that image in my mind for the rest of my life,' Bruno complains as he and Nicholas leave the Palazzo Bo around noon. 'You might have warned me.'

'I thought you had the stomach of a lion?' Nicholas replies, trying not to laugh.

The early mist has burned off and the sky is cloudless. The light paints the buildings a pale gold. In the arcades of the Piazza delle Erbe the fruit and vegetable stalls are a blaze of greens, oranges, reds and purples. The citizens parade in their finery. Only Bruno's face is without colour.

'I think I might forget about the statue,' he says sadly. He squeezes his eyes tight shut and shakes his head vigorously. 'One thing's for certain: I'll never be able to eat oysters again.'

They have arranged to meet Bianca by the Palazzo del Podestà. She has been shopping for supper. They find her waiting for them, a wicker basket by her feet. Bruno makes another of his extravagant bows. 'Cousin!' he cries. 'Your beauty outshines bright Phoebus himself. Once again you look positively blooming.'

Bianca replies with a little bob of a curtsey. 'I've bought some fine *folpetti*,' she says proudly, and then to Nicholas, 'That's octopus.'

'Oh, *good*,' says Bruno quietly.

A few minutes' walk takes them back to the house in the Borgo dei Argentieri. The conversation is inconsequential, lazy exchanges of friendly banter in the sunshine. Carefree laughter. Past moments revisited. Nicholas's attention wanders to the colourful city. Three times on the journey he sees a man in a grey coat and a black cloth cap, and three times he knows he is looking only at a shadow, or a trick of the light.

At the Barrani house the three Corio cousins whom Bruno has hired as guards are sitting against the street wall playing knuckle-bones. The street door is open, giving a view through the passageway into the sunlit courtyard beyond. Nicholas can see figures standing around the table by the mulberry tree. One is Galileo's pupil, Matteo Fedele. He is in animated conversation with Bruno's servant, Luca. Judging by the rolls of parchment on the table, he has brought more calculations from Signor Galileo's house.

As Nicholas, Bianca and Bruno emerge into the bright theatre of the courtyard, Luca turns towards them and says, 'Master, we have company.'

Now Nicholas can see more clearly the other two figures standing around the table. One is Alonso. The other is a young woman with fair hair, wearing a plain brown cloth kirtle. He senses Bianca freeze at his side.

'Master, we have a visitor,' says Alonso, making a careless bow to Bruno Barrani. 'This pious signorina has come from the Beguinage at the Seminary Maggiore. She says she is a friend of your guests. She has come to be remembered to them.'

Bruno is already making another extravagant bend of the knee, his habit whenever he meets a female unknown to him, be she six or sixty. But Nicholas and Bianca are rooted to the spot.

'Good morrow, Meneer Nicholas... Mevrouw Bianca,' says Hella Maas, presenting them with one of her cold, emotionless smiles. 'Praise be to God! He has brought you safely to your destination.'

30

'What are you doing here, Hella? This is not Rome. Have you decided the Pope no longer needs you to pray for him?' Bianca's voice is frostier than Nicholas has ever heard it.

'What manner of welcome is this?' Hella Maas says in quiet voice. 'After all the weeks we spent together on the Via Francigena, and after all the effort I expended finding you.' She tilts her head towards Nicholas, her eyes widening as though searching for a friendly face. 'Surely you are pleased to see me, even if your wife isn't.'

'I think you should answer my wife's question.'

Bruno's eyes flick from the stranger to Nicholas, then to Bianca. The tension in her body isn't lost on him. She's as rigid as if she's just spotted a viper at her feet.

'I changed my mind,' Hella says, suddenly cheerful again. 'Rome can wait awhile. Padua is such a fine city. Much finer than Den Bosch, don't you think?'

'How did you know where to find us?' Nicholas asks.

'Easily. Bianca mentioned her cousin more than once in all those weeks we were together. I am lodging at the Beguinage. All I had to do was ask the Sisters to enquire after one Bruno Barrani. It seems he has some small fame in this city. So now here I am – though I must confess I had thought to find a warmer welcome.'

Bruno looks perplexed. 'You don't seem joyful to see your friend, Cousin – and after such companionship on the road. Is there something wrong?'

Bianca doesn't answer him. Her eyes remain locked on the newcomer. 'What is it you want with us, Hella? I thought we had said all we have to say to each other.'

'I wanted to see Nicholas again. I have need of a physician's skill.'

'You are ill?'

'I am sick of heart.'

Bianca lets out a stunted laugh of derision. 'There are numerous churches in this city, Hella. If you need your heart healed, any one of them will service your needs. Just light a candle and leave a coin. God knows, it's not as though you don't know how to pray.'

'Cousin, are you not being uncharitable to Signorina Maas?' Bruno asks, his fine black eyebrows lifting in surprise. 'It seems she has come a long way to meet only coldness.'

'Signorina Maas is a young maid who hasn't yet learned how to curb her tongue in adult company. I thought we had heard the last of her.'

'Cousin, this is unlike you. When did your own tongue become so heartless?'

'You don't know her, Bruno. On the journey here, she said things – bad things... hurtful things.'

Hella adopts a contrite expression that neither Bianca nor Nicholas has seen before. 'I confess it,' she says. 'On occasion the demands of the journey brought about a certain ill humour in me.'

'Only on occasion?' Bianca mutters under her breath.

Hella seems not to have heard her. 'My feet were sore. I was not as kind as I could have been. That was wrong. Every day since we parted at the hospice of St Bernard I have prayed to God to forgive me.'

'There, you see,' says Bruno, pleased by the result of his impromptu diplomacy. 'All is now made up. Greet your friend kindly, Cousin, and Alonso will prepare us a tasty dish of that *folpetti* you bought in the Palazzo delle Erbe. If Signorina Maas has expended so much effort in finding us, the least we can do is offer her some proper Paduan hospitality. Let no one say of Bruno Barrani that he sent a Sister of charity from his house empty-handed and hungry.'

Hella says to Bruno, in Italian, 'You are generous, Signor Barrani. God likes generosity, especially to a stranger. Will you permit me to help your servants prepare the meal? It would be an honour for me to recompense your kindness.'

'Can you cook, Signorina?' Bruno says, flattered.

'Well enough.'

Matteo Fedele chips in. 'That's not all she can do.' He points to the rolls of paper on the table. 'We've been having a discussion about the calculations I've made for the gearing for the orbit of Mars. She has a rare grasp of mathematics – for a maid.'

'Then you are doubly welcome, Signorina,' Bruno says. 'Do you plan to stay long in Padua? We could well put your skills to use, in the *Arte dei Astronomi*. Poor Matteo is a slow fellow unless the whip is applied liberally, or so Signor Galileo tells me.'

Bianca opens her mouth to protest. But Bruno and Matteo, engaged in an impromptu bout of mock-sparring, are too distracted to notice. She drops her shoulders and shakes her head in slow despair.

'Bruno is a fool where women are concerned, even ones dressed in plain kersey and brimful of dubious piety,' she says softly to Nicholas. 'Hella's up to something. I know it. And I have a very bad feeling that you are at the centre of it.'

✠

The supper, taken in the warm afternoon air, is a torture. For Nicholas and Bianca, it is like being the only two people at a revel who have realized how the illusions are performed, or who know that the singers are out of key and the dancers clumsy. They eat unenthusiastically, while Bruno and Matteo take turns to fawn over the new arrival. Both men seem entranced by Hella's ability to converse on matters mathematical, though Bianca suspects most of it is lost on her cousin, who is only pretending in order not to look less able than Galileo's pupil.

It is the first time in all the weeks since leaving Den Bosch that they have seen Hella in the company of men other than priests. She displays a worldliness that neither is expecting. She speaks when not actively invited to do so, does not lower her gaze submissively when either man declaims. She takes the conversation where she chooses, rather than following. If Bianca did not know any better, she would admire it. What is certain to her is that this is not the character of a maid who has given herself up to prayer and humility in the service of God. When Matteo and Bruno boast of the great sphere they are building for his Serene Highness the doge, there is no stern lecture on the folly of seeking knowledge, no hectoring about curiosity opening the door to the Devil's designs. Instead Hella appears to have adopted the technical mind of a student of astronomy.

'How will the retrograde motions of the planets be depicted?' she asks. Then, when the answer has been given to her satisfaction by a beaming Matteo, 'How have you calculated the representative distance between their orbits?' And when this has been explained, 'How far into the future will you show the precession of the equinoxes?'

Bianca chews noisily on a piece of octopus and tries to stop herself pulling a face. What game Hella is playing she cannot determine. But there is no question in her mind that a game is exactly what it is. Nor is there any question about the meaning of those not-so-discreet glances she keeps throwing at Nicholas.

✠

'Forgive me for sounding harsh, Cousin, but I cannot remain here in this house if that woman is to be your guest.'

The supper is over. Alonso and Matteo Fedele are accompanying Hella back to the Beguinage. She has left them as the latest addition to the *Arte dei Astronomi*, proposed by Matteo and unreservedly approved by Bruno. 'If they had a crown, they'd have anointed her queen,' Bianca whispered angrily to Nicholas after she'd departed.

'Did Signorina Maas's offer of reconciliation not move you?' Bruno asks.

Bianca's amber eyes blaze dangerously. Nicholas can see she has that set to her jaw that those who know her well recognize as a warning to tread carefully.

'It was not hers to make.'

'Surely it could have been no more than a minor falling-out, Cousin,' Bruno says. 'She would not have taken the trouble to seek you out otherwise. I see no poison in her.'

'If there isn't – there ought to be. You weren't there, Bruno.'

But Bruno is nothing if not a conciliator. 'Come, it is a warm evening and we have had good company. This is not the time to harbour ill will.'

'I wish to say no more on the matter. If you would prefer that we sought lodgings elsewhere—'

Bruno looks hurt. 'Of course not. You are kin. I would not think of it.' Then, with the merest hint of an astute smile, he turns to Nicholas. 'Is it perhaps that Signorina Hella is in need of a cure that has nothing to do with medicine? A cure that only you can provide?'

Nicholas opens his mouth to deny it, but Bianca breaks in. 'Please, Cousin, if you bear any love for Nicholas and me, keep that woman away from us.'

And with that, she kisses Bruno demurely on the cheek, thanks him kindly for the meal and sets off for the chamber she and Nicholas share, as though it has all been nothing but a foolish misunderstanding. Though from the tautness in her stride, Nicholas knows that inside she is screaming.

'Was Bruno right? Are you frightened I'll let Hella lead me by the hand to adultery? Why would you even think that?'

Nicholas has asked because Bianca has started to cry. She is crying only softly, and were it not for the slight movement in her shoulders he would never know it. It is something he has seen her do only rarely, and never when they are lying together in a tangle of sheets, the fire of lovemaking cooling on their bodies. The window shutters are thrown open to air the chamber. It is almost night. Outside in the Borgo dei Argentieri comes the sound of young gallants singing praise to wine, women or honour.

Bianca does not answer him.

'Is it what she said in Reims, about a dead child? Is that still preying on your mind?' He runs a soothing hand through her hair.

Still no answer.

'Listen to me, Bianca. When she spoke those words, yes, I admit it, they brought back old memories I thought I had buried. But only for a while. I have had plenty of time on the road since then to consider their effect. I have made peace with my past. I have let Eleanor's memory go. You must, too.'

Bianca draws a slow, steadying breath. She thinks: what can I say to you? What can I confess that will not cause my fear to burst free from its chains? Like a ghost whispering in a graveyard, the words Hella had spoken on the road outside Mouthier-Haut-Pierre insinuate themselves into her mind: *It will break his heart when the child you are carrying is stillborn...* No, she thinks, I cannot tell you what I truly fear. Because to do so will mean acknowledging the utterly unacceptable truth, which is that Hella isn't the street-huckster I thought she was, a charlatan peddling tricks to turn a husband away from his wife. It means considering the possibility that she has somehow cursed me. That she knows what the future holds for a body that isn't hers – *my* body. Which means she has control over *my* happiness. *Our* happiness. And that I will never do. Especially now that my menses are overdue and – according to Bruno, who seems to be the only one of us who has noticed – I am apparently *blooming*.

31

Rose Monkton hurries up Woodroffe Lane on a windy morning in late September. The trees in the gardens of the fine houses north of Tower Hill are starting to lose their summer bloom. Soon the leaves will begin to fall, to die.

Death has been much on Rose's mind of late. She has come across London Bridge today determined that if he is to take anyone in the coming days, it will not be her husband Ned.

She has visited him every day since he was returned in chains to the Marshalsea from the Queen's Bench, a condemned man with a very temporary stay of execution. In her presence Ned has been unconvincingly jovial, almost unconcerned. But she knows from the gaoler that he spends some of the money she provides, to keep him free of manacles and in a private room, on jugs of fiery bingo to numb the fear. Sometimes she can smell the spirit on his breath. Once she noticed an empty pitcher in his room. He told her he used it as a piss-pot. It is the only time, she is sure, that he has ever lied to her.

The past few days have not been easy for her. The work on the Jackdaw, though progressing well, cannot be left entirely unattended, and Mistress Bianca would not want her weeping into her sleeve all day. Rose has tried hard to be ordered and restrained, but it is not in her nature. After all, she knows Mistress Bianca is wont to refer to her as *my Mistress Moonbeam* and – when irritated – likens her brain to a cauldron of pottage: full of scraps and constantly bubbling. But since the day the magistrate set down his awful sentence, Rose has shown a determination that would astound Bianca – wherever she is.

Rose has decided that Lord Lumley is her only hope. Until last summer she had never been in close proximity to a lord, let alone served one his roast mutton pie and discussed the state of the beans and lettuces in his kitchen garden. But a year ago, when the plague was still rife in London and Mistress Bianca was recovering from the injuries she had sustained in the destruction of the Jackdaw, Lord Lumley had generously agreed to Master Nicholas's plea that they all decamp to the relative safety of his magnificent palace in the Surrey countryside. And thus Rose had discovered – though she was sure the example was not universal – that Baron Lumley of Lumley Castle in Northumberland was a thoroughly decent man with a generous and kindly heart, even if he did have the long, grey outward appearance of a rainy week in January.

To her immense relief, when she reaches Lumley's town house – a fine oak-timbered place barely a stone's throw from the old city walls below Aldgate – she finds him in the orchard garden.

'Why, God give you good morrow, young Mistress Monkton,' Lumley says with a smile, turning from his pruning at the sound of her discreet cough. 'I have informed the lawyer I asked to make young Ned's defence that he will have no more instructions from me. Apparently, on the day, he thought it beneath him to defend a common man. I trust the judge ordered an acquittal?'

Several minutes later Rose has regained a measure of composure. A small mound of sodden kerchiefs lies on the ground beside Lumley's pruning knife. She takes a noisy gulp from the glass of warm hippocras he has ordered brought to her. He can barely bring himself to look into her eyes. The agony there is too much for him to bear.

'When is he to hang, Rose?' Lumley asks. 'I assume we have very little time.'

'The magistrate said something about sending the case to the Privy Council, to put Ned to the hard press. I fear they mean to rack him before they 'ang him.' The tears begin to well in her eyes again. 'There must be *something* you can do, m'lord. I 'ave no hope in the world but you.'

'I will do what I can, of course. But I don't want to give you false cause for hope. It will require a considerable amount of luck. It is a shame there was no immediate family to offer a financial settlement, in return for a plea to the magistrate for clemency. I would have paid that for you in an instant. And I will make an immediate appeal to Chief Justice Popham and Attorney General Coke to overturn the judgement.'

Lumley tries to sound positive, but his great fear is that Coke and Popham, knowing of his Catholic faith, will disregard his plea out of spite. He cannot bring himself to tell Rose that. He raises his hands to his bearded face, almost as though he would shut out the look of grief in her eyes. He is a thoughtful man, prone to melancholy, and her presence at Nonsuch brought a welcome brightness to the days he spends amongst the books in his formidable library. He wishes now that he had found a more practical knowledge there, something that might bring comfort to this frightened young woman.

✳

'You Caporetti women have always been rumoured to be notorious poisoners, Cousin Bianca,' Bruno Barrani says with only half a smile, laying aside his book of Boccaccio poetry and looking up from the divan that Luca and Alonso have set in a shady corner of the courtyard for their master's relaxation. 'I have no intention of putting it to the test. I accede to your wish.'

It is the first time Bianca has heard her mother's maiden name spoken since she was a child. But she has always been aware of the rumours: that it was a Caporetti who mixed the poison Agrippina used to murder Claudius, and that the women of the line have been skilled in lethal distillations ever since. She smiles wanly at her cousin's little joke.

'I'm not asking much, Bruno – only that you deny Hella a welcome in this house, at least while Nicholas and I are here.'

Bruno shrugs in acquiescence. 'Very well, Cousin. As you wish. But I cannot prevent her from visiting Signor Galileo and Matteo Fedele. Young Matteo seems greatly enamoured by her. And her quickness in mathematics is clear. The *Arte dei Astronomi* has need of her. Signor Galileo is too much in demand at the Palazzo Bo, and too easily distracted when he's at home.'

'Then let her trouble *them* with her gloomy talk. I ask only that she is kept from my sight, and away from my husband.'

'If it pleases you, Cousin,' Bruno says, admitting defeat with a spreading of his palms. He goes back to his book of Boccaccio.

Am I being honest? Bianca wonders as she walks away. Is it Nicholas's tranquillity I am concerned for, or my own?

Her menses are now well overdue. If she is with child it is a prospect that should, by rights, fill her with unbounded joy. And it would do so, had Hella Maas not uttered those cruel words in Reims and on the road below Mouthier-Haut-Pierre. They alone should qualify Hella as a beneficiary of the Caporettis' art. And it would not be so very hard to do, Bianca thinks. It would be an easy thing to purchase a little hemlock or wolfsbane, masking the taste with something sweet. Her mother might be in her grave, but there are still apothecaries in Padua who would help. Some might even remember her. She recalls now what she had said to Nicholas on Bankside when he told her about the denunciation. In jest – and before the true

321

danger of the slander had dawned on her – she replied: *There can be but one poisoner in our union, Nicholas. You're the healer, I'm the poisoner, remember?*

Yes, she thinks, for Bruno's sake I will forbear. But if that woman dares to show she has any further designs upon my husband, then it might well be time to consider taking up the old trade once more. After all, what can be more honourable than maintaining a family tradition?

✠

The next morning Matteo Fedele leads Hella Maas across the stone bridge by the Ponte Portello. A rain shower has left the white stone busts of Padua's nobility gleaming like polished marble, and the brickwork of the storehouses along the grassy riverbank the colour of overcooked mutton. Proudly brandishing a heavy iron key, he does battle with the lock on the side-door of the storehouse.

'Tell me, sweet Matteo,' she says, 'are you *sure* Signor Barrani said nothing more about why I was not to go to the house in the Borgo dei Argentieri again?'

He gives her a look of regret. He does not care to disappoint a maid whose humility, both in dress and demeanour, he admires. She is a revelation to him. Where in all Italy could he find a maid whose eyes don't glaze over when he speaks of Euclid, Pythagoras, Plato and Aristotle? She can almost match him in discourse – and in a language that is not even her own. And there is an intriguing beauty hidden away beneath all that severity. She is a catch, and no mistake. Indeed, the mask of piety she wears will make the chase all the more exciting.

Not that Matteo Fedele is thinking of anything serious. She clearly has no dowry, and his father would cut him off without a *scudo* to his name if he so much as suggested marriage to her.

Time enough, he thinks, for marriage when he's an established figure in the *Arte dei Astronomi*.

'He said only that it was improper for an unmarried maid to visit the house of a man who would be Master of the Spheres for His Serenity the doge,' Matteo answers. He tries not to smile. Such an explanation might hold water if the doge's Master of the Spheres was any man but Bruno Barrani.

'I hope Signor Barrani's sense of decency will not prevent me from assisting you and Signor Galileo? God did not give me the gift of understanding such things only for it to rot away like windfall.'

Matteo grins. Is she playing an opening gambit? he wonders. Is there fire under the ice?

'I fear that Signor Galileo's house is a lot more disreputable than Signor Barrani's.'

She gives one of her chilly smiles. 'Our Saviour did not walk only amongst the pure, Signor Matteo. Quite the opposite.'

Inside the storehouse all is silent. The forge in the corner is cold. Tiny flecks of dust turn gently in the air, glinting in the shafts of light streaming in from the high windows. The wooden cradle of the sphere stands in the centre, like some giant antediluvian sea creature lying dead on its back after the flood has receded. A single brass meridian ring hoops towards the roof, twice the height of a man. Around the base lie the innards of the beast: the segments of rings etched with signs of the zodiac; the discs of varying diameters; the cogs, wheels, brass globes to represent the planets... Matteo watches as Hella circles the neat stacks of metal and gilded wood. She has a curious look on her face. She seems intrigued, but appears to be frowning. For just an instant he has the extraordinary impression of a predator circling a disembowelled carcass. She looks across at him from the other side of the cradle. The frown has gone from her face, but it still lingers in her eyes.

'This is only a small fraction of the whole,' Matteo says defensively. 'It will take many months to fabricate everything.'

The maid circles the cradle in silence until she is standing beside him again. Then she says, 'Do you think it is wise for mankind to build a machine that mimics God's works?'

This surprises Matteo, because until now he has assumed the maid wholeheartedly approves of the new learning, of enquiry and experimentation, of seeking the limits of what may be known. Now she sounds almost censorious.

'But how else may we understand those works, if not through science?' he replies. 'By this engine, we will be able to see the cosmos as it will be in days, even years, ahead – if Maestro Galileo and I can contrive the movement of the mechanism correctly.'

The maid's gaze drops from his, as though she doesn't want him to see into her thoughts. 'I have seen a representation of the future, Signor Matteo,' she says, so softly he barely hears, 'in Brabant. It does not end well.'

'What do you mean?'

'It ends in death.'

'Of course it does. But then there is resurrection and eternal life. Surely you believe that? You're not a heretic, are you?'

She looks up, as though the words she has just spoken were someone else's. 'How could a Beguine be a heretic, Matteo? I am God's child as much as you.'

'Then there is nothing to fear by seeking to look into the future, is there?'

A change seems to come over her. Something in her eyes makes Matteo think of a child who has woken from a nightmare and fears the return of sleep.

'Tell me, Matteo,' she says, 'if you could make the sphere turn enough times, do you think it might one day replicate the positions of the planets and the zodiacs on the last day?'

Now it is Matteo's turn to frown. 'What do you mean, "the last day"?'

The stare she gives him lances into his mind like a bolt fired from a crossbow.

'Judgement Day, Matteo. The *last* day.'

For a moment he doesn't know what to say. Her intensity unnerves him. 'I... I suppose it *might* be contrived. But only a man like Maestro Galileo could imagine the calculations required to achieve it. It would be beyond my skill. And I wouldn't dare do it, anyway. It would be blasphemy.'

'But it *could* be done?'

'In theory, I suppose it might.'

'What would it look like?'

Matteo is beginning to feel uncomfortable. 'How would I know? Perhaps if one could turn the sphere through enough cycles until the planets and the stars were all constrained in alignment, or were no longer visible from your chosen latitude – *that* might indicate an empty cosmos. But if the Holy Office of the Faith knew the sphere was capable of such a calculation—' He breaks off, shuddering as he imagines the flames beginning to lap around his legs as the Inquisition has him burned in the middle of the Piazza dei Signori. 'But I cannot imagine why anyone would want to know such a thing. I think it would be best to speak of any other matter but *that*.'

✠

'I've had her banished, Nicholas,' Bianca says proudly. 'It's the best thing all round, don't you think?'

She has just this moment met her husband in the university botanical gardens. Nicholas has been attending another of Professor Fabrici's lectures.

'Banished? You sound like Queen Elizabeth or Catherine de'

Medici,' he says, trying not to smile. Bianca has a familiar glint in her eye, the one that's often there after she's had Ned Monkton eject a quarrelsome customer from the Jackdaw.

'Well, it's a compromise. Bruno has some silly notion Hella can be of use to the *Arte dei Astronomi*. Fine, let her haunt Signor Galileo's house then. I think it was Matteo Fedele's idea. The lazy rascal wants to make use of her ability at mathematics, so that he can put his feet up while Hella does all the work for him. They'll soon grow tired of her, when she starts telling Signor Galileo he's going to spend eternity being crushed in a wine-press for living a life of debauchery.'

They find a place by the canal bank to sit awhile in the sunshine. Bianca leans forward over her knees, watching the brown water slide eastwards on its journey to the Venetian lagoon.

'I thought when I came here that we would find peace, Nicholas. At least for a while,' she says. 'But that woman is like some cold, dead hand on my shoulder that I cannot shake off.'

'This isn't like you, Bianca,' he says, taking her hand, his face troubled. 'You've never let a soul cower your spirit: not Robert Cecil, not Cat Vaesy, Tyrell, Gault... None of them could match you, when it came down to it. Even the pestilence took one look at you and thought better of it.'

She gives a half-hearted laugh at his attempt to console her. 'This is different. I don't know why, but I feel it in my bones.'

'Is this to do with what passed between you and Hella on the Via Francigena? You still haven't really told me what happened.'

'I *can't*,' she says, tears welling in her eyes.

'Why not? How bad could it be?'

'It would make it real. Words are like stones, Nicholas. Once made, they are indestructible.'

He holds her close, knowing that to press her further will only add to her distress.

'There are people on Bankside who believe I have second sight,' she says, wanting his embrace, yet afraid it might feel like the embrace of a stranger. 'Do you believe it?'

'I wouldn't put it past you, Bianca Merton.'

'And do you believe Hella can see into the future, the way she claims?'

'I think she has suffered greatly in the past, and blames herself for it. I think she looked too deeply into grief and found patterns there, when there were no real patterns to be found.'

'You're defending her?'

He lets go of her and stands. Bianca follows, watching him as he chooses the right words.

'I'm a physician. I know that maladies are not confined to the body alone. The mind and the soul can sicken, too. Professor Fabrici can dissect all the cadavers he wants, but he cannot see inside a single human thought.'

'Are you going to try to heal her, if she comes to you?'

Nicholas takes her in his arms again, running a hand through the thick, dark waves of her hair, brushing away a strand that has fallen wilfully over one eye. 'I cannot turn away someone who is sick. It is not in my nature. You must trust me to know what is right.'

'I thought that is what you would say.'

She sinks into his chest, laying her face alongside his neck. On the gravel path behind them, two white-haired men in professorial gowns walk past, casting scowls of disapproval at the show of intimacy. Neither Nicholas nor Bianca notices them.

'Nicholas,' she says after a while, 'I believe I am pregnant.'

Releasing her, he holds her at arm's length as though he's inspecting something he has long coveted, but can only now afford. Then he steps back, throws his arms wide and makes three joyous circles on the path, hopping from one foot to the other as he turns, silently, though his grin is wide enough for all the words in the world to spill out.

Bianca watches him. She wants so much to sense the swell of joy in her own heart. To match his unbridled happiness. But all she can feel at this moment is fear.

32

At the house in the Borgo dei Argentieri, Bruno has ordered a feast in celebration of Bianca's news. Alonso and Luca are dispatched at the double, returning laden with gleaming hams, vegetables bright enough to dazzle the eyes and glistening *sardele* and *orata*, which they swear on their lives arrived on ice from the Venetian lagoon this very dawn. Bruno's collection of best plate is carried ceremoniously from his chamber, where it is kept in a locked chest on account of his servants' propensity to forget about the rules of ownership.

'A black bean or white bean?' asks Bruno, grinning like a carnival mask.

Nicholas looks perplexed.

'It's the way the city used to record births,' Bianca explains, sounding oddly subdued to Nicholas. 'Beans placed in a box: black for a boy, white for a girl.' Then, to Bruno, 'It will be a white bean.'

'Or a black bean,' says Nicholas, smiling.

And then Bianca says, with a harshness that makes him glance at her in surprise, 'White or black, as long as it's a bean and not a poison berry.'

That evening, in their chamber, he says, 'You have to tell me what's wrong. You are beginning to trouble me – deeply.'

'Do you believe in curses, Nicholas?' she asks, in an absent-minded way. 'I suppose not. Your vaunted new learning will tell you to believe only what you can see... touch... *measure*.'

'Is that what this ill humour is about? Has Hella Maas laid a *curse* upon you?' he asks, astonished.

But Bianca does not answer. She turns away from him, and he can tell by the way her shoulders are tightly hunched that she is on the verge of either tears or an explosion of anger. He is unsure which he fears most.

✠

In the dormitory of Padua's Beguinage, the Sisters dream their pious dreams. The squat, stripped-down villa just outside the walls of the Seminary Maggiore is home to some twenty of them, the youngest seventeen, the oldest eighty-six. Being neither nuns nor wholly secular, they are a constant worry to the seminary's praeceptor and a source of endless speculation by his young male students. If they are not exactly brides of Christ, he tells them, you may at least regard them as loosely betrothed.

As the Seminary bell marks midnight, its deep bass voice sending tremors through the Beguinage like spasms through a dying body, only two of the Sisters are still awake, sharing their mattress with two older women who snore contentedly in the darkness. One is Hella Maas. The other is a plump raven-haired girl, a year or two younger.

'Madonna Antonella asked me where you go each day,' Sister Carlotta says, her voice breathless with excitement. In the Beguinage, Madonna Antonella represents authority and, like young women everywhere, Sister Carlotta enjoys the thrill of defying it, even though she does so only in the smallest of measures. 'I told her that you go to the Basilica of St Anthony, to be nearer to God. But I know that's not it. I saw you yesterday in the Borgo dei Vignali, going into a house.'

'Have you been spying on me, little Carlotta?' Hella asks.

'No! I was taking a message from Madonna Antonella to

Father Giuseppe at St Angelo's. I happened to see you, that's all.' A thought occurs to Carlotta, sending a tremor of vicarious pleasure through her body. 'Are you seeing a *man*, Hella? Tell me! I promise I will keep your secret.'

It has taken Hella some time to bend little Sister Carlotta to her will. She has done so carefully, so as not to raise her suspicions. She has played on Carlotta's gullibility, and her desperate need for a companion who can make her days a little more exciting. It could prove useful, Hella thinks, to have a tame creature to do my bidding, run my errands, lie for me.

'We're not living in a nunnery, or a prison, sweet little Carlotta,' she says enigmatically, watching the tallow candle flicker weakly in the corner of the dormitory, set there that the older Sisters might find the night-soil pot without kicking its contents over the floor. 'Don't you want to know what it's like?'

Carlotta almost squeals. 'I don't *believe* you. How can you be truly pious and yet give yourself in lust?'

'What do you think the priests and bishops do? What do you think the Pope does?'

Another slack-mouthed gasp of excited horror. 'You cannot say such things! It is blasphemy! You'll be damned to the everlasting fires.'

Hella tries to stop herself smiling. *Captured*, she thinks. She arches her back in readiness for sleep, stares at the darkened ceiling and imagines a great golden sphere of planets and stars turning inexorably through the years towards the end of days. 'Oh, sweet Carlotta,' she whispers knowingly, 'have no fear on my account. I won't be the only one.'

✠

In the storehouse by the river, old Bondoni the goldsmith watches anxiously while the Corio brothers hammer a series of cog-wheels onto an iron spindle the length of a man's arm. In his hand is a gleaming brass ring from which extend a series of wires, each with a small gilded ball on the end. From each ball flows a fiery wavy tail of beaten copper. In the corner, a Corio assistant is pumping the bellows of a forge, sending showers of sparks dancing through the dusty air.

'If my cometary ecliptic fits first time *anything* the Corios have made, I'll forsake wine and women and take up holy orders,' Bondoni says with a wink to Nicholas and Bianca. 'I wouldn't trust them to make me a fork with the tines all pointing the same way.' He gives the ring a final polish against one yellow-hosed thigh, his lank white hair falling over his brow as he rubs.

Bianca recalls the goldsmith's fearsome mistress and six children, and wonders if secretly Bondoni might be deliberately holding himself hostage to fortune.

'We've brought the next set of drawings, for the equatorial ring,' Nicholas says, setting down three rolls of parchment on the workbench. 'Signor Barrani received them this morning, from Signor Galileo.'

'I don't suppose he mentioned a payment – for my last work?' Bondoni says, rolling out the drawings.

'No, I'm afraid he didn't.'

To Bianca, the diagrams look bewildering, with their lines of axis and fan-like graticules, tangents, arcs, Roman numerals and strange equations. She suspects they're even more meaningless to her cousin Bruno. She has the sneaking feeling that he only insists on signing them off so that his name appears on them, establishing for posterity that from the start this was always the Barrani Sphere.

'I must say, young Matteo's work is splendid. Very precise,' Bondoni continues. 'It's come along no end. Of course that's probably down to Signor Galileo's teaching.' He gives Nicholas a knowing, men-of-the-world-together look. 'But it's the maid who's cured him of his laziness. I wonder why that might be.'

Feeling Bianca stiffen at his side, Nicholas takes his leave. As they walk back towards Bruno's house, she says, 'So you weren't the only one to be taken in by Hella Maas.'

'What do you imply by that?'

She puts on a derisive sing-song voice, parodying Bondoni. '*I must say, young Matteo's work is splendid... very precise... I wonder why that might be.*'

'You really must put Hella out of your mind,' Nicholas says, as kindly as he can manage. 'It's not healthy for you to hold this animosity against her. Forget about her. I have.'

Bianca casts him a hard look. Her amber eyes gleam with an intensity that unsettles him. He can see anger brimming there, and exasperation.

'You... Bruno... Galileo... Matteo Fedele – you've all fallen under her spell like children at the Bartholomew Fair,' she says. 'Yet not one of you has bothered to ask yourself the obvious question.'

'And what question would that be?'

Hands on hips, Bianca turns to face her husband.

'Have any of you stopped for a moment to wonder why someone who preaches that seeking knowledge is akin to inviting the Devil into your house should be helping my cousin build a sphere that can see into the future?'

33

In the closing days of September the weather breaks. Grey clouds drift down from the mountains to the north. At night, it is easier to sleep. For Nicholas and Bianca, this does not, however, lead to an increase in ardour. A distance has opened up between them.

By day, Bianca has taken to making solitary visits to the places of her childhood: the old lodgings where her mother and father lived, the little church where they are buried and where old Father Rossi – eighty if a day – still tends the graves. She walks the lanes through which, as children, she and Bruno would carry secret letters for Cardinal Fiorzi, the perfect messengers for a cardinal enmeshed in political conspiracies they themselves were too young to understand.

For his part, Nicholas attends the Palazzo Bo, to hear lectures by Professor Fabrici. His friendship with Galileo is burgeoning. Aware that his visits to the house in the Borgo dei Vignali are a source of tension between him and Bianca, he tries to time them for when Hella Maas is not there.

One evening the physician and the mathematician share a jug of wine together at a tavern called The Fig, close to the part of the university where Professor Fabrici is building his anatomical theatre. Nicholas takes a deep breath and asks after Hella Maas.

Galileo raises one bushy eyebrow, wipes the wine from his lips with the back of a hand and says, 'Why do you ask? You already have the handsomest wife in Padua. You can't have tired of her already.'

'Of course not. I'm a physician. I'm concerned for the maid, nothing more.'

'You think she is ill?'

Nicholas shrugs. 'Perhaps not in the body. But in the soul—'

Galileo turns the wine jug in a circle, as though inspecting it for faults. 'Well, I must confess she is a little – how shall I describe it? – *fervent*.'

Nicholas takes a thoughtful sip of wine. The hubbub of the tavern washes over him while he considers his words.

'I think some ill has passed between Hella and my wife, during their time together on the Via Francigena – something to which Bianca refuses to make me privy.'

'Have you no idea what it could be?'

'Hella seems convinced that the end of days is very close. I think all her talk of judgement has brought a heavy melancholy down upon Bianca.'

Galileo lets out a sharp, contemptuous laugh. 'There are plenty of people who believe that, Niccolò. The churches are full of them, in front of and behind the altar. Every time there's a storm or a bad harvest, or a comet appears in the sky, down they go on their knees. The Church makes a fortune out of it. When it actually happens, the Pope will have to go back to being an honest man.'

Smiling, Nicholas says, 'All I know is that this young woman has suffered a great tribulation in her life and been witness to great violence. And something happened on the journey here, something between her and Bianca.'

'I can solve complex mathematical questions, Niccolò; but marriage problems—' He feigns a look of bewilderment. 'My brother-in-law demands I pay him more for my sister's dowry... my sister calls me a wastrel and a drunkard... If you'd come to

335

me earlier, I'd have advised you to avoid the condition of marriage entirely.'

'I believe I must speak directly to Hella,' Nicholas says. 'I must confront her – find out what has passed between her and my wife. I'll not learn it from Bianca; she can barely bring herself to speak of the maid.'

'Then we shall agree a day and a time,' the mathematician says, draining his cup. 'I'll give you an hour. I'll contrive to send Matteo on an errand, if I can rouse his lazy arse. As for me, I shall retire to my chamber and make eyes at the signorina who sits in her window opposite, watching what goes on in the street all day. Like Signor Purse's sphere, she is a work in progress.'

✠

'Rejoice at the wonderful news,' Bruno says when Nicholas returns to the Borgo dei Argentieri. For a moment he thinks Bruno is speaking of his cousin's pregnancy. But he is not.

'His excellency, the Podestà, has agreed to allow the *Arte dei Astronomi* to march with all the other city guilds in the great parade on the Feast of the Holy Rosary.'

'I'm pleased to hear it,' says Nicholas, contriving an unconvincing interest.

Bruno explains, barely able to contain his excitement. His little frame almost quivers like a spaniel catching sight of a partridge. 'Every first Sunday in October we celebrate the victory of the Venetian fleet over the Turk. There is a grand procession, ending with the blessing of the guilds' banners at the Basilica of St Anthony. We are recognized at last! I will have to buy a decent cloak. And I insist on finding Cousin Bianca a pretty new gown to wear.'

'That is generous of you, Bruno, but I will pay.'

'No! I insist. It will be a gift from me to her, to celebrate all our good fortune: your presence here, her pregnancy, my success...'

Nicholas concedes graciously. When he goes in search of Bianca, to tell her of her cousin's gracious offer, he finds her in the courtyard, writing a letter. It's to Rose and Ned, she says – asking after the Jackdaw's resurrection, telling them she will not be returning to England for some time. They are to open the tavern as soon as it is ready and run it without her. He considers asking her if she's told them of her pregnancy, but he has second thoughts. He thinks he already knows the answer.

✠

October slinks in like a starving wolf, wet and miserable, yet still able to bite. In the narrow lanes of Bankside yesterday's rain has filled the open sewers with a scummy, stinking brown soup. A brisk wind flails the trees in the Pike Garden, blowing the dying leaves into sodden piles around the white plaster walls of the Rose theatre. It has rained for most of September. This, in conspiracy with the violent storms of spring, has pushed the price of wheat to almost eight shillings a bushel. Money is scarce. Rose Monkton is beginning to fear that when the Jackdaw does reopen, few in Southwark will have much above a farthing left over to spend in it. On top of everything else, the cost of keeping Ned in even a small measure of comfort at the Marshalsea is eating into the purse that Mistress Bianca entrusted to her for the rebuilding. Only yesterday Jenny Solver asked her if she'd lost weight. Rose just smiled. She hadn't the courage to confess that she hasn't slept soundly since the constable came and took her husband away.

Shortly after breakfast a liveried servant brings a message from John Lumley. He wants to meet her at the public fountain at the top of Fish Street Hill, on the north side of the Bridge. Noontime, if that is not inconvenient.

Wrapping herself in her thick winter cloak, Rose hurries across the river. She knows she will arrive ridiculously early, but thinks it better to fret there in the open air than alone in the Paris Garden lodgings.

She waits for more than an hour and a half, the minutes dragging by, not one of them bringing her the slightest ease. By the time she sees the tall figure in the dark cloak and the neatly starched ruff making his way towards her from Grass Street, a black cap with a jaunty peacock's feather in it upon his head, Rose's eyes are red from the constant rubbing of the kerchief that is now wedged, cold and wet, between her forearm and the fabric of her kirtle, as if something unpleasant from the river has crawled up her sleeve.

'Forgive me if I am a little late, Mistress Rose,' Lumley says. 'My endowment of the chair of anatomy at the College of Physicians requires me to attend the occasional formal function. They tend to be tedious and last longer than I would prefer.'

Knowing there cannot be many other nobles in the land who would bother themselves for an instant with the problems of a former servant, Rose makes what she hopes will be a dignified curtsey. Her right foot slips on the cobbles and she ends up at a tilt on one knee, one hand around Lumley's shin to stop herself from tumbling. Calmly he reaches down and lifts her to her feet.

'Are you hurt, Rose?'

'No, my lord. Well, *yes*, my lord, but in my heart, not my ankle.'

A troubled look floods his old grey eyes. 'I fear I have not made the progress I had wished. You must be brave,' he says gravely, like a priest attending a deathbed.

Rose feels as though she has just stepped off a cliff. She is tumbling, spinning to destruction, yet the buildings around the fountain remain fixed and constant in her sight. Her eyes well with tears again.

'Do not give way to despair, Rose,' Lumley says. 'There is, perhaps, still hope. Come with me, and I will explain.'

The tavern he takes her to is on the east side of Fish Street Hill, at the corner of Little Eastcheap. It is a place Rose could never afford to drink in. The taproom boys are all smartly dressed, the customers languid and oddly silent. One or two glance her way with looks of disapproval. At any other time than this, she would probably stick her tongue out at them for their presumption that she is the old gentleman's whore.

Lumley sits her down in an alcove and calls for two glasses of sack. Rose drinks with an unsteady hand.

'Firstly, Rose,' he begins, 'we may give thanks that the Privy Council moves exceeding slow. It has not yet considered the magistrate's suggestion that Ned be investigated for having sympathy with Dr Lopez's alleged crime. They haven't racked him yet, thank God.'

Rose emits a heavy sigh of relief. Lumley raises a hand to forestall any undue optimism.

'I have appealed to Chief Justice Popham and Attorney General Coke to reconsider the verdict. I told them I believe your husband is innocent of manslaughter and acted merely in self-defence. I even offered to purchase an acquittal. I fear they refused. I think they did so in order to spite me. They cannot bear the thought that Her Grace the queen can favour an old papist like me. They were adamant. Ned must go to his death – by hanging, at Tyburn.' He tries to calm another burst of noisy weeping by laying one hand gently on Rose's arm. 'Hush, child. I have more to tell you.'

Lumley takes a silk kerchief from his gown and dabs at her eyes. 'I then sought an audience with Her Majesty,' he continues. 'She has read the letter of retraction that Vaesy wrote. She is confirmed in her belief that Dr Shelby is innocent of the charge made against him. But she has refused to pardon Ned.'

Rose's face crumples with injured indignation. 'But... but... 'e's innocent too! Why will she not show us mercy?'

339

'She fears that if a person of Ned's humble station is excused the violent death of a knight of the realm, then any man of the lowest order might think it but a small matter to kill a duke – or a queen.'

'Then my man is going to 'ang?' Rose says in a small voice.

Lumley's long grey face contorts in pity. He takes her hands in his, feels them tremble as though he were grasping a little animal that he might crush in error without even realizing. He says gently, 'They haven't sentenced him yet, so there could be a way to save him. It is not certain, and it will take luck and not a little skill – on all our parts. And it must be instigated quickly, before the sentence is formally given.'

'What way?' Rose mumbles miserably.

'Ned must claim Benefit of Clergy.'

The sound that comes out of Rose's mouth is a strangled mix of disbelief and desperation, as though Lumley has just suggested her husband sprout wings and fly away to safety.

'Ned – plead the 'Oly Book?' she gasps.

'It is the only way. If he claims Benefit of Clergy, he will be exempt from temporal law. It will then fall upon the ecclesiastical courts to define the sentence. But it must be done between the verdict and the sentence. So I have taken the liberty of entering the plea for him. Thank God the magistrate did not pass an immediate judgement or he would already be dead.'

'But no one could confuse Ned for a *priest* – no one!'

Lumley offers her a gentle smile of hope. 'I know a chaplain who served my late father-in-law, the Earl of Arundel. He owes me a rather large favour. He has agreed to hear Ned's submission. If all goes well, a branding is the customary sentence for a first crime, so long as it is less than treason. A severe hurt, I know, but a lot better than the alternative.'

'What will be required of my Ned?' Rose asks doubtfully.

'All he has to do is appear before the ecclesiastical court and recite the opening verses of the fifty-first Psalm, in Latin.'

Expecting her face to lighten, all Lumley sees in her brimming eyes is more misery. Her chest heaves. She says, in a tortured voice, 'But... but Ned *cannot* read, my lord. He 'as not the letters in his 'ead.'

Lumley covers his nose and chin with one palm as he digests the news. 'Can *you* read, Rose?' he asks, looking at her over the tip of his fingers.

'Yes, my lord – and write, too. Mistress Bianca gave me the skills.'

'Do you possess a Bible, Rose?'

'Of course, my lord,' Rose snorts tearfully.

'Then we had better pray that your Ned's memory is as sharp as his temper.'

34

On the day of his meeting with Hella Maas, Nicholas leaves Bruno's house on the Borgo dei Argentieri after breakfast. He has told Bianca that he is going to the Palazzo Bo, to attend another of Professor Fabrici's lectures. A lie told in order to protect, he convinces himself, is hardly a lie at all. Bianca, suffering the indignities of the tailor who has come to check the measurements for the new gown that Bruno has insisted she have for the Feast of the Holy Rosary, seems barely interested in his explanation.

He arrives at Galileo's lodgings in the Borgo dei Vignali just as the bell in the nearby church tolls eight. The street door is open. Under the gaze of the pretty young woman watching from the first-floor window opposite, he enters.

Professor Galileo is sitting in the courtyard, one knee providing support to a heavy leather-bound book on Euclid's theorems by Benedetti, the other stuck out at a jaunty angle, the foot tucked round a leg of the chair. With his free hand, the mathematician is munching a peach.

'Fortunate she's a Beguine,' he says, spitting out the stone, 'or else the university's rector might accuse me of running a bordello and rescind my appointment.'

'Where is she?' Nicholas asks, wondering if he dares ask Galileo for a cup of wine to fortify his resolve.

'Inside, with Matteo. They're working on something for Signor

Purse. We think the Corio brothers might have erred: they've produced some cogs for the orbit of Saturn that will have it colliding with Jupiter after three revolutions, and that will never do.'

'I will need privacy.'

'You shall have it, Niccolò, never fear.' He lays the book aside. 'You're lucky she's here, mind.'

'Why?'

'Yesterday Matteo took her to the Palazzo Bo, to show her the work on the anatomy theatre that old Fabrici is spending all the university's money on. I was beginning to wonder if they were coming back. I think Matteo is smitten. Odd choice, if you ask me. She's too serious for my liking. A woman who can count is all well and good, but only if she smiles occasionally.'

Galileo leads him up a flight of stairs to a plainly furnished chamber set back from the first-storey loggia. Matteo and Hella are stooped over a table on which Nicholas can see papers bearing calculations and diagrams. When the maid looks up, he thinks he detects a faint glint of satisfaction in her eyes, though her face remains still.

'Matteo, I need some papers I left at the Palazzo Bo,' Galileo says.

The pupil begins to protest. 'But, Maestro, I—'

'I haven't notated the other side of the equation yet. "Matteo, I need some papers" *equals* "Do as I command, or I'll recommend to your father that you study theology instead of mathematics." How would a chaste life in holy orders suit you?'

When the professor and his pupil have gone, Nicholas says, 'Walk with me awhile, Hella. I wish to speak plainly with you.' He beckons her to follow him out onto the loggia that runs along all four sides of the house, a shady colonnade encompassing the courtyard below. He puts a hand to his mouth and gives a fast double cough, as though he has a diagnosis to deliver that might not be what the patient wishes to hear.

But before he can start, Hella says, 'I knew that eventually you would come after me, Nicholas.'

'*Come after you?* What do you mean?'

'It was inevitable.' She gives him another of her mirthless smiles. 'We are but opposite sides of the same card, you and I. And you want to know what is on its face: the Lovers or the Hangman.'

'This is not a *game*, Hella. Not to me. Not now that you have hurt Bianca so.'

'I am not responsible for your wife's jealousy, Nicholas.'

He manages to calm a sudden surge of anger. 'She isn't jealous – she's frightened. And I want to know why.'

'I have told you both: once something is known, it cannot then be unknown. In consequence, all that then befalls the discoverer is theirs to own.'

He stops. 'Listen to me, Hella. I've come here to try and help you.'

'I do not need your help, Nicholas. I am not sickly.'

'I think you are, in your heart. I believe the grief you have suffered – the loss of your sister and the others in your family – has brought a great melancholy upon you. I understand that. I, too, have chosen in the past to live in darkness rather than in light. But you were *not* to blame for what happened, whatever you have told yourself. You did not see the future any more than I did. You didn't foresee what was going to befall those you loved. I didn't foresee what was going to happen to my first wife and the child she was carrying, but in the pain that came afterwards, I too convinced myself that it was *my* fault, that there were signs I should have seen: warnings. But I was wrong. If there is a Purgatory, Hella, Bianca led me out of it. You, too, must seek the way out of the Purgatory you have built inside your mind. I can help you – if you let me.'

344

Her eyes have been locked on his throughout. They have not faltered for a moment. 'Why were you hiding in that chamber in the cathedral at Den Bosch, Nicholas?'

Surprised, he asks, 'What does it matter now?'

'What was it you really feared?' she persists. 'Being discovered somewhere you shouldn't have been? Or had sight of that painting driven you into the darkness?'

'It is of no consequence now,' he says, realizing that she is stealing the resolve from him.

'I think you hid because, in your heart, you had gone into that chamber to seek knowledge of what lay within. I've told you before how dangerous that can be. Do not blame *me* for the consequences.'

'And my coming here now – I suppose you could divine that, by the patterns of the arches in the arcades around the Palazzo Bo, in the lines of geese flying overhead or in the fall of the numbers you hold such store by?'

'Don't mock me, Nicholas.'

'If you had any foreknowledge of why I have come here, it is only because you knew that eventually I would learn what it was you said to Bianca on the Via Francigena.'

'She has told you?'

'No. That is why I am here.'

'Then you should look to your wife for the answer,' she says airily. 'Do not seek it from me.'

He cannot stop himself reaching out to seize her arm. 'What did you tell her? She thinks you have cursed her.'

Hella pulls herself free. She stares back at him defiantly.

'If I tell you, Nicholas, I warn you now: you will not be able to unhear my words. They will stay with you for ever.'

'I *have* to know. I have to find a way to bring Bianca back to me.'

Her eyes lift a little, staring out of the loggia as though seeking divine approval. 'I told her that your baby will be stillborn. I told her that she will be barren thereafter. It is what I have seen. It is what Hannie has seen – my sister, my *dead* sister.'

Nicholas thinks the floor of the loggia has given way. He feels as though he is plunging to destruction, that he will go on plunging – through the earth itself – in a descent that will never stop. The sensation is suddenly all too familiar to him. It is not a loggia in Padua he is falling from, but the wet planks of a Thames river stairs. It is not a warm morning in Italy, but a chill night in London, some four years ago. And it is not someone else's actions that have made him fall, but his own. He is falling towards icy water, waiting for its cold embrace to drown out the voice of his dead wife, Eleanor, as she whispers in his head. She is pleading with him to perform a miracle with his physic – a miracle that will save her and the child she is carrying. And though in reality he knows she never spoke a word when she slipped towards oblivion, in his head he is waiting for the river to cleanse him of her accusing voice, cleanse him of all the useless knowledge that failed them both.

And then he is no longer falling. He is lying in a sweat-stained bed in the attic of a Bankside tavern. His eyes are focusing on reality for the first time in days, trying to make out the features of a young woman who has just appeared in the doorway. She has strong, almost boyish features that narrow to a defiant chin. A face that could be stern, if it wasn't for the generous mouth and the astonishingly brilliant amber eyes. Her hair is a rich ebony, burnished by a foreign sun. An exotic flower, he thinks, blooming in the wasteland that is his recent memory. 'You're awake,' the young woman observes dispassionately in a faint accent he can't quite place. 'I imagine you must be hungry. Can you manage a little breakfast? There's larded pullet. We have some baked sprats left over, too. I'll have my maid Rose lay out a trencher...'

As the image fades, Nicholas knows his resurrection is complete. Nothing Hella can say to him – nothing she can say to Bianca – can unlock the door he has chosen to close behind him.

'How much hurt must you have suffered to be so cruel?' he says, as gently as he can. 'If that is the future you think you saw, why in the name of all that is holy did you not just keep your thoughts to yourself?'

'You were sent to me, Nicholas,' Hella says, as though trying to reason with a distracted child. 'You were sent as confirmation that I am right. I knew it from the moment I saw you step out of the shadows in that chamber in the cathedral. That could not have been mere chance. If you had not wanted the knowledge, you would have remained in hiding.'

He lets out a snort of derision. 'It was chance. Nothing more. We shouldn't even have been in Den Bosch. We were bound for Antwerp.'

'But can't you see the pattern, Nicholas? Every little piece falls into place when you look at the whole.'

Unable to control the sudden wave of disgust that sweeps over him, Nicholas says coldly, 'Take back the curse, Hella. Take it back! Or by God, I'll finish what that Dutch rebel failed to.'

But she doesn't even blink. 'No, you won't, Nicholas,' she says with frightening calmness. 'You want to know if I'm right. You're driven by the same appetite as I – to seek what lies behind the curtain. You're not so much of a coward that you will turn away for fear of what you will find there. But I have looked already. I *know* I am already damned.'

He turns and walks away towards the stairs.

'You will come to me eventually, Nicholas,' he hears her call out, even as he raises his hands to his ears. 'Why do you think I am here in Padua? It isn't to help Galileo and that fool Matteo with their calculations; it's to be where *you* can find me. You will come back to me – it is written. The signs are all there, like the signs that foretell what is coming: the rains, the storms, the comets, the war, the pestilences... They are all telling us that time is running out.'

He tries to shut out the sound of her voice as he goes. But her parting words are a cold breeze blowing in his ears.

'Don't delay, Nicholas. Don't leave it too long. I cannot face what is coming alone. And there is very little time left.'

35

The Marshalsea Prison, Bankside,
2nd October 1594

In the sickly grey light filtering through the rain that streams down the leaded-glass window, Rose Monkton eases herself out of her husband's embrace. She can feel his reluctance to let her go, as though his great fingers are already beginning to stiffen after the long drop from the gallows.

'How is your memory, 'Usband?' she asks, taking stock of how he seems a little diminished since last she saw him. His great auburn beard will require a good trimming, she thinks. And he'll need a clean linen shirt. The ecclesiastical court will take a lot of convincing, but it will be down to Ned alone to save himself.

'My memory?'

He seems confused by her question.

'Yes, your memory. How is it?'

'Have I forgotten something, Wife?' he asks, perplexed. 'I know it's not our anniversary. An' it's not your birthday...'

'No, 'Usband. You have forgotten nothing. It is a simple question. How good are you at remembering things?'

'Why do you ask, Rose?'

'I have been to see Lord Lumley. He says there is no hope for us – but one. He would have you plead Benefit of Clergy.'

'He wants me to call a priest?' Ned asks, misunderstanding her. 'Does he think giving me papist absolution before I 'ang is going to help?'

Rose looks horrified. 'No, 'Usband. If you plead the Book, sentencing will fall to the Church authorities, not a temporal court. A first offence will be punished only with a branding upon the thumb – an M, to show you've been judged guilty of slaying a man – so that you cannot plead mercy again, should you commit another felony. Not that you did commit a felony – you're innocent... I know that... but it's the only way.'

Ned lays a steadying hand upon Rose's shoulder to stop her words running away with her. 'Well, what's a sore thumb, Wife, if it joins what has been torn asunder?'

The tears begin to flow again. 'Oh, but dearest Ned, it is not that easy. You must sermonize from the Bible – Psalm fifty-one – like you was a parson. An' there's you without the readin'...'

Ned offers her a huge smile that stops the tears mid-flow.

'So you want to know if my memory is up to learning what you will read out to me – is that it?'

Rose snorts a rapid volley of watery breaths. 'I... I lie abed at night, unable to sleep for weeping. I know Mistress Bianca thinks I'm an addle-pate an' can't keep one thought in my head longer than an 'eartbeat, but I 'ave tried *so* hard to think of a way of saving you from the noose. An' now Lord Lumley offers this chance, but you can't read. So I must read to you, an' you *must* remember it, Ned – perfectly. If you gets it wrong, all is lost. And I know how hard remembering is. I fear you will forget.'

Ned guides her to the mattress. He eases her down gently, her body folding compliantly to the pressure of his hands. He sits beside Rose, pulls her head into the cushion of his armpit.

'There, sweet, *there*. Trouble yourself no more. You will sleep easy tonight.'

She looks up at him. 'How?' she asks. 'How shall I sleep, when all I think about is losing my Ned?'

'Let me tell you of the time before I met you, Rose,' he begins. She feels the great rumbling of his voice through his shirt, as it flows from the wellspring deep inside him. 'You know well that I was a solitary man...'

She nods.

'My days and my nights were not spent like other men's. I lived amongst the dead – in the mortuary crypt at St Tom's hospital. You know that.'

Another nod.

'The dead were all I had for company. They were poor, for the most part: men, women, children... vagrants, vagabonds, out-casts... sailors drowned in the river... suicides destined to lie alone in unconsecrated ground. They were my only company. An' when they left the crypt for a pauper's grave – an unmarked pauper's grave – they had only me to remember them, to mourn them. So I remembered their names. An' if they had no name, why, I would give them one. An' every day I would take a moment to speak those names – a score or so in a sitting – so that they would not be forgotten.'

Ned pulls Rose even closer. She can smell his unwashed body and the musty smell of his linen shirt. It is like a balm to her. He could be a father soothing his child to sleep, telling her a tale of knights and princesses, dragons and queens. She feels safe for the first time in weeks.

'So fear not for my memory, Rose Monkton,' he whispers softly as he kisses the top of her head, inhaling the clean scent of apple from the pomatum she uses to tame her wild curls, ''tis as sharp as it ever was.'

✠

As Bruno Barrani approaches the stone bridge to the Porta Portello in the early evening of the following day, his thoughts whine like the clouds of *zanzare* rising from the surface of the canal. And, like their bites, they cannot be ignored. Until the Podestà acceded to his request for the *Arte dei Astronomi* to take part in the great parade to celebrate the Feast of the Holy Rosary, he hadn't appreciated how much there would be to consider.

For instance: where in the parade should the *Arte* be permitted to march? At the front, naturally, Bruno had suggested boldly. The Podestà had laughed at that, pointing out that the vanguard was reserved for the most influential guild – the *richest* guild. The best Bruno had been able to screw out of the pompous old clown was a position in the rear third, between the water carriers and the basket weavers. That had stung. But he could live with it; next year, perhaps...

Then there was the matter of a suitable banner. After much consideration, he had decided upon a field of dark-blue silk, with a pattern of stars woven out of gilded thread. It would be carried on a cross of spruce.

Livery was something else he hadn't thought about until now. The city's newest company could not possibly march in its present attire. Look at the Corio brothers: they dress like bandits. Bondoni can't afford to dress any better than a beggar, because his mistress and their six children leave him without so much as a *scudo* for clothes. So Bruno has had to pay through the nose to get them fitted out. And finding a tailor at this late hour who can stitch a straight seam has taken all his ingenuity. Still, he thinks, it will all be worth it when his own bust is placed with great ceremony upon the balustrade of this bridge, beside the other great men of Padua.

He has called a meeting of the *Arte* to let its members know how diligently he has been working on their behalf, and to dismiss their usual complaints and objections. He is early. This is because first he wishes to see if Pasolini the carpenter has delivered the corrected segments of the mount that carries the sphere's equatorial ring. He doesn't trust Pasolini's eye. He intends to lay out the segments himself, checking that they fit together and that, once assembled, they form a circle and not something resembling a child's doodle.

So engrossed in these practicalities is Bruno that it is only in the instant before they collide that he notices the man hurrying towards him from the opposite direction.

They meet at the crown of the bridge. Bruno opens his mouth to apologize. Or to protest. Later, he won't be able to remember which. He catches only an indistinct impression of someone in a plain grey coat, his leather half-boots playing a staccato drumbeat on the pavement, a black cap of Germanic style on his head. He might have heard a muttered apology, but there again he might not. And if he did, it was in a foreign language. *Sotto voce.*

The collision is glancing, shoulder-to-shoulder. But it is enough to make Bruno – by a good margin the smaller of the two – stumble.

When he has regained his balance, he turns. But all he sees is the man's back, disappearing into a lane adjacent to the one from which he himself emerged just a few moments before. He utters a coarse condemnation of the foreign students at the university and their deplorable manners. It does not occur to Bruno for a moment that he might have veered into the man's path because he was distracted. Nor is his mind clear enough to connect the man in the grey coat with the description Nicholas had given a few days before.

The man who rents the storehouse – from another man who rents the storehouse – has provided Bruno with a key to the side-door. Bruno has become concerned that the theatrical rapping of an appropriate code on the big entry doors at the front is too likely to attract attention. But when he follows the side-wall, he sees that the smaller, single door is ajar.

He hears the buzzing of the flies – smells the blood – even before he puts one smartly booted foot across the threshold.

The interior is hot and stuffy, neatly partitioned by columns of evening sunlight lancing down from the high windows. They fall upon the cradle of the great sphere, remaking it as an altar or tabernacle dedicated to some ancient pagan god. Lying across one of them is a body, the arms stretched out in the stance of a diver caught mid-plunge. As Bruno approaches, the little cloud of flies lifts and disperses, like fragments of a soul fleeing heavenwards. He stops a few paces away, his heart pounding.

Face-down, the youth's head has been battered against the floor, the bloodied tangled hair dishevelled. Lying discarded across the neck is an iron bar, part of the sphere's internal mechanism. Even before he moves closer to kneel beside the body, Bruno knows he is looking at the corpse of Matteo Fedele.

36

Searching for a pulse seems pointless. The back of Matteo's head looks as though it has been savaged by the claws of a wild beast. A broad trail of blood smeared across the flagstones marks his desperate but ultimately futile attempt to crawl away from his attacker, even as the blows rained down and the life drained out of him. But in forlorn hope, Bruno does so. He finds nothing. But Matteo has not been dead for long. Warmth still lingers in the flesh.

Leaving Matteo's body, Bruno embarks on an inspection of the storehouse. His first thoughts, to his shame, are for the sphere. He checks to see if any of the stacks of parts have been smashed or stolen. He finds them intact, save for a few sections of gilded wooden rings – now bloodstained – that have been scattered during Matteo's desperate struggle to escape. He offers up a brief prayer of repentance to the nearest beam of sunlight for his insensitivity and turns his attention back to the crime.

Following the winding wake of smeared blood, he comes across the place where he assumes the attack began. It is in a corner, well away from the main entrance or the side-door, marked by a sudden spray of crimson droplets. A surprise attack then, after Matteo invited his killer in. No chance to defend himself.

Nearby, Bruno notes a collection of iron rods propped against the wall. They are identical to the murder weapon. He pictures the sequence: Matteo and the killer walking in conversation around the cradle of the sphere, Galileo's pupil no doubt boasting of his accomplishments. He can hear Matteo's voice, imagine his words: *It will eclipse the Medici sphere of Florence, and I – Matteo Fedele – was, in good part, the architect...* Close to the wall Matteo turns his back, still singing his own praises. Behind him, the killer lifts one heavy rod from the stack...

Returning to the body, Bruno sees something he missed when he'd walked in: a pattern of bloodstains leading to the side-door. Not footprints exactly – too indistinct for that. But evidence of the killer's flight.

And then he remembers the figure in the grey coat who pushed so carelessly past him on the bridge. But again he does not connect it with Nicholas. Instead, he imagines only Matteo's boasting: *It will eclipse the Medici sphere of Florence...*

Bruno freezes. He feels a hot rage course through his little body.

Santucci!

That jealous bastard, the master of the Medici spheres, has sent an assassin to Padua, he thinks. *He would see us all dead, and my great plan laid in ruins.*

Leaving Matteo Fedele to the gathering dusk and the returning flies, Bruno Barrani hurries out of the storehouse to raise the alarm. But not before checking that the stiletto he likes to wear on the belt of his black satin Venetian hose, and which – until now – he has considered mostly for show, can easily be drawn, should he have sudden need of it.

✠

At the house in the Borgo dei Argentieri the three cousins of the Corio brothers – hired in case of an attempt by agents of the English Privy Council to snatch Nicholas – have been warned to be on their guard against another threat. After the murder of

Matteo Fedele, an attempt on Bruno's life by the same Florentine assassin that he encountered on the bridge must be expected. They sit in the lane by the street door, playing dice, their rapiers oiled and sharpened. Inside, around the courtyard, torches are burning in their mountings. Plump brown moths play frenzied hazard with the flames. Luca the servant stands a little apart from the figures around the table, batting away the more reckless insects with his hand. He has not seen his master so perturbed for a long time.

At the head of the table sits the captain of the Podestà's police, a beak-nosed man in a brocaded tunic with a face as cold and thin as shattered ice. His style of questioning, thinks Bruno, has been downright disrespectful, given his subject's position as head of the *Arte dei Astronomi* and the doge's Master of the Spheres in-waiting. But he doesn't appear to mind supping on someone else's wine. Alonso is refilling the wine jug for the second time.

A call from one of the Corio cousins announces the arrival of Signor Galileo, summoned by Luca. The mathematician has come hot-foot from his local bathhouse. His face gleams with sweat in the torchlight.

'Luca told me. I can't believe it,' he says, easing himself onto the bench beside Nicholas. 'Poor Matteo wouldn't hurt a fly.' He catches Alonso's eye and drains an imaginary wine glass into his throat.

'And you are—' asks the captain.

'Galileo Galilei.'

'Oh, him.'

'Yes, *him*,' says the mathematician.

'I've heard of you. You're that smart-arsed fellow from the university – the one who drops metal balls off the top of the clock tower. What's all that about then?'

Galileo accepts the cup Alonso is offering and drinks without looking at his interrogator. Smacking his lips, he says to no one in particular, 'To see if I can hit a passing captain of the Podestà's police squarely on his empty noddle.'

'Forgive my friend's tetchiness,' Bruno says apologetically to the captain. 'He's from Pisa. They're not used to law officers there. And we've all had something of a shock.'

'Matteo was a fine lad,' Galileo says dispiritedly, staring at his wine as though he's suddenly lost his thirst. He takes a sip. 'As bone-idle as a cardinal in Conclave, of course, but a good fellow for all that. He might even have made a half-decent mathematician. What am I going to tell his father?' He takes a second, deeper draught. 'I suppose I'll have to find a new pupil to help with the rent.'

'I'm sorry, Signor Compass. This is a very bad thing all round,' Bruno says contemplatively. 'Very bad indeed. I liked Matteo, too. His loss will set the *Arte* back in its endeavours.'

'Is that all you two can think about?' Bianca demands. 'A shortfall in rent, and a setback to your plans? Shame on you!'

Chastened, Masters Compass and Purse turn their attention to the tabletop.

'That poor, poor boy,' Bianca continues, shaking her head. 'He seemed a kindly young fellow. To die so young, slain so brutally... Who would *do* that?'

The captain says, 'I do not need a woman to ask my questions for me. Remain silent until I have completed my enquiries.' He looks at Nicholas. 'And who is this?'

Nicholas explains that he is a member of the English Nation, the group of English students at the university. It is, after all, a sort of truth.

'English... Germans... Poles... Swiss – all drunks and trouble-makers,' the captain sneers. 'You're not a Lutheran or a Calvinist, are you?'

'He's a physician,' Bianca says proudly, as though it's the best religion of them all.

Bruno thinks it best to steer the captain's attention away from Nicholas. 'That scoundrel Santucci is behind this,' he says. 'I'm sure of it. He cannot bear the competition. Jealousy, that's all this is: naked Florentine jealousy. I wouldn't be surprised if the Medici put him up to it. Fancy sending an assassin to take the life of an innocent young lad, just because a Paduan steals a march on you. It's monstrous.'

The captain points a finger at Bruno, staring down it as though he were aiming a crossbow. 'You say, Signor Barrani, that you encountered the man you suspect was the assassin as you crossed the Porta Portello bridge. Is that so?'

'He was coming from the direction of the storehouse. He was in such a hurry he almost barged me into the water.'

'Would you recognize him again?'

'Not by his face. But I can describe his dress. It wasn't Paduan. A cheap grey cloth coat, black leather half-boots. And he had a black cloth cap on his head.'

Nicholas stares at the tabletop to stop the captain noticing his expression. He feels Bianca stiffen beside him.

'What made you think he was the murderer, Signor Barrani?' the captain asks. 'Was he wielding the iron bar? Was he uttering blood-curdling oaths? Was his grey coat spattered with gore?'

'No, he just pushed past me,' Bruno says, looking a little foolish.

'Then I'm sure that description will be of immeasurable help,' the captain says caustically. 'Let us hope the assassin omitted to bring a change of clothes with him from Florence.'

No one around the table laughs. 'I'm sorry I cannot be of more assistance,' Bruno says. 'I recount only what I saw.'

Like bullies everywhere, the captain sniffs weakness. 'Have you wondered why this professional killer sent from Florence failed to take the opportunity to kill *you*, when you crossed his path on the bridge?' he asks. 'Or was it that he felt intimidated by your size?'

Bruno says through gritted teeth, 'Perhaps he thought it too public. Maybe he didn't recognize me until it was too late. Maybe Santucci simply picked the wrong man for the job.'

'Just like the Podestà has,' Bianca mutters under her breath.

If the captain hears her, he doesn't show it. Nicholas smiles and squeezes her hand.

'Well, Signor Barrani,' the captain says, 'I see you have placed guards at your gate. If you come across this man again, let us hope *you* have picked the right men for the job.'

'Is that it? Am I to be afforded no other protection?' Bruno asks.

Satisfied that he has investigated the crime thoroughly – and downed enough of the witness's wine – the captain rises from the table. 'I do not profess to understand for a moment the precise nature of what you are engaged upon in that storehouse, Signor Barrani, but His Excellency the Podestà seems to think it is worth something to him. As for me, I will have enough on my plate keeping the public safe from felons and criminals on the Feast of the Holy Rosary. I can do without some foolish spat between you clever-dick men of learning. Therefore I would prefer it if there were no further outbreaks of *jealousy* in this city. Do I make myself clear?'

'Completely,' says Bruno.

The captain turns to Galileo. 'And that includes *you*, Signor Mathematician.'

As the captain departs, Galileo makes an obscene gesture to his back. Then he pats Bianca's thigh in a manner she assumes is meant apologetically, but can't be sure.

Bruno orders Alonso to recharge everyone's cups. When it is done, he lifts his own. 'Drink up, Signor Compass, Cousin Bianca, Nicholas – to the memory of Matteo Fedele, may God welcome his soul into His everlasting peace.'

Amens are said around the table. Alonso is dispatched for another jug. But although the wine is good and the night warm, in the house in the Borgo dei Argentieri nothing can lift the sense of disbelief and sadness.

✠

'The fellow you chased into the church and the one Bruno encountered on the bridge – can they really be one and the same man?' Bianca asks later in their chamber. Beyond the window the night is lit by flashes of lightning as a silent storm rages far off over the distant mountains.

'If they are, one thing is certain: he didn't come from Florence to murder Matteo Fedele.'

Bianca sits up in bed and props her chin on her bended knees. 'He follows us all the way from Brabant without so much as an uncivil word, and then murders someone we barely know?'

'Perhaps it wasn't us he was following.'

A lightning flash paints Bianca's face a deathly white. 'Hella? You believe he was following Hella?'

Nicholas nods. 'I think I've had it wrong all along. He's no more an agent of the Privy Council than Luca or Alonso.'

'But why kill Matteo, of all people?'

'I don't know,' Nicholas confesses. 'But the lad was close to her. Therefore Hella could well be in terrible danger.'

'That might explain why he didn't try to kill Bruno.'

'Probably.'

Bianca eases herself over the end of the bed. She goes to the window. By the flickering lightning Nicholas can see the form of her body through the thin linen of her nightgown. He imagines a slight swelling of her belly, but knows it is only a fancy. It is too early. He wonders if he should tell her about his meeting with the maid, tell her he knows why she thinks herself cursed. But he suspects that if he does, there will be a storm right here in the chamber that will put the one over the mountains to shame.

'You're going to warn her, aren't you?' Bianca says presciently, looking out into the darkened street.

'I *have* to. I can't simply leave her to an assassin. My conscience—'

'I know, Nicholas. I *know*.'

He puts the sudden squirm that infects his spine down to the sweat trickling along his back. 'It doesn't have to be face-to-face,' he says. 'I'll send her a note.'

'No, you won't. That isn't your nature.'

'One meeting, that's all. Just to warn her. I'll get Bruno to ask the Corio cousins to look out for her.'

Bianca turns back from the window. 'And then we put her out of our lives for ever. Do you promise?'

Nicholas climbs out of bed and takes his wife in his arms. The first audible rumble of thunder rolls down across the valley and over the walls of Padua like the secret marauders of an advancing army.

'As if she had never existed,' he says.

37

Assurances, promises, denials... in the last half-hour Nicholas has made them all. None have appeared to ease Bianca's heart. Over breakfast she has listened to him with a face of stone. In desperation he says, 'You agreed. One visit. Then we will forget her for ever.'

She looks at him for what seems like an hour, her eyes unreadable to him. Then she says, 'I agreed. What else needs to be said?'

He thinks, how about: *I know why you fear the maid so much.*

But he knows that if he turns his thoughts to words, they will very likely raise a fire in her that will burn them both.

'I will be brief with her, I promise,' he tells her. 'I will be back before you know it.'

'Take all the time you need,' she says. 'I'm going to pay another visit to the place where I grew up – my parents' house.'

'Will you wait until I return? I would like to see it.'

She shakes her head. 'Another time, perhaps. This journey I need to take alone.'

It feels to Nicholas as though Bianca has slammed a door in his face. He lays his knife down amongst the peach stones and leaves the table. When he reaches the stairs he looks back, only to see that her attention is not on him, but on something he cannot know or see. Something far away.

✠

At the Beguinage, Nicholas is shown into Madonna Antonella's office. She is a doughty woman of fifty with canny, generous eyes and severely crimped grey hair that makes the simple linen coif she wears on her head look like a kerchief stuffed with hazelnuts. Though she welcomes him cordially enough, he detects wariness in her eyes, a suspicion honed through experience that sometimes the men who come here enquiring after her Beguines are not always truthful about their motives. He gives her the story about him being a Catholic recusant, fleeing English tyranny. At first he tells her only that Hella Maas accompanied him and Bianca on the Via Francigena, omitting any mention of what happened in the cathedral at Den Bosch. Then he tells her about Grey-coat and the murder of Matteo Fedele. As he speaks, Madonna Antonella's face darkens.

'You sincerely believe her life could be in danger?' she asks when he has finished speaking.

'Yes, Madonna. I thought at first he might have been an English bounty-hunter – that it was me he was following. Now I believe Signorina Maas is his intended quarry.'

'Have you come to any conclusion as to why this man should want to harm her?' Madonna Antonella asks.

'I believe it has something to do with a crime she witnessed, in the Duchy of Brabant.'

'A crime?' Madonna Antonella echoes with a lift of her brow, as though crime is something indistinct and living only on the far edge of her memory. 'What manner of... crime?'

'A double murder, Madonna. A Catholic priest and a Spanish officer. I can only assume that the assassin believes Hella can identify him. Perhaps that is why he has followed her here. Perhaps he killed her friend Matteo Fedele whilst trying to force him to reveal where she is sheltering.'

'Forgive me, Signor Shelby,' she says, lifting a small silver bell from her desk. 'Sometimes men come here trying to convince us they have their women's interests at heart when in fact they seek only to regain their influence and dominion over them.' She gives the bell one brisk shake. An elderly Beguine enters. 'Is Sister Hella with us, Sister Giulia? Or is she at the Basilica, telling God how to behave?'

'She is in the dormitory, Madonna – with Sister Carlotta,' the Beguine says, casting a doubting look at Nicholas.

'Then please be so kind as to bring her to me.'

While he waits, Madonna Antonella asks him about the trials of life as a Catholic in a heretic land. Nicholas pilfers uncomfortable answers from his memory, things he's heard Bianca and John Lumley say. Now, in Padua, they seem more damning to him than when first spoken in England, where he has never had to feign humility to keep himself safe, or deny his faith lest someone close proves not to be the friend they claimed, but an informer.

When Hella arrives, she bows stiffly to Madonna Antonella. Nicholas is favoured with little more than mild curiosity.

'This gentleman says he is an English physician, and that you spent some time together on the Via Francigena,' Madonna Antonella says. 'Is that true, Sister Hella?'

'It is, Madonna Antonella,' she says.

'Do you wish to hear what he has to say to you? Do you trust him, child?'

'With my life, Madonna Antonella. And even beyond it.'

Satisfied that Nicholas is neither a vengeful lover nor a bullying relative, Madonna Antonella gestures to Nicholas to speak. He chooses English, for discretion. Immediately it proves to be a wise choice.

'I need to talk with you,' he says brusquely. 'It is of some considerable import.'

'Have you finally found the courage to cast off Bianca?' she says coldly. 'Have you come to take me away?'

He cannot stop himself glancing at Madonna Antonella. To his relief, she has retreated into studying a leather-bound psalter.

'I've come to warn you that you may be in grave danger.'

Her smile is so weak it can live for no more than a moment. 'We are all in danger, Nicholas. Haven't I convinced you of that yet?'

'Young Matteo Fedele is dead,' he says brutally, seeing no gain in gentleness. 'He was murdered.'

He studies her face, expecting emotion. He sees none.

'You don't seem troubled by that. I thought you were close to him.'

'I told you before, I only indulged the boy in order to stay close to you.'

'Do you feel no pity?'

She shrugs. 'Why should I pity him, Nicholas? Matteo is at peace. He will remain at peace until the time comes when he faces what we must all face.'

'Don't you want to know who killed him?'

'Does it matter?'

Nicholas struggles to rein in his anger at her indifference, lest Madonna Antonella has second thoughts about letting an English stranger into her Beguinage.

'It matters, Hella, because the man who killed him might think to play hazard with *your* life, too. I believe it was the same man I saw at Reims, and again at the hospice in the mountains. He wore a grey coat... black boots... a black cloth cap on his head. I am sure now that he spoke to you in the cathedral square when we joined the Via Francigena. But that morning we left the mountains you denied it, when I asked if you had seen such a person. So I ask again now, in a place of holiness where God hears every word: do you know why this man would follow you to Padua and murder Matteo Fedele?'

Nicholas is aware that Madonna Antonella has put down her psalter and is regarding him with new-found suspicion. She can tell by the tone of his voice that his words to the maid are not words of reassurance.

'I have told you before, I do not know this man, Nicholas. And I cannot imagine that he has come all this way to kill me.'

'I fear he believes you recognized him in the cathedral at Den Bosch. I think he may be the man who killed Father Vermeiren and the Spaniard. Are you not at least afraid?'

'I am not afraid to *die*, if that is what you mean. Like poor little Matteo, it would bring a period of peace before the Day of Judgement.'

Stunned by her utter lack of emotion, Nicholas opens his mouth to protest. Madonna Antonella lifts a hand to stop him. She says, 'Enough! I do not know what you are saying to Sister Hella, but it does not seem to me to be kind counsel. She will be safe enough here in the Beguinage; we are well used to dealing with men who have violence in their hearts towards the Sisters who have sought refuge here. We will look after her. You may rely upon it. Now, Dr Shelby, I think it best we consider this audience at an end.'

✠

Bianca Merton stands in the lane and looks up at the stuccoed wall of the house she was born in. Since she left, it has been painted a garish yellow. She knows her mother would be horrified.

The wooden double doors on the ground floor are as crooked as she remembers them. She wonders what lies behind them now. In her childhood it had been sacks and crates of the herbs and spices Simon Merton imported from the lands of the Ottoman Turks. Above was the accommodation: two bedrooms, a living space and a kitchen. On the top floor her father had a curtained space where he set down on paper the strange notions he had about the world and the cosmos, notions that had eventually earned him a dank cell and the attention of the Inquisition. At the rear of the house her mother had a chamber with a table and a basin, where she could mix her balms and medicaments, her syrups and her poisons. Looking up at the little windows beneath the eaves, Bianca finds it almost amusing: the notion that her father's harmless pursuits proved fatal, whereas her mother's dangerous ones made her reputation.

Taking Simon Merton's silver Petrine cross from her gown, she holds it against her chest, the crucified figure of St Peter facing outwards, as though house and cross might somehow be united again, at least for a brief moment. Or is it, perhaps, an offering? A gift, to seek approval from her mother for what she intends to do? Then she turns and walks away.

She does not go far. Just two lanes away, in the direction of the Piazza delle Erbe, she stops before a narrow shop front. It is a place so ancient that she imagines the first transactions here were made in Latin. Tentatively, as though afraid its substance is no more solid than her recollection of it, she pushes at the door.

Inside, the shop is exactly as she remembers it, dark and reeking with heavy pungent scents. Moving further in, Bianca smiles with recollection, half-expecting to see the eyes of forest nymphs peeping at her from between the profusion of leaves, sprigs, bunches, roots, tubers and stems.

'Signor Tiziano,' she calls out. 'It is I, Signorina Bianca.'

At the back of the shop, as if emerging from a fairy glade, a very old man in a pale, discoloured cloth gown, tied at the waist with a cord, emerges. As he moves, Bianca hears the slow clack of wooden clogs on flagstones. She closes the distance, because she knows his eyesight is not good.

'Is it really you – little Bianca Caporetti?' the apothecary says, reaching out to take Bianca's hands in his. 'Or am I dreaming?'

'You never did call me by my father's name,' Bianca says with a gentle smile as she grasps what feels to her like two sprigs of dried reed wrapped in fragile parchment. 'Why was that, Signor Tiziano?'

'Because your mother was a Caporetti, and the Caporettis have been known in Padua since before the Venetians came here, before the Carrara even.' The old man gives her a toothless grin. 'Nothing against the Englishman, your father, of course. A good fellow; but he wasn't one of us. Have you tired of his land, Daughter? I hear they are all heretics there. Is that why you have come home?'

'Something like that, at least for a while.'

She helps him back to his chair. They talk of old times, though Bianca is pretty sure that, for Tiziano, time was only young in her great-grandmother's day. When they have reminisced enough, and he has recounted all those from the neighbourhood whose bones have been interred in her absence, she says, 'If I was in need of *cantarella*, Signor Tiziano, could you provide a vial for me?'

He peers at her, almost as though she is beginning to dissolve slowly before his watery old eyes, as if she has been nothing but an apparition from the moment she walked into his shop. '*Cantarella*,' he says at length. 'The Borgia poison.'

'I'm only asking – for the present. But if other remedies for my... malady... don't work, I might have to think again.'

He gives a wise, slow nod. She hears the cartilage in his thin neck grind.

'Is it for a man or a woman? The weight will matter.'

'It is for a maid.'

'You wish the consequences to be speedy? Or lingering?'

'Oh, speedy,' she says. 'I am not a vindictive woman.'

He smiles again. 'They always said that crossing the Caporettis

369

in love was never a wise idea.' He raises Bianca's hands to his mouth and bestows a dry kiss upon them with his ancient lips. 'I always knew I was right to call you Caporetti. It is good to see you taking up your mother's trade again.'

38

St Paul's, London, 6th October 1594

I f Ned Monkton is awed by his surroundings, he shows no sign when the guards lead him into the Long Chapel of the old Norman cathedral of St Paul's. He looks around at the un-adorned stone and the simple furnishings with little more than mild interest. Watching from her place on the shadowed side-benches, Rose wonders if it is courage he is showing or a failure to understand the consequences of error. She can cry no more tears for him; her eyes are raw from two days with little sleep, schooling him in the one thing that stands between her husband and the gallows.

Before bidding him farewell at the Marshalsea – harder even than she had expected – she handed him the clean shirt she had brought and checked him over for loose straw. Looking at him now, chained at the ankles and the wrists, she is pleased to see that his great auburn beard and his hair are as neat as they have ever been. First impressions are important, and never more so than when making a plea to escape the noose.

Lumley's tame chaplain is a stooped, sad little fellow. He looks to Rose like a country parson who's attended too many funerals. Dressed in a formal clerical gown, with a broad flat cap across his head, he sits behind a table covered in ecclesiastical linen, flanked by his clerks. One of them reads the temporal charge, the verdict and the sentence. The other restates the plea of Benefit of Clergy made on Ned's behalf by Lord Lumley, who observes silently from his place next to Rose. She wonders how she could bear this for a single minute if Lumley's calming presence were not beside her.

'Does the accused claim to be a member of the clergy?' the chaplain asks Ned doubtfully.

Ned looks to Lumley for guidance.

'No, most reverend sir, Master Monkton is not of the clergy. But he is literate, and can therefore plead benefit of the same. That is the law, as amended by Her Grace the queen. I can confirm it with her, if you wish.'

The chaplain smiles graciously. 'That will be unnecessary, my lord. You are correct in your interpretation of the law. Let us proceed. Step forward, Accused.'

Ned shuffles closer to the table. One of the clerks look up. Rose notices the sudden nervous jump of his Adam's apple.

'Here is the word of God,' says the chaplain ominously, lifting a large heavy leather-bound Bible from the table. 'Open it to Psalm fifty-one and prove your Benefit of Clergy.' He offers the Bible slowly and with great dignity, as though offering a sacrifice at an altar.

'Excuse me, most reverend sir,' Lumley interjects with a discreet cough. 'A word—'

'My lord?' the chaplain says, turning his head in Lumley's direction.

'That is a very large Bible, and the accused's manacles will prevent him from opening it fully. I would like to offer the court my own, personal one.' He holds it up, a neat little volume bound in calfskin, with worked brass cornerpieces. 'I have taken the liberty of opening it to the appropriate place – for the court's convenience.'

'That is very generous of you, my lord,' says the chaplain. With a wave of his hand, he dispatches a clerk to retrieve it. Rose can feel her heart thumping as the man carries Lumley's open Bible towards Ned.

And then the clerk stops.

Rose knows by the hunching of his shoulders that something is troubling him. He turns to face the chaplain. He shows him the open pages.

'As you may see, sir, it is a true Bible.'

The chaplain leans forward to study the offering. Satisfied, he nods gravely.

'But it should be presented shut,' says the clerk.

'Is that strictly necessary?' Lumley enquires.

The clerk's eyes remain fixed upon the chaplain. 'It *has* been known for an appellant who is illiterate to memorize the psalm, in order to deceive the court,' he says.

'*Oh merciful Jesus*,' Rose whispers into her hand.

'It *is* the law, my lord,' the chaplain says to Lumley, with the faintest trace of an arched eyebrow. Then to the clerk, 'Please be so kind as to continue, Master Broxton.'

Her mouth as dry as dust, Rose stares helplessly as the clerk closes the Bible. The slap as the pages come together has a dreadful finality that makes her shudder. She can barely bring herself to watch as he hands the book to Ned, a smile of officious triumph dancing on his weak lips. She offers up a silent, desperate prayer. If God can't hear me in this place, she thinks, there is no hope to be had anywhere.

His great fiery face impassive, Ned Monkton takes the little book in his huge hands. He flips through the pages one way, then the other. Then he starts again at the beginning.

'Is the accused having... *difficulty*... finding the correct psalm?' the chaplain asks Ned.

Ned does not answer. He carries on shuffling the pages. To Rose, the noise of the parchment turning sounds like the flapping wings of a vulture descending upon its prey.

And then Ned stops. He opens the Bible to its full extent. To

Rose's mind, he seems to grow another couple of inches, dwarfing the trio behind the desk even more. He begins to speak, his voice clear and resolute:

'*Have mercy upon me, O God, according to thy great mercy... And according to the multitude of thy tender mercies blot out my iniquity... Wash me yet more from my iniquity, and cleanse me from my sin.*'

He never once stumbles. He doesn't even appear to draw breath. His deep basso-profundo voice rolls around the chapel as though he were delivering a sermon to God Himself. After a few more lines, the chaplain says, 'I think we have heard enough. The plea of Benefit of Clergy is accepted. The sentence of the ecclesiastical court is that the guilty man be removed to the Marshalsea prison to suffer a branding upon the thumb. After that, he is free to go.'

Rose has never embraced a baron before, and it is likely Lord Lumley has never had a plump, curly-headed maid of the lower orders hurl herself upon him like a demented spaniel. But both put aside their social constraints for just long enough to celebrate the joy of the moment.

As Ned is led away, Rose calls out across the chapel, 'Be brave, sweet!' Then, as a practical afterthought, 'If the hurt proves too much, I still have some of the balm we used for burns when the Jackdaw burned down.'

''Tis little but a trifle, Wife,' Ned calls back with a grin. 'A bee sting is worse.'

As Rose and Lumley make to leave the benches, the chaplain comes over to speak with them.

'A satisfactory outcome, I trust, my lord?'

'We sought only justice, most reverend sir.'

'The slate of our obligations to each other is wiped clean, I trust.'

'Spotless.'

The chaplain gives Lumley a wry smile. 'I wouldn't have taken him for such an educated man, my lord.'

'It's a common mistake.'

'Well, from now on I shall presume that Ovid and Virgil are common fare amongst the reprobates on Bankside.'

'I don't know what you mean, reverend sir,' says Lumley.

The chaplain gives him the briefest hint of a knowing look. Then he says, 'For such a fellow to read the fifty-first psalm so cogently is one thing, my lord. But to give a faultless translation in English of a text that was printed on the page in Latin – now, that truly is remarkable.'

✠

John Lumley waits until he and Rose are safely outside. A blustery wind tugs at the hem of his gown. There are goosebumps on Rose's arms, but she's too ecstatic to notice.

'My dearest Rose, can you *ever* forgive me?' Lumley says as he steers her through the St Paul's churchyard towards Paternoster Row. 'I almost undid *everything*.'

'Why say you that, my lord?'

'I thought I had it all in hand. I checked the width of his manacles before he was led before the court. I even put a little dab of gum arabic on the appropriate page of my Bible, so that he might find it, should the book be closed. But it had never occurred to me that you would school him in English, while my Bible is printed in Latin.'

'No harm was done by it, m'lord,' Rose says. 'My Ned is returned to me, and for that I thank you from the depths of my soul. I just 'ope your conscience isn't troubled by 'aving to lie to the court.'

Lumley smiles, something Rose has hardly ever seen him do before.

'It was a very small deceit, Rose.'

'But a deceit in God's own house, nonetheless.'

Lumley takes her arm in his. 'Fear not, Goodwife Monkton. The court is adjoined to the Protestant Church, whereas I am a Catholic. Therefore what I say in it doesn't count.' He raises his eyes heavenwards. 'Besides,' he says, 'I think the Almighty would approve of a very small deceit, if it was made in order to save the life of a good man.'

✠

Madonna Antonella has agreed the Beguines may attend the horse race planned for tomorrow, the feast day of the Holy Rosary. 'To give charity and counsel to the poor amongst the crowd, mind – not to gamble,' she says sternly. 'Or... Sister Agnes' – and here she sends a cautionary glance in the direction of the oldest member of the order of Beguines – 'to lust over the handsome riders.' This causes much amused twittering, most of all from Sister Agnes herself, a sweet-faced biddy of eighty who, even on tiptoes, stands less than five feet tall.

Madonna Antonella dismisses the Sisters to their duties, reminding them not to let their excitement make them late for Vespers. As they scatter into the cloisters, Hella pulls little Carlotta into the cover of the doorway to the refectory. It is time to put the last pieces of her plan into motion.

'Do you have the two messages I gave you?' she whispers. 'Have you kept them safe?'

'As safe as if they were my own honour,' says Carlotta, laying her hand just below the neckline of her plain cloth gown to show where she has hidden them.

'You haven't read them?'

'Of course not! You made me swear an oath not to.'

'If you *have*, I promise you this: at a moment of my choosing, your eyes will begin to burn, and they will go on burning until they are as black and shrivelled as raisins. Now, repeat the instructions I gave you.'

Half-thrilled, half-terrified, Carlotta does as her friend commands her. She finishes with a gabbled, 'Shall we go to the race together? Please... Hella... say yes.'

'No, sweet Carlotta, *we* shall not.'

Carlotta's happy expression crumbles. Hella tries not to laugh.

'But... but... it is not safe to go on your own.' Carlotta's protest has more to do with her own disappointment than her concerns for her friend's welfare. 'It's a horse race. There will be men there – common men, the sort who have no respect for the honour of a pious maid.'

'You are right,' says Hella, relenting. She lays a consolatory hand on the other's shoulder. 'I hadn't considered that.'

'Then I may accompany you?'

But the young Beguine's sudden surge of relived joy is only fleeting.

'No, Carlotta, you may not accompany me,' Hella says. 'But you may fetch me a sharp knife from the kitchen.'

'A knife? What need do you have of a knife?'

'To set your mind at rest, of course. So that, if accosted, I shall be able to defend myself. What else would I need a knife for?'

39

Padua, 7th October 1594, the Feast of the
Holy Rosary

Bianca wakes to the sound of raised voices. They pull her from a troubled dream in which she saw herself as an ugly demon in the painting at Den Bosch, forcing a draught of fatal *cantarella* down the throat of a sinner on Judgement Day.

As she looks around the chamber in the dawn light she cannot help but feel a sense of power. In the dream she felt guiltless. Pouring the clear liquid into the gaping mouth – prised open by the fiery fingers of her demonic accomplices – she experienced nothing but cold triumph. She whispers, or perhaps just imagines that she does, *Never seek to curse a Caporetti, or those they love. And especially not their unborn children.* Yes, she thinks, without question I am my mother's daughter.

Noticing the space beside her is empty, she curls herself up on the part of the rumpled sheet that Nicholas has vacated. She can smell the scent of him, feel the heat of him still trapped in the linen.

He has not spoken to her about his visit to Hella Maas, and she has not prompted him. But she can trace – to the very moment – when the strength returned to her, the strength to shake off the strange servitude the maid had imposed upon her mind; to defy the curse. It had occurred the day before yesterday when Nicholas had taken her in his arms, after she had agreed to his meeting with the maid on the condition they would then put her out of their minds for ever. *As if she had never existed*, he had told her. And then the thunder had rolled down from the mountains – like one of the omens that Hella was forever going on about. That had convinced Bianca. It was indeed a sign. Not a sign that Hella had power over her, but rather confirmation that if the curse was to be lifted, it would be down to her to do it; down to a Caporetti.

She sat at breakfast yesterday wrestling with her new-found determination. Whatever the outcome of Nicholas's meeting with the maid, she has decided to give Hella a warning of her own. She will tell her that danger does not come in the form of a stranger in a grey coat, but in the form of the woman with whose mind she has so recklessly toyed. *Withdraw the curse, leave our lives – or I will bring about your own personal Judgement Day. And this one will not be made of paint: it will be made of poison.*

From the courtyard the raised voices reach her again. She can make sense of them now: Bruno is chiding Alonso and Luca for some crime of indolence or omission. Her cousin has become ever more agitated in the past few days, consumed by his determination that the *Arte dei Astronomi* shall be accorded its rightful status in the forthcoming festivities. She smiles. At least one person close to her has an unswerving and thoroughly optimistic view of what the future holds.

When she has washed and dressed, she goes down to breakfast. The courtyard is enveloped in a sullen mist, like a bathhouse after the fires have been doused. The sound of Bruno's chivvying seems to come from some distant place, flat and listless with the travelling. She finds Nicholas inside, at the dining table. He offers her bread and cheese from the plate Luca has laid there.

'You haven't told me of your meeting with Hella Maas,' she says, taking the chair opposite.

'There is nothing to tell. I warned her she might be in danger. She didn't seem to care. Even poor Matteo's death seemed hardly to move her.'

'Then we are done with her?'

He looks at her, his head slightly tilted, his eyes uncertain. 'I am done with her. The question is: are you?'

'This is Bruno's day, Nicholas. I refuse to let her sour it.' Aware she hasn't answered his question, she adds, 'I wish to go to the Basilica of St Anthony, before they close it to prepare for the procession. I want somewhere where I may sit quietly in contemplation.'

'Do you wish to be alone?'

'You may come, if you want. But I will not speak of... her. So do not waste your breath asking.'

They walk together mostly in silence, each unable to unburden themselves, both acutely aware that silence is not the natural state they share. In the mist, Paduans of all shapes and sizes, colours and estate surge around them. Priests and clerks hurry here and there on missions of organization, like black wraiths moving through a churchyard. Streets are being cleared of obstacles and sanded for the horse race scheduled in the afternoon. Vendors are setting up their stalls. The city heaves with a common expectation, as though it is a single organism stirring after hibernation.

At length they emerge into the cobbled Piazza del Santo. Nicholas knows enough of the city now to recognize Donatello's great bronze equestrian statue of the warrior Gattamelata. Skirting the plinth, they approach the stern brick façade of the Basilica. To Nicholas, it looks like a Moorish temple that has drifted in on the tide of mist. Flanking its six domes, two spires lance into the opaque heavens, each more like a minaret than a Christian bell tower.

'Are you going to make confession?' Nicholas asks as they enter the echoing interior.

'Why, do you think I might have committed a sin?'

'No, of course not, I...' He stops, unable to breach the walls of Bianca's reserve.

'If I do, promise me you won't go wandering off. Remember what happened in Den Bosch.'

'If I had my time again, I would have left Hella there,' he says. 'You must know that?'

'We are both responsible for what has happened, Nicholas. Perhaps the maid is right: once knowledge is out, it cannot then be put back in its cage. We must each deal with it as we think best: either placate it or defy it.'

As she walks on towards the altar, leaving Nicholas in the doorway, Bianca wonders if perhaps she should make confession. But how could she admit what is in her mind, even to a faceless priest behind the confessional screen? How much penance will he expect from her for the sin of wishing someone dead? How much more for actually planning it? And she suspects he could never answer the question that has plagued her since the notion first came into her head: if Hella dies, will the curse she has laid die with her? Or will it live on, like a malignant pestilence, waiting for the moment to strike?

She settles quietly in a pew near the altar rail and tries to calm her racing mind. She imagines she must glow with guilt, visible to all around. Yet no one pays her attention. The roof does not fall in upon her. The flagstones do not crack and gape beneath her feet. God does not whisper even the softest condemnation to her. In the end, she thinks He must understand that she is no murderess, but simply someone trying to protect her husband from a threat she cannot quite put shape to. And more than that, even – protecting the child growing inside her.

Eventually a peace she hasn't felt for weeks comes over Bianca. She rises, genuflects, crosses herself and walks back to where Nicholas is waiting. As they leave the Basilica, she takes his hand. 'Whatever happens, Nicholas,' she says, 'I did not bring you back from your darkness only to let another have you.'

He is about to ask her what she means when they notice, simultaneously, a small band of citizens gathered in the mist by Donatello's statue. A woman's voice reaches them, throaty and insistent.

Hella Maas is standing with her back to the plinth, her face transfused with righteous vehemence, her words laden with warning. The small crowd stares at her in appalled wonder.

Before Nicholas can stop her, Bianca lets go of his hand and pushes her way forward. He follows, fearing what she might do. The crowd parts for them. In an instant Bianca is within striking distance of the maid. Startled by the sudden movement, Hella glances at her. Her eyes widen in recognition, but her voice does not falter.

Bianca stops for a moment. Nicholas reaches out to grab her sleeve, to restrain her. But then she steps forward again, not aggressively, but calmly, until she is close enough to the maid to embrace her.

Hella stops her ranting. She lowers her arms and regards Bianca with a quizzical expression. Bianca leans in close and says something Nicholas cannot hear. He knows it cannot be a threat, because Bianca's body remains loose and calm. There is no anger in the way she holds herself.

Hella bows her head in thought. Then she replies – in Italian, and too softly for Nicholas to catch. Bianca turns, walks back to him, takes his hand once more and leads him out of the Piazza del Santo.

'What did you say to her?' he asks.

'What does it matter? I have already forgotten her,' she replies. 'What was the phrase you used? *As if she had never existed.*'

✳

Bianca's new gown has arrived in the nick of time. She takes one look at the pearl-coloured brocade with red lace trimmings and proclaims it the most exquisite thing she has ever seen. Nicholas thinks he has never seen her looking more beautiful.

'I wish Rose were here to see it,' she says, after thanking Bruno so profusely that he has begun to blush.

'I insist on paying you,' Nicholas says, drawing him aside. 'This is too generous to stand, even for you.'

Bruno pats his arm. 'I told you before: it is my way of thanking you both for saving my life when I came to London. If you want, you can pay for the panels when they're needed.'

'The panels?'

Bruno's hands spread outwards from his doublet, in imitation of a swollen belly.

'Oh, yes, I see what you mean: when she's... *larger.*'

'Exactly,' says Bruno.

✳

The mist still clings to the city like a spurned lover. The sun has not been seen all day. Those citizens who have listened to the warnings given by the strange maid in the Piazza del Santo go about the streets with troubled faces, wondering if her predictions are coming to pass even sooner than she had claimed. Their mood does not improve when word spreads that the hour-hand of the great clock on the face of the Torre dell'Orologio has stopped moving.

It's just nesting birds, gumming up the mechanism with straw and mud, the Podestà's men announce. We'll have it fixed in time

383

for the horse race. But their assurances find little purchase with those who prefer a more supernatural explanation.

In the race stables, the favourite stallion suddenly rears without warning. Panicked, its flailing hooves break the skull of the groom's thirteen-year-old assistant. The groom lays the blame on a rat seen running across the cobbles. Highly strung stallions are prone to such terrors, he tells the owner – who has him soundly flogged for trying to spook the horse on behalf of a competitor in the hope that it might injure itself. But by the time the news is common knowledge, another explanation is already in play: the mount reared in terror when an eagle – the colour of the darkest night – alighted upon the rail of its stall.

The wise men at the university on the Palazzo Bo laugh at these stories. The common people do not. Italians, Bianca reminds Nicholas as they walk to the Piazza dei Signori to watch the start of the race, often have superstition running in their veins more thickly than blood. But it doesn't make them stupid.

The piazza itself is too packed for Bianca's liking, so they find a place in a nearby street where there is still room to stand in relative safety, their backs to the stucco houses. The make-up of the crowd has Nicholas imagining that the entire population of Padua has been poured into a bucket, stirred with a ladle and decanted into the streets. Gallants in satin doublets and striped hose rub shoulders with artisans in broadcloth; women in vibrant gowns stand beside friars in brown sackcloth; children shelter between the steel knee-guards of men-at-arms, glancing up at them with wary fascination.

The Podestà's men have proved to be overconfident. The hour-hand of the clock on the Torre dell'Orologio is still jammed. But the bell in the tower works. As it begins to toll, the Podestà drops his official baton. In the side-street where Nicholas and Bianca are standing, heads turn expectantly towards the great roar coming from the Piazza dei Signori. Bianca clings tightly to Nicholas's arm.

And then the ground seems to sing, as though an invisible tide is beginning to flow over the cobbles. Bianca senses the people around her holding their collective breath. From the direction of the piazza comes a noise that she can only liken to barrels of ale rolling down the ramp to the Jackdaw's brewhouse. Faint at first, it swiftly rises to a frightening roar.

At the end of the side-street where it gives onto the Piazza dei Signori, a tight phalanx of horses bursts out of the mist. Heads tossing, jaws grinding on iron bits, nostrils gaping, spume flying, they plunge forward like creatures fleeing out of hell. Their jockeys ride bareback, stirrupless. Clad in vibrantly coloured silk tunics, they crouch low over the necks of their mounts, gripping the reins with one hand, lashing furiously with a leather crop held in the other. For Nicholas, it is impossible to distinguish the crowd's shrieks of terror from its screams of encouragement. He has the brief impression of a dark wall of rippling muscle bearing down upon him, then a roar like a mountain falling into a wild ocean.

And then they are gone. Almost as one, the crowd lining the street turns to watch them go. Catching his breath, Nicholas says, 'I've never seen the like. It was terrifying.'

'I don't like the way they whip the horses,' Bianca confesses. 'And you wouldn't want to be a bull in Italy.'

He looks at her quizzically. 'A bull? The Paduans race bulls, too?'

'No, Husband,' she replies, grinning. 'The *whips*. If you're a bull, they cut off your pizzle, dry it out in the sun, stretch it and make a lash out of it.'

'I'll bear that in mind, next time we argue,' he says, realizing that it's the first time they have laughed together in a long while.

And then he notices, further down the street, people beginning to break away from the crowd. They are running in the direction of the vanished horses, and something about the agitation in them tells him these are not merely supporters trying to follow the progress of the race. Something is amiss. A woman's scream pierces the mist.

'Oh, Jesu, there's been an accident,' Bianca says, raising a hand to her mouth.

Without even thinking, Nicholas runs towards the commotion, Bianca at his heels. Rounding the bend at the end of the street, he runs into the back of a throng of spectators, all jostling for a view. He calls out in Italian, 'I'm a physician, let me pass.' Grudgingly, the crowd separates and Nicholas finds himself at the front.

A crumpled, bloodied figure in bright-yellow Venetian hose lies face-down in the street, his awful stillness a rebuke to the agitation of the people gathered around him. Rivulets of blood snake out through the spread of white hair, finding the easiest path through the cobbles like the first tentative signs of a turning tide. Too old to be a competitor, Nicholas thinks.

A quick glance around tells him he is right. Two horses stand a short way off. One is being calmed by his rider, who stands beside his mount's sweating neck, cursing his luck. The other is riderless, his head making great sweeping bows, vapour pluming from his nostrils. A spectator struggles to hold him steady by the reins. The jockey sits propped up against the wall of a house, his face screwed up in agony, one leg twisted outwards at a sickening angle. Someone has torn away the hose from the injured limb and an elderly, grey-haired man in a black gown has his ear close to the flesh, listening for the telltale noise of bone fragments moving. Nicholas recognizes him from his visits to the Palazzo Bo as a colleague of Professor Fabrici.

Satisfied the jockey is in good hands, Nicholas turns his attention to the body in the street. As he does so, a woman and a clutch of children break out of the crowd and fall upon the inert form lying on the cobbles, wailing and lamenting with piercing cries. The woman, stout and plump-cheeked, rolls the body onto its back. She cradles it in her muscular arms, turns her tear-drenched face to the opaque sky and begins to harangue an uncaring God.

'Merciful Mother of Jesus,' Bianca whispers at the same instant that Nicholas recognizes the dead man. 'It's one of Bruno's people – it's the goldsmith, Signor Bondoni.'

40

The people emerging from the mist, heading towards the Piazza dei Signori to watch the start of the parade, or to the Basilica of St Anthony to catch its end, barely notice the couple passing in the opposite direction towards the Borgo dei Argentieri, heads down, lost in their own thoughts.

'Are you *sure*?' says Nicholas for the third time in ten minutes.

'As sure as I may be,' Bianca replies wearily. 'I asked everyone who was standing close to Bondoni the same thing. No one saw him pushed, certainly not by a man in a grey coat and a black cloth cap.'

'But all eyes were on the horses and riders.'

'Perhaps it really *was* just an accident, Nicholas. Every year *someone* gets injured – even killed – during these races.'

Nicholas lets out a short, brutal laugh. 'Mind you, with a wife who looked as though she would happily wrestle an armed brigand, and six children with mouths like hungry sparrow-hawks, perhaps Bondoni stepped under the horses by choice.'

Bianca rebukes him with a sharp look. 'Nicholas! You of all people should not make light of the sin of self-destruction. Besides, she wasn't his wife. Bruno said he has a *mistress* and six children.'

'Well, there we are then. He was over sixty. Perhaps the poor man had an apoplexy and stumbled.'

They walk on in silence for a while. Then Bianca says, 'It wasn't chance, was it?'

'No, of course it wasn't.'

'Or suicide.'

'Doubtful.'

'So he was pushed?'

'Very likely. First Matteo dead, now Bondoni. Who amongst Bruno's little guild will be next?'

'I don't understand,' Bianca says. 'If the assassin intends Bruno harm, why didn't he take the opportunity when they passed each other on the bridge by the Porta Portello? And he's had weeks in which to make an attack against you and me. I can see no common explanation anywhere.'

'Nor I,' Nicholas admits. 'But one thing in certain: we must counsel Bruno to withdraw from the procession.'

'Bruno – withdraw? He'll never agree. He might be small in stature, but he has a great heart.'

'Well, we cannot keep him in ignorance.'

Bianca laughs. 'Bruno would risk a whole army of assassins to march at the head of his *Arte dei Astronomi*. You know how much it means to him.'

Nicholas shrugs in resignation. 'There is someone else we should warn, too.'

Bianca stops. The edge in her voice cuts through the mist like a sword through gossamer. 'We promised each other, remember?'

'I know, but—'

'Nicholas! No more of this!'

'Is that what you want of me: to leave her to her fate? Will your conscience lie easy if she is next?'

An anger blazes in her amber eyes that Nicholas has never seen before. He could almost believe it murderous.

'Enough!' she cries, so loudly that heads turn. A passer-by

frowns: a public altercation on a holy feast day – do some people have *no* respect? Relenting, Bianca takes Nicholas by the arm, her hand stroking his wrist in conciliation. She drops her voice. 'That woman has done little but lecture *us* on fate since the day we met her. You have done all that could be asked of any compassionate man. I will *not* countenance you doing more. We have promised each other to forget her. Do you now break your oath?'

He shakes his head like a scolded schoolboy and sighs. 'Of course not. You are right. I *have* warned her. She chose not to listen. What more can I do?'

Bianca releases his arm. As they set off again through the strange, ominous vapour that muffles their footsteps and robs those who pass of a distinct outline, she says softly, 'We agreed: *as if she had never existed.*'

✠

'He went to the Podestà's office, hours ago, Signora Bianca,' Luca says as he brushes the creases out of the new livery that his master has provided for the procession: a tabard of lockram dyed midnight-blue, with a long-tailed star picked out in yellow thread arcing across the breast from shoulder to hip.

'Did he go alone?' she asks tentatively.

'Alonso is with him.'

'Did he say when he would return?' she asks, casting a worried glance at Nicholas.

'He will not return, Signora. He told me that once he'd done at the Palazzo del Podestà, he would send Alonso to summon the Arte dei Astronomi to assemble beneath his banner in the Palazzo dei Signori. If you need him, that's where you will find him.'

'Are you sure?'

'Absolutely. The Master will guard that banner with his life, lest the guild of shit-shovellers tries to move it to the back of the procession.'

'Why would they do that, Luca?'

'To usurp our rightful place in the parade, Madonna. That's the sort of low-down trick the guild of night-soil removers always tries to play on holy days.'

Rather than risk sending Luca into a panic, Nicholas waits until he and Bianca are alone in their chamber before he says, 'I'll go to the Palazzo dei Signori and warn Bruno to take care.'

'Surely you don't think this man will make an attempt on Bruno's life in broad daylight, do you?'

'But it *isn't* broad daylight, is it?' Nicholas points out. 'And it will start getting dark before long.'

'All the more reason for you not to go stumbling about a city you don't know, Nicholas. Send one of the Corio cousins instead.'

'They sit outside in the street all day playing dice. I can't imagine they'll suddenly discover alacrity.'

'It may be a holy day, Nicholas, but this is still Padua. The cut-purses will be busy.'

Nicholas's eyes narrow. 'I know what this is about: you want me not to go alone because you fear I'll sneak away to see Hella Maas.'

For a moment Bianca just glares at him. Then she purges herself with a stream of Italian vocabulary that Nicholas may not yet have learned, but whose coarse, contemptuous meaning is clear.

He waits for her range to dissipate. Then, calmly, he asks, 'What was it you said to her – when we saw her this morning preaching by that statue in the square?'

'It is not important.'

'Oh, but I think it is. What is it about Hella that still troubles you – even while you tell me we must forget her?'

Tears begin to well in Bianca's eyes. Her face twists in pain, becomes almost ugly. With a desperation in her voice that alarms him she says, 'I'm trying to protect you, Nicholas – just as I protected you from yourself when I found you half-drowned by the river four years ago. Just as I have protected you from all the ills that have come upon us since, in your work for Robert Cecil. It is what we Caporettis do: protect those we love, whatever the cost to body or soul.'

'I don't know any Caporettis,' he says. 'I know only Bianca Merton. And I fear that some vile melancholy is stealing her from me.'

She shakes her head wildly, as though trying to block out a scream that her ears cannot bear to hear. 'No! It is *not* so,' she sobs.

Nicholas takes her in his arms, feeling the heave of her despair against his chest. He says, 'I know what it was that Hella said to you on the Via Francigena.'

He feels her body go still. She looks up at him, her eyes brimming.

'She told you?'

'Yes. And see for yourself: I am still here. The words she spoke had no more potency to harm me than did the images on that painting in Den Bosch. I can hear the words – I can see the images – and I am not destroyed. *We* are not destroyed. They cannot harm us, not unless we let them. There is no curse that Hella Maas can lay upon us that would be worse for me than the curse of a life without you, *whatever* she has foretold.'

There are two Biancas who lay their head against Nicholas's chest. The first, Simon Merton's daughter, allows the fear to drain out of her. She understands now, finally and completely, that his Eleanor and the child she carried are locked away securely in his past – a past that cannot now harm either of them. But the second, the daughter of Maria Caporetti, feels no such happy resolution. Because a Caporetti knows that regardless of what the new learning teaches, there are old fears – old curses – that can only be expunged by the old, reliable methods.

✠

The call to Vespers rings out from the bell towers of Padua, strangely muted in a mist that has, if anything, grown thicker with the onset of dusk. Torches are set, bonfires lit. Through the chamber window the evening air has a fiery hue to it, as if the city is being sacked. Shadows dance against the stucco walls of the house opposite as people pass below.

'Look at me,' Bianca says with a sad, disparaging laugh. 'This fine new gown Bruno has bought for me – the lace around my neck is all damp.'

'Even so, you will be the brightest star of the evening.'

'It is a pity I may not march with you and Bruno in the procession. I should like that. If my parents' ghosts are still here, they would be so proud. And I should like them to see my handsome English husband.'

'Can you walk beside us in the crowd?'

'I will try. The parade is always stopping and starting, so I should be able to keep up. And I know the route well. I know the shortcuts, if I need to use them.'

'I'm going to leave now, to find Bruno. Are you ready?'

Bianca sits up against the bolster. She studies his face carefully, almost as if she doubts her eyes. Then she lowers her head, almost evasively.

'I need to rest a little longer. I'll follow, with Luca. But promise me that you'll take one of the Corio cousins. I know this city, remember?'

Nodding his acquiescence, he says, 'You're tired – I understand.'

She places a hand over her belly. '*We* are tired.'

He rises, makes a gallant's bow and – smiling – says, 'Then I will see you in a while, in the Palazzo dei Signori... *my ladies.*'

'I shall look out for you by Bruno's banner, with its bright comet. A long-tailed star.'

She leans up to bestow a gentle kiss upon his mouth. When he opens the door, she calls to him, 'A comet is a portent, is it not?'

He turns. 'So it is said.'

'Then I name Bruno's comet as a portent of good fortune to come.'

The door closes. She hears the soft fall of the latch. She waits until she hears voices below the window – Luca ordering one of the Corio cousins to accompany her husband. Cautiously Bianca leans out a little way and watches until the two shadowy figures have been consumed by the mist. Then she closes the shutters, tidies the trim of her gown, covers her face with a lace veil, throws a cloak across her shoulders and goes downstairs to the street door, where she too exchanges pleasantries with the two remaining Corio cousins.

And then, rather than turn left to follow the general drift of people heading towards the Piazza dei Signori, she turns right – in the direction of the Porta Portello and the storehouse beyond.

✠

Time has begun to run again. The *Arte dei Orologiai* has sent its best artisans to repair the clock in the Piazza dei Signori. Around its face – the colour of a Paduan sky in summer and rimmed with the signs of the zodiac – the hour-hand restarts its sweep just as Nicholas arrives in the square. He is welcomed by the deep tolling of the tower's bell.

The piazza is filling up with people. In the mist they look like figures painted on a faded fresco, softened, indistinct. Torches bloom like fiery raindrops on glass, though it is not yet fully dark.

In the centre of the square, set upon a trestle, a wooden replica of a Venetian galley awaits its bearers. When the parade begins, it will be carried to the Basilica of St Anthony, where the victory over the Turks will be commemorated and the banners of the Arti blessed.

The Podestà's men have organized things with practised efficiency. The banners have been set out for the guildsmen to muster beneath, the senior guilds directly beneath the triumphal arch of the clock tower, the rest in the order of march.

It takes a while for the Corio cousin to help Nicholas locate Bruno's banner – halfway down a side-street. Alone, Alonso holds onto it grimly as if he's the sole survivor of a doomed last stand. Of Bruno himself, there is no sign. 'No need to fear, Signor Shelby,' Alonso says. 'We have almost an hour before the procession will be fully assembled. He'll get here in time.'

'He's probably in the piazza, trying to sell the Podestà a new clock,' Nicholas says, trying hard not to let his concern show. 'I'll go and look for him.'

As he sets off, the Corio cousin makes to follow. Nicholas raises a hand and smiles. 'I'll be fine. Stay here with Alonso, in case someone tries to steal the banner.'

Re-entering the square, he walks among the swelling crowd, taking in the aroma of cooking meat from the vendors' braziers. A corps of drummers in vividly striped tunics is practising its staccato tattoos. A nun pushes an old man in a wooden wheelbarrow, careless of who she barges aside in the effort to find a good spot. And all the while, more and more guildsmen in their fine livery gather to their banners like soldiers mustering for battle.

Nicholas has almost completed two laps of the piazza without sight of Bruno when he hears a male voice call out, 'Physician – heal thyself!'

He turns and sees a familiar, bearded figure sitting on a bench, his back against the stucco wall, feet up on the table in front of him. He is waving a half-empty flask of wine at him, like a patient inviting him to check his urine for an imbalance of the humours.

'Professor Galileo! Are you not marching with the rest of the learned gentlemen from the Palazzo Bo?'

The mathematician swings his feet off the table. 'Are you mad? An hour of being kicked in the heels to see some overfed priest bless a toy ship? Besides, they expect me to wear that ridiculous toga. If I don't, they look down their noses at me and call me a peasant.' He nods at the flask. 'This is far better company. You look at a loss. Join me. I'll call for another cup.'

Nicholas comes to the conclusion that as the *buchetta* is close to the side-street where Alonso is guarding the banner, it is as good a place as any to keep a lookout for Bruno. With this thickening mist, he could wander the Piazza dei Signori for a week, pass him ten times and still not catch sight of him. Besides, he thinks, if two of its members have already been murdered, then the mathematician is as much in danger as any in the *Arte dei Astronomi*.

'Just for a moment, Signor Galileo,' he says, walking over. 'Purely to rest my feet before the parade, you understand.'

✠

The bridge to the Porta Portello curves ahead of her into the darkening night. Torches set into the parapet turn the faces of Padua's heroes into lurid carnival masks. On the far side, Bianca can see barely a hint of the squat stone gatehouse. The storehouse a little further along the bank is invisible. She hurries across, the soles of her shoes tapping out a metallic rhythm, like the workings of one of Signor Mirandola's clocks.

Reaching the far side, she breathes deeply to steady her resolve. She is determined to remain calm. Once more she commands herself not to scream, not to rail. Tell Hella to her face that you seek only to put aside what has passed between you. Then ask her to lift her curse.

'And if she refuses? What then?'

Bianca wonders where the question has come from. Because it seems not to have come from inside her head. She could swear it came out of the fog. And there is no mistaking whose voice it is: Maria Caporetti's. It is her mother's voice.

'What will you do then, my daughter?'

'Then I will walk away,' Bianca answers out loud. 'I will seek out the apothecary, Tiziano. I will have him procure that *cantarella* we spoke of. Then I will do what we Caporettis have done down the long centuries, ever since we gave Agrippina the means to poison Claudius.'

'Then be at peace, my daughter,' says the voice.

And then its echo fades, leaving Bianca to wonder if her mind – or the fog – is playing tricks with her. She turns along the canal bank. The water murmurs as it flows past, mocking her with teasing little sucks and gurgles, as though preparing to digest her. When a twig snaps underfoot, Bianca has to suppress the notion that Hella is pouncing from the night, arms outstretched to push her into the river.

In their brief exchange beside the Gattamelata statue, they had agreed to meet outside the storehouse. But when it looms out of the fog, Bianca can see no trace of Hella. Looking upwards, she notices the glimmer of a torch or taper burning within.

She tries the huge wooden main doors, but they are locked. Slipping cautiously down the side of the building, she finds the door there ajar.

'Hella? Are you there?' she calls out softly.

Receiving no answer, she steps inside.

Hella is waiting for her in front of the empty cradle of Bruno's great sphere. In the light from a lantern set upon a stack of large iron cog-wheels, she stands legs akimbo, her plain hessian gown reminding Bianca of the tougher girls who lived around her family's lodgings and used to challenge her to fight, calling her the bastard prodigy of a Paduan mother and a heretic foreigner. She has the same swagger, the same spoiling for a brawl. And she is as unlike the pious maid from Den Bosch as Bianca can imagine. She could almost believe the maid has been possessed.

'So you've found the courage to come?' Hella says. 'I wasn't sure you would.'

'We agreed to it. We Caporettis keep our promises.'

'What do you want of me, Bianca? I have things to do. Time is running out.'

'So you keep telling us.'

Hella allows herself a wry smile, the bestowing of respect on an adversary she might have misjudged.

Bianca forces a stillness upon herself. 'I have come to make amends,' she says. 'To ask you to lift the curse you have laid upon me.'

'Have I cursed you? I don't recall.'

'In Reims, and upon the pilgrim road – you foretold a tragedy for Nicholas and me. I want you to renounce it. I ask you to take back your curse.'

'And if I don't?'

Bianca tightens her jaw. *Then I will ask Tiziano to make the venom linger in your body, so that my judgement is worse than any you might have seen in that painting, worse than any you already fear.*

'Or nothing,' she says, as pleasantly as she can manage. 'I ask simply as a woman who loves her husband and would see him happy.'

Hella smiles. It is the coldest of any smile Bianca has yet seen her give.

'Nicholas *will* be happy,' she says. 'Once he is with me.'

'Is that what all this has been about?' Bianca snaps. 'All the cruel talk of dead children, stillbirth and barrenness? Was it all just to send me into a confusion, so that I would doubt myself? So that you could drive a shard of ice between me and the man I love?'

Hella steps forward until she is close enough for Bianca to touch. Her pupils seem as large as golden florins, reflecting the lantern light. One corner of her mouth cracks open, like a pike about to snatch a minnow.

And then Bianca hears a sudden movement behind her. A voice calls out, guttural and harsh. The words mean nothing to her. They are shouted in a language she cannot understand. She turns.

Framed in the doorway is the figure of a man.

A man in a grey coat.

41

'You seem untroubled by the thought of an assassin in this city,' Nicholas says, surprised by Galileo's airy dismissal of the warning he has just delivered. The mathematician has listened to his recounting of the death of the goldsmith Bondoni with little more than mild interest.

'You have no proof that Bondoni was pushed. Every year someone gets hurt or killed in that horse race. I think you're reading too much into it. And as for Matteo, he was a young fellow with a roving eye. This is Padua, Nicholas, feuds are our meat and drink. There's always someone who thinks he has a legitimate quarrel with you – even if you've never met him before.'

Nicholas remembers the altercation he'd had with the youth outside the church. Perhaps Galileo is right. 'But what about the man in the grey coat that Bruno saw before he found Matteo Fedele's body?'

'A man in a grey coat – which, according to Signor Purse, had no bloodstains on it.'

'Bianca and I were followed from Reims by such a man.'

'That doesn't make him an assassin, does it? Besides, why would anyone follow you and that comely wife of yours all the way from France and then start murdering associates of Signor Purse – in Padua? It makes no sense.'

'I don't know,' Nicholas confesses. 'But I fear Hella could be in danger. Indeed, so could anyone in Bruno's new guild. Speaking of Bruno, have you seen him of late?'

'Not since this morning, but there's nothing remarkable in that.'

'I still think you should be careful.'

Galileo studies the bottom of his empty wine cup. 'I thought the English were supposed to be unexcitable fellows.'

'Are you not troubled by the possibility I might be right?'

The mathematician shrugs. 'In all honesty, I have had little to do with Bruno's wild scheme, other than to lend my name to it. It was Matteo who put in the hard effort. Besides, I'm accomplished at avoiding characters who wish me ill. I've been dodging my brother-in-law over my sister's dowry for months. He still hasn't caught me, and let me tell you: Signor Benedetto Landucci is a *very* persistent fellow.'

'A dowry can't stab you between the ribs, Signor Galileo.'

Galileo gives a snort of appreciative laughter. 'Maybe not, but I'm safe enough here. Who in their right mind would attack a peaceable fellow like me, in the middle of the celebrations of the Holy Rosary? Unless he was a creditor, of course. There's a whole army of those.' He sets down his cup. 'Talking of credit, mine's run out. Fancy more wine? I'll pay you back tomorrow.'

Exasperated by the mathematician's *sangfroid*, but at the same time amused by his audacity, Nicholas calls to a waiting servant, orders another jug and pays for it. From across the Piazza dei Signori comes a sudden thunder of drums. Looking up, Nicholas sees the liveried bearers hoisting the Venetian galley aloft. He rises from the table.

'Not going to help me drink it, Master Physician?' Galileo asks in surprise.

'I'm supposed to be marching with Bruno. I've probably missed him in this fog. He'll be wondering where I am.'

Galileo fills his cup and raises it in a toast. 'You're a good fellow, Niccolò – for an English heretic. But I think you're seeing goblins hiding under tables.'

'Perhaps I am,' Nicholas says with a smile, though underneath he feels a sense of unease. 'But I'd still counsel you to take care. There may be people here tonight more dangerous than brothers-in-law.'

✠

In the Piazza dei Signori and the adjoining side-streets the members of the city guilds have assembled beneath their banners. The sound of drumming fills the night. There is expectation in the foggy air. Nicholas is reminded of an army flushed with the thrill of conquest, preparing to march out for the final battle, exultant.

He does not share this exhilaration. The hour has come, and still there is no sign of Bruno Barrani. Worse still Luca has arrived, and he has come alone. 'But the Signora was not in your chamber,' he protests, looking about uneasily as though he has mislaid something precious entrusted to his care. 'I knocked, but she had gone. I assumed she had made her own way here.'

'It's not your fault, Luca,' Nicholas says, taking in the faces gathered beneath the banner of dark-blue silk emblazoned with its shooting star. They drift across his vision like half-remembered acquaintances from the past: Alonso, Mirandola the clockmaker, Pasolini the carpenter, the Corio brothers, the engraver Carlo Pomponazzi, and a gaggle of accompanying apprentices and servants. There must be almost a score of them. But no Bruno. No Bianca. The unease he'd experienced when leaving Galileo Galilei in the Piazza dei Signori a few minutes ago suddenly has the weight of lead about it.

The guild ahead of them in the procession is hoisting its banners and preparing to follow the sound of the drums. The crowd lining the walls breaks out into sporadic clapping and cheering. The *Arte dei Astronomi* must either march or stand down.

In the event it is Alonso – entrusted by his master with the banner – who takes command. He has the little group form into an orderly file, two abreast. Then, as the guild in front begins to stride out, he calls out in what he imagines is the voice of a Caesar, 'Astronomi – *avanzare!*'

The only man not to obey is Nicholas. Wishing them well, he slips away into the crowd.

At once he is jostled by bodies. He feels as though he's jumped from the safety of a shore into waters whose depth he cannot judge. Although the throng is moving with him, it does so with a slow, jerky, hesitant progress. This far down the procession, the guilds are stopping and starting unpredictably. And he needs to hurry. He is sure now that something is terribly wrong.

From his bench in the Piazza dei Signori the mathematician watches the vanguard of the march move off into the mist. The drummers raise their hands high in a blur as they hammer out a martial beat. Behind them comes a squad of the Podestà's guard. Their breastplates of burnished steel reflect the numerous flaming torches, making them appear like a squad of small suns on the move. Behind them, the replica Venetian galley sways precariously on its way to do battle with the heathen Turk.

Galileo pours himself another cup of the Englishman's wine. And as he does so, a young maid barely out of her teens – dark-haired, plump and dressed in pious brown hessian – slips onto the bench beside him. She has a folded sheet of paper in her hand.

'Are you Signor Galileo, the professor from the Palazzo Bo?' she asks tentatively. She seems to be searching his face as though she thinks she might have met him before, but isn't sure.

'I am he... Sister. Who are you?'

'My name is Carlotta.'

'You look like a nun. I'm a little short on coin, if it's charity you're after.'

'I'm not a nun. I'm a Beguine. And I have a letter for you.'

'It's not a bill for votive candles, is it – for my father's soul?'

'I have been instructed by Signor—' Carlotta stops, as though trying to make sure she has the name right. 'By Signor Barrani to give you this.' She hands him the paper.

'Why is Signor Purse entrusting his letters to a Beguine?' he asks.

Her reply sounds stilted, like a bad actor who has trouble memorizing lines. 'He said... you would surely want to hear the news... but he was too busy at... the Palazzo del Podestà... to give it to you in person. It's an errand. The payment will go to the poor.'

'I'm glad to hear it. Perhaps I should give up mathematics and take to delivering letters.'

Unfolding the note, Galileo finds the misty twilight insufficient to read by. He moves across to a torch burning in its sconce against the wall.

> *... a great purse full of His Serene Highness's ducats has this day arrived from Venice... your labours on the sphere rewarded... wherein this very place I may see you soundly recompensed.... be there, when the bell in the clock tower strikes the said hour...*
>
> *Your friend and fellow seeker of knowledge,*
>
> *Signor Purse*

Galileo reads it a second time, to savour the meat of it and capture the detail that his first, hurried glances have missed. The hand is new to him. He cannot recall receiving a letter from Bruno Barrani before, and on reflection he wonders if perhaps the writing is a little too feminine to be his friend's. But then

Bruno is a small man and is as particular as a woman about his appearance. A measure of delicacy might be expected. And it is signed Signor Purse. By that measure alone, he can see no reason to suspect one of his pupils of playing a trick on him.

Tucking the note into the sleeve of his tunic, Galileo Galilei walks back to the bench, ready to thank the messenger and explain – regretfully – that he cannot afford to tip her for her troubles.

But when he reaches the spot, he finds she has not waited.

✠

The mist is thickening. Night has the upper hand now as Nicholas pushes on through the lanes towards the Borgo dei Argentieri. Soon he is all but alone. He passes only the occasional citizen late for the festivities and the odd scrawny, prowling cat. More than once he takes a wrong turning, straying down stuccoed canyons whose ends are lost in darkness. So far he has realized his error before becoming irretrievably lost. But the prospect of wandering into the heart of this vaporous labyrinth and losing all sense of place is frighteningly real to him. When he spots the two Corio cousins sitting on the cobbles outside the entrance to Bruno's house, a flask of wine and a dice board lying beside them, he feels like a mariner who's spotted land on the very day the food runs out.

He asks, 'Where is Signor Barrani? Have you seen him?'

One of the cousins points back up the street. 'He's in the procession, Master.'

'I've just come from there,' Nicholas says, trying hard to stifle the fears that are marching inside him now with a din that would put the Piazza dei Signori to shame. 'They started without him.'

The man shrugs. 'That's what he said when he left. We haven't seen him since.'

'And Signora Bianca? You must have seen her leave. Which way did she go – towards the Piazza dei Signori?'

The other cousin shakes his head. To Nicholas's horror he points in the opposite direction – towards Porta Portello.

✠

Along the riverbank the mist has turned to fog. The narrow margin of black water that is visible to Nicholas is shot through with a golden weave from the torches burning here and there in their mounts. As he crosses the bridge, his fears rise up from the surface like monstrous sea creatures. He can think of only one place Bianca could have headed for in this quarter of the city: the storehouse. And he can think of only one reason for her visit. He sees again in his mind her brief exchange with Hella in the Piazza del Santo this morning, and he recalls only too clearly her refusal to reveal what had passed between them.

The brickwork of the storehouse looms out of the fog, like the walls of a prison so grim that he cannot stop himself imagining the torturers at work within. The fact that he can see a glimmer of torchlight in the narrow window beneath the eaves gives him no comfort. A torturer needs enough light to work by, but not so much that he can see too deeply into his victim's eyes. Unless, of course, he has no soul.

The wide doors at the front look securely barred. Slipping down the side of the building, he sees the smaller door ajar. His heart pounding, his mind flinching at all the horrors presented to it by his imagination, he slips quietly around the door and inside. He is certain now that something very wrong has happened tonight, and that Hella is at the centre of it.

What he sees confirms the very worst of his fears.

Bianca is lying against the cradle of Bruno's great sphere, clad in the pearl-coloured gown Bruno had brought her. Only it is no longer pristine. It is stained with blood. And looming over her is the man in the grey coat.

42

Nicholas is upon him even as the man turns, alerted by his footsteps and his sudden, agonized intake of breath. Indifferent to the near-certainty that the assassin has a blade, Nicholas hauls him off Bianca's body, smashing his fist into his upturned, startled face. He doesn't feel the damage done to his own knuckles. The rage, the despair, makes pain meaningless. He strikes again, driving the man down as though he would batter him into the very earth itself and bury him. He raises his fist to strike a third time, all restraint gone, only raw murder in his mind.

And then Bianca's voice stays his hand.

'Nicholas, for the love of Jesu, leave Ruben be! You're killing him.'

His right elbow thrust out at an acute angle, his balled fist held at the instant before he smashes it home, Nicholas freezes. The man slithers away from him, groaning, his face bloodied.

'Ruben?' he repeats, confused beyond measure. 'You know him?'

'I do, now,' Bianca says. 'His name is Ruben Maas. He's Hella's brother – the priest. And he wasn't trying to harm me. In fact I owe him my life.'

For a moment Nicholas does not understand. Then he remembers the conversation he and Hella had in the forest outside Clairvaux Abbey, when she told him of the Spanish fury at Breda and the slaughter of her family: *The day of the massacre I was with my twin brother, Ruben... I didn't see him more than once or twice after that... He became a priest.*

Nicholas hauls the cowering Ruben to his feet. 'Is this true?' he asks, still half-consumed by a murderous anger.

Ruben Maas answers in passable English, distorted only by a Dutch accent and the fact that blood from his nose and lips has found its way in no small quantity into his mouth.

'Yes, it is true. I try my best to protect your woman. But I am not a man of action. I am a man of God. Violence does not come readily to me.'

Nicholas fishes a kerchief from his doublet and hands it to the man to clean his face. 'If you're a priest, why aren't you dressed like one?'

Ruben tries to smile. 'I have no stomach to be a martyr. I am a Lutheran. And while I may be a coward, I am no fool. Only a fool would flaunt his Protestant faith in a papist country.'

Another fragment of the conservation in the Forest of Troyes comes back to Nicholas: *He refused to countenance that God could be a Catholic, like the Spanish who had murdered our family...*

'Why have you been following us all the way from Reims?' he asks.

Ruben Maas lets out a bitter laugh that bubbles through the blood seeping from his mouth. 'Reims? I've been following you from Den Bosch.'

'But *why?*'

The young priest struggles to force himself upright. Nicholas's assault has taken the strength out of his legs. He sways precariously. Nicholas puts out a hand to steady him and Maas flinches, as though he anticipates another blow.

'It's alright,' Nicholas assures him. 'I will not strike you again. But tell me why you've been following us all this way.'

Ruben Maas looks into Nicholas's eyes with the pain of a man who knows he cannot meet the measure he has set for himself. He says, 'Because I wanted to stop my sister from committing the sin of murder – again.'

✠

'Are you too elevated to march with us tonight, Professor Galileo?' calls a voice teasingly from the Piazza dei Signori. 'Is our company too dull for your exceptional mind? Or are you too drunk to walk in a straight line?'

Looking up from his wine, the mathematician sees the procession has come to one of its frequent halts. Directly in front of him, grouped in an untidy gaggle around the university's banner, are the senior men from the Palazzo Bo. In the fog, their black scholastic togas soften their outlines, making them look as though the darkness of the night has taken on a solid, human form. By the light of the torches their servants carry, he can see them grinning at him.

'Maestro Fabrici,' he calls back, recognizing the speaker, 'our august professor of anatomy! Off to do some butchery, are you? Bring me back a good slice of fresh pork.'

'I'll bring you back a dozen, if you like – but I doubt you'd be able to count them accurately.'

Galileo raises his cup in a good-natured salute. 'Tell me, Professor, is the door to your new anatomy theatre locked?'

'Locked? It doesn't have a door yet. And I intend to take that up with Signor Fassolato of the *Arte dei Carpentieri* straight after Mass. Why do you wish to know?'

'An assignation, Professor Fabrici,' Galileo says, picking the first fiction that comes into his head. 'You must remember those – though, in your case, it would be a very ancient memory.'

'You're a disgrace to the university, Professor Galileo,' Fabrici replies with good humour, bringing mutters of agreement from his companions.

'So anyone can just walk in?'

'Holy Mother of God! Don't tell me you're inviting an audience to watch you in your rutting? Are you *that* desperate to raise money?'

'Just wondered. It doesn't sound very secure.'

'We have a watchman, so you'll have to bribe him.' Fabrici gives him a foxy stare. 'If that's beyond even your limited resources, I can only suggest you find a convenient wall, like the lecherous rogue you clearly are.'

The drums have started up again, echoing from the head of the procession somewhere on the way to the Basilica of St Anthony. The professors gather up the hems of their togas and prepare to resume their un-martial shuffling.

'If there should happen to be any sign of...' Fabrici screws up his face in disgust, 'fornication... in my anatomy theatre tomorrow morning, Professor Galileo, I shall have stern words with the rector.'

'Why?' says the mathematician, making a farewell flourish with his free hand as the professors move off. 'Does the rector use it, too?'

✼

The blood on Bianca's dress comes from a glancing slash to her shoulder.

'It's not deep,' Nicholas says, after a careful inspection. 'But it needs binding.' He unlaces her sleeve, removes his own doublet, rips one sleeve off his linen shirt and tears a makeshift bandage. When he has tied it in place, he turns his attention to Ruben Maas. The priest's right eye is half-shut, the socket bloodied from where Nicholas's first blow landed. He is dabbing his mouth with his kerchief to staunch the bleeding from the gash in his lower lip.

'Forgive me,' Nicholas says, 'but I had every reason to think you were an assassin. You must see how it looked—'

The priest nods slowly through the pain. 'There is no blame, I have brought all this on myself,' he says miserably. 'I am a weak man. A man of faith, not of violence. But even I should have had the courage to have acted earlier, in the cathedral at Den Bosch. Then perhaps I could have stopped all this in its tracks.'

Nicholas stares at him. 'In the cathedral at Den Bosch? It was *you* in that chamber? *You're* the one I caught a glimpse of as you fled?'

'I had no idea Hella was going to kill the priest, or the Spaniard. It all happened so quickly. But then, ever since Breda she has been like that: one moment calm and placid, the next a raging she-devil. I believe it is because she has Satan inside her heart. He makes her hate herself.'

'Hella?' Nicholas breathes. '*She* killed them?' He shakes his head in disbelief. 'Why was I so blind? She wasn't screaming in that chamber because of what she'd witnessed. She realized it was too late to run, and the knife was out of reach on the floor. She was screaming to fool *me*.' He stoops to retrieve his doublet from the floor and slips it on, leaving the points unlaced. 'Help me get my wife to the Borgo dei Argentieri,' he says curtly, his face creased with self-recrimination. 'I can bathe her wound properly there – and yours. You can explain everything as we go.'

✠

The fog is so thick now, the night so dark, that they almost miss the bridge. Only the torches burning on the parapet show the way back into the city. Bianca refuses the help of either man. Nicholas clumsily persists.

'I'm not an invalid, Husband. I can walk perfectly well. It's my shoulder – there's nothing wrong with my legs.'

'But the child—'

'The child will be fine, Nicholas. I know it. After what Ruben just said, Hella's curse does not frighten me any more.' She stares up into the fog, as though it might contain dark creatures floating out of sight. 'But I fear what she is capable of: the Dutch priest... that Spaniard... poor Matteo Fedele... Bondoni the goldsmith.'

'Were you in the crowd today, when she pushed Bondoni into the path of the horses?' Nicholas asks Ruben.

The priest covers his face with his hands. 'Oh, sweet Saviour, not *another* one.'

'I think it is time for you to give a full account of yourself, Father Ruben,' Nicholas says as they hurry across the canal and into the narrow lanes beyond. 'And your troubled sister.'

✠

'It began after Breda,' Ruben begins. 'Until then we were a fortunate family – gifted not in riches, but in our minds. Hella was the cleverest by far. She ate numbers as hungrily as others eat sweetmeats and sugared comfits. Soon she started to believe that she could foretell events because of the patterns she saw in numbers – she thought numbers were the underlying structure of all that she saw around her. But after the Spanish came to Breda, she began to blame herself for not foreseeing the greatest threat of all.

'Afterwards I could not bear to remain in a place with so many terrible memories clinging to it. When Hella took refuge with the Beguines, I went north, into the Protestant territories. I still believed in God, but I knew He could not be a Catholic God. I became a Lutheran priest.'

'How did you come to be in Den Bosch cathedral then?' Nicholas asks.

'Eventually I gathered the courage to go back to search for Hella. I tracked her down to the city, found her sitting in a doorway like a prophet who's been cast out by those she would warn. She told me of the painting, and that she was going to plead with Father Vermeiren to remove it. When we entered that little chapel, I thought that's what she was going to do. Then she drew a knife. It all happened so quickly. Vermeiren was dead before he knew what was happening – before I knew what was happening. When the Spaniard tried to take the blade from her, she struck him across the throat.'

'And then you fled?'

'What could I do? If they'd found out I was a priest from the Protestant states, they would have hanged me. I looked to my own safety – and for a second time I abandoned my sister.'

Walking in step between the two men, Bianca says, 'Why did she not kill you, Nicholas?'

'She had dropped the knife before I stepped out into plain view,' Nicholas answers. 'As Ruben says, Hella has faster wits than most. She probably realized that by the time she got to it, either I would have overpowered her or the commotion would have brought others running. So she decided to play the innocent victim. She started screaming.'

'Why did you decide to follow us, Father Ruben?' Bianca asks the priest.

'I thought perhaps I could help my sister find redemption. But at Reims, when I tried to speak to her, she would have none of me. I was not deterred. I would not let myself forsake her again, not like I had after Breda. And to be truthful to you – and God knows it's time to be truthful to myself – I feared she might kill again.' He gives a sad, reflective laugh. 'I thought I could stop her. What a fool I was.'

Nicholas says, 'That's when I saw you first, when you stopped her in the cathedral square. And then again at the hospice of

St Bernard's in the mountains. You could have spoken to us. It would have been better if you had.'

Father Ruben finds another failing in himself. He adds it to the list with a slow shake of his head. 'Alas, I am not accomplished at intrigue. Besides, Hella told me I should not trust you.'

'Hardly a fortnight after we saved her life,' Bianca says, as though she's known it all along.

'Why did you run – the day I saw you in that side-street by the Basilica?' Nicholas asks.

'I told you: I am a coward. That's what cowards do. They run.'

Bianca lays a hand on Ruben's forearm. 'You are not a coward, Father Ruben. A coward would not have risked his life to seek out his sister in a land dangerous to him. And a coward wouldn't have done what you did in that storehouse.' She turns her head to Nicholas. 'Hella pulled a blade. She would have killed me. As it was, she landed a strike on my shoulder even as I was trying to get away from Ruben – whom I believed at that moment was the true assassin. He stood over me. He told her that if she was determined to take my life, she would have to take his first. If that isn't courage, I don't know what is.'

'It took me long enough to find it. When I followed Hella to that same place a few days ago, on the day she murdered that poor young fellow, I fled again – like a frightened child.'

'At least I know now why she's doing it,' Nicholas says. 'Warning us about the dangers of seeking knowledge is no longer enough for her. She's come to the conclusion it's better to stop us altogether. If we're dead, we can't look behind the curtain. We can't open the door and risk letting the Devil in.'

Ahead of them, the two Corio cousins rise up out of the fog, their dice and their wine forgotten. Staring in disbelief at the apparitions emerging from the night, they begin to draw their rapiers. Bianca stays them with a brief call of reassurance. Once inside the house, Nicholas dispatches one of them to fetch a flask of *aquavite di vinaccia* from the credenza in the parlour. He uses the grape spirit to clean Bianca's wound and the lacerations that his fury has inflicted on Ruben's face.

'Where did your sister go?' he asks, dabbing the spirit-soaked cloth against the priest's mouth.

'She didn't say.'

'She walked out into the fog without a word?'

'Not exactly. She said something about an audience?'

'She wants an *audience* for whoever in the *Arte dei Astronomi* she intends to kill next?' Nicholas asks, horrified.

'I heard what she said,' Bianca chimes in. 'I'm not quoting her exactly, but it was along the lines of: It is bad enough people opening the door to the Devil's knowledge without scholars making a theatre of it and inviting an audience.'

'Then I believe I know where she's gone,' Nicholas says. The sense of dread that has been with him ever since the *Arte dei Astronomi* began its march without its leading light has become a hard, cold stone in his stomach. 'I'm going back to the Palazzo Bo.'

Bianca rises from her chair.

'No, stay here,' Nicholas says, sounding harsher than he intended. 'She has already tried to kill you once. At least here you have the Corio cousins to keep you safe.'

He turns to Ruben.

'Forgive me for the hurt I did you, Father. Do you feel well enough to come with me? You may be the only man able to avert further tragedy tonight.'

Ruben tries to smile through the swollen corner of his lip. 'I've come this far,' he says. 'Only a true coward would give up now.'

✠

The streets around the Palazzo Bo are almost empty. The tail of the procession is somewhere off to the south, towards the Basilica of St Anthony, mired in the fringes of the great crowd filling the Piazza del Santo. But Nicholas can still hear the echoing of drums and the occasional roar of public approval.

By day, the arcades that line the university are teeming with students and scholars, arguing, debating, sometimes even brawling. But tonight they stand empty, like the cloisters of an abandoned monastery. The mist drifts around the arches like a mournful sea lapping at an uninhabited shore. The watchman's brazier burns unattended. Nicholas calls out, but receives no answer.

'Perhaps he's slipped away to watch the procession,' Ruben says as he and Nicholas lift torches from an iron rack bolted to a pillar and light them in the brazier. Nicholas doesn't answer. His fear is that the watchman has been lured away not by curiosity, but by some clever deceit – or, worse, that he has met the same fate as the Spaniard at Den Bosch, paying with his life for being in the wrong place at the wrong time.

On the way from the Borgo dei Argentieri he has had plenty of time for dark images to crowd his mind. Now he understands Bruno's failure to join the procession. He is certain that Bruno and the mathematician have somehow been lured to this place by Hella Maas. The knowledge fills him with dread. The fact that she is one young woman, alone, does not ease that dread for an instant.

Torch in hand, the flames casting devilish patterns on the plastered walls, he approaches the empty hole in the night that is the open doorway to the uncompleted anatomy theatre. He senses Ruben hesitate.

'Be careful,' he warns the priest. 'This place is full of workmen's gear and rubbish. I've caused you enough hurt already, without you planting your face on the floor or walking into a beam.'

'There is no room left in my heart for any further hurt,' Ruben says grimly. 'It is too full of pain for what my sister has done.'

On either side of the open doorway a flight of wooden stairs curves away around the elliptical body of the auditorium, creating a narrow space between the inner and outer walls. Ahead of him, through the entrance, Nicholas can see the railed enclosure where Professor Fabrici will carry out his dissections when the anatomy theatre is in use. It is not a large space, just long enough to take a cadaver, with enough room for the lecturer to stand between his subject and the first tier of his audience.

To his horror, he sees the dissection area is not empty. By the torchlight he can make out a figure lying on the platform. He moves cautiously closer, holding up the torch. Suddenly the figure sits up. In Nicholas's mind, he has just seen a corpse rise from its grave.

'You've left the procession, Signor Physician,' says Galileo, his voice a little slurred. 'Wise fellow. Who wants to listen to a priest blessing a toy boat when there are taverns still open?' He jabs a finger in Nicholas's direction. 'I was expecting Master Purse,' he adds as an afterthought. 'Has he sent you instead? Have you brought the money with you?'

'Money?' echoes Nicholas, confused.

'Bruno sent me a note to meet him here. He said he had a heavy purse of the doge's coin to give me.'

'Did you receive this note from his own hand, Professor?' Nicholas asks.

'No, it was a maid. She looked like one of those Poor Clares, clad in sackcloth and brimming with piety.'

Nicholas covers his face with his free hand for a moment, as if to stop his thoughts from spinning and fix them in one place.

'From Hella Maas?'

'No, it wasn't her,' Galileo says. 'I'd have recognized *her*.'

'I fear greatly for Bruno's life, Professor – and yours,' Nicholas tells him. 'I think you should come away from this place, now. There is great danger here.'

Galileo gets to his feet. He peers at Nicholas in the torchlight, trying to read his face. 'You're serious, aren't you?'

'Never more so.'

'What sort of danger?'

'Of murder.'

'You're still fretting about that, are you? I told you before, no one in this city would bother themselves making an affray upon my life. Apart from dear old Fabrici – and my creditors, of course.' He frowns at his own reasoning. 'But then what good would murdering me do *them*? You can't get blood out of a stone, and you can't get a dead man to pay his debts.'

'The one you have to fear is the maid with the clever brain.'

'Signorina Maas?' Galileo says, astonished.

'It was she who killed Matteo Fedele. Today she murdered the goldsmith, Bondoni. And she would have killed my wife, Bianca, too – had not Ruben here stopped her. I fear you and Bruno are next on her list.'

Galileo seems to chew the air as he digests what Nicholas has told him.

'*Why?*' he demands. 'I have done her no harm. What does she want to murder *me* for?'

And then, out of the darkness from one of the tiers above, comes a woman's voice, calling out in a guttural English.

'Tell him, Nicholas. You understand the truth. *You* tell him why he must die.'

In the flickering torchlight, three heads move as one. Three pairs of eyes fix on the figure standing, barely visible, behind the wooden balustrade of the third tier. Hella Maas, dressed as plainly as a martyr at the stake, her hands away from her sides to grip the rail, leans out of the darkness as though intending to address an assembled crowd of loyal followers.

'I think we should hear the justification from you, Hella,' Nicholas answers. 'Do not seek to make *me* complicit in your madness.'

'I have to stop them, Nicholas,' she cries out. 'The curtain has to be drawn. The door has to be closed. We have let the Devil in too often. If we let him in again, there will be chaos. Judgement Day will be upon us all soon enough. The world must have a little peace before it does. A little rest. How else may we ready ourselves for what is coming?'

Nicholas jams his torch into the narrow gap between the dissection table and its surrounding rail, then climbs up onto the balustrade of the lower observation tier. He reaches out to steady himself against the edge of the tier above, his head tilted back so that he can look up directly into Hella's face.

'You are suffering a terrible malady of the soul, Hella. I understand that. But this insanity cannot continue. Come down and let your brother help you.'

Her head turns towards where Ruben stands with Galileo. 'So the courage you found in the storehouse hasn't deserted you yet, little brother,' she says, a sad smile on her face. 'You couldn't help me after Breda, and you cannot help me now.' She leans further out to look down at Nicholas. 'Only *you* can help me,' she says. 'You, alone, can see a little of what is in my heart. No one else has that faculty.' She looks puzzled as – beneath her – his face contorts with rejection. 'You know I am right, Nicholas. Admit it.'

'That I can see a little of what is in your heart?' he replies contemptuously. 'Did you really believe that killing my wife would help me to see more?'

'She was in the way, Nicholas. She has been in the way since we met. Discard her.'

'Discard her – for you?'

'This close to Judgement Day we have to make brave choices.'

Nicholas jumps back down from the rail. 'Ruben, go to the doorway. Take the steps on the right; I'll go left. Be careful. I think her mind is so disordered she might strike at either of us without even realizing she's doing it.' He turns to the mathematician. 'Professor, you go to the Piazza del Santo. Tell the first of the Podestà's night-watch you come across that we need help here. Tell him I fear the doge's Master of the Spheres is in danger. Hurry!'

Perplexed, Galileo shakes his head. He seems to have sobered up rapidly. 'Don't you want me to stay and help? The maid knows me. Perhaps I may reason with her.'

'There has been nothing resembling reason in that poor maid's mind for a long while, Professor. And speaking of what is reasonable, getting yourself stabbed as a way of avoiding paying your sister's dowry is not it.'

With a harsh laugh, the mathematician heads for the doorway, his body silhouetted there by the light of the brazier burning in the mist beyond.

Nicholas takes up the torch from where he planted it and follows him, taking the left-hand flight of wooden steps. Ruben takes the right.

Hemmed into the narrow space between the wall of the auditorium and the outside masonry, Nicholas begins the steep climb into the blackness. Shoulders hunched, he thrusts the torch out ahead of him, moving within its dancing sphere of light into an otherwise impenetrable cosmos.

He climbs the first flight and reaches a curved landing barely wide enough to allow him passage. To his left is an open space

to enable the audience of students to spill out and fill the observation tier; to his right, the brickwork of the building's shell.
He hears movement on the tier above, the clatter of footsteps on
timber. From the far side of the auditorium comes the sound of
Ruben pleading with his sister to stay where she is.

Moving forward, he stumbles upon the next flight of stairs.
He begins to climb once more. Again he hears movement above
him, a desperate and doomed slithering of shoe leather on
freshly planed timber. A crossbeam support left in place by the
carpenters springs out of the darkness and almost brains him.
And then, out of the wall to his left, Hella emerges.

'Come with me, Nicholas,' she says in a pleading voice,
holding out her hand, staring at him in the torchlight. 'Come
with me and we will find our rest together, before the last day.'

Turning her back on him, she hurries ahead. He catches a
shadowy glimpse of her climbing the next flight of steps. Then
he loses her again in the pitch-black confinement of this seemingly never-ending prison.

He does not count the tiers they climb together in this
strange pursuit. But then suddenly there are no more steps, just
an opening to his left. He turns to face it and steps forward.

By the light of the torch, Nicholas sees he is standing on
the very top tier, looking out into space. There is no wooden
balustrade here, only an elliptical, uncompleted walkway of
planking held up by scaffolding. Two steps forward and he
would go over the edge. He feels the unsecured planks move
under his feet. Looking down, he sees glimpses of the tiers
of the auditorium set out beneath him, as though he were
peering over the edge of an elliptical stairwell, forty or more
feet down into the darkness. A faint, single wash of yellow
from the brazier in the courtyard falls on the now-empty dissection table. He feels his knees weaken, his stomach lurch.

His free hand clutches at the wall in a bid to stop the reeling of his senses.

From his right he hears the rasp of planks raking against each other. Turning his head, he catches a glimpse of Hella lunging towards him, her arms outstretched to carry them both over the edge. She moves so quickly, so suddenly, that he doesn't even think of stepping back out of the way. He closes his eyes and waits to feel the brief moment of fatal freedom as he falls.

The night rings to the sharp crack and clatter of un-nailed planks sprung out of place by the impact of careless feet. A scream. A sickening glissando of impacts as Hella's body strikes the rails of the lower tiers as it plunges. A final crack – mercifully brief – of a human skull striking the unyielding edge of the dissection table.

Then silence, save for the sound of his own breathing and the faintest *rat-a-tat-tat* of drums, like the sound of a victorious army leaving the battlefield to the defeated and the dead.

43

A disturbance at the Palazzo Bo – even one involving a fatality – is just another irritant in a busy night for the Podestà and his staff. The night-watch has had its hands full ensuring that the Feast of the Holy Rosary passes off without the great and the good of Padua having their purses lifted by the larcenous, or the honour of their wives and daughters insulted by the impertinent. Thus it is daylight before Bruno Barrani's body is found in the chamber below the dissection table of Professor Fabrici's almost-completed anatomy theatre.

Found in the new black silk doublet he wears – purchased specifically for the procession, but now stained with dried blood from a single knife-thrust to the back – is a letter claiming to be from the rector of the university. In it, Bruno is asked to meet him in the seclusion of the anatomy theatre, the more privately to discuss the prospect of Signor Barrani taking a leading position on the university's Studium, in reward for his tireless work on behalf of the city's reputation. When the letter is shown to the rector, he barely reads beyond the first line before pronouncing it a forgery. 'It's not even in my hand,' he says, before adding dismissively, 'Anyway, why would Padua want a chancer like Signor Barrani for an exemplar?'

Bianca is almost inconsolable, and for a while Nicholas is racked by the fear that she will lose the child. He realizes that if she does, it will prove the power of Hella Maas's curse, and he blames himself for not seeing through Hella's deceit from the very start.

'You saw what you thought was another human soul in distress,' Bianca tells him. 'You're a physician. What choice did you have?'

Madonna Antonella allows the Podestà three days' grace before she seeks an audience. He receives her in his palazzo with all the grace due to her piety. But as she tells him why she has come, his podgy face clouds over.

'Heresy – here in our city? How did you learn of this, Madonna?'

'A young Beguine, Sister Carlotta, who knows her duty to our Lord, has come to me,' Antonella tells him from a kneeling position, adopted because, in his red gown, the Podestà looks to her very much like a cardinal, and she thinks it better to be safe than sorry. 'She heard, apparently from our poor sister who had that dreadful accident in the Palazzo Bo, that this blasphemous device is able to predict events that God – and our Holy Mother Church – would wish impressionable minds not to know of.'

'What manner of events, Madonna?'

'The precise date, for instance, of the day of our final judgement.'

The Podestà manages a weak smile through the grinding of his jaw. When he regains control of his face, he reaches out to raise her to her feet. 'You are right to have come to me, Madonna,' he says generously. 'But you need have no fear. None whatsoever. The device is not heretical, merely scientific.' And with a benign smile he sends her on her way. He is a practical man; 4 per cent of the money His Serene Highness in Venice has set aside for the late Signor Barrani's scheme cannot be endangered by the concerns of one unworldly woman, however pious.

But the Podestà has judged Madonna Antonella unwisely. She has contacts. She uses them. Ten days later he receives a visit from Cardinal Lorenzo Priuli, the Patriarch of Venice, who carries with him not only the doge's authority, but that of God Himself.

'If what Madonna Antonella tells me is true, this engine is heretical,' he tells the Podestà, having failed to offer him one single smile since he walked through the door. 'What is more, if the common people were to get hold of it, understand its workings, use it to determine matters the Almighty desires to remain unknown, then no prince in all Christendom would be safe from insult and overthrow.' Then Priuli reminds him that while the Serene Republic likes to consider itself open to the new learning, it has its limits. Was not the heretic prior, Giordano Bruno, arrested in Venice only two years ago, after spreading his vile theories on the universe – and man's place in it – throughout Europe? He will surely burn before long. And Podestàs, the cardinal observes ominously, are no more immune from God's wrath than are heretic friars.

That very afternoon the Holy Office of the Faith descends upon the storehouse by the Porta Portello. By sunset it is empty. The timbers are burned, the iron carried away to be melted down for more practical usage, and the brass and gilt handed to the Church to be turned into something less troublesome. Nothing of Bruno Barrani's great sphere remains. By order of the Council, the Arte dei Astronomi is struck from the roll of city guilds.

When the Patriarch departs for Venice, he leaves the Podestà with a written order from the doge's treasury: return all monies as yet unspent.

✳

Throughout the following weeks Nicholas keeps a careful eye on his wife. Slowly her grief subsides. Together, they take long walks along the banks of the Bacchiglione. The leaves lie scattered around the trees like fragments of discarded memories. But he is pleased to see that the dark, underlying mood that had preceded the events of the night of the Feast of the Holy Rosary seems to have lifted from her. He puts it down to the death of Hella Maas.

At the end of October, Ruben takes his leave of them. He has it in mind to join the Protestant community at Montreux. Bianca wishes him well, and keeps the conversation she had with his sister there to herself.

In November Nicholas is approached at the Palazzo Bo by a young student of law, an Englishman, though his dress is distinctly Paduan. He hands Nicholas a letter. 'Don't open it here,' he says. 'Should a reply be needed, seek me out.' He doesn't stay to give his name.

Upon opening it, in the privacy of Bruno's study at the house in the Borgo dei Argentieri, Nicholas is confronted with a meaningless jumble of letters written in a neat, professional hand, the sort of hand a clerk at Cecil House might favour. Bianca watches as he sets to work decoding the cipher. She resists the desire to look over his shoulder to see what manner of future his quill is revealing. Don't interrupt him, she tells herself sternly. Give him time. Thoughts of returning to England have begun to fade from her mind of late, but for Nicholas's sake she would rather see him exonerated.

Eventually he begins to smile. He lays down the pen. 'Mistress Merton, you'll be relieved to know that you're no longer married to an accused regicide,' he tells her, the smile on his dependable jaw in severe danger of becoming a grin. 'Apparently it was Fulke Vaesy who denounced me. He's written a confession, admitting it was all a lie. We are free to go home.'

'With a child well on the way?' she says. 'Shall we pack her in a crate like a set of pewter?'

'I didn't mean *now*, of course. Not at this very moment.' He holds up the paper on which he has deciphered the letter. 'Sir Robert says he could do with a second set of eyes and ears in Padua. More importantly, in Venice – England has no ambassador there.'

'A *second*?'

'The English law student who gave this to me—'

'And Cecil is suggesting you?'

'Not officially.'

'Does he intend to pay you?'

'Not officially.'

They decide to put off a decision, at least until the child is old enough to travel safely.

In December Bianca's old family house unexpectedly comes up for rent. They move out of the Borgo dei Argentieri, taking Luca and Alonso with them. Nicholas can afford servants now: there are enough well-heeled foreign students at the Palazzo Bo for an English physician to take on as clients. And thanks to Professors Galileo and Fabrici putting the word about that there is a competent young man of physic new to the city who might be just the fellow to consult for your current troublesome malady, he has Paduan patients, too.

In the new year, Girolamo Fabrici's revolutionary anatomy theatre opens to great acclaim. Nicholas attends a lecture there. Watching the cadaver being dissected by the great man, he cannot help but think back to the night of the Feast of the Holy Rosary. Wherever she is now, he hopes Hella Maas is at peace. Given the hurt and pain she has both suffered and inflicted, he thinks she will need a little rest – before she faces her Last Judgement.

✠

In the courtyard of her parents' old house, Bianca writes her will. Made on this, the first day of June, in the year of our Lord 1595, and being possessed in all respects of sound reason and health... She does not plan to die, but when childbirth is imminent one has to take precautions. Nicholas finds it hard not to weep at her bravery.

A little before sunrise on the fifth day of the month, with a soft wash of light gilding the domes of the Basilica of St Anthony, Nicholas and Galileo wait outside the lying-in chamber in the house where Simon Merton and his wife, Maria Caporetti, once lived. Nicholas has spent several hours in a state of unrest. But not once has Eleanor called to him through the haze of anxiety in his head. And whenever his thoughts have wandered briefly in her direction, she has somehow never quite materialized into any identifiable form.

When he hears the laughter of the midwives, followed almost immediately by a robust, high-pitched howling, he finds it almost impossible not to weep.

'That's a lusty boy, or Galileo Galilei can't count,' his friend says, clapping him on the shoulder. 'By what name will he be christened?'

'Bianca wants to name him Bruno. That's good enough for me.'

The mathematician purses his lips in approval. 'You should thank the saints for your good fortune. If you need any help spending the money you've saved on a dowry, I'll be your man.'

Nicholas would laugh – were it not for the fact that he is too busy giving thanks that curses have power only over those who believe themselves cursed.

✠

A cold wind is blowing off the River Thames, stirring the leaves on the trees in St Saviour's churchyard. Towering over his wife,

Ned Monkton draws her to him, placing himself between her and the small wooden cross. They have been coming here every week after Sunday sermon since early April. Ned holds her until he feels her sobbing ease a little.

'We wasn't cursed, Rose. It was God's will,' he says softly. 'We cannot know what is in His holy plan. Perhaps He has more need of her than we do.'

'But couldn't He 'ave given her a minute or two of life?' Rose asks, red-eyed. 'Enough for us to bid her welcome, and tell her she was loved?'

'There will be another child, Wife,' Ned says gently. 'An' more than just another.'

He tries hard to sound as though he believes it. Having spent so many years amongst the dead, he has often thought he would be inured to the pain of loss. But the murder of his young brother, Jacob, five years ago had shown him that familiarity is no protection. He holds Rose even closer, to draw some of her own strength into him, then releases her because he knows she needs it even more than he does.

'We must pray that will be so,' she says, stepping back and wiping her eyes on her sleeve. 'And I know I should not be angry with God. More than once I pleaded with him to spare you, even at the cost of our unborn child. Was that wrong of me, Ned?'

'Nay, Wife. I would 'ave made the same bargain, had it been you on your way to Tyburn.'

Rose takes his hand in hers. The weight of it surprises her, as it always does. She marvels at how something so hard and powerful can caress her so gently. Yes, she thinks, surely there will be others.

Lifting his branded thumb towards her mouth, she bestows a kiss upon the recently healed scar tissue, sensing the puckered M against her lips. Then she lets it fall.

'Come, Ned Monkton,' she says, trying to smile through her tears. 'We cannot tarry here amongst ghosts. We 'ave a tavern to run.'

Historical Note

The extraordinary triptych *The Last Judgement*, painted by Hieronymus Bosch, went missing from his home town and was only catalogued, some sixty-five years after this story is set, when it appeared in the private collection of the Archduke of Austria. It is now on public display in Vienna. A congregation in the sixteenth century must have found its phantasmagorical images – intriguing and compelling even today – terrifying.

Pilgrims have been walking the Via Francigena to Rome for more than a thousand years. Archbishop Sigeric made the journey from Canterbury around eighty years before the Battle of Hastings. The story of his journey is told in a splendid audio-visual presentation in the Entry Point Museum in the beautiful Italian town of Lucca.

Girolamo Fabrici – or, to give him his Latinized name, *Fabricius ab Acquapendente* (I have used his Italian name throughout for ease) – held the chair of anatomy and surgery at Padua for fifty years. He is responsible for the construction of Europe's first custom-built anatomical theatre, which can still be visited today at the Palazzo Bo. Dissections were performed there until the last quarter of the nineteenth century.

It was only about fifty years earlier than that when Ned Monkton's ruse to escape the gallows was removed from English law. The actor and playwright Ben Johnson relied upon Benefit of Clergy to avoid being hanged for the manslaughter of a fellow actor, though he didn't need his wife to coach him in his lines.

In 1597 Galileo Galilei, professor of mathematics at Padua, perfected his military compass. It was a bestseller. It enabled him, amongst other things, to pay back the two hundred ducats he had borrowed to settle the issue of his sister's dowry. His subsequent career needs no further exposition here.

Which brings us, finally, to Antonio Santucci's great armillary sphere. At 3.7 metres high – more than twelve feet – it towers over the modern-day visitor to the Museo Galileo in Florence. It looks, at first glance, like something from the set of an episode of Dr Who. What a sixteenth-century Florentine must have made of it, we must leave to the mists of history.

Acknowledgements

Once again, my deepest gratitude to Susannah Hamilton, Sarah Hodgson and everyone at Corvus Books for their hard work and encouragement, and to my agent, Jane Judd. If there was ever to be a medal for saving authors from their own howlers, one must surely go to copy-editor Mandy Greenfield, whose eagle eye and uncanny memory have once again avoided far too many embarrassments on my part.

Also due my sincere thanks are Penny and Brian Osborne, Annie and Pete Williams, Di and John Richardson, Lisa and Chris Seabourne, Sue Stirling, Gill Stringer, Naomi and Darren Standing, Mike and Sian Simpson. I must thank, too, the Chapman family: Rachel, Jeremy, Joseph and Sian; Val and John Holloway, and all those book-club members around the Worcestershire Lenches who have been generous enough to support my writing and have enjoyed and championed the Jackdaw series.

As ever, my heartfelt thanks and appreciation to my wife Jane, who inspires me, encourages me and tolerates with such good grace her husband's frequent sojourns in the sixteenth century.

Since the Jackdaw series began, one character has actually made the journey in the opposite direction, from fiction into real life. In a few short months Buffle (who appears in two of the books) has apparently been so inspired by Elizabethan history that he's taken to digging up the garden, in an effort – I presume – to be the first cocker spaniel to become an archaeologist.

Read on for an extract from ...

PART 1

✠

The Death of Kings

1

The Atlantic Ocean, sixty leagues south-west
of Ireland, September 1598

Since the sandglass was last turned, the storm has stalked the *San Juan de Berrocal* from behind the cover of a darkening sky. It has sniffed at her with its blustery breath, jostled her with watery claws, spat at her with a sudden icy blast of rain. Along the western horizon where the twilight is dying, flashes of lightning now ripple. Whenever the carrack rises on a wave crest, they seem brighter. Nearer. It is only a matter of time, thinks Don Rodriquez Calva de Sagrada, before the accompanying thunder is no longer drowned by the roaring of the sea and the screaming of the wind.

Drowned.

Don Rodriquez has faced death before in the service of Spain. He has made voyages longer and more uncertain even than this one. But to drown... that, he thinks, would be an ignominious death for a courtier of The Most Illustrious Philip, by the Grace of God, King of Spain, Aragon, Valencia, Mallorca, Naples, Sicily and Sardinia.

The deck cants alarmingly as the *San Juan* plunges down a vertiginous slope of black water. Don Rodriquez flails wildly for something to hang on to. His hands seize the wooden housing of the ship's lodestar, brightly painted red and gold – the colours of Castile. Beneath his numb fingers, the wet timber is as slippery as if the paint were blood. But to let go, he is sure, would result in him sliding off the deck and into the maelstrom surging mere feet below. He is beginning to wonder if the captain – fearful of interception by one of those sleek English sea-wolves bristling with cannon and possessed of Lucifer's luck – has made a fatal error of judgement.

As the deck soars upwards again, leaving Don Rodriquez's stomach somewhere in the depths of the ocean, the captain – a short, taciturn fellow with the darting eyes of a scavenging gull, and whose seaman's contempt for the landsman who chartered his ship has not abated since they left Coruña – pins his chart against the lid of the lodestar box. The corners thrash wildly in the gale like the wings of a bird trying to escape the hunter's net. 'Be not dismayed, my lord!' he says with an insulting smile as the index finger of his free hand, encased in the thick felt of his glove, makes landfall in the pool of dancing light cast by the helmsman's lantern. 'God, in his infinite mercy, has provided us with a safe anchorage – here.'

Don Rodriquez leans forward to study the map. It is a portolan chart, purchased in Seville for more maravedís than he had cared to pay. Everything on it – from the compass bearings to the harbours and inlets, promontories and coves – is based upon reports from Spanish fishermen who once plied these waters. But since the outbreak of the present war between the heretic English and God-fearing Spain there have been few enough of those in these waters. What if the map is out of date, and the English have built a castle where the captain's finger now rests? Besides, it will be utterly dark soon. Not even a lunatic would consider a night landfall on such a treacherous coast. And only a lunatic who was heartily tired of life would do so in the face of an approaching storm.

'Here' turns out to be some distance from Roaringwater Bay, where the captain had promised to put them ashore at first light.

'Is there nowhere closer? Every extra hour I am ashore is an hour given to the English to contrive our ruin.'

With an impertinence he would never dare risk on dry land, the captain says, 'We made a pact, my lord, did we not? I am not to ask why a grand courtier of our sovereign majesty wishes to interrupt his voyage to the Spanish Netherlands to spend a night in Ireland. In return, the same grand courtier shall leave all decisions of a maritime nature to me. Yes?'

'Yes,' admits Don Rodriquez despondently. 'We agreed.'

'Trust me – I know these waters,' the captain adds. 'I have sailed them before, with the Duke of Medina Sidonia.'

The man's familiarity with the coast of Ireland is why Don Rodriquez hired him in the first place. Now, thinking on the fate that befell the commander of the grand Armada, he is beginning to have second thoughts.

Another wave of watery malevolence sends the *San Juan* into a plunge even more sickening than the last. The sea breaks over the elegantly carved Castilian lion on her prow, and for a moment Don Rodriquez fears she will go on plunging into the deep, never to rise again. From beneath the deck planks, a shrill female scream carries clearly against the clamour of the gale.

'You had best go below and comfort the noble lady, your daughter, and leave me to my duties, my lord,' says the captain, fighting the wind for possession of the chart as he tries to tuck it back into his cape.

Don Rodriquez, being a man of honour, objects.

'You may think me a cosseted courtier, Señor, but I am also a soldier, and I have voyaged in His Majesty's service before. My arms are still strong. Let me stay here. Direct me as you will.'

The captain glances at his passenger's well-manicured hands, the fingers laden with bejewelled rings. He looks at the pretentiously styled black curls on his head, the conceit of a man just

7

a little too old to carry them off. A landsman of the worst kind, he decides. A danger on a storm-tossed deck, not only to himself but to all around him.

'Voyaged where?' he asks. 'On the Sanabria, in a pleasure barge?'

'To New Spain. To Hispaniola.'

The captain looks Don Rodriquez up and down, wondering if this is little more than a courtier's boasting. 'You never told me that at Coruña. Was this recently?'

'Twenty years ago,' Don Rodriquez admits.

'Ah,' the captain says, barely bothering to keep the scorn out of his voice. 'In that case, your place is not here, my lord. I suggest you go below and leave me and my crew to our profession.' Then, with the sly smile of a Madrid street-trickster, he adds, 'I hope you and the women have strong stomachs. We're in for a tempestuous night.'

✠

Beyond the shuttered windows of the smaller of the two grand banqueting chambers at Greenwich Palace, on the southern bank of the Thames some five miles downriver from London Bridge, the early-September dusk is troubled by no more than a few high wisps of cloud, as insubstantial as an old man's breath on winter air. Inside, the candles have been lit, the dining boards and trestles cleared away, the covers of Flanders linen folded up and carted off to the wash-house, the plate and silverware removed. As for the diners, if indigestion is in danger of making its presence publicly known, they are doing their level best to suffer in silence. Elizabeth of England does not appreciate having her masques interrupted by vulgar noises off-stage.

Dr Nicholas Shelby and his wife Bianca have removed themselves to the gallery, amongst the other palace chaff who don't

8

merit a place closer to the players. As a consequence, they have an uninterrupted view of the assembled courtiers bedecked in their late-summer plumage: satin peasecod doublets and venetians for the men, low-cut brocade gowns cascading richly over whalebone farthingales for the women – all striking languid poses around a raised dais covered in plush scarlet velvet. In the centre of the dais stands a gilded wooden chair emblazoned with the English lion and the Welsh dragon. Upon the chair lies a plump cushion covered in the finest cloth of gold. And upon the cushion, like a petite pharaoh perched on a ziggurat, sits a woman with the whitest face Bianca has ever seen.

'She's smaller than I expected,' Bianca whispers into her husband's ear.

'Smaller?' Nicholas answers. 'What did you expect – an Amazon?'

The court has assembled tonight to enjoy a recital of excerpts from Master Edmund Spenser's *The Faerie Queene*, performed by the best actors the Master of the Revels has contrived to drag out of the Southwark taverns and transport – standing fare only – on the ferry from Blackfriars.

On the assumption that mirth at the expense of royalty is probably treasonous, Bianca stifles a giggle. 'Has she let you see what she hides behind all that white ceruse yet?'

'Of course not. I'm not allowed to actually touch the sacred personage of the sovereign.'

'Then how can you treat her if she falls ill?'

'That's only half the problem,' Nicholas replies. 'What if I have to cast a horoscope before making a diagnosis? If it turns out to be inauspicious and I say so out loud, or write it down, I could be sent to the Tower for imagining her demise. At the moment, that's treason.'

'But you don't believe in casting horoscopes before making a diagnosis, Nicholas. You never have.'

'But the College of Physicians will insist on it. Otherwise they'll accuse me of not doing my job properly. Remember what happened to poor old Dr Lopez? Being the queen's doctor didn't save him from his enemies.'

'How can I forget?' Bianca says, rolling her eyes. 'I see his head on the parapet of the gatehouse every time I cross London Bridge. It's been up there since before we went away.' She pulls a face. 'Except for the jaw, of course. That must have dropped off and fallen into the river while we were in Padua.'

Nicholas rests his elbows on the balustrade and turns his face very close to hers. 'If you want the truth, I don't believe she ordered Sir Robert Cecil to call us back to England because she wanted *me* to be her physician. She can call on any number of the senior fellows from the College. They'd stab each other with a lancet to get the summons.'

Bianca pushes a rebellious strand of dark hair back under the rim of her lace caul. Holding his gaze, she whispers mischievously, 'Well, it wasn't because she was in need of a good dancing partner, was it, Husband?'

Nicholas feigns hurt feelings. 'It's not *my* fault I can't dance a decent pavane or a volta. My feet spent their formative years wading through good Suffolk clay.'

'Are you telling me that we subjected ourselves and our infant son to several uncomfortable weeks aboard an English barque all the way from Venice just to satisfy the passing fancy of an old woman who wears whitewash on her skin?' Bianca asks. Then, as an afterthought, 'And if that's her own hair, then I'm Lucrezia Borgia.'

Given his wife's known skills as an apothecary – and the long line of Italian women on her mother's side whose art in mixing poisons is still infamous throughout the Veneto – Nicholas winces at her choice of comparison.

'She likes to hear reports from foreign lands,' he says, 'particularly concerning the new sciences. She was very interested to hear about my studies with Professor Fabricius at the Palazzo Bo. She understood everything I told her about the professor's views on the mechanisms in the human eye.'

'Mercy! Who could possibly have imagined such a thing: a woman – a queen – understanding the musings of a learned professor?'

Nicholas has learned not to rise to the bait. 'Besides, I believe she's grown weary of being nagged by her old physicians,' he says. 'It is my diagnosis that she has chosen to discomfort them by favouring someone they all hold to be a dangerous rebel – someone young; someone who still has all his teeth.'

'You're her *plaything*,' Bianca announces with sly enjoyment. 'My husband – an old woman's sugar comfit.'

'It hasn't done the noble Earl of Essex any harm, has it?' Nicholas counters, nodding in the direction of Robert Devereux, lying like a favoured greyhound at the foot of the dais. At thirty-two – four years younger than Nicholas – he makes an elegant sight, only slightly less pearled and bejewelled than the queen herself.

'No, too thin in the calf for me,' Bianca says, surreptitiously running the instep of her right foot along the back of Nicholas's leg. 'And *far* too primped.'

On the floor below, two slender youths in gleaming breast-plates are striking heroic postures. One declaims as loudly as his adenoidal voice will permit, 'Upon a great adventure he was bound, that greatest Gloriana to him gave, that greatest Glorious Queen of Faerie land—'

'Tell me again, Husband: which one is the Gentle Knight?'

'Him – the one with the broken nose.'

'Why does he have that silly painted horse's head between his legs?'

'Didn't you catch the line about his angry steed chiding at the foaming bit?'

'Foaming bit? It looks to me as though someone's stuck a giant painted wooden pizzle onto his codpiece. It's the sort of thing I expect to see on a Bankside May Day, not at Greenwich Palace,' Bianca says, making a play of fanning the embarrassment from her cheeks.

'Just try to imagine it's an angry steed, *please*.'

'So, the other one – the one with the superior look on his face – that's Gloriana.'

'Correct.'

'And Gloriana is really Elizabeth.'

'You have it in one.'

'And this fairy land they're in – that's really England.'

'It's an *allegory*,' Nicholas says slowly, a hint of weariness in his voice.

'It's a delusion, that's what it is – a woman in her sixties being played by a boy who's barely plucked his first whisker.'

'Edmund Spenser is our finest poet,' Nicholas protests, not altogether convincingly.

'I'll take Italian comedy – Arlecchino and Pantalone – over your Master Spenser's allegory today and every day, thank you, Husband.'

A portly factotum from the Revel's office, lounging unnoticed against the wainscoting, leans forward. 'Some people prefer to listen to quality verse,' he mutters, 'rather than the bickering of other people who are clearly devoid of any artistic appreciation whatsoever.'

'Sorry,' says Nicholas.

'How long will this go on?' Bianca whispers.

'It's a *very* long poem.'

'Do you think anyone will notice if we sit down against the wall and take a nap?'

'Don't worry,' Nicholas tells her. 'Gloriana herself will have nodded off long before the end.'

'Then we can all go to bed?'

'Bed?'

'That painted pizzle has given me an idea.'

'The players will all pretend she's wide awake. So will the court. You can't escape Edmund Spenser that easily,' Nicholas says despondently. 'I fear we're in for a long night.'

To be continued...

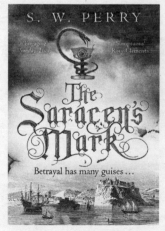